CONTENTS

OF

THE FIFTH VOLUME.

THE

INFANT'S PROGRESS

FROM THE

VALLEY OF DESTRUCTION

TO

EVERLASTING GLORY.

INTRODUCTION

TO

"THE INFANT'S PROGRESS."

My little children,—

The intention of this story is to make you acquainted, in an agreeable manner, with many of those awful mysteries of our holy religion, the knowledge of which is necessary to your salvation.

You do not yet know what it is that has separated you from your God: nor do you fully understand what it was that induced the Lord our Redeemer to descend from heaven for the purpose of assuming our nature, and dying upon the cross. You have, perhaps, never yet been informed that the sin of man's heart is very great, very prevalent, and very hateful; and that, except it be overcome, it will subject him to everlasting perdition.

Many long sermons have been preached, and many learned volumes have been written, in order both to describe the nature of this sin, and to guard us against its influence: but little children cannot understand these grave and elaborate discourses. I have therefore written for your instruction on this subject a story about some little children, who, like yourselves, were born in a state of sin. And in this story I have personified the sin of our nature, and introduced it as the constant companion of these children.

The relation is given under the form of a dream, the various incidents of which are so contrived as to show

how incessantly sin assaults even those who are truly devoted to God, and what unhappiness it causes them from the beginning to the end of their days.

Through the whole of this dream, the present life is compared to a *pilgrimage*, which signifies a journey undertaken for some pious purpose; and in every part of it especial care has been taken distinctly to mark the straight and only way to the kingdom of heaven,—viz. the Lord Jesus Christ, who himself hath said, "I am the way, the truth, and the life; no man cometh unto the Father but by me."

Now as nuts and almonds are hidden under rough shells, and as honey is concealed in the bells and cups of flowers, so there is a hidden meaning in every part of my allegory, which I hope you will be enabled to draw forth for your profit. In the mean time, my dear children, I pray God to seal instruction upon your hearts, and fill you with that heavenly wisdom whose price is far above rubies.

I will just add, that this little work was composed in the East Indies during the year 1814.

THE

INFANT'S PROGRESS, &c.

CHAPTER I.

One night as I lay upon my bed, I dreamed a dream. Methought I was sitting upon some high place, resembling a cloud; beneath which there was spread out a very large plain, called the Plain of Destruction, containing all the towns, and villages, and dwelling-places of the children of men, with their kings' houses, and the temples of their gods.

Some of these places possessed many external advantages, and were not unpleasant to look upon; for *God maketh his sun to rise on the evil and on the good, and sendeth rain on the just and on the unjust.* Matt. v. 45. Nevertheless, no man could remain in safety in any of the habitations of this plain; because, from time to time, the earth opened, and there came out fire and smoke, hell itself lying close underneath: the place therefore was properly termed the Plain of Destruction. Moreover, occasionally, dreadful storms of thunder and lightning broke over the plain; where I saw some as they travelled through the country stricken with thunderbolts from heaven—*For the Lord looked down from heaven upon the children of men, to see if there were any that did understand, and seek God: but they are all gone aside, they are all together become filthy; there is none that doeth good, no, not one.* Psalm xiv. 2, 3.

Now, while I looked, behold, a certain person appeared clothed in white, and bearing in his hand the Book of God. This person's name was Evangelist; and being sent from God, he went from city to city, and from house to house, warning men to flee from the wrath to come. And these were the words in which he addressed them—"Ye are all sinful, ye are all unclean; ye have departed from the service of the Lord your Maker, and are under the condemnation of hell: nevertheless, the Lord hath prepared for you a way to escape; 'for God so loved the world, that he gave his only-begotten Son, that whosoever believeth in him should not perish, but have everlasting life.' John iii. 16.

I saw, then, that to such as were disposed to inquire further into this matter, being content to turn their backs upon the world, and to take Christ for their portion, Evangelist pointed out certain hills at a great distance, over which there was stretched, straight as an arrow, and as far as the eye could reach, a narrow path, having so upward a tendency that I could not distinguish the farther end of it, by reason of the glory and brightness which were cast thereon from the heavens. Now at the entrance of this path there was a narrow pass or cut through the hills, where a little gate was placed, the Lord Jesus Christ himself mercifully providing this way for the escape of sinful men, and setting *before them an open door, which no man can shut.* Rev. iii. 8. So I continued to look on Evangelist; and behold, he went to the door of a small house in a certain little village, and, as his manner was, he knocked thereat.

The name of this village was Family Love. Many parts of it lay in ruins, having been destroyed by successive tempests and the heaving of the earth: nevertheless, what remained thereof was exceedingly fair and lovely, so that in all the plain I saw not such another village.

Now, as I before said, Evangelist knocked at the door of a certain small house; when presently one coming and opening the door, he entered in.

In this house dwelt a certain young man, with his wife and their three little children. So I saw, in my dream, that Evangelist delivered his message to the young man and his wife, saying, "Flee from the wrath to come."

These young people then put certain questions to Evangelist, saying, "Whither shall we flee? or who shall help us?"

Upon which Evangelist gave them a book, and bade them read therein. So they opened the book, and read these words: *Let not your heart be troubled: ye believe in God, believe also in me. In my Father's house are many mansions: if it were not so, I would have told you. I go to prepare a place for you. And if I go and prepare a place for you, I will come again, and receive you unto myself; that where I am, there ye may be also.—I am the way, the truth, and the life: no man cometh unto the Father but by me.* John xiv. 1–3, 6.

Then said the young man, "Where shall we find him of whom this is written?"

In answer to which, Evangelist opened his mouth and taught them many things concerning the Lord Jesus Christ: how *God was manifest in the flesh, justified in the Spirit, seen of angels, preached unto the gentiles, believed on in the world, received up into glory.* 1 Tim. iii. 16. And behold, while Evangelist yet spake, the Holy Spirit of God entered their hearts, and they cried out, as with one voice, "*Lord, we believe; help thou our unbelief.*" Mark ix. 24.

Evangelist then pointed out to them the means of escape, even the little door which the Lord had opened at the head of the way; and behold, a very bright light issued from thence. Then said Evangelist, "Keeping that light in your eye, go up directly to it; and when ye come to the door, knock without fear. *Christ is the door: by him if any man enter in, he shall be saved.*" John x. 9.

So while I continued to look, the man and his wife began to put themselves in readiness for their journey; busying themselves, at the same time, in teaching their little ones such things as they had themselves learned from Evangelist. But, while they lingered, Evangelist hastened them, saying, "Escape for your lives; for the time is short."

To which they replied, "Must we leave our little ones behind?"

"It is the will of God," answered Evangelist, "that, for the trial of your faith, you should give up these little ones for a season. 'For every one that hath forsaken houses, or brethren, or sisters, or father, or mother, or wife, or children, or lands, for my name's sake, shall receive an hundred fold, and shall inherit everlasting life.' Matt. xix. 29. 'Leave thy fatherless children; I will preserve them alive, saith the Lord.'" Jer. xlix. 11.

Now the poor parents, in obedience to the will of God, kissed their pretty babes, and with many tears and prayers charging them to follow their steps, they hastened away, because the messenger of God was exceedingly urgent. So turning their steps towards the shining light, they speedily reached the wicket-gate: where the Lord of the way having graciously received them, and washed them from their sins, and clothed them in fair white garments, and set them in the narrow path which leadeth unto the city—they were shortly and safely conveyed through the black river of death unto everlasting glory.

Upon this I turned my eyes towards the little ones, who were left behind in their father's house—the eldest of which was a boy named Humble Mind, being not quite ten years old; and he had two little sisters, whose names were Playful and Peace, the younger of whom was of very tender age.

I saw, then, that, after their father and mother had left them, very little care was taken of these poor babes: so that their clothes were little better than rags; while, like the prodigal son in the gospel, *they would fain have filled their bellies with the husks which the swine did eat.* Luke xv. 16. Moreover, I saw that they had for a companion one who had been brought up under the same roof with them, as ill-favoured and ill-conditioned an urchin as one could see, whose name was *Inbred* or *Original Sin.* His great forefather, a child of hell, came into this world at the time when Adam ate the forbidden fruit; and from that very moment he became the constant companion of our first parent. Moreover, as Adam's family increased on the earth, in like manner the family of Original Sin multiplied, filling the whole earth with violence, and leading men to the commission of every evil work (Galatians v. 19); insomuch that the history of all the kingdoms of the earth, ay, and of every individual in them, from the fall of Adam till now, is filled up with the ill-doings of this apostate family. And even now, so entirely are the sons of Adam under the power of *Inbred-Sin,* that they cannot even wish to do well, without the help of God; but the Lord Jesus Christ, having by his death upon the cross obtained for us the assistance of the Holy Spirit of God, we are enabled, through his help, to subdue our inbred corruption.

Having said thus much concerning the family of this *Inbred-Sin,* I shall now proceed to describe what I observed of his habits and tempers, wherein he differed so little from other individuals of his hated race, that in describing one of the family I cannot fail to convey a tolerably correct idea of all the rest.

In the first place, I remarked that he never slept; but that he was on the alert, and, as it were, on the look-out for occasions of action both day and night, neither observing any Sabbath-day himself, nor allowing any season of rest to those with whom he familiarly associated: *for the wicked are like the troubled sea, when it cannot rest, whose waters cast up mire and dirt.* Isa. lvii. 20. His grand work was that of contriving mischief, and setting others to execute it; and from this work he never ceased. Even while the children were in their beds, he would sit on their pillows and whisper all manner of evil in their ears, filling their fancies with idle dreams, and suggesting such a variety of unholy thoughts, that on their awaking they were prepared for every evil deed.

Another quality of *Inbred-Sin* appeared to be this, that he was a stranger to shame, and could neither be put out of countenance, nor thrown off his guard; so that when pursuing any object, if baffled in one way, he would instantly wheel about and come to the very same point by some other way, and that, perhaps, such a round-about one, as would make it believed that he had given up the very purpose which he was then actually carrying into effect. He had also this further quality in common with others of his family, that the more he was submitted to, the more unreasonable he became in his demands; frequently requiring such compliances as led, not only to great inconvenience, but to imminent danger.

It is true that the children had no desire to contend with him; nay, they had, in fact, great pleasure in obeying his commands. Nevertheless, there were occasions, as I said before, when he would require them to do such things as necessarily exposed them to the danger of immediate punishment; and, on these occasions, something like an argument or discussion would arise between them, when it was marvellous to observe how he would proceed till he had brought about his design.

It was also wonderful what devices he would put the little ones upon, in order to avoid detection: and if at any time they were found out in a fault, he was never at a loss to gloss it over, by putting some plausible falsehood into their mouths. And if nothing else could screen them from punishment, he would put them upon seeming humble and sorry for the offence they had committed; merely for the purpose of bringing themselves out of present trouble. At other times he would set them to quarrel one with another, instigating each one to set up himself in opposition to the rest.

Moreover, I saw that this *Inbred-Sin* never left the children; dwelling in their house, lying in their bosoms, walking out with them when they went abroad, and sitting down with them at all their meals: neither indeed was there any thing done in the family, great or small, in which this busy one did not meddle and make.

I perceived, further, that this *Inbred-Sin* loathed and hated all that was good, influencing the children to do the same; so that, if by chance they heard any one of their neighbours reading a good book, or speaking a word for God, they would shut their ears and run away; choosing rather to wallow with the swine in the mire of the streets, than to give their hearts to any good. And in proportion as *Inbred-Sin* influenced the children to hate and loathe all that was good, he caused them also to desire and eagerly long after all manner of evil; so that "they gave themselves over to work all uncleanness with greediness." Ephes. iv. 19.

Then began I to fear for these little ones, and to consider by what means they might be delivered from the power of this *Inbred-Sin*—"for the wages of sin is death." Rom. vi. 23.

CHAPTER II.

After awhile I looked again at these three children, to wit, Humble Mind, Playful, and Peace; and behold, Evangelist again came up to the door of their dwelling, and knocked.

Then said *Inbred-Sin*, "Behold, Evangelist knocks at the door. Open not to him; for Evangelist is a hard master, and he will bring us to judgment for our faults."

Now I saw, in my dream, that while the children stood doubting whether they should open the door,

Evangelist *put his hand in by the hole of the door*, and entered the house. Cant. v. 4. Then were the hearts of the children moved towards him; and behold, *Inbred-Sin* shrank back and hid himself.

I heard then that Evangelist opened his mouth and spake tenderly and comfortably to these little ones. And first he showed them, that although they were under the dominion of *Inbred-Sin*, and by their unholy living were prepared for eternal punishment, yet it was not the will of their heavenly Father that one of them should perish. After this he explained unto them, as his manner was, what God had done for the salvation of men; how he had sent his only Son, the Lord Jesus Christ, to take upon him a human form, and to die upon the cross for the salvation of all such as believed in him. Moreover, he showed them how Christ had, by his death, procured for mankind the assistance of the Holy Spirit of God, through which every man might be enabled to war with and finally to overcome his inbred or original sin. He then pointed out to them the only path to everlasting happiness, even the narrow pass cut through the hills, which openeth into the way of salvation; after which he gave to each of them a book, even the Book of God, bidding them to read therein, and pray for *the Spirit of Truth* (that is, the Holy Ghost), *that he might guide them into all truth.* John xvi. 13. So he departed for a while.

Now I saw, in my dream, that, as soon as Evangelist was departed, *Inbred-Sin* came forth from his hiding-place, and behold, he was in a fearful rage.

"What," said he, "has this man been saying? Would he have you to leave all your friends and neighbours, your playmates and companions, your sports and pleasures, in order to take up the life of a pilgrim? Would he have you to spend all your time in reading dull books, and in saying your prayers? I hate this man, and his books, and his counsels."

"But," said Humble Mind, "if we do not hearken to the words of Evangelist, and if we remain in this place until we die, shall we not go to hell?"

Upon which I heard *Inbred-Sin* pleading thus with the children: "Are you not very young, and will it not be many years before you become old? and when you are old, will it not be time enough to think of dying?"

"But many *children* die," said Humble Mind.

To which *Inbred-Sin* replied, "If you should happen to die while you are a child, God will not punish you for your faults as he will punish those of maturer age who know better."

"But I know that I ought to be good," answered Humble Mind, "though I am not yet a man."

"Well, then," said *Inbred-Sin*, seeing that he could in no other way prevail, "if you cannot be satisfied to stay here, and live like other children, but must go on pilgrimage; why then you must needs go. It is not necessary, however, that you should set out to-day; to-morrow will be time enough: let us therefore, for the present, put away Evangelist's books, and go to our sports."

"Yes," said Playful, "do, Humble Mind, put away the books now. Let us spend this evening in play, and to-morrow we will begin our journey to the Celestial City."

So Humble Mind did as *Inbred-Sin* advised him. He laid down the book which Evangelist had given him; when I saw that the three children immediately went to play, and *Inbred-Sin* went with them.

The next day I was anxious to observe whether the children would bethink themselves of obeying the commands of Evangelist: but I found that *Inbred-Sin* would in nowise allow them so to do.

Now Humble Mind could read very well, having been carefully instructed by his father: neither were Playful and Peace bad readers, considering their tender years. Nevertheless, I saw that they gave no heed to the books which Evangelist had given them; for although they took them up several times, yet before they could get through a single sentence of their contents, *Inbred-Sin* expressed such a loathing and abhorrence of their employment, that they were glad, for the sake of quietness, to put the books aside again.

Then as to forsaking their home and going on pilgrimage, they seemed altogether to have lost all thought of such a thing. Observing this, I looked again for help for these children, crying out in a sort of unbelieving despondency, "How can these sinful little ones be saved!" But I considered not that "God is faithful, by whom they were called unto the fellowship of his Son Jesus Christ. For God hath chosen the foolish things of the world, to confound the wise; and God hath chosen the weak things of the world, to confound the things which are mighty; and base things of the world, and things which are despised, hath God chosen, yea, and things which are not, to bring to naught things that are: that no flesh should glory in his presence." 1 Cor. i. 9, 27–29.

Now when things had remained for some time in this state, I perceived that the Lord began again to deal with Humble Mind, but after a manner somewhat different from his former dealings with him; and behold he sent another messenger unto him from on high, who appeared before him at night, and this messenger's name was *Conviction-of-Sin.* While Humble Mind was lying upon his bed, I saw that *Conviction-of-Sin* stood before him. "Fear came upon him, and trembling, which made all his bones to shake. Then a spirit passed before his face; the hair of his flesh stood up: it stood still, but he could not discern the form thereof: an image was before his eyes; there was silence, and a voice was heard, saying, Shall mortal man be more just than God? shall a man be more pure than his Maker? Behold, he put no trust in his servants: and his angels he charged with folly: how much less in them that dwell in houses of clay, whose foundation is in the dust, which are crushed before the moth? They are destroyed from morning to evening: they perish for ever, without any regarding it." Job iv. 14–20. So this *Conviction-of-Sin* stood before Humble Mind, and laid all his iniquities in order before him; at which Humble Mind was so dreadfully alarmed that he trembled exceedingly, while the water stood in cold drops upon his forehead.

Now when this new messenger first appeared, I perceived that *Inbred-Sin* hid himself in Humble Mind's bosom. But after a while he began to look up, till by degrees gathering courage, he sprang from his place, and flying at the throat of *Conviction-of-Sin*, griped and squeezed him after such a fashion, that I verily thought he would have utterly destroyed him—the other however exerting himself manfully, they continued struggling and fighting till sunrise; each party in his turn, as he obtained the superiority, attacking poor Humble Mind in so vehement a manner, that I feared the poor boy would be killed between them. But, as I have just intimated, when the sun arose, the contest ceased, *Conviction-of-Sin* then spreading his wings, and mounting upwards; for *Conviction-of-Sin* is of heavenly birth, and unto him it may truly be said, *Blessed is the man whom thou chastenest.* Psalm xciv. 12. So Humble Mind was left lying on his bed, sorely distressed, and bitterly lamenting.

After this, I saw, in my dream, that it began to be noised abroad in those parts, that *Conviction-of-Sin* had visited Humble Mind; and thus the neighbours discoursed thereupon:—"What is this *Conviction-of-Sin* which is come unto the child? What sin can this little boy have been guilty of? But that same Evangelist, who turned the heads of his father and mother, is, it seems, frequently meddling with him; so that, unless we can hit upon some method of diverting his thoughts from the communications of that enthusiast, the boy will never be good for any thing as long as he lives."

Then one neighbour said to another, "Come, let us go and talk with this boy, and try to put other thoughts in his head: for, if this Evangelist and his counsels prevail in our streets, what will become of the honour of our town; or how shall we preserve our credit among men?"

So the neighbours agreeing together, they came to Humble Mind's house; where, having knocked at the door, they speedily obtained entrance, and found the children preparing to be gone: for the pain and anguish which Humble Mind had suffered from the attacks of *Conviction-of-Sin* rendered it altogether impossible for him to rest in the place where he was.

Accordingly, on rising from his bed, he had opened his mind to his sisters, in spite of *Inbred-Sin*, who vehemently opposed him, declaring his determination, by God's help, to set out on pilgrimage. He had also, through the Divine blessing, obtained his dear sisters' consent, to accompany him: so that, when the neighbours arrived, they found the three children preparing to be gone.

Now I perceived that there arose a very vehement dispute between the children and the neighbours who were come to dissuade them from going on pilgrimage; and behold, *Inbred-Sin* very resolutely sided with the neighbours, applauding and seconding their carnal reasonings.

The neighbours represented to the little ones, that the profession of a pilgrim was a profession as despicable as it was unprofitable; since nothing could be gained by it, while much might be lost: "For," continued they, "he that stays at home, and does his duty, is in as sure a way of salvation as he that forsaketh all to follow his own fancy."

Now Humble Mind knew not every argument proper to be used against this false reasoning of his neighbours, on account of his youth and inexperience; but he made answer to the best of his ability, and said, "I have not only been made to know my sins, but am convinced that I can do nothing to save myself, all my best actions being marred and spoiled by sin. I find therefore that the assistance of one who is both able and willing to save me is absolutely necessary to my deliverance; and to such a deliverer I must fly. I do not however presume to judge or decide for other people: there may, perhaps, be some who do not stand in such need of a Saviour as I do; but, for my own part, I have been made to know that I am dead in trespasses and sins."

"And these little ones, thy sisters," said the neighbours, "what have they done, that they should be exposed to all the hardships of a pilgrim's life?"

To this Humble Mind replied, "I have heard it said, and have also read in my book, that we are all born in sin; and that, unless our nature is changed, and a right spirit renewed within us, we must all surely perish. It appears, then, that the youngest among us stands in as much need of a Saviour as those who have committed more actual offences; and hence it becomes the duty of every child, as soon as he has any discernment, to inquire after this Saviour. On this account, therefore," continued Humble Mind, "I, who esteem myself the chief of sinners, am, with God's help, about to leave all things, in order to seek the way of salvation pointed out in this holy book which I hold in my hand."

I perceived then, that, when the neighbours saw the firmness of Humble Mind, after ridiculing and mocking him, they proceeded to loud abuse, invectives, and threatenings: but *Conviction-of-Sin* had dealt with Humble Mind to such purpose, that his determination to go on pilgrimage was not to be shaken. Nevertheless, the little girls were much terrified by the harsh language of their neighbours; and their trouble was not a little increased by the whisperings of *Inbred-Sin*, who would have it that they were running themselves into a thousand needless snares and troubles, by giving heed to the advice of Evangelist.

Now I saw, in my dream, that, when the neighbours perceived that they could prevail nothing, they took counsel aside one with another; and this was the purport of their consultation:—

There dwelt in those parts a certain schoolmaster, one who was countenanced by the king of the country, even the prince of this world; and one who stood high in favour with all the chief inhabitants and honourable men of the land. This schoolmaster, whose name was *Worldly-Prudence*, was descended from an ancient family, and could boast of a long line of ancestry, all of whom had been employed by the prince of this world in the instruction of youth. He was a person of a venerable appearance, and knew how to make himself agreeable to all ranks and orders of men, having wit at will, and arguments always ready to support his opinions. He was well skilled in ancient learning, had much to say in favour of human wisdom, and could speak largely of the dignity of the human mind; but if he did not utterly despise religion, as some confidently assert, he at least gave it but a secondary and inferior place in all the concerns of life.

Now as this schoolmaster was held in general respect and fear by the children of the land, it was proposed by the neighbours, when they discovered Humble Mind's unyielding inclination to a pilgrim's life, that this schoolmaster should be brought to him and his sisters; "For," said they, "the children will assuredly acknowledge his authority, although they despise our arguments."

So they made haste; and when they had found Mr. *Worldly-Prudence*, they brought him to Humble Mind's house. Then I hearkened to what should pass between the schoolmaster and Humble Mind, confidently expecting that Mr. *Worldly-Prudence* would begin to rail at religion and pour contempt upon a pilgrim's life; because I knew that he was in the service of the prince of this world. But I was mistaken; for he went more cautiously to work, opening the conversation by speaking highly of the religion of Christ, and praising those men who faithfully devoted themselves to his service. And having thus thrown Humble Mind off his guard, he proceeded in a more direct manner to the accomplishment of the business he had undertaken, namely, to turn the child from that way of salvation which Evangelist had pointed out.

"Have you been informed, my son," said Mr. *Worldly-Prudence*, addressing himself to Humble Mind, "that this way, into which you are so rashly and hastily determined to set your foot, is a way abounding in all manner of snares and dangers; and that if you go unprepared to meet these dangers, you must inevitably perish?"

"I know, sir," replied Humble Mind, "that the way of the pilgrim is thickly set with dangers, and that I am weak, and unprovided with any means of self-defence; but Evangelist has taught me to trust in Him for help who will assuredly bring me through every trial."

"The Lord our God," said Mr. *Worldly-Prudence*, "as Evangelist has taught you, will no doubt ultimately become our Saviour; but this consideration is by no means to prevent us from exerting ourselves in the use of those powers which God has given us for the promotion of his glory, and for our own preservation. In the way which Evangelist has persuaded you to take, you will meet with thieves, with wild beasts, with giants, and dragons; with adversaries who will ridicule and scoff at you; with some who will endeavour to shake your faith by learned and wily arguments; and others who will endeavour to mislead you by cunning misrepresentations.

"Now, in order properly to meet all these difficulties," continued Mr. *Worldly-Prudence*, "you ought to understand the whole art of offence and defence as it is taught in my school; and this I can speedily put you in the way of acquiring, if you will but delay for a short time your perilous undertaking, and put yourself under my care. Moreover, you should have a familiar acquaintance with such facts and objections, such reasonings and representations, as your adversaries are likely to produce; lest, by your ignorance, you should bring the Christian profession into disgrace. For the enemies of our Lord are often found to be men of such deep learning, ready wit, and shining talents, as enable them very readily to perplex and confound their opponents. And how, I ask, can a child like you expect to prevail against such wily antagonists?"

"Is it not written," said Humble Mind, "*Out of the*

mouths of babes and sucklings thou hast perfected praise?" Matt. xxi. 16.

"It is so written," said Mr. *Worldly-Prudence*, "and it doth so happen, sometimes, that even babes in Christ appear to triumph over the wise and learned of this world. But these are extreme and rare cases; and such results can only be expected where the ordinary means of improvement have not been enjoyed. But can the blessing of God be expected to follow a youth who, on being offered the advantages of human learning, rejects them all, either from the indolence of his nature or from his false notions of religion? Come with me, therefore, I entreat you, Humble Mind," continued the schoolmaster; "remain but a while under my tuition, and you shall then go forth not unprepared for that mighty warfare with demons and infidels, which he must needs engage in who becomes a pilgrim."

Now I perceived that Humble Mind did not thoroughly understand all these big words which were used by Mr. *Worldly-Prudence;* but so far he thought he understood their meaning, viz. that the way of salvation was an extremely dangerous way, and such a one as could not be safely travelled by an ignorant or untutored child. Here therefore the poor boy felt himself in a strait, not knowing what to do or say: for as he was pressed on one side by the dread of *Conviction-of-Sin*, from whose assaults he was still exceedingly sore; so on the other he was vehemently urged by *Inbred-Sin* and Mr. *Worldly-Prudence*, which last held him at this moment by the arm, and seemed by no means inclined to leave his hold.

Now after a while I looked again, and, behold, the enemy had prevailed; so I saw Mr. *Worldly-Prudence* leading away Humble Mind to his school, having quieted Playful and Peace by a promise that their brother should soon return to them completely armed and prepared to be their defender in the perilous journey which they were desirous to undertake.

Then I looked again after Humble Mind, whom Mr. *Worldly-Prudence* had conveyed to his school-house, a very ancient building, situated on an unenclosed ground, among wild olives and other trees, which had never been grafted, and which therefore produced but little fruit. And behold, many boys were passing to and fro through the courts of the school-house; and I hearkened to the language which they used, but it bore no resemblance to the language of Zion.

So Mr. *Worldly-Prudence* led Humble Mind into his study; and having examined him concerning what he had learned, he directed him to lay aside for the present the book which Evangelist had given him; instead of which he put into his hands certain heathen writers of ancient date, which he assured him it was necessary that he should study, in order effectually to refute the adversaries of religion. So having finished the examination, the schoolmaster brought Humble Mind into the school-room among the other boys—and *Inbred-Sin* was with him.

There Humble Mind remained for a season in the school of Mr. *Worldly-Prudence*, studying such books as were placed before him, and playing with his school-fellows at their customary games.

Now I perceived, in my dream, that all who belonged to the school were called Christians, and that certain moral forms were observed by the master: while the religion of Christ was never mentioned in the school; neither was any reference made to our Lord's will and pleasure in the conduct either of scholars or masters; nor was I able to discover how that which was taught the boys could have any tendency, either directly or indirectly, to the advancement of religious knowledge.

Then anxiously watching to observe what effect this mode of life would have upon Humble Mind, I speedily remarked, that he grew utterly dull and dead with respect to the concerns of his soul; that he conversed with *Inbred-Sin* as with a bosom friend and brother; and that *Inbred-Sin* ruled him as entirely as he formerly had done. Thus the enemies of the Lord for a while were permitted to triumph. In the mean time I looked around for help: but, for the present, could perceive none.

CHAPTER III.

Now I saw, in my dream, that it pleased the Lord of pilgrims, after a time, to stretch forth his arm for the preservation of the child. And behold, Evangelist came to him as he stood before the door of the school-house, and said, "Humble Mind, what doest thou here? Did I not visit thee in thy father's house? and did I not warn thee to flee from this country? Knowest thou not that sure destruction awaits such as continue to dwell in this place?"

On hearing the words of Evangelist, Humble Mind began to tremble. *Inbred-Sin* also drew into the background; still however keeping close enough to the ear of Humble Mind to whisper therein the answers which he should make to Evangelist.

"Did I not point out," said Evangelist, "the dangers which awaited thee on remaining in this place? and did I not charge thee to flee by the gate which is erected at the head of the way of life? What, then, art thou doing here?"

To this Humble Mind replied, "Sir, fearing that I might be too weak to wrestle with the enemies which I was told would meet me in the way, I was persuaded to come hither, in order to learn the art of attack and defence, and to obtain such other kinds of knowledge as might fit me to contend with the adversaries of our Lord."

"And what is that art of war? and what is that knowledge," asked Evangelist, "which thou hast been acquiring in this place? Knowest thou not, my son, that he only is strong who walks in the strength of the Lord? and that he only is mighty in arms who puts on the whole armour of God?"

"I have acquired the knowledge of many estimable things in this school," replied Humble Mind, "where my master has endeavoured to confirm my belief in the holy Book of God by making me study the writings of ancient authors; several of whom are found so far to agree with the sacred Scriptures as to cast some light upon them."

"And hast thou not," said Evangelist, "while looking at these lesser lights, forgotten to fix thine eye on that diviner light which will not fail to shine brighter and brighter unto the perfect day?"

I heard also that Evangelist proceeded to pronounce certain dreadful threatenings in the ear of Humble Mind; under the terrors of which he broke into tears and cries, saying, "Sir, I confess that I have done amiss, and desire to do better: but I am held in such a state of bondage by this my companion, even this sin which so easily besets me, that 'the good that I would, I do not; but the evil which I would not, that I do.'" Rom. vii. 19.

Then spake Evangelist—"Know, my son, that this *Inbred-Sin* which dwelleth with thee is so exceedingly powerful, that no man hath ever been able, by his own strength, to break the yoke of that wicked one from off his neck. When Adam transgressed the law of God by eating the forbidden fruit, this *Inbred-Sin* was then conceived in his heart; and from thenceforward the nature of every man, who is of the offspring of Adam, has been very far drawn aside from original righteousness, and strongly inclined to evil; so that the flesh lusteth always against the Spirit. Moreover, this contrary tendency so far prevails in every person born into the world, as to deserve God's wrath and damnation. Wherefore no man is counted righteous before God, excepting and only for the merit of our Lord and Saviour Jesus Christ, by faith, and not for his own works or deservings. That holy Book therefore which I delivered to thee doth set out unto us only 'the name of Jesus Christ, whereby men must be saved.' (*Articles of the Church.*) The Lord Jesus Christ hath mercifully opened a way for sinners unto salvation—He is 'the way, the truth, and the life;' and 'no man cometh unto the Father but by him.' John xiv. 6. Now I formerly pointed out to thee this way of salvation, which is thus described—'Strait is the gate, and narrow is the way, which leadeth unto life; and few there be that find it: but wide is the gate, and broad is the way, that leadeth to destruction; and many there be which go in thereat.'" Matt. vii. 13, 14.

I heard then that Evangelist spake of Mr. *Worldly-Prudence* and his followers. "These are the men," said he, "who think themselves wiser than their Maker, and who turn aside many young persons from the right way, in order to fill them with such knowledge as only puffeth up, and tendeth to destruction. They take the sling and the stone from the hand of the youthful pilgrim, and put on him the armour of Saul; they rob him of his Bible, and fill his mouth with the words of man's wisdom: so that more young pilgrims are destroyed by this *Worldly-Prudence* than by thousands of the open enemies of our Lord."

In this manner spake Evangelist; after which I saw, in my dream, that he again put into Humble Mind's hand the Book of God, bidding him beware, and never again part with it; "For it shall be," said he, "a lamp unto thy feet, and a light unto thy path." Psalm cxix. 105.

So Humble Mind received the book; and, placing it in his bosom, he gave his hand unto Evangelist; saying, "God be merciful to me a sinner!"

Then Evangelist took the hand of the child, and drew him forward towards the gate which led from the school-yard.

Now I perceived that, when those scholars who were in the yard saw Humble Mind going out from among them in the hand of Evangelist, they raised such a hue and cry, that the master and his assistants, with all those who were in the school-house, came running out to see what was the matter.

I heard also that there arose a very warm and vehement dispute between Mr. *Worldly-Prudence* and Evangelist; wherein Mr. *Worldly-Prudence* maintained that he was one of the best friends of young pilgrims, and that the object of his instructions was to bring them so far acquainted with the writings of the best and wisest of the ancients that they might have a decided advantage in arguing with the enemies of religion.

In reply to which, Evangelist read from his book the following passage—"I will destroy the wisdom of the wise, and will bring to nothing the understanding of the prudent. Where is the wise? where is the scribe? where is the disputer of this world? hath not God made foolish the wisdom of this world?" 1 Cor. i. 19, 20.

Upon which, I heard that Mr. *Worldly-Prudence* charged Evangelist with enthusiasm and folly, saying that he was the friend of indolence and ignorance, a hater of learning, and a despiser of all the wisdom of past ages.

At this the whole school broke forth into loud taunts and scoffs; whereat Humble Mind trembled exceedingly, more especially as *Inbred-Sin* began, at the same time, to whisper in his ears such things as filled him with shame, and brought the blood up into his cheeks. Nevertheless, through the secret help of God, he drew not his hand from Evangelist, but kept close to him, till that divine instructer had conveyed him out of the school-yard, and brought him to a place from whence the gate which leadeth to salvation might clearly be distinguished.

By this time Humble Mind had got out of the sound of the scoffings and blasphemies of his late companions in Mr. *Worldly Prudence's* school. Notwithstanding which, his mind was as yet by no means at ease: since no sooner had he begun to move towards the Way of Salvation, than such a strife arose between him and *Inbred-Sin* as would surely have proved too much for him, had not the child received assistance from on high, although he knew it not. *Inbred-Sin* first sprang upon his back, where he lay like a drag upon a wheel; so that the boy could hardly advance at all. I saw then that Humble Mind tried to shake him off; but as fast as he freed himself from him in one part, this tormentor fixed upon some other; now hanging on him by one limb, and now by another; sometimes taking him by the hair of the head, sometimes twitching him by the back; sometimes by one elbow, sometimes by the other; but still, as it were, in a sly and underhand way, though without rest or intermission; for, as I said before, one of the qualities of this family of *Inbred-Sin* is, that they know not what it is to be fatigued or weary. In spite, however, of the tormentor, Humble Mind, being led by Evangelist, proceeded towards the gate which is at the head of the Way of Salvation.

Then said Evangelist to the child, "My son, what seest thou?"

Humble Mind. I see a light, which grows brighter and brighter as I look thereon.

Evangelist. I am well pleased that thou art enabled to discern that light. "Blessed art thou: for flesh and blood hath not revealed it unto thee, but thy Father which is in heaven." Matt. xvi. 17. This is "the root and offspring of David, the bright and morning star"

(Rev. xxii. 16); the leading star which hath brought many to Zion.

Then Evangelist rejoiced in spirit, and said, "I thank thee, O Father, Lord of heaven and earth, because thou hast hid these things from the wise and prudent, and hast revealed them unto babes. Even so, Father; for so it seemed good in thy sight." Matt. xi. 25, 26. So Evangelist kissed the boy; and bidding him hasten to the gate, and there knock boldly for admission, he withdrew himself from the eyes of the child.

Now I saw, in my dream, that when he which was sent from God, to wit, Evangelist, had departed, *Inbred-Sin* immediately faced about: and coming before the little pilgrim, began openly and without disguise to impede him in his way. And first, he would have him to stand still while he argued with him; and so pressing was he, that the boy for quietness' sake, stood still to hear what he had to say. Then began he to plead and argue with Humble Mind, and that after such a fashion as I had never witnessed before. He assured him, that if he persevered in following the counsel of Evangelist, he would become the laughing-stock of all the country; that he would lose all the good things of this world, and be generally considered as a fool and a madman. And when he found that these arguments would not prevail, he was for having Humble Mind just to go back and take a handsome leave of his master and his school-fellows: "For who knows," said this arch-tempter, "but God may give you power to persuade a few of your old playmates to come on pilgrimage with you?—and thus you may become the instrument of saving some whom you love." He spake unto him also of his sisters, and those of his father's house, earnestly pleading with him to turn back, for the purpose of securing their company. Thus *Inbred-Sin* sought to entice and entangle Humble Mind through the affection he bore to his earthly friends. But when this would not do (for Humble Mind was too hot upon his journey to be thus put by), *Inbred-Sin* shifted his ground again, and asked him how he could think of appearing before the Lord of the gate clothed in those filthy rags, and with *Inbred-Sin* as his companion? "for," added he, spitefully, "wherever thou goest I will follow thee, Humble Mind, and will be thy torment and thy shame; for I am thy brother, the son of thy mother, and I have had dominion over thee ever since thou wast born, and now will I bring thee to disgrace in the presence of thy King."

I perceived then, that when *Inbred-Sin* became thus outrageous, Humble Mind trembled exceedingly, neither had he power for some time to look towards the shining light. After a while, however, he recovered himself so far as to recollect the book which Evangelist had given him. So he plucked it out of his bosom, and read these words—"I find then a law, that, when I would do good, evil is present with me. For I delight in the law of God after the inward man: but I see another law in my members, warring against the law of my mind, and bringing me into captivity to the law of sin which is in my members. O wretched man that I am! who shall deliver me from the body of this death? I thank God, through Jesus Christ our Lord." Rom. vii. 21–25.

When he had read these words, he was comforted; and crying mightily unto God, he pressed forward, overthrowing *Inbred-Sin* to clear the way before him. So he hastened towards the gate, and *Inbred-Sin* followed swiftly behind him.

CHAPTER IV.

Now I looked again after Humble Mind; and behold, he was come unto the gate which is at the entrance of the Way of Salvation. That gate is cut in a rock hard as adamant; beyond which I saw the Way of Salvation walled on each side, and straight as an arrow, sometimes ascending dangerous heights, at other times descending into deep valleys, and passing through dreary wildernesses, bogs, and quagmires. Nevertheless, the tendency of that way was, for the most part, upwards, till at length it reached the utmost boundaries of the everlasting hills; where the glory of it became too dazzling for mortal eyes—for "the path of the just is as the shining light, that shineth more and more unto the perfect day." Prov. iv. 18.

I saw then, in my dream, that when Humble Mind came up to the gate, he was so spent by his struggle with *Inbred-Sin*, that he fell upon the step like one fainting, having no power to knock for entrance: nevertheless, the door was speedily opened by a venerable person called *Good-Will*, who lifted the child from the ground, and carried him in to his Lord. Then thought I on these words—"And it shall come to pass that before they call, I will answer; and while they are yet speaking, I will hear." Isaiah lxv. 24.

I could not discover in what manner the Lord of the gate revealed himself unto Humble Mind; for he showeth himself in various forms unto pilgrims, according to his own good pleasure, and in the manner which he deemeth most suitable and profitable to their tempers and conditions. Sometimes he showeth himself crowned with thorns, with bleeding hands and feet; sometimes he appeareth full of sorrow, and clad with mourning-garments; and at other times he discovereth himself in the glory as of the only-begotten of the Father. But in whatever form it pleaseth him to reveal himself, he is found to be all lovely, without spot or stain of sin.

So Humble Mind came out from the presence of the Lord, and I wondered at the change which had passed upon him. His Lord had caused him to be washed in a pure fountain of water; and stripping him of his rags, had clothed him in beautiful garments, even the garments of salvation, washed and made white in the blood of the Lamb. Moreover, the Lord had set his signet on the brow of the child, which was an ornament so exceedingly becoming that it made him look like unto the sons of God. One thing, however, grieved me, which was, that *Inbred-Sin* still accompanied the boy; though he carried it not so imperiously towards him as before, but conducted himself more modestly, restraining his tongue and putting on a demurer look.

Then Humble Mind set his face to go forwards; when I saw that certain servants of the Lord of the gate went with him a little way, and gave him directions for his journey. They bade him beware of turning aside, either to the right or to the left. Moreover, they told him that he would find many quiet resting-places in the way, which the Lord of pilgrims had prepared for the reception of his servants. "The first of these," said they, "are the pleasant pastures and flowery fields belonging to the shepherd Sincerity, by whom infant pilgrims are received and fed many days with the fresh milk of the

Word. Next to these sweet fields, and a little farther on, is the house of the Interpreter, where young pilgrims also receive wholesome instruction and nourishment. Beyond this is the palace called Beautiful, where certain holy virgins dwell, and where many rare and excellent things are to be seen. And still farther on are to be found the sweet Valley of Humiliation, where lilies grow in shadowy places—the house of Mr. *Orthodox*, in the very town of Vanity—the hills upon which the shepherds dwell, and which are called Immanuel's Land—also the lovely land of Beulah—together with sundry little peaceful valleys and verdant solitudes scattered over the pilgrim's path, where the weary traveller may obtain sweet refreshment, freely drinking of the living stream, and gathering honey from the stony rock." After acquainting Humble Mind with these things, and giving him their blessing, the servants of his Lord went back to their Master's house.

I perceived then that Humble Mind went joyfully on his way, even along the Way of Salvation. Now the way was exceedingly beautiful, even like a garden enclosed on each side, and shaded with cedar-trees and lign-aloes; while many fountains of water gushed out beneath the trees, and ran murmuring along by the wayside. The high-road also was visible in the remote perspective, ascending the blue heights, till, at length, it was lost in the distant clouds.

So Humble Mind pursued his way, sometimes breaking into songs of praise, sometimes leaping for joy like a young hart, and sometimes reading in his book. Thus he passed on for a whole day, being filled with the love of him whom he had lately seen, even the Saviour that bled for him upon the accursed tree. And as night approached, he drank of the water of the fountain by the way-side, and laid him down to sleep under the shadow of the trees till morning-light; when he arose and pursued his journey, hoping soon to reach the pastures of the shepherd Sincerity, which were then not half a day's journey before him.

Now all this while, to wit, from the time that Humble Mind had left the gate till he arose on the second day of his journey, *Inbred-Sin* had followed close upon his steps; but so softly and cautiously, that during the whole of the first day Humble Mind knew not that he was there. And herein is often displayed the subtlety of *Inbred-Sin*, in seeming to withdraw himself in seasons of peculiar consolation, by way of lulling the soul into a state of security and carelessness. Thus was it with Humble Mind: during the first day of his pilgrimage, *Inbred-Sin* was so quiet, that Humble Mind, trusting he had taken his leave for ever, was ready to say in his prosperity, "I shall never be moved: thou, Lord, by thy favour hast made my mountain to stand strong." Psalm xxx. 6, 7. But on the second day, I saw that *Inbred-Sin* became bolder, bestirring himself betimes in the morning; and not being properly checked at first, he speedily put an end to all the comfort which the little pilgrim had lately enjoyed.

Inbred-Sin began his operations by disturbing Humble Mind while reading his Bible; for the little pilgrim used to read and meditate upon his holy Book as he walked along the way. *Inbred-Sin* at these seasons got close behind him, and peeping first over one shoulder into the book, then over the other, he whispered strange words into his ears, drawing back as quick as lightning whenever Humble Mind turned to discover whence those whisperings proceeded. These suggestions were repeated whenever Humble Mind attempted to read; and I perceived that they generally had some reference to the passage of Scripture which the boy was perusing. On such occasions, a poor pilgrim has nothing for his support, except earnest prayer: Humble Mind did not, however, fly to this remedy; but, finding that he had not the same delight in reading as at other times, he shut up his book, and put it into his bosom.

Upon this, *Inbred-Sin* became more daring and proceeded to pluck and twitch Humble Mind, as he had done several times before, when the boy showed an inclination to go forward in the way from which he was anxious to withdraw him.

Now I saw, in my dream, that these pulls and twitches had been many times repeated before Humble Mind was aware whence they came. For he had so buoyed up his mind with the assurance that *Inbred-Sin* would not be able to follow him into the King's highway, that he was for attributing all his unpleasant feelings either to the malice of Satan who is the declared enemy of the Prince of pilgrims, or to bodily disorder, or indeed to any other outward circumstance, rather than to his own *Inbred-Sin*, which he supposed had been left on the outside of the gate at the head of the way. He was therefore much hurt, and cruelly mortified, on finding that his struggle with sin was not to end where the work of grace began—and going on to infer from his late experience that this warfare might probably continue till the work of grace should be finished at the hour of death, he was hurried into an agony of mind, crying out in his distress, "Who shall deliver me from the body of this death?" Rom. vii. 24.

In answer to this, *Inbred-Sin*, coming forward, began to plead with Humble Mind; and thus he addressed him:—"Wherefore, Humble Mind, do you cry out against me, who am no other than a part of yourself? Was I not born with you? was I not bred with you? have I not always slept in your bosom? have I not provided you with sports and pleasure from the days of your infancy until very lately? And now will you cast me aside for ever?"

"Nay, but," said Humble Mind, "if I separate not from you, I shall surely perish for ever: for 'the wages of sin is death.' It was you, and such as you, who crucified the Lord of glory; and I know that nothing less will content you than my absolute ruin, both of body and soul."

"Nay," said *Inbred-Sin*, "you wrong me, Humble Mind: I am not what you think; I am your friend, your brother, nay, I am your very *self*. And would any man, think you, seek his own ruin? More than this, if I was evil-inclined in former days, it was because I knew no better; but I am now changed, and have received a new nature from the Lord of the gate which is at the head of the way. Therefore, Humble Mind, you have no occasion to fear me any longer; I am become a servant of the High and Mighty One, I have submitted my will to his, I am anxious to obey his commandments, and am set upon doing his service. Therefore, do not be afraid, but treat me as your friend, and take me as the companion of your pilgrimage."

In this manner *Inbred-Sin* pleaded a long while, and that with so much importunity, that Humble Mind at length ceased to argue with him, or to resist him: so *Inbred-Sin* took his place by his side as boldly and familiarly as ever.

Now, while I wondered how the little pilgrim would pursue his course with such a companion, I saw a man come into the King's highway, climbing over the wall, and with him came his sons, two boys about the age of Humble Mind.

This man's name was Mr. *Lover-of-Novelty*, and he was come to make trial of a pilgrim's life, having been told that it was a pleasant one. And such indeed it is, with all its troubles, to those who are introduced to it by the right way; but to those who do not enter it by the gate which is at the head of the way, it is neither agreeable nor profitable. "I am the door," saith Christ, "and he that entereth not by the door into the sheepfold, but climbeth up some other way, the same is a thief and a robber." John x. 1.

So Mr. *Lover-of-Novelty*, having entered the King's highway, presently espied Humble Mind, who was a little before him; and, calling aloud to him, invited him to join their company.

Now Humble Mind had no inclination to make any acquaintance with this man or his children, because he liked not the manner in which they had entered the Way of Salvation. *Inbred-Sin*, however, suffered not Humble Mind's better judgment to prevail, but insinuated that Mr. *Lover-of-Novelty* might be a good pilgrim, though he conformed not altogether to the ancient rules set down for pilgrims; and, moreover, he insisted that Humble Mind should accept his invitation. So he held him in debate till Mr. *Lover-of-Novelty* and his sons came up and joined them.

Then thought I—This *Inbred-Sin* is a bold one, and, as the ancient saying is, "Give him an inch, and he will take an ell." A little while ago, he did not dare to show his face; and now he is become so bold, and loud, and vehement, that he must have all things his own way; and this, too, on the King's ground, and in company with one of the chosen ones of the Lord. Then I recollected these words—"If they do these things in a green tree, what shall be done in the dry?" Luke xxiii. 31.

It is true, that Humble Mind, being young and inexperienced, could not be supposed to have skill enough to contend with this child of hell: but it is well known, that neither age, wisdom, nor experience has ever yet enabled any man to overcome his inward corruptions. He that would conquer *Inbred-Sin* must contend with him, not in his own strength, but in the power of the Holy Spirit; he must watch unto prayer, and go forth in the strength of the Lord. God the Holy Spirit hath power sufficient to overcome and cast out this our inbred enemy; since it is his peculiar work to purify the heart, and to set it free from the dominion of sin.

I perceived then that Humble Mind had not gone far with Mr. *Lover-of-Novelty* and his sons, before they came to a little rising ground; from which, just before them appeared the pastures of the shepherd Sincerity, an exceedingly fair and lovely region, adorned with groves of tufted trees, shady fountains, and delicate flowers. This place was provided by the Lord of the way for the reception of young pilgrims; and here the lambs of the Lord's flock "dwell safely in the wilderness, and sleep in the woods." Ezek. xxxiv. 25.

Now these delightful pastures of the shepherd Sincerity had proved so peculiarly beneficial to many young pilgrims, that the enemy of their Prince had long looked upon them with a very evil eye. And not only so; but, in order to divert the attention of youthful travellers from that attractive scene, he had planted a garden on the left-hand, close by the way-side, on that very spot where these beautiful fields first present themselves to the view: and behold, he had adorned it with all kinds of fanciful decorations. He had also opened a door from it into the King's highway, where he stationed one *Light-Mind*, a fair-looking gay damsel, to entice young pilgrims into his garden.

I saw then, in my dream, that Mr. *Lover-of-Novelty* was mightily taken with the appearance of this garden on the left-hand: and Humble Mind, too, thought it looked very pretty; for it was ornamented with all manner of gay flowers, together with little pavilions made of filagree work. So they stopped before the garden-gate; when the damsel *Light-Mind* immediately opened it, and invited them to enter.

Now I observed that Mr. *Lover-of-Novelty* and his sons went in at once; but that Humble Mind made a kind of stand, and would know of the damsel, who she was? and whether the garden belonged unto the King? and wherefore she so pressingly invited him to come in?

To these questions the damsel thus answered:—"This garden has been planted here for the advantage of young pilgrims. This is a place of refreshment and education. Here all kinds of desirable accomplishments are taught, and that in a manner the most easy and pleasing. We have also in this place all kinds of musical instruments," added the damsel, "with every other possible device to render study delightful. Only come in, and you shall speedily be taught every thing which can make you an agreeable and accomplished pilgrim."

Then answered Humble Mind, "I thank you for your invitation, but I am upon a journey of life and death. I am a poor sinner, travelling from the place of my birth, which was the Valley of Destruction, to the Celestial City."

The damsel then replied, "Wherefore should you be in such haste? have you not many years before you for this journey of which you speak? You are but a child; turn in here, and rest a while, and when you are a little older, you may proceed with more confidence on your intended course."

Humble Mind. I know not how many years are before me, nor at what hour it may please God to require my soul: but what I most fear is, that, if I once turn knowingly out of the right way, I may never be able to discover it again. For this I have found, that we cannot turn into the right way when we please, but must wait for the leadings of the Spirit of God; "For that which I do, I allow not: for what I would, that do I not; but what I hate, that do I." Rom. vii. 15. Therefore I dare not come in, lest hereafter, like Esau, I should seek repentance with tears, and find it not.

Then I saw that *Light-Mind* laughed, and said, "Who has filled your head, my son, with these grave conceits? There is a time for all things: youth is the time for pleasure, and old age for religion. Methinks it is a pity that so fine a boy as you are should not be taught every thing that might enable him to pass well through the world. Cannot a man serve God without being awkward and ignorant?"

In this manner *Light-Mind* pleaded and reasoned with Humble Mind. Neither was *Inbred-Sin* quiet all this time; but while the damsel continued urging her request, he was gently drawing Humble Mind towards the gate of the garden, and whispering in his ear such things as he thought would add force to her arguments. So that, at length, through the open persuasions of the damsel, and the secret influence of *Inbred-Sin*, Humble Mind was sufficiently overcome to turn aside and follow *Light-Mind* into the garden.

Now I remarked that the walks in this garden were artfully disposed into a labyrinth; so that he who once set his foot therein could find no passage out again. Here also, among all kinds of vanities, were seen teachers of every superficial accomplishment, together with many children and young persons whom *Light-Mind* had beguiled from the right way. Then I saw that certain of these teachers of vanities came and spread forth their toys before Humble Mind, to wit, pencils and paints, maps and drawings, pagan poems and fabulous histories, musical instruments of various kinds, with all the gaudy fopperies of modern learning. Whereupon *Inbred-Sin* insisted that Humble Mind should take possession of these things; which indeed he himself was so greedily disposed to do, that he filled his pockets and his bosom therewith, overloading himself in such a manner that he dropped the book which Evangelist had given him among the rubbish of the place, without perceiving that he had lost it.

Immediately upon this, *Inbred-Sin* gathered strength and courage; so that, taking Humble Mind by the hand, he led him along the mazy windings of this garden, still farther and farther from the Way of Salvation: while Humble Mind, being puffed up with the fine things he had gotten, adverted not to the situation in which he was placed. He continued therefore till towards evening, strolling about the garden, amusing himself with the baubles it presented, and playing with the children and young people who were there assembled.

Now I beheld that, at the back of the garden, there was a howling wilderness full of wild beasts, which used to come in the night and commit dreadful ravages in the place; there being no secure fence or wall between the garden and the wilderness. So about sunset the beasts began to howl in a frightful manner; till all who were in the garden, being filled with consternation, fled some one way, some another—but there was no place of security to be found in the whole garden.

Hereupon Humble Mind became sensible of the fault he had committed in leaving the right way, even the Way of Salvation. He then looked about for some passage by which he might return: but, alas! he could find none; and the dark night was coming on apace. At length I heard that he broke out in angry reproaches against *Inbred-Sin*, which the other as angrily retorted; so that their words ran very high on both sides.

And first Humble Mind spake. "Oh, child of hell!" said he, "to what have you now brought me! You have beguiled me from my straight, my safe, and pleasant path, into this forbidden place; where I am in danger every moment of being devoured by wild beasts. Oh, *Inbred-Sin!* you will never be content till you have plunged me, soul and body, into hell."

In answer to this, *Inbred-Sin* replied, "Am I not a part of yourself? am I not indeed your *own self?* How then can you reproach yourself?"

To this Humble Mind answered, "I well know that you are a part of myself; I know that you were born with me, and bred with me: and, more than this, I fear that I shall never get quit of you, till we go down together into the grave."

"Nay, but," said *Inbred-Sin*, "are not the things which I have shown you very excellent, and worthy of the most serious attention?"

Humble Mind. But, if I should gain the whole world, and lose my own soul, what would it profit me? Matt. xvi. 26

"As for the welfare of the soul," said *Inbred-Sin*, "I am not so much concerned about that."

"But are you not afraid of hell-fire?" asked Humble Mind.

Inbred-Sin. I love to indulge my own longings—the things in this garden please me.

Humble Mind. You are, I see, no better than a brute.

Inbred-Sin. What *I* am, *you* are: if I am even a devil incarnate, you are the same.

Humble Mind answered, "I know that I am exceedingly vile, and altogether filthy, and that no good thing dwelleth in me: nevertheless I will not submit to your control; since He who died for me upon the cross intended thereby to deliver me from your dominion. So, take my defiance."

"We shall soon see which is the stronger," said *Inbred-Sin*. So they rushed together; and *Inbred-Sin* showed himself mighty in war. There was no beating him off. Although Humble Mind did his utmost, he could by no means prevail; because, as I said before, *Inbred-Sin* was a stranger to fatigue. He required no time to take breath or gather strength, but heaped blow upon blow, and stroke upon stroke, in such sort, that Samson himself would have been no match for him; since what he wanted in strength was more than made up by his perseverance. They continued struggling therefore for a long while. At length *Inbred-Sin*, grasping Humble Mind in his arms, and entangling him with his feet, tripped him up and laid him at his full length on the ground: by which unlucky fall the poor boy was so disabled, that he had not power to lift himself up. In that place therefore he lay all the night, moaning and crying; while *Inbred-Sin* stamped upon him with all his might, triumphantly exulting over him, and whispering in his ears evil words against the King of pilgrims. During this sad interval Humble Mind had no power to pray, being filled with horror at the blasphemous suggestions of his own inbred corruption. Thus he lay all that night; but the Lord of pilgrims would not suffer the evil beasts to come near him. "For the Lord will not cast off for ever: but though he cause grief, yet will he have compassion according to the multitude of his mercies. For he doth not afflict willingly, nor grieve the children of men." Lament. iii. 31–33.

CHAPTER V.

Now it was an extraordinary thing, that this same night, towards dawn of day, the shepherd Sincerity (the same who has the care of the little ones of our Lord), dreamed a dream as he lay asleep on his bed. And in his dream there was presented to his view a fair white lamb in the jaws of a dreadful wolf, that was just about to devour him: when lo, a voice from heaven awakened the shepherd, saying, "Save my lamb."

At this he arose in haste, and taking his crook in his hand, he went forth in search of him that was in the power of the wolf. So at break of day he came to the door of the garden into which Humble Mind had strayed; and turning in thither, he soon espied the child lying groaning on the ground. Now the shepherd knew by his white garment and the mark upon his forehead, that he was one of the lambs of his Lord.

Therefore stretching out his staff, and bidding him take hold thereof, he raised him up, and drew him towards himself. Then taking him by the hand, all trembling as he was, he led him through the winding ways of the garden towards the King's high-road.

The shepherd was so well known in these parts, that no one dared to ask him what he did there, or wherefore he meddled with the child. When the shepherd, however, had passed on a little way, I heard that all the inhabitants of the garden broke out into loud hissings and mockings—but Sincerity heeded them not.

Now when the shepherd had brought Humble Mind to the place where he had dropped his book, causing him immediately to cast away all the toys and trifles with which he had loaded himself the day before, he made him take up his book again. So he led the boy on, till he had brought him out upon the King's highway, where he smartly corrected him with his shepherd's crook; agreeably to the words of holy writ—"Correct thy son, and he shall give thee rest; yea, he shall give delight unto thy soul." Prov. xxix. 17. After this the shepherd addressed him in the following manner.

Shepherd. How has it come to pass, after being so kindly received by the Lord of pilgrims, after being invested with the white garments of salvation, and sealed with your Lord's own signet: how comes it, I say, that you have so speedily turned aside from the right way? Have you so quickly lost the remembrance of your Lord, and how lovely he appeared in your eyes when you were first admitted into his presence? How is it, that you have so soon forgotten your first love?

Then Humble Mind began to weep; and, as he wept, he thus replied:—"It is my wish to do well; I have no desire to have any other king than the Saviour Christ. 'His ways are ways of pleasantness, and all his paths are peace.' Prov. iii. 17. But though I wish to do well, I find I cannot; 'for to will is present with me; but how to perform that which is good I find not.'" Rom. vii. 18.

Shepherd. Can you tell what it is that holds you back from doing that which you wish to do?

Humble Mind. Yes, sir, it is my *Inbred-Sin*, the sin that was born with me, and which I fear I shall never get quit of, till I go down into the grave. Oh, sir! you know not what a deceitful, dangerous companion this *Inbred-Sin* is.

Shepherd. Perhaps I know more of him than you think, my child; nevertheless, I should be glad to hear in what way this deceiver has dealt with you.

Humble-Mind. If I were to tell you, sir, all the tricks and contrivances of this *Inbred-Sin* it would take me till sun-set, ay, and all the night too; but if you please, sir, I will mention some of the chief things, with which I have to charge him. And first, before I was effectually called by the Lord (for the Lord sent several messages to me before I could be persuaded to answer the call), this *Inbred-Sin* was altogether my master: and I am shocked on recollecting to what a state of hardness and sinful desperation he had reduced me at that time, and what crimes he caused me to commit. When I was a very little child, I remember that I loved my father and mother, and that very dearly: but after they were gone, this *Inbred-Sin* so hardened my heart against them, that I heeded no more the commands they had left with me than if I had never received them: neither had I any wish to follow my dear parents, or to be joined to them again; and all this through the instigation of this *Inbred-Sin.* And more than this (continued Humble Mind), I was persuaded by this same *Inbred-Sin* to go to Mr. *Worldly-Prudence*, and to forsake my little sisters, of whom I now know not what has become. But *Inbred-Sin*, as I before said, exercised an absolute dominion over me in those days.

Here Humble Mind looked very sorrowful; for he remembered his sisters, and his heart was greatly moved for them.

"This *Inbred-Sin*, my child," said the shepherd, "as you have found, offereth such violence to the nature of man, that he often subverts and destroys all natural affection. He produces hatred between husbands and wives, brothers and sisters, parents and children; ay, and such hath been his power, that he has sometimes induced parents to 'sacrifice their sons and their daughters unto devils, shedding innocent blood, even the blood of their sons and daughters.' Psalm cvi. 37, 38. But now go on with your account."

I heard then, that Humble Mind informed the shepherd how *Inbred-Sin* had led him to neglect the warnings of Evangelist, to despise the remonstrances of *Conviction-of-Sin*, to throw aside his Bible, yea, and to turn his back altogether on the Way of Salvation.

"And, I doubt not," said the shepherd, "but that this same *Inbred-Sin* would have you to brave hell-fire itself, for the sake of half an hour's pleasure in the present world."

"Oh, sir! the fear of eternal punishment has no power at all over him; he more than once as much as told me, that nothing would satisfy him, but my resolving to lay aside all concern about my soul."

"I could have shown you," said the shepherd, "had I then been present with you, what were the views and purposes of this *Inbred-Sin:* for he is not only the enemy of God, but he is *enmity itself*, and his nature can never undergo a change."

"But I have not told you, sir," said Humble Mind, "that, troublesome as this *Inbred-Sin* was before I became a pilgrim, he has been much more so since; nay, from the first hour that I entered upon this course, he has been the very torment of my life. He has occasionally made my very existence a burden to me—sometimes pulling me back; sometimes pinching and rending my very heart; and then hanging upon me like a drag upon a wheel, so that I could scarcely go or stand—at other times whispering evil words in my ears, arguing and contending, lying and pleading, without intermission—and lastly, in a furious onset he brought me to the ground; where he kept me sorely bruised, and not daring to cry out for help; till you, sir, came in to my assistance."

The shepherd answered, "Give the glory to God, my son, and not unto me; for unto him you owe your present deliverance." He then explained to Humble Mind the reason why *Inbred-Sin* had appeared more troublesome to him of late than formerly. "You have now," said the shepherd, "by the power of the Holy Ghost, received a new and spiritual nature, which is directly contrary to your old nature; and thus a warfare between flesh and spirit is begun within you, which will continue till your sinful body turns to corruption in the grave. Formerly, you and *Inbred-Sin* pulled one way, and were of one mind. You were then dead in sin, and had no power to turn to that which is good. But now you are become a new creature; and this has given rise to the contest of which you complain: 'For the flesh lusteth against the Spirit, and the Spirit against the flesh: and these are contrary the one to the other: so that ye cannot do the things that ye would.'" Gal. v. 17.

"I had hoped," said Humble Mind, "that, after obtaining admittance at the gate, and receiving forgiveness of sins, and being clothed in garments made white in the blood of the Lamb, I should be freed for ever from the assaults of this vexatious enemy."

"It is not the will of God," replied the shepherd, "to deliver his children, while they are in the flesh, from the importunities of sin. Although he sets them so far free from the dominion thereof, as to prevent its tyrannizing over them as in former times (Rom. vi. 14.); yet he leaves their inward corruptions as a thorn in the flesh, to humble and mortify them; teaching them, by experience, that they are nothing, and can do nothing, but must look for salvation to Christ alone."

"But, sir," said Humble Mind, "if sin is no longer to have dominion over us, how came I lately to meet with so dreadful an overthrow?"

"Because," said the shepherd, "you had given this *Inbred-Sin* a temporary advantage over you, by yielding unto his deceitful arguments, and forsaking the King's highway: moreover, you encountered him in your own strength, without seeking assistance from on high."

I heard then that Humble Mind put several further questions concerning the manner in which *Inbred-Sin* might be best mortified and kept in subjection: to all of which the shepherd thus concisely answered, "By deep humility and self-abasement, by prayer for the assistance of the Holy Spirit, and by looking to the cross of Christ."

Humble Mind, being still anxious to obtain further information from the shepherd, inquired of him wherein lay the sinfulness of such things as were taught in the garden to which he had turned aside.

"The things in themselves," answered the shepherd, "are not actually sinful; but they are rendered so by their abuse. It is written, 'Whether therefore ye eat or drink, or whatsoever ye do, do all to the glory of God' (1 Cor. x. 31.): therefore all those elegant arts and acquirements which are not directed to this end are, to say the least, dangerous pursuits."

In this manner the shepherd and Humble Mind conversed together as they walked along the Way of Salvation towards the shepherd's abode. In the mean time

Inbred-Sin followed Humble Mind softly and cautiously, stealing silently along, and, as it were, on tip-toe, yet close upon the boy's steps, and listening curiously to what the shepherd said; but he avoided showing his face, on account of the shepherd's staff, of which he was sore afraid.

By this time they had come close upon the pasture-ground, and a more inviting or lovely prospect my eyes never beheld. The Way of Salvation passes through these fields. They are called the fields of holy Peace, where, as I before said, infant pilgrims are received in order to be fed with the pure milk of the word, until they have attained strength to continue their pilgrimage. At which time, it is strictly required of them all to take up their cross; to crucify the flesh, with its affections and lusts; to wrestle against principalities and powers; and to put on the whole armour of God, that they may be able to stand against the wiles of the devil. Eph. vi. 11–13.

The air of these fields is soft and refreshing, and Humble Mind was well pleased to see many young children, clothed in white, scattered over the green lawns: some sporting on the velvet turf; others walking, with books in their hands, under the shade of the waving trees; and others sitting apart on the hill-side, or near the cool fountains, hymning their morning praises: for as yet it was but early day. Here the larger and stronger children watched over the little ones with tender love, while the little ones gave due honour to their elders, all of them preferring one another; and the weak, and the humble, and the lowly among them were had in respect by all their companions. Their garments were pure and spotless, their complexions fresh and ruddy, and their eyes as the eyes of young doves.

As soon as the good shepherd appeared, these little ones came joyfully skipping towards him, like so many young roes and harts upon the mountains; yet their love was sweetly mingled with awe; so that when they came near, they bowed humbly before him and were silent. Their good shepherd then smiled upon them, and gave them his morning blessing.

Moreover, I saw that, when the children were gathered round their shepherd, Humble Mind looked, and behold Playful and Peace stood in the midst of them. Then indeed did the young pilgrim forget all the sorrows he had endured; and while his heart leaped for joy, he wept aloud, and ran towards his sisters.

Now Playful and Peace, when they first saw Humble Mind holding the hand of the shepherd, knew him not to be their brother, by reason of the number of children that were gathered around him; but on his coming towards them, they recognized him in a moment, and hastened to meet him. At this there was a joyful cry set up among the other children, "This is their brother, their beloved brother! he is come at last, and has found his little sisters"—for Playful and Peace had often spoken of their brother, frequently wishing for his arrival, and often watching for his approach as far as they could see along the King's highway. And behold, there was joy through all the little flock, because that Humble Mind was come: for their shepherd had taught his young disciples to "rejoice with them that do rejoice, and to weep with them that weep." Rom. xii. 15. The shepherd Sincerity also rejoiced with his flock, thanking God for the lamb that had been lost and was found.

I saw then, in my dream, that the shepherd caused all the children to sit down upon the grass, giving to each of them a bowl of sweet milk, with honey and fine wheaten cakes: so the children received their food thankfully, and with hands lifted up to heaven.

Now I especially noted Humble Mind and his sisters, as they sat close together on the green grass. And behold, *Inbred-Sin* was skulking behind them, evading the notice of the good shepherd, but not less busy or troublesome than if the shepherd had been absent. I heard him whispering in the ear of one and another of them; and though they encouraged him not, but, as I observed, kept pushing and shaking him off, yet could they by no means rid themselves of his company. Nothing could be more absurd and false than the words which he whispered in their ears; and yet I perceived that he thereby greatly troubled the peace of their minds. I will repeat a few of his spiteful whisperings, as a specimen of the whole.

And first, he said to Humble Mind, "So, your sisters, who are younger than you, have got the start of you, and have been enjoying sweet peace in these pleasant fields, while you were tossed about, enduring all manner of troubles and disquietudes. Your sisters are, certainly more beloved by the Prince of pilgrims, than you are."

Then shifting his place, he whispered to Playful, "Now your brother is come, he will rule over you, and will not let you play in your bower every day, as you used to do." Then, quick as lightning, he was at Peace's ear, saying, "See you not that your brother loves Playful better than you? he kissed her first, and now he has got hold of her hand." Then again I heard him at Humble Mind's side, whispering something about certain of the children of the shepherd who were sitting near him, how much prettier they were than himself, and how they appeared to despise him, because he was but newly come. He had something also to say against the children's breakfast. This was not proper, and that was not good; your sister's bowl of milk is larger than yours, and that boy's cake is whiter than yours: and so he went on. But I was pleased to observe that the children, through God's grace, gave him at that time no encouragement.

Now breakfast being finished, the shepherd led the children into a lovely grove of tall cedar-trees; where, placing them again around him, and taking the smallest and most tender of the infants upon his knees, he delivered to them such instructions as their young minds were capable of receiving. "Look up, my beloved children," said the good shepherd, "through the opening boughs of those trees which meet in lofty arches above your heads; look at the blue sky beyond those white and shining clouds. Beyond that sky there is a celestial country, in which the throne of God is placed. God is One: he is an all-powerful Spirit, who had no beginning, and shall have no end; of infinite power, wisdom, and goodness; the maker and preserver of all things both visible and invisible. In this one God there are three persons, of one substance, power, and eternity; the Father, the Son, and the Holy Ghost. These three holy persons are called the Trinity—'There are three that bear record in heaven, the Father, the Word, and the Holy Ghost.' 1 John v. 7. 'Whosoever denieth the Son the same hath not the Father.' 1 John ii. 23. And again, 'Whosoever transgresseth, and abideth not in the doctrine of Christ, hath not God.' 2 John 9.

"The holy angels are glorious spirits, who wait upon God; they sing his praises, and obey his commands. At the appointment of God they watch over young children, and preserve them from harm; as it is written in the holy gospel—'Take heed that ye despise not one of these little ones; for I say unto you, that in heaven their angels do always behold the face of my Father which is in heaven.' Matt. xviii. 10.

"The angels live in heaven, where they enjoy all the inconceivable glories of that holy place. And if such things are written of us in the book of remembrance as are pleasing in the sight of God, we shall, in the morning of the resurrection, be received into heaven, there to dwell for ever with God the Father, God the Son, and God the Holy Ghost. The devils once were glorious angels; but they rebelled against God, and were cast down to hell. And if your names are at the last day not found in the book of the Lamb which was slain from the foundation of the world, you will be cast into the lake of fire, there to dwell with the devil and his angels.

"Therefore, my beloved children," added the good shepherd, "kneel down with me, and call upon your God; beseeching him, for the Lord Jesus Christ's sake, to have mercy upon you, to deliver you from the influence of your own evil hearts, and to make you his children for ever."

So the shepherd knelt upon the grass, with his children all around him; and they prayed to God that he would bless them for the sake of Him who died for them upon the cross, and that he would send his Holy Spirit to dwell with them and deliver them from the power of their inward corruptions. I saw then that the shepherd took a harp in his hand; and, while he prayed, the children accompanied him with one accord: and the burden of their song was the praises of the Lamb without blemish and without spot.

Now, while the shepherd was delivering his instructions to the children, and while they prayed and sang their hymn, I could not but observe the various tricks and antics of *Inbred-Sin*, who was in his usual place between Humble Mind and his sisters, but drawn rather behind them, for fear of the shepherd's eye. There he sat quietly till the shepherd began to speak; when immediately he began to whisper in the children's ears, at the same time giving them sundry pushes or sly pulls to draw their attention to himself. "What's yonder?" said he; "See there! look at that bird! There comes a mouse! I hear a cricket! Look at that butterfly! How tall those trees are! I see a bird's nest! Mark how the leaves quiver! I hear a dog bark! How fast that crow flies!"

In this way he ran on, whispering all manner of impertinences in the ears of the children, and disturbing them so much, that they could not hear half of the shepherd's discourse: and when they went to prayers, he began to yawn with all his might, thereby constraining the children to do the same whether they would or not. So that I could not help crying out, "There is no end of the mischievous ways of this *Inbred-Sin;* he 'is deceitful above all things, and desperately wicked: who can know him?'" Jer. xvii. 9.

But, to leave speaking of this *Inbred-Sin* for a while, I must say that I never heard any sound more sweet in all my life, than the voices of the little ones singing the praises of their Redeemer.

So, the hymn and the prayer being finished, the shepherd proceeded to give instructions to his little ones of a somewhat different kind, and more particularly suited to their different ages and capacities. He caused the little ones to repeat certain portions of Scripture which he had allotted to them as their several tasks, making the elder children to read certain passages of that holy book in the original languages in which they were first delivered to man. And now I perceived that he had recourse to all the assistance which could be derived from the works of the ancients: but he used them only as books of reference, treating them as literary handmaids preferred to wait upon that sacred volume, of which he never suffered his scholars to lose sight for a moment.

These duties being fulfilled, this faithful shepherd called Playful and Peace to him, bidding them take their brother to the bower which he had given them for a resting-place during their abode with him; "And there, my children," said he, as he smiled kindly upon them, "you may tell each other what things have happened to you since the day of your separation. And you, the rest of my children," added he, turning to the others, "go and feed the young birds that were lately hatched: remember also to take some new milk to the white fawn whose mother is dead; and forget not to carry food to the fair hind which yesterday broke her leg." Some other little commands to the same purport he gave them: then waving his hand, his little flock were soon scattered over the green hills and pastures, all hastening to fulfil their various duties of love and kindness; while the good shepherd sat upon the hill under the shade of the cedar grove, conversing with his God in holy meditation, and still watching his scattered charge as they wandered about the flowery pastures, lest some enemy should break in, and by any means hurt one of those unsuspecting little ones

---

CHAPTER VI.

THEN I looked again after Humble Mind: and behold, his sisters were leading him towards the bower which the shepherd had given them. And as they walked along, they sometimes kissed each other, and sometimes questioned each other concerning the things which had happened since the day of their parting.

Now I saw, in my dream, that this bower was exceedingly lovely and fresh, shaded from the noonday sun by the tufted branches of the trees; and there was a soft bed of spring herbs, on which the little ones were accustomed to sleep. So the children broke off their conversation relating to past circumstances, in order to show their brother such things as they loved in and near their bower. Peace showed him a little valley adorned with lilies; and told him that, early in the morning, while the dew was upon the grass, the young fawns would come and feed among the lilies.

"Here," said Playful, "you may sit in the heat of the day, and hear the voice of the turtle-dove (Sol. Song ii. 12); here too are 'brooks of water, and fountains, and depths that spring out of valleys and hills' (Deut. viii. 7); and here are 'beds of spices and sweet flowers.'" Sol. Song v. 13.

Then spake Peace: "Our good shepherd tells us, that all these things were made by God for the use and entertainment of those who love him. But there are more beautiful things than these in heaven; for he showed me where it is written in my book—'Eye hath not seen, nor ear heard, neither have entered into the heart of man, the things which God hath prepared for them that love him.'" 1 Cor. ii. 9.

To this Humble Mind made answer, "O my beloved sister! 'let us bless the Lord at all times, and let his praise be continually in our mouths' (Psalm xxxiv. 1.): for 'as a father pitieth his own children, so hath the Lord pitied us.'" Psalm ciii. 13.

I beheld then, that the children sat down in their bower, and related to each other every thing that had happened to them during their separation. First, Humble Mind gave an account of himself; after which Playful related to her brother the history of her and her sister's pilgrimage. And thus she spake:—

"When Mr. *Worldly Prudence* had taken you away from us, sweet brother," said she, "Evangelist came again to us while we were crying at the door of our house, bidding us to take our books in our hands, and, leaving all, to follow him. Now our hearts clung not to our home, as in days past; for our father was gone, and our mother was gone, and you, our dear brother, had also left us: so we followed Evangelist, who brought us from our own dwelling-place, and set us in the way where the shining light and the gate of salvation were directly before us; then bidding us hasten towards that gate, he departed.

"Now we had not gone far, before we were overtaken by a young woman carrying a very little baby in her arms, and her steps were turned, like our own, towards the shining light: so she looked affectionately at us, and said, 'My little ones, whither are you going?' And when we had answered her, she kindly said, 'Come with me, my children, and what little assistance I can afford you shall be freely given.'

"So, as she hastened on, with her little one in her arms, certain idle persons passing that way, said to her, 'Woman, wherefore are you in such haste?'

"'I am going,' she answered, 'to yonder shining light, to seek admittance there of the Lord of the gate for this my little boy: for whereas, through the disobedience of his first father Adam, this my baby is counted worthy of death, I, his mother, anxiously seek for him the righteousness of the Lord Jesus Christ, whereby he may be rendered meet for eternal life.'

"Whereupon these strangers, being enemies of the

Lord, and wishing to trouble the pilgrim, thus answered: 'That outward sign of the Lord's acceptance which was formerly appointed by him and administered by his servants, to wit, Baptism, hath for some time past been denied to such little ones as thine in that place, through failure of the ministers of the Lord's ordinances.'

"With that the young woman began to weep, crying out, 'O my Father! grant to this child admittance at thy gate: whether living or dying, make him thy own child, O my Father! my Father! I ask this inestimable favour at thy hand in my Saviour's adorable name.'

"So we hastened towards the gate," continued Playful, "where we met with no hinderance: for we were there most kindly received; after which we were washed with pure water, and clothed with white garments, and had the seal of our Lord set in our foreheads. Then did the mother of this little baby give thanks, and weep for joy.

"After leaving the gate, we came on our way, Peace and I, with the young woman and her little baby: and she talked sweetly to us as we passed along, and was unto us like our own mother. And in this manner we went on a day and a half: she from time to time kissing the little fair one who lay in her arms, and making the way pleasant with cradle-hymns and songs of praise, which she sang almost continually as we journeyed along.

"But behold, as we went on, there came after us a winged messenger, on whose brow the word *Death* was written. At sight of him we began exceedingly to tremble, while the poor woman pressed her baby closer to her bosom. But the messenger showed her a token, which was a silver cord broken. And more than this, he told her that he came from God, and that these were the words which he had orders to speak in her ears: 'If you love this child you will rejoice, because he is going to his Father.' John xiv. 28.

"On hearing this she wept bitterly, and delivered her baby into the messenger's hand, saying, 'O God, take my child, and make him thine own for ever!'

"The little baby smiled, and looked upon his mother, as she delivered him to the messenger; and O! how sweet was his smile! O! how lovely was his pale face!

So the messenger of God took away this little fair one, and we saw him no more."

I perceived then in my dream that Playful's account was for a time interrupted by her sorrow. After a while, however, she thus continued her story.

"So we walked on weeping and mourning, till we came to this place. Here we found the good shepherd, and to him our loving companion very earnestly commended us, saying, 'Kind sir, I beseech you, take care of these lambs, and feed them with milk till they have gained strength to continue their journey.' And with that, kissing us and blessing us, she was about to depart; when the shepherd asked her, wherefore her countenance was sad, and her eyes red with weeping?

"So she told him all that had befallen her sweet baby: 'And now, my little fair one,' said she, 'being removed from me, I cannot but go on my pilgrimage mourning.'

"With that the shepherd rebuked her, yet with kindness; for the water stood in his eyes while he spake—'My daughter,' said he, 'despise not thou the chastening of the Lord, nor faint when thou art rebuked of him: for whom the Lord loveth he chasteneth, and scourgeth every son whom he receiveth. If ye endure chastening, God dealeth with you as with sons; for what son is he whom the Father chasteneth not?' Heb. xii. 5-7. Dost thou well, my daughter,' he added, 'to grieve, because thy little son is gone to Him who loved him so well as to die for him upon the cross?' Then drawing from his pocket a perspective glass, and bidding her put it to her eye, he bade her look upwards. So she did as he required.

"Then said the shepherd, 'What seest thou?'

"She answered, 'I see nothing, sir, by reason of the tears which dim my sight.'

"'I feared as much,' he replied: 'cast away, therefore, this 'sorrow of the world which worketh death.' 2 Cor. vii. 10. Wipe away thy tears, and pray to God for help.' So she wiped away her tears; and kneeling down with the shepherd, he prayed that the God of all consolation would comfort her.

"After rising from their knees, the shepherd bade her put the glass again to her eyes, and look towards the heavens. So after looking awhile, she put on a smile of satisfaction.

"'Wherefore smilest thou, my daughter?' said the shepherd.

"She answered, 'For this my son was dead, and is alive again; he was lost, and is found.' Luke xv. 24.

"Then said the shepherd, 'What sayest thou, my daughter?—explain thy words.'

"She replied, 'The glass which you gave me, sir, has brought my baby again to my sight. I have seen my little fair one! He is without spot or blemish! He is clothed with beauty and glory such as no tongue can describe! He is with his Redeemer! 'The Lord is his Shepherd: he will never want. He maketh him to lie down in green pastures; he leadeth him beside still waters.' Psalm xxiii. 1, 2. O my baby! my sweet baby! thou art happy, my child! 'As one whom his mother comforteth, so doth the Lord comfort thee, and thou art comforted in Zion.' Isaiah lxvi. 13. I will no longer sorrow as one without hope, but will go on my pilgrimage rejoicing. 'O magnify the Lord with me, and let us exalt his name together. I sought the Lord, and he heard me, and delivered me from all my fears.' Psalm xxxiv. 3, 4.

"At this the shepherd was greatly pleased; and he said, 'God be with thee, my daughter!' But before she went forward, he gave her the glass, and bade her keep it for her comfort by the way, and rather lose her life than part with it. Now this glass was called Faith; and she received it thankfully.

"She then said to us, 'My dear children, fare ye well! God in his mercy grant that we may meet in that happy country whither my baby is gone before, and where he dwells with the children of the King.' Then again bidding us farewell, with many tears, she took the road to the Celestial City; and by this time she has doubtless proceeded very far on her way. Thus she departed, and left us in this pleasant place, where we have ever since been very happy, though often wishing for you, my dear brother; but now you are with us our joy is complete." So they kissed each other again, and seemed to be filled anew with joy.

About this time, putting his pipe to his mouth, the shepherd Sincerity played a sweet air; which sounding over the green pastures and rising grounds, the little ones soon knew the call, and came running together at the signal. I saw then that, having first given thanks, he distributed to each child a portion of such sweet and nourishing food as was most suitable to their tender ages. After which, having joined in blessing God for this seasonable repast, he made them sit down round about him upon the grass, while he thus held discourse with them. They were seated on a hill-side which faced the west, lovely and airy, and sweetly overlooking the flowery vale below. The shepherd bade his children look at the sun, which having run his daily course, was going to set; while many golden and purple clouds rested on the hills. "Look, my little ones," said he, "look at that glorious sun—it is a mighty world of light and heat. It is fixed in the heavens by the same great God who formed you all. Many worlds like this which we inhabit take their yearly courses round that sun, receiving from it light and warmth. These worlds are the work of our Redeemer Jesus Christ, by whom God made them all. The sun will soon disappear behind yonder hills: when we shall see in the heavens millions of stars. Those stars are themselves supposed to be suns, which shine on other worlds, which the same God created, and over which the same God is the universal Ruler. In those worlds, no doubt, there are creatures more numerous than the sands of the sea. God is the Father of them all; and such of them as submit to his will are happy everywhere; while they who rebel against him are everywhere miserable. By God the Son 'were all things created that are in heaven, and that are in earth, visible and invisible, whether they be thrones, or dominions, or principalities, or powers; all things were created by him and for him: and he is before all things, and by him all things consist.' Col. i. 16, 17.

"In the Book of Psalms these words are addressed to the Son of God; 'Of old hast thou laid the foundations of the earth: and the heavens are the work of thy hands. They shall perish, but thou shalt endure; yea, all of them shall wax old like a garment; as a vesture shalt thou change them, and they shall be changed; but thou art the same, and thy years shall have no end.' Psalm cii. 25–27.

"But although the mighty God who made these myriads of worlds hath the constant rule and charge of them all, yet his fatherly care extends to the minutest of his creatures. He numbers every hair of your heads and clothes the lilies of the field with all their beauty. There is not a little flower, nor a tender herb, nor leaf of the forest, but it is the workmanship of his hand. At his command each little blossom unfolds its enamelled leaves, and sheds sweet odours through the air. Wherefore if God so clothe the grass of the field, how much more shall he take care of you, my little children? Matt. vi. 30. Love him therefore with all your heart, and serve him in the way that he has commanded in his Holy Book; so shall you be safe from evil of every kind. For the Lord is your compassionate Father, and he loves you even more than your mothers ever did; as it is written—'Can a woman forget her sucking child, that she should not have compassion on the son of her womb? yea, they may forget, yet will I not forget thee.'" Isaiah xlix. 15.

Now the good shepherd took his harp in his hand, while his children accompanied him in a song of praise. They then knelt down upon the grass, and joined him in an evening prayer; which being finished, they all betook themselves to rest in their several bowers: and I saw that an aged woman, whose name was *Careful*, watched over the little ones.

CHAPTER VII.

Now, perhaps, some curiosity may be excited to know how *Inbred-Sin* was employed all this time; since he seems to have allowed the young ones to enjoy a little quiet. But the truth is, that finding himself in a place where he had so many enemies, and seeing that the shepherd was always ready to put the children on their guard against him, he judged it best to keep back and be quiet for a season, that the children, being freed from his importunities, might be thrown off their guard: that so, ceasing to watch, they might the more easily be surprised, and led astray. Accordingly, I saw that although he had followed the children all the afternoon close upon their steps, he had refrained from meddling with them, even so much as by a whisper. At night also he came with them to their bower, where stretching himself upon the grass, he pretended to fall fast asleep; though he was, in reality, as wide awake, and as full of mischief, as it was possible for him to be. So Humble Mind and his sisters seeing *Inbred-Sin* asleep, as they thought, they rejoiced, sitting down and chatting together by the light of the moon, till they felt the need of repose; when being tired with the duties and amusements of the day, they laid themselves down and slept soundly.

Now, hard by the shepherd Sincerity's pleasant fields, the enemy of pilgrims, to wit, that old serpent the devil, had planted an orchard, to the intent that the little pilgrims might be tempted by the beauty of its forbidden fruit to leave their safe and peaceful abodes. This orchard was situated in a valley, where it might be seen from many parts of the pasture-ground; and in fruit-time it presented so very fair and inviting an appearance, as to have become the means of drawing aside several young pilgrims, to their great harm and distress.

Playful and Peace had often seen this orchard at a distance, and had admired the beautiful red colour of the apples; but being warned by the shepherd, they had never ventured a step towards it. Nevertheless, it was with the fruit of this orchard that *Inbred-Sin* resolved to beguile the children. And now I will tell you how he went to work. He first began with Playful, as being the gayest and least thoughtful of the three children, and consequently the most liable to be drawn aside by vain fancies. As soon as he perceived that she was asleep, up he got, and with a soft stealing pace crept close to her side: where quietly seating himself, he began to stir up false and sinful imaginations within her, by setting forth in secret whispers the deliciousness of the fruit that grew in the enemy's orchard. I saw also that, while the tempter sat at her ear, she frequently started and turned about, as if in trouble, yea, and talked in her sleep. So the night wore away, till at length the dawn began to appear.

The little ones were awakened by the notes of the lark; when Humble Mind and Peace got up light and gay, while Playful appeared heavy, and full of thought. And behold, *Inbred-Sin* kept close by her side wherever she moved, lodging vain thoughts in her mind concerning the fruit, and causing her to think upon it with pleasure. Thus he worked upon her mind all the day; and in the evening, when the shepherd gave the children leave to play, *Inbred-Sin* put it into Playful's heart to lead her brother and sister to that side of the pasture-ground, from whence the orchard and its fair fruit might be seen. Thence I perceived that she pointed out the orchard to Humble Mind, and bade him look at the beautiful colour of the fruit. So Humble Mind looked till his mouth watered, and little Peace did the same. Upon which *Inbred-Sin*, seeing that he had got them at an advantage, came boldly forward, and put in his word, saying that he thought it very hard indeed that the children should be kept back from such desirable fruit. He further took upon him to call the shepherd by some hard names in the children's ears; to which he added, that the shepherd's Master himself dealt too hardly with little pilgrims, in denying them such pleasures as were peculiarly adapted to their time of life. The children therefore stood looking at the orchard till sunset; when they went back to their bower—but so troubled in mind that they could not pray. So they betook themselves to sleep without going to prayer.

Now I saw, in my dream, that, while the children slept, *Inbred-Sin*, having so far obtained influence over them, grew bolder still; till at length he ventured to call in the Wicked One, to wit, Satan, to his assistance. For this Wicked One is ever ready to obey the call of *Inbred-Sin*, and is always waiting, as one may say, at the door of the heart, prepared to come in at the slightest invitation. So he came forward, and a most frightful creature he was, such as my eyes never before beheld: but his figure admits of no description. He eyed the children for awhile, as they lay sleeping, just as a wolf would contemplate so many sleeping lambs; after which he began to use his enchantments. And first, he caused a thick darkness to be shed over the bower, so that the light of the moon and the stars was quite extinguished thereby; he then caused to arise before the children a representation of the forbidden fruit, after which they lusted; and the vision was exceedingly beautiful and tempting, insomuch that it surpassed the reality by many degrees. And now the children lay as in a trance; nevertheless, the eyes of their mind were opened, and fixed upon the representation of the fruit.

Thus were the imaginations of these poor children so excessively inflamed through the arts of sin and Satan, that at day-dawn up they got, and regarding neither th fear of hell, nor the hope of heaven, nor yet the expectation of punishment in this present life, away they posted towards the orchard, being violently urged forward by *Inbred-Sin*. So they ran hastily over the pasture-ground, till they came to a little lane, which opening out of the King's highway, led directly to the orchard. Down this lane ran the children as fast as they could go—when Playful, who was the first of them, having got into the orchard, suddenly felt her foot caught in a trap; that orchard being thickly set with traps and snares of various sorts. Upon this she cried aloud, but Humble Mind could not then help her; for in his haste he had fallen over-head into a ditch—nor was Peace in any better plight, she having plunged into a bog or quagmire, where the more she strove to get out, the deeper she sunk—so that all the three being in a terrible fright, their cries were very pitiful.

Now, while they were in this sad state, they heard a growling near them, like that of a wild beast. This was their "adversary the devil, who goeth about like a roaring lion, seeking whom he may devour." 1 Pet. v. 8. So as he came towards them, the poor children screamed aloud, repeatedly praying to their Redeemer, and calling upon his servant the shepherd! Neither did they pay any heed to *Inbred-Sin*, who was for stifling their cries by assuring them that neither their Redeemer nor their shepherd would hearken to them, after the great sin they had committed. The lion then came on apace: but at the very moment when Playful believed that he was about to seize upon her, the voice of the shepherd was heard, who forthwith came running into the orchard with his staff in his hand; and behold his staff bore the semblance of the cross. But the lion being on his own ground, neither fled at the voice of the shepherd, nor feared the sight of his staff, as he would have done had he been on the King's highway; but came on growling and roaring to attack the shepherd himself. Then I saw that a dreadful battle followed between the shepherd and the lion, which lasted for a considerable time; insomuch that the poor shepherd was covered with blood; nevertheless, the servant of the Lord at length prevailed, through the power of him who gave up his life to destroy the works of the devil. Whereupon the lion fled growling away; while the good shepherd, having set the children at liberty, removed them with speed from the enemy's ground.

Now I saw, in my dream, that when they were come into a safe place, to wit, into the King's pasture-grounds from which they had strayed, the children fell at the shepherd's feet and kissed them, shedding many tears, and humbling themselves in the very dust before him.

Then spake Humble Mind, "'We remember our ways, and all our doings, wherein we have been defiled; and we loathe ourselves in our own sight for all the evils that we have committed' (Ezek. xx. 43.); and more especially we hate ourselves for having caused you, dear sir, those grievous wounds; nor can we ever cease to detest these our vile and sinful inclinations, which have brought such distress upon our kindest earthly friend."

"Remember, my son," said the shepherd, "that these your sins crucified the Lord of glory: it was for these he bled and died upon the accursed tree; yea, it was for your sakes that he fought with this same lion, there being none to help him: on these accounts, therefore, you ought to loathe your sins, and to humble yourself in dust and ashes before God."

Immediately I saw that the shepherd went to a certain tree which grew thereabout, and taking some of the leaves thereof, he bound them upon his wounds: when behold, the pain was assuaged, and the flowing of the blood was stayed. The shepherd then drank of the spring of water which ran sparkling by the way-side, giving also thereof unto the children, who were greatly refreshed thereby in their fainting condition. After which the shepherd gave thanks, saying, "All my fresh springs are in thee." Psalm lxxxvii. 7. Which done, he would know of the children by what means they had been tempted to the commission of so great a sin.

So Humble Mind and Playful told him how they had been enticed by *Inbred-Sin* to commit the great offence of which they had been guilty: and they lamented, at the same time, the exceeding sinfulness and vileness of their own hearts.

I heard then that the shepherd took occasion to speak more largely and fully than he had ever before done upon the nature of *Inbred-Sin*, that deadly enemy and tormentor of pilgrims. And first, he declared unto them that the place or seat of this *Inbred-Sin* is the heart of man. "He dwells," said the shepherd, "in the heart of every one of the children of Adam, and hath always done so, excepting only in the case of Jesus Christ, who, though the son of man, 'was yet without sin.' Heb. iv. 15. Every man, before he turns to God," continued the shepherd, "is under the entire rule and governance of *Inbred-Sin*, which actuates all his members, possesses his whole heart, and influences his whole conduct; so that, without help from God, no one can do that which is right and good. But when men have once turned to the living God," proceeded the shepherd, "when they have received forgiveness of sins, through the blood of the Lord Jesus Christ, and the Spirit of God enters into their hearts, *Inbred-Sin* no longer rules over them with absolute power: because the Spirit opposeth him, and counteracts his devices. Nevertheless, this our enemy, which lurks within our hearts, ceaseth not still to strive for the mastery, though he be sensibly weakened by the prevailing power of the Spirit of God. And since he cannot domineer, and carry it so high as in times past, he has recourse to all manner of stratagems and contrivances in order to regain his lost power, and to check the workings of the Holy Spirit. In these circumstances he promises all kinds of pleasures and rewards to such as will obey him, in like manner as he promised you the fruit of yonder orchard; he withdraws men from their duties, especially from prayer and holy meditation; puffing up pilgrims with high thoughts of themselves, or persuading them to rest contented with outward forms and shows of religion.

"But," added the shepherd, "time would fail to enumerate all the frauds and artifices of this *Inbred-Sin*. Remember, my children, what we have suffered this day, and entreat your heavenly Father for grace to watch against that dreadful enemy who has his hiding-place within you: and fight not with him my children, in your own strength, but in the strength of the Lord; for 'God resisteth the proud, but giveth grace unto the humble. Submit yourselves therefore to God. Resist the devil, and he will flee from you. Draw nigh to God, and he will draw nigh to you.'" James iv. 6–8. Then the shepherd kissed Humble Mind and his sisters, and brought them back unto his fold.

Now I saw, in my dream, that the three little pilgrims remained many days with the shepherd, under whose fatherly care they grew in wisdom and in stature; and the blessing of God was upon them. At length it was signified to the shepherd, by the almighty Ruler of all things, that Humble Mind and his sisters should proceed on their pilgrimage. So, with many tears, they bade adieu to their little companions, and their pleasant bower, and the sweet pastures in which they had been so delightfully entertained. After which the good shepherd, tenderly bidding them farewell, and giving them a note to the Interpreter, whose house was not far distant, set them forward on their journey.

CHAPTER VIII.

Then I looked after the children, and saw them wiping away the tears which ran down their cheeks. So they walked on their way, even the Way of Salvation; and *Inbred-Sin* was with them. But for a while they took no notice of him, not even making the least reply, good or bad, to any of his suggestions. At length, coming to a rising ground, towards evening, they saw before them two houses at a little distance, one to the right-hand, and the other to the left; and behold, the way parted in this place, one path leading to the house on the right, and the other to that on the left. Now the children knew that one of these houses must be Mr. Interpreter's; but whose the other was, they could not tell.

Moreover I perceived, in my dream, that, while they were at a stand, knowing not which way to take, they saw a man, with two little boys, coming over the fields on the left-hand; upon whom when Humble Mind had looked for a while, he knew them to be Mr. *Lover-of-Novelty* and his sons. "Here," said Humble Mind, "is one coming whom I have met with before; but we shall get no good of him. He set me wrong on that occasion; and if we hearken to him, he will do so again."

Then spake *Inbred-Sin*, "Nevertheless, as you are

now at a loss, it would be as well to hear what this gentleman can say upon the subject: perhaps he may know this part of the country better than you do, and may be able to point out which of these two houses is the one belonging to Mr. Interpreter."

"No, no," said Humble Mind, "I have had enough of his counsels; I will have no more of them."

Inbred-Sin therefore finding that he could not persuade Humble Mind to do as he would have him, fell to whispering in Playful's ear; and so greatly did he gain upon her, that she said to her brother, "Do as you please, Humble Mind; but, for my part, I shall stay in this place till the good gentleman comes up, that I may ask his advice: for I do not see, although you are older than I am, that I should always be entirely governed by you."

"That's right," said *Inbred-Sin*; "that is well said; that is showing a proper spirit." Then stepping over to Humble Mind, he whispered in his ear, "Do you stand like a tame fool, and allow your sister, who is so much your inferior, to address you after this fashion? Have you no courage?—no spirit in you?"

In this strain he went on for some time; but Humble mind, being inwardly assisted by the Spirit of God, would by no means hearken to him. Upon which the tempter faced about again, and put Playful upon provoking her brother more, to the intent that he might be urged to speak harshly to her.

So she went on challenging him to answer, saying, "Why, this gentleman must be a foolish person indeed, if he is not fit to give advice to such children as we are. Surely, brother, you do not think yourself wiser than all the world beside! You cannot certainly be much of a pilgrim, if you hold so high an opinion of yourself as that comes to." And in this manner she went on provoking her brother, being instigated thereto by *Inbred-Sin*, till Mr. *Lover-of-Novelty* and his sons came up.

Then spake Mr. *Lover-of-Novelty*, "Well met once again, brother pilgrim! and where have you been since we parted company? and who are these little ones with you?"

When Humble Mind had answered these questions, Mr. *Lover-of-Novelty* further inquired, whither he was going? "If," said he, "you are going to the house of the Interpreter, I shall have great pleasure in accompanying you; for I am going thither myself to place these my little boys for a while under his care, being informed that he has many curious and profitable things to exhibit."

"But, sir," said Playful, "seeing before us two houses, with two ways *both* straight and even, we are quite at a loss how to proceed. Can you, sir, inform us which of those two houses belongs to the Interpreter?"

"I am very glad," said Mr. *Lover-of-Novelty*, "that I happened to come up just at this time, to help you out of your trouble. If you will hearken to me, I will inform you why you see two houses here instead of only one, as you expected; and I will direct you to which of these houses it will be advisable for you to go. You must know that yonder house which is on the right-hand, is the house of the old Interpreter. It was built by the Lord of pilgrims for the refreshment of his people; and the task allotted to the master of the house, to wit, the Interpreter, was to expound the Bible to pilgrims; for which purpose he was allowed to take similes and examples from all the creatures under heaven. That house has stood where it now stands from the time of the apostles: and in his younger days the Interpreter was a man of such rare and excellent speech, that it was delightful to hear him converse. But of late he is become so superannuated and full of wild fantasies, that he speaks of the Bible as containing a *hidden* as well as a *plain* meaning; pretending, it is thought, to see more in it than ever was intended. On this account few pilgrims at present repair to his house; suspecting that he is either mad, or sunk into a state of hopeless dotage. So that now travellers, for the most part, frequent the house of the new Interpreter, which is that to the left; where they not only find good board and lodging, but receive also the most wholesome instructions; the new Interpreter very properly maintaining, like a man of sound judgment, that the Bible has no meaning but the plain straight-forward one. To this last house, therefore, my children, I am anxious to lead you: so, come forward; for night draws on apace."

Now I saw that Playful and Peace were willing to accompany Mr. *Lover-of-Novelty;* for they understood not the real purport of what he had been saying; and *Inbred-Sin* was all on tip-toe to follow him. But Humble Mind, remembering the trouble he had fallen into once before by hearkening to Mr. *Lover-of-Novelty*, bethought himself of consulting his book: so plucking it out of his bosom, and opening it, he read these words —"If any of you lack wisdom, let him ask of God, that giveth to all men liberally, and upbraideth not; and it shall be given him. But let him ask in faith, nothing wavering." James i. 5, 6. "Here," said Humble Mind, "I have found what I wanted;" then kneeling down and praying, he said, "O God, give us now wisdom and knowledge; for we are little children, and foolishness is bound up in our hearts." Prov. xxii. 15.

Upon this I saw that one more beautiful than rubies, and more precious than silver or choice gold, came towards them, and thus addressed them:—"I love them that love me; and those that seek me early shall find me. I lead in the way of righteousness, in the midst of the paths of judgment. Now, therefore, follow me, my children: for blessed are they that keep my ways." Prov. viii. 17, 20, 32.

Now Humble Mind knew that this was Wisdom, and that she was from on high. At sight of her, Mr. *Lover-of-Novelty* and his sons made off as fast as they could, while *Inbred-Sin* slunk behind; leaving the children to follow her without interruption. So they went with her rejoicing; and she led them to the house on the right, to wit, the dwelling of the old Interpreter.

As the little pilgrims drew nearer to Mr. Interpreter's house, it appeared to them more and more pleasant and desirable. It was a large old-fashioned house, standing in a fruitful and flourishing garden enclosed with a wall and containing great choice of fruits and flowers. Here were also olive-yards, and fig-trees, and vineyards, with blooming orchards, and little cottages, and fields covered with bees. In short, all things seemed to flourish under the hand of Mr. Interpreter, who took great delight in the culture of his grounds, and would plant no seeds therein but what were of the right sort.

Mr. Interpreter was walking forth to meditate at evening-tide, when he perceived Wisdom leading the little pilgrims towards his house. Upon which he hastened to meet them; and receiving the children at her hand, he led them into the house. He conducted them first into a large parlour, where bidding them to be seated, he immediately entered into discourse with them. "Welcome, my little children," he said, "welcome to this house; and here I hope, through the good pleasure of God, that ye may abide for a season, to the end that I may show you such things as may be profitable to you." Then I heard that he called to his servants, and ordered them to prepare such tender meats as were best adapted to the state of his guests, saying at the same time, "Ye have hitherto been fed with milk, my children, but now I shall set before you a little solid food; for every one that useth milk is a babe." Heb. v. 13.

So Humble Mind thanked him for his kindness, and added, that they should rejoice to tarry awhile with him, if God permitted.

"Well, my children," answered the Interpreter, "I trust that it will so please him: and now, while you are waiting for your evening meal, I must request you to relate unto me such things as have happened to you both before and since you became pilgrims."

The little ones therefore immediately began their histories: and the Interpreter spake not until they had finished.

Now when they had done speaking, he said unto them, "My dear children, give glory to God, 'who hath delivered you from the power of darkness, and hath translated you into the kingdom of his dear Son; in whom you have redemption through his blood, even the forgiveness of sins.' Col. i. 13, 14. For ye were born in sin, 'and were by nature the children of wrath, even as others' (Eph. ii. 3.): but now are ye made the children of grace. While you yet dwelt in the land of your nativity, you trod the ways of sin and death: and not you only, my children, but all the sons of Adam do the same, being by nature utterly depraved; as it is written—'Who can bring a clean thing out of an unclean?' Job xiv. 4. 'What is man, that he should be clean? and he which is born of a woman, that he should be righteous?' Job xv. 14. These are the words of that book which cannot lie; which also saith in another place, 'without holiness no man shall see the Lord.' Heb. xii. 14

"This being the unhappy state of mankind, all men being sinners by nature, and the wages of sin being death—according to that which is written, 'Behold, all souls are mine; as the soul of the father, so also the soul of the son is mine: the soul that sinneth, it shall die' (Ezek. xviii. 4.)—such being as I said, the unhappy state of all mankind, the Lord Jesus Christ gave himself for them, that he might endure the punishment which they had incurred.

"This blessed Saviour, the Son of God, who is equal with God, and one with God, took man's nature upon him in the womb of the blessed Virgin; so that two whole and perfect natures, the *divine* and the *human*, were joined together in one person. And this holy person was crucified, in order to reconcile offending man to his offended God, actually dying on our account, and descending into the grave; from whence he afterward triumphantly arose, and ascended up into heaven, where he is now seated at the right hand of God. Moreover, at his departure, he left with his disciples this gracious command—'Go ye, therefore, and teach all nations, baptizing them in the name of the Father, and of the Son, and of the Holy Ghost.' Matt. xxviii. 19.

"This is He who opened that door of salvation through which you were admitted to the divine favour, and received into the congregation of Christ's flock. The assurance that your sins are forgiven you, and that you are become the adopted children of God, was signed and sealed upon you at that time; and the promise of the Holy Spirit, which proceedeth from the Father and the Son, and who is also equal with God and one with God, was also granted to you at that time."

I heard then that the children lamented in the presence of the Interpreter, the many hinderances and drawbacks which they experienced continually in their pilgrimage, from the secret enemy they carried about them, even their own inbred corruptions. "Why, sir," said Playful, "it was but this very day that I was secretly inclined to turn out of the right way; on which occasion I was influenced, though I knew I was doing wrong, to speak many reproachful words to my brother."

"Sir," said Humble Mind, "our *Inbred-Sin* seldom allows us any peace; and if he seems to be quiet for a while, he is sure at that very time to be contriving further mischief: so that when we think ourselves most secure from his attacks, he is then most to be feared."

"Very true, my children," answered the Interpreter: "it is not when we are on the watch, and up in arms, as it were, against our sins, that they are most to be feared; but rather when they cry, 'Peace, peace,' and persuade us to think that all is well within."

"Oh!" said little Peace, "what would I give for a complete deliverance from this tormentor!"

"My child," answered the Interpreter, "after this life thou shalt behold the face of thy Redeemer in righteousness; and awaking in his likeness, thou shalt be satisfied. Psalm xvii. 15. Then, and not till then, thou wilt be completely freed from this inbred enemy." The Interpreter then proceeded to point out to the children how, from the earliest times, this *Inbred-Sin* had made the saints of God to go groaning on their pilgrimage. "It was this *Inbred-Sin*," said he, "which made the patriarch Noah to drink of the wine, and be drunken in his tent (Gen. ix. 21.); and it was he which brought righteous Lot to commit the same crime in his old age. Abraham also, and Isaac, and Jacob, went mourning all their days, by reason of this same homebred evil. It was this *Inbred-Sin* which caused King David to cry out, in his anguish, 'O Lord, rebuke me not in thy wrath; neither chasten me in thy hot displeasure. For thine arrows stick fast in me, and thy hand presseth me sore. There is no soundness in my flesh because of thine anger; neither is there any rest in my bones because of my sin. For mine iniquities are gone over mine head; as an heavy burden they are too heavy for me. My wounds stink, and are corrupt, because of my foolishness. I am troubled; I am bowed down greatly; I go mourning all the day long. For my loins are filled with a loathsome disease; and there is no soundness in my flesh.' Psalm xxxviii. 1–7. And finally, it was this *Inbred-Sin* which rendered it necessary to our salvation, that God himself should take our nature upon him, and bleed and die upon the accursed tree.

Now I saw, in my dream, that when the Interpreter had ended his discourse, and supper was finished, he prayed and sang with his family; after which he charged one of the damsels of the house to see that the children were lodged in a comfortable chamber. Moreover, I heard him give commandment to the servants of the family, to take good heed to the children, and provide them with all such things as might be needful for them while they remained in that place; taking special care that their white garments should contract no stain. And I observed that the servants received their master's orders gladly; for they loved young children.

CHAPTER IX.

Now I saw in my dream that the children were up betimes in the morning; the Interpreter having promised to take them into his garden at an early hour. *Inbred-Sin*, as usual, rose with them; and while they waited the coming of the Interpreter, he began prating after a prodigious rate, and with as much pertness as ever. "And so," said he, "you are very comfortably situated! You are not here treated like babies, as you were at the shepherd's, and fed with milk; but you are fed with meat, which is certainly more suitable to your present state. For you are not now mere babes in Christ, as some would have you think; you have had a great deal of teaching, and have acquired much experience; so that you know more than many grown persons. There are many grown people," continued he, "who, though they seem wise, are very foolish, still seeking after trifles, and taking no care of their souls: but it is otherwise with you. What incessant thought and care do you take about everlasting things!"

In this manner *Inbred-Sin* went on chattering; while the children, one and all, seemed to listen to his flattering words with great satisfaction. Humble Mind smiled, and looked self-sufficient; and Playful assumed an air of much complacency. When the Interpreter, however, appeared, *Inbred-Sin* drew behind, and the children began to recollect themselves a little. So the Interpreter took them into his garden.

Now the Interpreter's garden, which was enclosed with a high wall, was watered with fountains of living water and streams from the hills. A south wind generally blew through this garden, and made the spices thereof to flow. The flowers now appeared everywhere in the green turf; the little birds were singing among the trees, and the voice of the turtle was heard all around. Sol. Song ii. 12.

The children wondered at the beauty of this garden, and inquired of the Interpreter, by what means he had rendered it so exceedingly lovely?

"This garden," replied the Interpreter, "was once

a wilderness; but after being planted with care, and watered with streams from the hills, the blessing of God came upon it. Man can cultivate the ground, and sow the seed, but God alone giveth the increase. For he maketh 'the wilderness and the solitary place to be glad; he causeth the desert to rejoice, and blossom as the rose.'" Isaiah xxxv. 1.

I saw then that one of the gardeners came to the Interpreter, bringing him a sprig of myrtle, to which rosebuds were fastened with thorns.*

When Playful saw it she was pleased: so the Interpreter bade the gardener to give it her. She had not however admired it long, before the buds began to fade, and their withering leaves to fall off. Then said the Interpreter, "Wherefore do those rosebuds fade so soon, my child?"

"I suppose," answered she, "because they have been parted from the branch to which they belonged, and fastened to another."

"True, my child," replied the Interpreter: "had those rosebuds remained on their parent stem, they would not thus have withered and fallen away, but would have unfolded their fragrant blossoms, and flourished as the rose of Sharon. Can you discover the meaning of this emblem? How do you apply this to yourselves?"

"I think," said Humble Mind, "I can answer this question."

"Do so, my son," said the Interpreter.

Then spake Humble Mind, "Our Saviour is the rose-tree, and we, his children, are the rosebuds. While we remain with him we flourish; but, parted from him, we fall away, wither, and die."

"Well spoken, my boy," said the Interpreter. "The Lord saith, 'I am the true vine. If a man abide not in me, he is cast forth as a branch, and is withered; and men gather them, and cast them into the fire, and they are burned.'" John xv. 1, 6.

I perceived then that the Interpreter showed the children a lily growing among thorns. (Sol. Song ii. 2.) And the children requested him to explain the meaning of that exhibition.

"The lily," replied the Interpreter, "represents a

* The Hindoostaunee mode of making nosegays, by fixing the blossoms of one flower upon the stalk of another with thorns.

Christian in this present evil world; for as his Lord and Master was not of this world, so neither is he; and if the world hated the Master, will it not also hate the servant?' John xv. 19, 20. After this the Interpreter conducted the children back to the house; where, after prayers, they all sat down to breakfast.

Now about noon the Interpreter again led the children abroad. *Inbred-Sin* also went with them; but being awed by the presence of the Interpreter, he cautiously kept himself for a while in the background. So as they walked through his fields and orchards, the Interpreter bade them look towards the east, where he showed them a milk-white lamb, lovely and fair, feeding on the side of a green hill. Around this lamb were many flocks of goats and sheep; but they were all spotted and speckled, and not one of them so lovely as this white lamb.

Little Peace appeared to be quite ravished with the beauty of this spotless creature; and she said, "O that he were mine!"

With that the old Interpreter smiled, and said, "He shall be thine, my little one, and thou shalt be his; and he shall take thee, 'and lead thee unto living fountains of water.'" Rev. vii. 17.

"When, sir?" said Peace.

"When God pleaseth, my child," replied the Interpreter.

Humble Mind then said, "Wherefore, sir, do I see that lamb white as milk, while all the rest of the flock have some spot or blemish?"

The Interpreter answered, "That lamb, my son, is an emblem of Christ, the Lamb of God, without spot or blemish, who by the sacrifice of himself once made, hath taken away the sins of the world. He, you observe, is without stain—but you see the rest of the flock to be spotted and speckled; this is to signify, that, although we are baptized and born again in Christ, yet we offend in many things; and if we say that we have no sin we deceive ourselves, and the truth is not in us." (*See* 15*th Article of the Church.*)

Now it came to pass, that while Humble Mind and Peace were talking to the Interpreter about this fair lamb which was without spot or blemish, *Inbred-Sin* drew himself close up to Playful's side, and began whispering foolish conceits into her ear: at which, when she had listened awhile, she began to smile; till, from smiling, she broke out into a downright loud laugh.

Her brother and sister looked hard at her; while the Interpreter said, " Methinks, my little maid, that you are very much diverted. Will you discover to us the cause of your mirth, that we too may laugh with you?"

Now Playful, being ashamed to tell the Interpreter what she laughed at, made no answer.

Then whispered *Inbred-Sin* in her ear, " Say that you did not laugh."

So she did as *Inbred-Sin* advised her, and said to the Interpreter, " Sir, I did not laugh."

Then being greatly grieved, the Interpreter replied, "Oh, my daughter! let not the evil of your heart lead you to the great sin of lying. When you have done amiss, why should you increase the evil, by adding to it a lie? Know you not what is said of lying in the Holy Book?—'Ye shall not lie one to another.' Lev. xix. 11. 'The mouth of them that speak lies shall be stopped.' Psalm lxiii. 11. 'All liars shall have their part in the lake which burneth with fire and brimstone.'" Rev. xxi. 8.

At this Playful was covered with confusion, and begged of God to forgive her: so *Inbred-Sin* was rebuked, and drew away from Playful for a season. But I saw him, shortly after, very busy at Humble Mind's ear, whispering therein flattering words, and telling him how much more wisely he had behaved than his sister, conducting himself with all possible decency and modesty, while she was giggling and tittering, like a foolish child.—Whereupon Humble Mind began to be puffed up, as I perceived by the pertness of his manner and a certain air of conceit which were not usual with him.

The Interpreter then having pardoned Playful, and taken her by the hand again, led the children on till they came to a vine-tree, fair and flourishing, enclosed with a paling. From this tree certain persons who had the care thereof were gathering clusters of grapes, and distributing to such as came to ask for them. I observed also that some of those who ministered before the vine were agreeable persons, possessing all the charms of external beauty and gracefulness of manner; while others were ill-favoured and unpolished. The Interpreter then called for grapes to be given the children: when behold, one of the ill-favoured persons went up to the tree, and gathered a few clusters for the children. So Playful and Peace received them thankfully: but

Humble Mind, being put upon it by *Inbred-Sin*, declined taking them, informing the Interpreter, that he would rather receive his grapes from the hands of one of the more sightly persons.

When the Interpreter heard this, he was displeased, and was about to order Humble Mind's portion to be carried back, remarking that he was not in a fit state to receive any thing; but Humble Mind instantly confessing his sin, the Interpreter forgave him.

As they continued their walk, the Interpreter took occasion to explain unto them what they had just seen, and wherefore he was so angry with Humble Mind for refusing the grapes from that ill-favoured person. "The vine which you saw," said the Interpreter, "is an emblem of our Saviour Jesus Christ (John xv.); and they who were gathering and distributing the grapes are his servants, who minister of the true vine unto the people. Now although in the church of Christ and among the true servants of the Lord, some are endowed with brilliant gifts and shining talents, while others are, as it were, without form or comeliness, possessing neither the charms of eloquence nor the graces of manner—but since all of them minister of the same vine in simplicity and truth, we ought to use their ministry thankfully, both in hearing the word of God, and in receiving the sacraments; remembering that the 'Lord is no respecter of persons, but in every nation he that feareth him and worketh righteousness is accepted with him.' Acts x. 34, 35. (*See 26th Article of the Church.*) Wherefore. my son, you greatly erred, when you listened to the whisperings of *Inbred-Sin*, who filled you with pride, and caused you to refuse the fruit of the Lord's vine, because you liked not the person employed to administer it. In this manner, very often," said the Interpreter, "do men refuse to go to church, because the minister pleases them not; and children, from the same proud spirit, refuse to receive holy instruction, because their teacher, perchance, hits not their fancies."

When Humble Mind heard these words of the Interpreter, he was ashamed—so passing on they came into the street of a little village. Now behold, at the door of a certain cottage there sat a knot of old women very busily spinning; and as they turned their wheels, they talked one with another. And behold their discourse was of the faults and failures of their neighbours; so that not an individual was mentioned, to whom some fault was not imputed.

Then said the Interpreter to the children, after they had passed on a little way, "Do you think that those old women spake the truth, when they imputed to each of their neighbours some particular fault?"

"Yes," said Humble Mind, "because we all have faults, and are none of us without sin."

The Interpreter answered, "True, my son. Keep this therefore ever in your mind, that, since we are all born in sin; yea, and even after our regeneration, fall very far short of the glory of God; it becometh us, in a kind and brotherly manner, rather to point out to one another the way of amendment, than to condemn and ridicule each other in absence. 'Therefore thou art inexcusable, O man, whosoever thou art that judgest: for wherein thou judgest another, thou condemnest thyself; for thou that judgest, doest the same things.'" Rom. ii. 1.

I saw then that, going a little further, they came to a house, where, by the buzzing sound of many young ones conning their tasks, they perceived that a school was kept. So the children stood still to hearken.

"Here," said the Interpreter, "dwells a schoolmaster, to whom I send all the children who occasionally sojourn with me. He is indeed a strict schoolmaster; but the rules of his school are so good, that if any one can keep them from his youth up, he is sure of salvation, and need go no further for it. But this venerable instructer hath this particularity, that if any one go contrary to the least of his commandments, it is the same thing with him as if the guilty person had offended against them all. He counts such a one a transgressor; and though he lets him remain in his school for instruction, he holds out to him no hope of reward."

"Surely, sir," said Peace, "he must be a very hard master! I should be much afraid of him."

The Interpreter replied, "This schoolmaster's name is *Law;* and it is written, 'Whosoever shall keep the whole law, and yet offend in one point, he is guilty of all.'" James ii. 10.

Then said Playful, "Who then can be saved?"

Interpreter. By the deeds of the law none can be saved. Rom. iii. 20.

"Sister," said Humble Mind, "have you forgotten

how often we have been told, that we cannot possibly be saved by any good which we ourselves can do?"

Now I saw that *Inbred-Sin* was very busy whispering in Playful's ear; and behold he was filling her with vainglorious conceits; so, after hearkening to his whisperings, she answered her brother accordingly. "Yes," said she, "the shepherd used often to tell us that we could do nothing well, and that there is no good in any person. But I am sure I have seen some good children, as well as some good men and women. Some days you are good, and some days I am good: and I think, if Mr. Interpreter would let me try a little while, I could keep all the rules of this school, be they ever so strict."

Humble Mind was surprised, when he heard his sister boasting in this manner, and little Peace looked hard at her: but the Interpreter wondered not; for he knew all the ways of *Inbred-Sin*, and how he influences mankind to commit all manner of follies, even while they "speak great swelling words of vanity." 2 Pet. ii. 18. So, without making any answer, he led the children into the school-room; where sat the schoolmaster *Law* at his desk, with his scholars about him.

Now the schoolmaster's brow was stern; yet withal he had a comely person, and his features were so well proportioned, that they who feared him most could not but look upon him with admiration. I saw then that the Interpreter requested him to show the rules of his school to Humble Mind and his sisters. When he pointed out two tables of stone, on which they were written; four on one table, and six on the other—and I perceived that all the books used in the school were but explanations of these rules.

Then Mr. Interpreter said unto the schoolmaster, "Declare unto us, sir, how many of all the children of Adam, who have received instruction from you, have been able to keep your rules."

To which the schoolmaster replied, "I have had millions, and tens of millions of mankind under my charge, Mr. Interpreter; but never had I more than one scholar who was perfectly obedient to me. He was one without a fellow; he was absolutely without fault—yea, without spot or stain."

"I know him well," said little Peace; "he was the Lamb without spot."

The Interpreter then looked at Playful, and, behold

she blushed; for she was ashamed to think of the boast that she had made. Whereupon she rebuked *Inbred-Sin* who had suggested it to her, insomuch that he drew behind, and kept himself quiet for awhile, perceiving that the children had no mind to hearken to him just then—for he was one who watched his opportunities.

After this the Interpreter spake thus: "I would have you to come, my dear children, for a few hours every day, while you remain with me, to study under this good master: for he will teach you to what extent you are sinners, and how far ye have fallen from all righteousness; which they are totally unacquainted with who, having never studied the righteous law of God, are filled with a conceit of their own innocence, even while living in all manner of sin. But this excellent master will make you to know the plague of your own hearts, to the end that you may the more speedily apply to him who alone can heal them."

The children then walked back to the Interpreter's house; and from that time they went, day by day, for a few hours to the school of *Law*. And behold, the schoolmaster caused the two little girls to work the laws of the school with their needle upon pieces of satin, while he ordered Humble Mind to copy them on vellum; which having finished, they received their master's directions to bind them upon their hearts.

CHAPTER X.

Now I saw, in my dream, that the time was come when the little pilgrims must leave the house of the Interpreter, and proceed on their journey: so the Interpreter bade the children to be ready at day-break on the morrow, saying that he himself would set them on their way. Accordingly, having prepared all things the night before, and taken an affectionate leave of such of the family as had shown them kindness, they were ready to depart before dawn of day: and *Inbred-Sin*, I perceived, was ready also to bear them company, though, it may well be imagined, not on their invitation.

On coming out of the room where they had slept,

behold, the Interpreter stood at the house-door, holding in his hands three little vessels of gold with their covers, having chains by which to hang them up, all curiously wrought, and very pretty. Of these golden vessels the Interpreter gave one to each of the little ones, bidding them fasten them by the chains to their girdles. So the children received them gladly, and would know of him their proper use.

"We will speak of this," said the Interpreter, "as we walk by the way."

Now the hour was so early that the morning light had hardly dawned in the east: but the little ones walked on cheerfully, having the Interpreter for their guide. And as they walked, their guide discoursed with them thus.

Interpreter. My children, you have a long journey before you, and many difficulties to overcome, ere you reach the Celestial City: hinderances from the enemy of souls, to wit the devil; hinderances from mankind; and more than all, daily, hourly hinderances from the sin that dwelleth in you, which ruleth in your members, and which warreth against your souls. Have you considered whether you have strength sufficient for this journey? The shepherd Sincerity will not be with you, to feed you with milk as heretofore; neither shall I be near you, to administer to your wants. The time has come when you are no longer to enjoy the stated assistance of your fellow Christians, as heretofore. You must now walk on your way with very little support from man, and encounter many dangers without human help. Tell me, therefore, my little tender ones, how do you expect to be sustained on this journey?

I saw then that the children were surprised and grieved at the words of the Interpreter; looking this way and that way, and not knowing what to answer.

At length *Inbred-Sin* whispered in Humble Mind's ear what he should answer; when Humble Mind spake to this effect: "We have been abundantly provided for, in your house, sir, of late; and I think we may go upon the strength of that meat a long time. We have also some dried fruits with a few biscuits in our bags, which we received out of your store-room; and these we can eat when we feel ourselves hungry."

Then I saw that the Interpreter sighed, and said, "My poor child, you say, 'I am rich and increased with goods, and have need of nothing; and know not that you are wretched, and miserable, and poor, and blind, and naked.'" Rev. iii. 17.

At this, beginning to be frightened, the children all cried out, "What then must we do? Where shall we find bread to keep up our strength? Surely we shall die by the way, and shall never reach Mount Zion!"

The Interpreter then replied, "In the Holy Book it is written, 'They that wait upon the Lord shall renew their strength; they shall mount up with wings as eagles; they shall run, and not be weary; and they shall walk, and not faint.' Isaiah xl. 31. And again, 'When I am weak, then am I strong.'" 2 Cor. xii. 10.

"Sir," said Humble Mind, "I remember these words, but I understand them not."

"By these words we learn," said the Interpreter, "that strength and power to do well and to walk uprightly in our heavenly course must be daily sought from God in sincere and earnest prayer. And God will assuredly hear our prayer, and give us the strength of the eagle, which alone, of all the birds of the air, can soar on high in the face of the sun. But before we can properly seek strength from God, we must know our own weakness, and cease altogether to trust in ourselves." Then I saw that the Interpreter knelt down, and with him the little pilgrims: and behold, he prayed: and the words of his prayer were, "Lord, give us day by day our daily bread."

On rising from prayer, he bade the children look upon the ground. And behold, upon the face of the ground there lay a small white thing, small as the hoar-frost, and the taste thereof was very sweet.

"This is manna!" exclaimed Humble Mind. Upon which the children were much delighted; and the Interpreter bade them hasten to fill their little golden vessels with the manna which God had given them, that they might eat thereof and refresh themselves on their journey. The children therefore made haste: and it was well they did so; for when the sun arose, all the manna which was left upon the ground shortly melted away.

Then cried Humble Mind, "I see that we shall be satisfied with bread, and shall want no good thing." And the children rejoiced.

"Remember then," said the Interpreter, "that Christ

is 'the living bread which came down from heaven.' John vi. 51. If ye feed on him, if ye seek him day by day in prayer, ye shall receive strength, and shall 'be strong in the Lord, and in the power of his might' (Eph. vi. 10); 'yea, out of weakness you shall be made strong' (Heb. xi. 34); 'and none shall be weary nor stumble among you.'" Isaiah v. 27.

Now by this time, the sun being pretty high, the Interpreter was minded to return to his house. So he kissed the little ones; and bidding them hold fast the book which Evangelist had given them, he exhorted them carefully to seek, day by day, the bread of life from heaven. After which he put into their hands a letter to be delivered to the damsels at the palace Beautiful, which is the dwelling of the Christian Virtues: and thus, bidding them God-speed, he went back to his house; while the little ones proceeded along the Way of Salvation.

In a short time I looked again after the children: and behold, they preserved an even course all that day, keeping *Inbred-Sin* under subjection, and refreshing themselves with the manna out of their golden cups. At night, coming to a place where there were much grass and many palm-trees, there they lay down to sleep —and *Inbred-Sin* was with them. And while they slept he was up and about, according to his custom, now perching by the side of one, and then of another, and busily whispering in their ears.

What would come of all this whispering I could not imagine; though I shrewdly suspected that it could tend to no good. So, before day-dawn, Humble Mind awaking called aloud to his sisters to arise and fill their pots with manna; but *Inbred-Sin* had so overcome them with the spirit of sinful sloth, that when Humble Mind called them they would not arise. Instead of this, they persuaded their brother to sleep a little longer, saying that they had manna enough left in their golden vessels for that day's use: upon which they all turned round and slept again. On awaking the second time, it was broad day, and they found themselves very hungry. Whereupon they looked into their pots for the manna which had been left the night before; but behold, it stank, and had bred worms; insomuch that they were forced to throw it away and to wash the vessels. They therefore began their day's journey fasting, and went sauntering along, as persons do when they are weak with hunger.

Now I saw that they had not proceeded far before they came to a place where a miry lane came up unto the King's highway, where there was a ladder set for climbing the separating wall. Then said *Inbred-Sin*, "Let us ascend that ladder, and look over the wall."

"For what purpose?" said Humble Mind.

"Just to see what is on the other side," answered *Inbred-Sin*. "We will only just look about, and then go on our journey."

"There cannot be much harm in just looking, to be sure," said Humble Mind.

So up the ladder they all climbed, and stood looking over the wall down the miry lane, which was shaded on each side with bushes of bramble and wild thorn. And behold, in a kind of bottom, at the end of the lane (which was very short), they saw one groping and grubbing in the ground for earth nuts.

When this man observed the children peeping over the wall, he invited them to come down to him, saying, "Here are some excellent earth nuts; and, if you are hungry, you may here eat and be satisfied."

"Let us go," said *Inbred-Sin*; "it is but little out of our way."

The children therefore went over the wall, and running down the lane, they began eagerly to grub up the ground for earth nuts, while *Inbred-Sin*, gayly crowing and clapping his sides, maliciously splashed the mud and mire of the lane over all their white garments.

Now, while they were in this bemired and evil condition, groping up to their elbows in the dirt with this stranger, whose name was *Filthy-Curiosity*, behold, one came behind them, and laid sorely on their backs with a scourge. Upon which they jumped up, and behold, it was the schoolmaster *Law*; at sight of whom *Filthy-Curiosity* fled, and *Inbred-Sin* hid himself behind the children. So the little ones stood trembling and quaking before their old master, filled with shame and confusion at their unseemly condition.

Then spake the schoolmaster, "What do you here? and why have you thus defiled your garments through the persuasions of this *Filthy-Curiosity*? Know you not these words?—'Behold, what manner of love the Father hath bestowed upon us, that we should be called the sons of God! therefore the world knoweth us not, because it knew him not. Beloved, now are we the sons of God; and it doth not yet appear what we shall be: but we know that, when he shall appear, we shall be like him; for we shall see him as he is. And every man that hath this hope in him purifieth himself, even as he is pure.'" 1 John iii. 1–3.

To all this the children had not one word to offer, by way of excuse; whereupon their schoolmaster reproved them again, and laid their sin in order before them; ay, and more than this, he corrected them severely too, insomuch that the blood ran down their backs amid many cries of sorrow and remorse. After which he led them back into the right way: and behold, they were sore distressed; for he pressed hard upon them.

So they ran forward till they came to a rising ground; and behold, just in the midst of the way before them stood a cross—the very cross of our Lord—to which his holy hands and feet were nailed; and upon which he poured out his soul an offering for sin. This is the cross to which all sinners must come for pardon, who hope to enter the kingdom of heaven. Now the glory of God shone upon this cross, and a divine light surrounded it.

At the sight of this cross the hearts of the children were gladdened; because they understood that here they should find refuge from him that smote them. But *Inbred-Sin* disturbed their joy: for while the schoolmaster *Law* drove them forward, he stepped in between them and the cross, and by casting large stones in their way, made them stumble as they ran. So that, through the terrors of the law on the one hand, and the resistance of *Inbred-Sin* on the other, they were reduced to a miserable plight; which at length constrained Humble Mind to cry out to *Inbred-Sin*, "Wherefore, O thou tormentor, dost thou harass us thus?"

To whom *Inbred-Sin* replied, "What! will you dare to appear before the cross of the Blessed and Holy One all unclean and filthy as you are? In such a case you will assuredly be cast forth into everlasting misery!"

Then were the children so much alarmed, that they began to beseech their old master to have patience with them. "O, sir!" said they, "allow us at least time to wash ourselves, and make ourselves clean, before we draw nigh unto the presence of our Lord."

But he answered them thus, "This suggestion is of

the devil: 'For though thou wash thee with nitre, and take thee much soap, yet thine iniquity is marked before me, saith the Lord God.' Jer. ii. 22. 'Go to your Father and say unto him, 'Father, we have sinned against heaven, and before thee, and are no more worthy to be called thy children.' " Luke xv. 18, 19.

Thus the "law was their schoolmaster to bring them unto Christ." Gal. iii. 24. So they came unto the foot of the cross, and there prostrating themselves in the dust "they sought the Lord, and he heard them, and delivered them from all their fears. They looked unto him, and were lightened; and their faces were not ashamed." Psalm xxxiv. 4, 5. For the Lord was graciously pleased to show them mercy, as they lay crying all night at the foot of the cross, and embracing it with their little arms; after which, towards morning, they fell into a sweet sleep. Moreover, while they slept the Lord caused a precious balsam to distil from the holy cross; which secretly falling upon them, suddenly healed all the bruises they had received, and cleansed their polluted garments from every stain.

The children then awoke from their sleep rejoicing; and rising up, they praised God together: when perceiving that the manna lay thickly scattered upon the ground thereabout, they gathered thereof and filled their golden vessels, eating at the same time till they were satisfied. This done they proceeded on their course with joyful hearts; and never did I see *Inbred-Sin* more cast down or inert than he was all that day. This however did not hold long; for while the children slept at night, he showed himself as brisk as ever: and on the morning appearing, when they should have been gathering manna for the day, he put them upon plucking certain curiously coloured flowers which grew thereabout—by which means they wasted their time till the rising sun had melted all the manna away.

So the children passed on, yet not so cheerfully as the day before, but with heavy steps, loitering, and lingering, and talking idly as they went. And behold *Inbred-Sin* was very busy among them, diverting their attention from time to time, with one trifle or another, till the day was far spent. Now towards evening, they perceived before them an exceedingly high hill which was called the hill Difficulty. The road to the Celestial City passes directly over this hill; and at the top of it stands the palace called

Beautiful, where dwell those three fair sisters, Prudence, Piety, and Charity, together with other wise and holy damsels, of whom mention is made in the histories of all such pilgrims as have travelled this way.

Now I saw that, having gazed for a while at the lofty hill before them, the children began to murmur and complain; and especially after *Inbred-Sin* had described the labour and pain it would cost them to ascend it. They stood still therefore for a time, considering what they should do. At length *Inbred-Sin* espying a pleasant grassy lane, which put itself into the highway just at the foot of the mountain, and which seemed to wind round it, he persuaded them to take that road. So being overcome by the entreaties of *Inbred-Sin* they made towards the lane, and came to it just about dusk.

This green lane was soft to the feet, and it was bordered on each side with sweet-scented shrubs and flowers. It was called *Idle-Lane*, and led to the house and gardens of a certain woman named *Indulgence*; one who has the training of many children, and who has enticed many young pilgrims from the Way of Salvation. This *Indulgence* is one of the daughters of the Evil One, and through her means many have been conducted down to hell; for she pampereth the flesh, and taketh part with the sin that dwelleth in us.

I looked therefore, and behold, the children went sauntering down the lane, the very air of which has a tendency to produce drowsiness and inactivity. And behold, the lane turned and turned, till, before it was totally dark, the little pilgrims found that they had quite turned their backs upon the hill: for the rays of the sun continued to illuminate the top of the hill some time after the lower lands were covered with darkness. Then I saw that, when the children perceived that they were getting farther and farther from the mountain, they began to be frightened; whereupon Humble Mind cried out, "We have turned our backs upon the Way of Salvation and have got into unknown paths; we have done amiss in wandering hither, and it would be our wisest course to return without delay."

Then spake *Inbred-Sin*, "How can you return to-night? is it not dark? and are you not weary?—it will now certainly be best to go on to the house which is right before us; where having lodged for the night, we may in the morning return to the King's highway."

The children therefore followed *Inbred-Sin*, who undertook to lead the way. Then I began to think—Is it not strange, that these children should let this *Inbred-Sin* lead them aside again, after having so often and so sorely smarted for following his counsels?—although they are so thoroughly acquainted with his vileness?—although they have lately spoken so prudently and wisely concerning him?—although they frequently lament his power over them, and that with so much anguish, as sometimes almost to wish for death to rid them of his tyranny?—and lastly, although they know whence assistance may be had to resist him? But then I thought again—Why do I wonder that this deceiver should have power so often to prevail against these little children, when I recollect the actual transgressions into which the most eminent saints of old time have been drawn by him? Truly this indwelling sin is so wonderfully powerful and armed with so subtile a poison, that it will bring leanness on the unguarded souls of men even amid all the precious means of growth and fruitfulness.

Now I saw, in my dream, that the children were come to the gate of a garden in which stood the house of *Indulgence;* and the gate being open, they entered without hesitation. And as they passed through the garden, although it was nearly dark, they could perceive that it abounded with flowers and fruits. But the fruit of that garden was not of a salutary sort; moreover it grew in the midst of many weeds and wild shrubs; for there was no care taken either to prune the shrubs or to clean the ground.

The pilgrims then passed on to the house, which was very spacious, but, like the garden, in bad repair; and knocking at the door, it was speedily opened by a damsel called *Thoughtless*, who welcomed the little pilgrims to the house of her mistress, the lady *Indulgence*. So she made them come in, and led them through an ample hall, where lay scattered upon the floor all manner of toys, such as tops, marbles, whips, coaches, wax babies, and every kind of plaything that could well be imagined. From the hall they passed into a large parlour, supplied with every description of convenient furniture, where sat Mrs. *Indulgence* herself. Now there was something in her appearance which pleased the children much at the first glance; nevertheless she was much bloated, and her dress, though costly, was yet negligent and slovenly. This lady received the children with many blandishments, and would know of them, whence they came?

To this inquiry Humble Mind made answer; and when he had done speaking, Mrs. *Indulgence* thus replied. First, she blamed those who had put it into their heads to go on pilgrimage, observing that children were little harmless creatures, in whom there was no natural depravity. After which she had something to say against the shepherd Sincerity, and still more against the Interpreter; while as to the schoolmaster *Law*, she scrupled not to call him a cruel tyrant. Moreover, she added, that as no child could possibly climb up the hill Difficulty, they could not do better than abide in her house till they should reach a maturer age, "when," said she, "you may, if you please, continue your pilgrimage."

Now, when Humble Mind knew not what answer to make, *Inbred-Sin* suggested that he should not only thank Mrs. *Indulgence* for her kind offer, but also express his willingness to accept it. Which he accordingly did; when Playful and Peace agreeing thereto, it was immediately determined that they should remain for a season at Mrs. *Indulgence's* house.

Then I saw, in my dream, that Mrs. *Indulgence* rang a bell; upon which her old housekeeper, named *Fondness*, came into the room, and received her orders to prepare supper and beds for the little strangers. These orders were very punctually obeyed, nor was it long before the cloth was laid, and the supper served up; whereat the little guests seemed to be mightily pleased, the table being covered with all manner of delicacies, and more especially with such sweet things as children love.

So they all sat down to supper, with *Inbred-Sin* among them; and never did I observe *Inbred-Sin* more troublesome than he was at Mrs. *Indulgence's* table. First, he put the children upon eating of every dish at the table, till their stomachs were quite full and uneasy: after which he engaged Playful in scolding Peace, and Humble Mind in rebuking Playful. Then when wine was set upon the table, *Inbred-Sin* would have them to partake of that also; which brought upon them so great a heaviness, that, on retiring to their chamber, they went to sleep without prayer. But while they were asleep, *Inbred-Sin* was uncommonly wakeful and active; for he was whispering in their ears all the night. Moreover, he admitted the Evil One among them, as he had done before at the shepherd Sincerity's, who went to work as aforetime with his enchantments, beguiling the imaginations of the children with vain and unholy visions. And in these visions he was especially careful to represent those servants and ministers of Christ, under whose charge the little pilgrims had formerly been placed, as hard and cruel masters, tyrannising over young children, and denying them every pleasure befitting their age.

Soon after rising in the morning, the children came again into the presence of *Indulgence*, who, when she had feasted them with all manner of delicacies, gave them leave to amuse themselves as they pleased till dinner-time. So they strolled forth into the garden, and *Inbred-Sin* went with them.

Now I saw in my dream that, when they had tired themselves with running about from place to place, they sat down, and fell into discourse upon their present situation. And first, Humble Mind said, "I should like very well to remain here all my days; but then, I am afraid."

"And wherefore are you afraid, brother?" said Playful.

"Because," answered Humble Mind, "we have forsaken the Lord and his ways, to satisfy our sinful lusts, through the instigation of our own evil hearts."

I perceived then that, after Humble Mind had thus spoken, *Inbred-Sin* began to rage and storm among them in a wonderful manner. For he knew that he had the children now at a double advantage: first, because they had forsaken the King's way, and were in the enemy's grounds; and secondly, because they had given away to him for some time past, indulging him in all his demands, so that he had acquired an unusual ascendency over them. He therefore ventured to speak his whole mind. "It is my pleasure," said he, "that you stay in this place; and here I shall expect you to grant all my demands, and satisfy all my desires."

"Nay but," said Humble Mind, tremblingly, "we shall surely lose our souls if we remain here."

"I care not for your souls," replied *Inbred-Sin*, "neither do I fear God; but I will, at all hazards, please myself."

Humble Mind then attempted to reason with him; but *Inbred-Sin* refused to hear him: neither would he listen to any thing which Playful or Peace could say, but put them all to silence with his imperious ragings. Insomuch that they ceased to oppose him; upon which he became perfectly good-humoured, and proceeded to jest with the young people. But his jestings were always of such a description as are never convenient; nevertheless, he succeeded in making the children laugh heartily, which I was greatly grieved to see.

Thus the little pilgrims remained awhile in the house of *Indulgence*, under the dominion of *Inbred-Sin*. And behold, they were entangled in the snares of the enemy, neither had they any power to deliver themselves. Their bodies were pampered with luxurious living, and their days passed away in idleness. Moreover, they were surrounded with all manner of playthings and toys: yet were they very unhappy, by reason of the sin which dwelt in them. For *Inbred-Sin* meddled more and more with them every day: insomuch that pride, and selfishness, and malice, and envy, successively exercised a complete dominion over them.

Then they remembered the days that were past, and wished it were with them as formerly; nevertheless, *Inbred-Sin* suffered them not to call upon the Lord. Whereupon I began to fear that these little ones would be utterly lost; not remembering the faithfulness of Him who had called them by his grace. 1 Thess. v. 24.

CHAPTER XI.

Now it was a custom, and had been so, as I found, from time immemorial, for such of the Lord's servants as were stationed along the way for the reception and assistance of pilgrims, to hold communication with each other, by letter, concerning the affairs of pilgrims: by which means all the pilgrims on the road were well known in all those places, and a vigilant watch was maintained, lest any of them should fall into the hands of the enemy.

In consequence of this established rule, the damsels

at the palace Beautiful having about this time received a letter from the Interpreter, giving them notice that certain little pilgrims were upon the road, they sent forth a faithful servant, called *Discipline*, to meet them, and bring them up the hill Difficulty. *Discipline* therefore set forth, and sought the children up and down. At length, receiving information that they were in Mrs. *Indulgence's* house, he went immediately thither, and demanded of her, how she dared to detain those chosen little ones under her unholy roof.

At this *Indulgence* trembled, well knowing that Discipline came not without authority; so she delivered up the children into his hands.

Then *Discipline* spake sternly to them, and asked them what they did there. Moreover, he took his rod and corrected them; after which he drove them before him into the right way. Neither did he spare them till he had urged them almost to the top of the hill Difficulty; and it was wonderful to observe how he caused the children to exert themselves. At first, indeed, they cried and complained piteously; but as they ascended higher and higher, they moved on with so much briskness, that although *Discipline* followed them up close behind, yet he forbore to use his scourge as he had done; till at last I perceived that, instead of employing the rod, he encouraged them to proceed by the kindest words he could use.

The sun was about to set when they came within view of the palace Beautiful: nevertheless, the loveliness of the place was plainly to be discerned, while the freshness and sweetness of the mountain air produced a very reviving effect upon the weary little travellers.

Now I saw that there were lions chained on each side of the way which led to the palace. But these creatures took no notice of the pilgrims as they passed, though the children trembled at the sight of them, and looked very pale.

So *Discipline* led them up to the gate of the palace: where I saw that the children turned to offer him their united thanks for having brought them to that place, and for all the assistance with which he had favoured them. Nay, I perceived that they kissed the hand which held the rod of correction, yea, and the very rod itself. And herein were the words of the wise man verified: "Foolishness is bound in the heart of a child;

but the rod of correction shall drive it far from him." Prov. xxii. 15.

Upon this *Discipline* smiled, and said, "I am the servant of the Most High, and have been employed by him to bring many pilgrims to this place. But without the aid of his Holy Spirit I can accomplish nothing: give, therefore, the glory to God. For such is the condition of man, since the fall of Adam, that he has no power of himself to come to this abode of the Virtues, nay, nor even so much as to desire to do so, without God's help." (*See 10th Article of the Church.*)

So after ringing the bell, behold, the gate was presently opened by Mr. *Watchful*, the porter. Now the old porter smiled on observing the youthful pilgrims before his gate: and laying his hands upon their heads, he thus spake:—"What! more fruit of your labours, Mr. *Discipline?* You are by far the most successful of all our agents: for by your means I have the pleasure of opening the gates of this palace to many fair little travellers, who would never, I am sure, have reached this place without your help."

"I had not brought you these, Mr. *Watchful*," returned *Discipline*, "without God's help. You know that I am but an instrument in His hands, and a very mean one, too; therefore, to God be all the glory."

"Very true," answered Mr. *Watchful;* "Paul planteth, Apollos watereth, but God gives the increase." 1 Cor. iii. 6.

By this time one of the damsels of the house having heard the porter's bell, had come to the door. The damsel's name was Humility; and she was one of the many lovely virgins who dwell there together in sweet harmony and love. Of these, Prudence, Piety, and Charity are considered as the chief; but there are several younger branches of this family who are not less lovely than their elder sisters. Humble Mind then delivered to the damsel Humility the note which he had received from the Interpreter, and which she immediately carried to those within. Whereupon the little pilgrims were called in, while Mr. *Discipline* went about other work.

Then such of the damsels as had received orders to introduce the little pilgrims, took them by the hand and led them first into the hall, which was a noble apartment, where were ranged upon pedestals near the walls many marble statues exceedingly beautiful and in fine proportion, representing the most holy and beloved of God among the children of men—Even such as "through faith had subdued kingdoms, wrought righteousness, obtained promises, stopped the mouths of lions, quenched the violence of fire, escaped the edge of the sword, out of weakness had been made strong, waxed valiant in fight, turned to flight the armies of the aliens. Women who had received their dead raised to life again: and others who had been tortured, not accepting deliverance, that they might obtain a better resurrection." Here were also the statues of such as "had trial of cruel mockings and scourgings, yea, moreover, of bonds and imprisonment: they were stoned, they were sawn asunder, were tempted, were slain with the sword: they wandered about in sheep-skins and goat-skins; being destitute, afflicted, tormented (of whom the world was not worthy); they wandered in deserts, and in mountains, and in dens and caves of the earth" (Heb. xi. 33–38); all of them silently suffering for the love which they bore to the Lord of pilgrims. Here also were the memorials of many pious and holy young persons, upon whom God had bestowed grace to serve him in spirit and in truth.

> "And there were those who pass'd life's blooming year
> Beside the mournful couch of parents dear;
> Renouncing all the joys of early days,
> To serve their God, and mind his strictest ways."

Here also were representations in marble of parents who, through the love they bore to their Redeemer, had yielded up their dying infants to Him that made them, rejoicing in the full assurance that their little sweet ones were about to be delivered from a vain and evil world; and submissively crying out, "Thy righteous will, most righteous Lord, be done!" "All these, having obtained a good report, through faith, received not the promise: God having provided better things for them" (Heb. xi. 39, 40);—even "an inheritance incorruptible, and undefiled, and that fadeth not away, reserved in heaven for them." 1 Pet. i. 4.

Through this hall the damsels led the little ones into a fair parlour, where sat Prudence, Piety, and Charity, with other virgins of the family. Each of these fair maidens was busied about some appropriate good work;

and as they wrought with their hands they beguiled the time in speaking to each other "in psalms and hymns and spiritual songs." Eph. v. 19. But upon the little pilgrims being brought in, immediately ceasing from their work and suspending their song, they gathered affectionately around them. Charity kissed them, and Piety gave them her blessing, while Prudence brushed the dust from their white garments. And one welcomed them, and another welcomed them, saying, "Blessed are you, ye chosen ones of the Lord."

So they were made to sit down, and a dish of wholesome food was speedily set before them; of which they were disposed to eat very heartily, since their exercise under Mr. *Discipline's* management had wonderfully sharpened their appetite. Then having prayed with the family, they were put to bed in a chamber called Peace; where they presently fell into a deep sleep.

Now it is not to be supposed, because the little pilgrims were safely lodged in the palace Beautiful, that they were also set free from the importunities of *Inbred-Sin*. No: for as that wicked one came with us into the world, so he will go out of the world with us. I had turned my eye upon him from time to time ever since the children were driven from the house of *Indulgence*. When Mr. *Discipline* set them running, I saw that *Inbred-Sin* kept close in with them; not indeed by running with them, but, as I had often observed before, by hanging upon them, and that so heavily, that the children were forced to drag him with great difficulty up the hill. And though he got many strokes from Mr. *Discipline's* rod, yet he never loosed his hold; but the more *Discipline* applied the scourge, the more he clung and held fast; giving the poor children many a sore pinch and many a painful twitch. On coming towards the top of the hill, where the way became easier, I saw that he ceased pulling and twitching, and went on quietly behind the children; keeping however quite close to them. He accompanied them also into the palace, withdrawing himself, however, as much as possible from the notice of the damsels of the palace; and when the children went to bed he went with them. Nevertheless he kept himself very quiet all night; and in the morning, just about the time that he expected the children to arise, he laid himself all along on the floor like one dead or fainting. And there he was when Humble Mind and his sisters, being awakened by the sweet singing of the birds before their window, got up and began to dress themselves.

Now the children, being busily engaged in conversation, never heeded *Inbred-Sin* till he began to make a low kind of moaning. Whereupon Playful perceiving him, said, "Why, here lies *Inbred-Sin* like one half dead. Well, well, I hope that Mr. *Discipline* has at last mastered him with his scourge; for he got many a hearty stripe yesterday."

Then Humble Mind turned to look at him; and little Peace actually began to touch him, in order to certify herself whether he was really dead or not.

"No, no," said Humble Mind, "he is not dead; for I believe that he will never die till we die, and that we shall never get quit of him till we sink into the grave."

"But," said Playful, "he cannot move: I think that both his legs and his arms are broken. Though he may not be absolutely dead, yet it appears to me that the severe blows he received have totally disabled him."

"Well, well, I wish it may be so," answered Humble Mind; "and then at least he will not torment us so much as he has done. For if he should grow weaker, and we become stronger, we shall soon be more than a match for him. I only wish that, if it were possible, he might die outright; and then how happy should we be!"

"O," said Peace, "in the condition he now is we need not fear him much; for I do not think he could even stand on his legs at present if he were to put forth all his strength."

By these means *Inbred-Sin* made the children believe that he was incapable of doing them any further injury, and that there was no manner of cause in future to fear him. So he filled them with vain confidence. Moreover, all the time that they remained at the palace Beautiful, he affected to be quite low and weak, like one in dying circumstances. And thus, notwithstanding all their experience of his subtlety in time past, and all that they had been taught concerning him by the Interpreter and others, the children were again deceived by this new device.

Now as soon as the young ones were dressed, their attendance was required at family prayers; after which all the maidens of the palace, together with the little pilgrims, sat down to breakfast in the parlour.

Breakfast being finished, every one went immediately to her proper work; for no one is idle in the palace of the Virtues, but all its inhabitants are employed in doing those things which are appointed by their King. So I saw that Prudence, Piety, and Charity, having called the three little ones, began thus to discourse with them. Prudence first spake. "My dear children," said she, "if you are so inclined, the Ruler of all things will, no doubt, grant you permission to remain for a season in this place; where you may, with God's blessing, attain unto the knowledge of all virtue. But while you remain here you must contentedly submit to the rules of the place, which, although they may appear strict, are by no means unpleasant; since they were laid down by Him who thus characterizes the service he requires, 'My yoke is easy, and my burden is light.'" Matt. xi. 30.

To this Humble Mind answered, that he and his sisters would gladly remain with them as long as the King should grant them permission; and that, in the meanwhile, they hoped very carefully to observe the rules of the house.

Upon which Piety remarked, "Of yourselves, my dear children, you cannot rightly observe the rules of this place; but ask of God, and he will assist you."

"I am glad," returned Humble Mind, "to hear that there are strict rules to be observed in this house; for while I was in the house of *Indulgence*, where no one exercised authority over me, I fell under the dominion of the sin that dwelleth in me—and of all masters, methinks, this *Inbred-Sin* is the hardest."

"Very true, my son," said Prudence; "whosoever is the slave of sin lives under the cruellest bondage: and it is in order to free children from the power of their evil passions that the Lord, among other means, hath appointed the rod of correction. Were children born without sin, no chastisement would be necessary."

I heard then that Humble Mihd, being questioned by the damsels, related all that had befallen him and his sisters, from the removal of their parents to that very day.

After which Piety thus addressed the little pilgrims: "I find, my children, that you have had your trials. But God has dealt very mercifully with you, in having brought you thus far on your journey; although, by your own account, from the time that you left your father's house you have not ceased to provoke him, through the suggestions of the sin that dwelleth in you. Nevertheless, while 'the Lord is merciful and gracious, slow to anger, and plenteous in mercy' (Psalm ciii. 8.), I would have you to remember that on no occasion have you ever turned to Him of your own free will and choice, but have been perverse and stiff-necked, being led continually by your own evil hearts to turn your back both upon him and his ways. Forasmuch, therefore, as you are come thus far on your pilgrimage, all the work and the glory of it belong to the Lord alone, while nothing is to be attributed to your own exertions. For had he not compelled you to follow Him, you would now be wallowing with the swine in the mire of the town in which you were born. 'Where is boasting then? It is excluded.' Rom. iii. 27. Give therefore, my children, all the glory to God; 'for who made you to differ from other children? and what have you which you did not receive?'" 1 Cor. iv. 7.

I observed then that the damsels conversed with Humble Mind concerning the several places of education in which he had sojourned. Whereupon Humble Mind would know of them which they thought most objectionable, the school of Mr. *Worldly-Prudence*, or the place wherein all manner of elegant accomplishments were chiefly taught?

"It is hard, my son," replied Prudence, "to tell which is the *worst*, or which is the *best*, of things that are manifestly evil. There is but one way to everlasting happiness; and 'Jesus saith, I am the way, and the truth, and the life: no man cometh unto the Father but by me.' John xiv. 6. We are therefore to hate every false way, however they may differ one from another, and choose the way of truth alone. Psalm cxix. Now 'the wisdom of the prudent is to understand his way' (Prov. xiv. 8.); and we have a promise that to the meek this way shall be pointed out—'The meek will he guide in judgment, and the meek will he teach his way.' Psalm xxv. 9. But they who seek their own glory, and the setting forth of their own selves, run into all manner of follies, and consume their days in vanity."

Then spake Charity; "Alas! alas! it even causes my heart to bleed, when I think of the many fatal mistakes into which mankind are prone to fall on this subject—

and all from the want of knowing the exceeding sinfulness of their own hearts."

"Now it comes into my mind," said Prudence, "that I have something to exhibit which will both please and profit these little ones; I mean the mirror or magic-glass, which was given me by Mr. *Spiritual-Man*." Then she ran up to her closet where she kept it, and brought it down; and behold it was a magic-lantern, such as children often play with. So when the damsels had shut all the windows, and lighted a candle (Prov. xx. 27.), they set forth the lantern in order; and behold, the things that were painted on the glasses of the lantern were represented on the smooth white wall in bright colours—at which the children were much pleased. And behold there was shown on the wall a wide plain full of large towns, all scattered over with heaps of mire and rubbish. *Above* this plain was a glorious heaven, and *beneath* it was a yawning grave going down to the very pit of hell. Moreover, in the midst of the plain stood a very unsightly old man clothed in filthy garments; and Satan stood at his right-hand. Zech. iii. 1, 3. "From the sole of his foot even unto the crown of his head there was no soundness in him; but wounds, and bruises, and putrefying sores." Isaiah i. 6. This man could neither stand upright (Micah vii. 2.), nor look towards the heavens to behold the glories therein displayed—for "the natural man receiveth not the things of the Spirit" (1 Cor. ii. 14.); but after looking downward for a time on the things which lay at his feet, he began anon to rake and scratch all the muck and the rubbish together; and while he was thus employed, he appeared not only to become vicious, but to be filled with an indescribable fury. At this, there came forward the appearance of one, whom the children knew to be the schoolmaster *Law*, and he laid upon the man many stripes, until he was glad to leave scraping the muck and rubbish together, and to sit down quietly upon the heap which he had already collected.

All this while *Inbred-Sin* was at the ear of Playful, though she knew it not. So, when she saw all these things, she began to smile; till, unable any longer to refrain, she burst into a loud laugh.

Then said Piety, "Wherefore do you laugh, my child?"

Playful. I could not refrain when I saw that ugly old man covered all over with rags and dirt, and so very ill-conditioned at the same time. I think such a vile old man is not worthy to live. If I had been Mr. *Law*, I would have put an end to him at once.

Then answered Piety, "In this case we may apply the memorable words of the prophet, 'Thou art the man!'" 2 Sam. xii. 7.

At which Playful blushed: whereupon Piety added these words—"What would have become of you, my child, if the Lord had said concerning you, 'She is not worthy to live?' And yet wherein do you differ from yonder old man?"

Then came the tears into Playful's eyes; for she was self-convicted: and Charity was pleased to observe her tears.

So they looked again at the old man, who had seated himself upon his heap of muck; and Satan began to make a great bustle about him. For Satan himself being the father of that old man, he called in his servants to support and adorn him. And first came one called *Art*, who painted the old man over with red and white paint, so as entirely to conceal all his wounds and his sores; moreover she taught him to smile. Then came one called *Fashion*, who put certain gaudy garments upon the old man's rags; which caused him to look somewhat more seemly. And after this came the damsel *Light-Mind* with her train, to wit, the teachers of elegant accomplishments, all of whom very busily engaged themselves about the old man: and it was wonderful to behold how vast a change they wrought in him. Insomuch that Playful began to like him better; and Peace observed that he was not half so frightful as before. "But," said Humble Mind, "perceive you not, my sisters, that his rags remain still beneath his fine clothes, that his wounds are not healed, nor is his filthiness washed away?"

Now, when all this was done, certain persons, wise in their own conceits, came to the old man with many learned professors, putting certain books into his hand. He received the books, and after reading therein, he rose up inflated with vanity; and his manner was as if he were mocking at the Most High. Then was he led up to the top of the heap of rubbish which he had collected, and which they that were about him had raised to an exceedingly great height—and there they put a crown upon his head, and bowed before him. And behold, even while they bowed, one came behind and struck him a deadly blow; upon which he lost both his crown and his rich garments, and suddenly falling down, he rapidly tumbled from precipice to precipice, till he sunk into an unseen pit and totally disappeared. At which Satan, who had stood by all the while, made outrageous merriment, and laughed the wretched sufferer to scorn.

The children then desired to see something more; but Prudence said, "It is enough." So the windows being opened, and the lantern put away, Piety proceeded, as the manner of the house is on all such occasions, to put certain questions to the children concerning what they had seen.

Piety. Whom do you suppose this old man to be, whose representation has just been exhibited to you?

Playful. I did not understand at first; but now I know that this old man is the emblem of what we all are by nature, and his wounds and sores signify the evil and uncleanness of our hearts.

Piety. Well spoken, my child: and this old man is thus described by St. Paul—"Being filled with all unrighteousness, fornication, wickedness, covetousness, maliciousness; full of envy, murder, debate, deceit, malignity; whisperers, backbiters, haters of God, despiteful, proud, boasters, inventors of evil things, disobedient to parents, without understanding, covenant-breakers, without natural affection, implacable, unmerciful." Rom. i. 29–31.

Then spake Prudence, "You saw all that Art, and Learning, and Fashion, and Elegant Accomplishments could do for this old man. But did it seem to be within their power to rectify his vile nature? or could they save him from destruction?"

Playful. To be sure, they made him look a little better; but as to any thing else, they left him much as they found him.

Then said Humble Mind, "When I saw them all so busy in painting the old man, and setting him forth in gaudy apparel, I thought of what our Lord said to the scribes and Pharisees—'Ye are like unto whited sepulchres, which indeed appear beautiful outward, but are within full of dead men's bones and of all uncleanness.'" Matt. xxiii. 27.

Prudence. Well spoken, my son: and herein we may perceive the folly of such as are continually striving to set forth and adorn their old vile and sinful nature, instead of coming to Him who alone can reform and renew it; even to Him who 'gave himself for them; that he might sanctify and cleanse them: and that he might present them to himself without spot or wrinkle, or any such thing; but that they should be holy and without blemish.' Eph. v. 25–27.

Piety. Well, let us have nothing more to do with our 'old man or his deeds.' Col. iii. 9. He is crucified with our Lord. Rom. vi. 6. 'If any man be in Christ, he is a new creature' 2 Cor. v. 17.

I perceived then that *Inbred-Sin* was very busy again with Playful, who thus vainly replied to Piety, "It is in truth a great pleasure to think that we have nearly done with our old nature; and that now having come so far on our journey, our *Inbred-Sin* loses ground very fast, while we are becoming every day wiser and holier. I am sure, when I think how wicked I used to be, and how much better I am now, I feel that I have great cause for thankfulness."

When Charity heard the child speaking after this fashion, she sighed deeply; nor could Humble Mind forbear blush; but Prudence rebuked her, and spake to this purpose: "When my sister Piety admonished us to have nothing more to do with our old man, she meant that it behooved us to shun him, and to fly from him; but, alas! though we would willingly have no more to say to him, we must not hope that he will so easily be restrained from having any thing more to do with us. O my child! how little, as yet, are you acquainted either with the decitfulness of your own heart, or with the subtile devices of *Inbred-Sin!* Be assured however of this, that *Inbred-Sin* is never more to be feared than when he would make you believe that you are in no danger from him."

Playful was now ashamed, and remained silent—while Piety entered further into discourse with the children, explaining unto them that, unless a man be born again, that is, born of the Spirit, he cannot see God. After which she caused Humble Mind to read aloud our Lord's conversation with Nicodemus on the subject of regeneration, recorded in the third chapter of St. John's gospel. Moreover, I saw that she made him kneel down and pray that the Lord would open the eyes of his understanding, in order to a due comprehension of this matter. And this she did, because herein is a great mystery, which they of this world cannot receive, a doctrine altogether despised and rejected of men, and which Christians themselves do not thoroughly understand, although they feel and know it to be true,—namely, how the old and sinful nature is destroyed in them that believe, while a new and heavenly nature is imparted to them.

Now I saw that Piety daily used great pains to make these little ones acquainted with this important doctrine: sometimes taking them apart into her closet and praying with them; at other times leading them by the hand when she walked out into the fields, and discoursing with them freely upon the new nature of man, when born again in Christ, and sanctified by the Holy Spirit. Among other statements, she represented to them, that the heart of the old man is continually full of abominable conceits with every kind of evil thought; while the heart of him who is born again and become a new creature abounds in "love, joy, peace, long-suffering, gentleness, goodness, faith, meekness, temperance." Gal. v. 22, 23. Moreover, she took especial pains to make the children comprehend that this work of regeneration is, for the most part, a slow or progressive work, and that the *old* nature will continue to contend with the *new*, until the work of grace be finished at the hour of death. Nor did she fail to point out *that* to which every Christian should carefully attend, namely, the necessity of supporting the new nature day by day, with heavenly food, in order to its growth and improvement; just as the natural body is fed by the fruits of the earth, in failure of which it grows weak and faint, and at length expires.

Thus Piety continued unweariedly to instruct the little pilgrims; insomuch that after they had been for a short space at the palace Beautiful, it was judged necessary to introduce them to certain other teachers, of whom I shall speak more particularly in the next chapter.

CHAPTER XII.

Now I saw in my dream that, when the little pilgrims had remained for a season in the palace Beautiful, the damsels took them, one morning, by the hand and led them through a long and shady cloister into a very large library, formed of various ranges of apartments of very ancient architecture, and filled with the works of the most esteemed writers, both ancient and modern, sacred and profane. Here was no sound of voices to be heard, but all was hushed and quiet, inviting to study and contemplation. And in one of the largest of these apartments two very venerable men were sitting at one table, before whom were spread many books, which they were busied in examining; and behold, from time to time they seemed to consult one another, and, as it were, to compare notes one with the other.

Then said Piety to the children, "Behold those venerable persons! they are brothers; and he that looketh most fresh and comely, is the elder by many years—for he is immortal, and time hath no power over him."

"May I," said Humble Mind, "presume to ask their names and characters?"

Piety. These brothers are the sons of one mother; whose name is Wisdom. The elder is called Divine Knowledge, and his age cannot be computed: for although he looks so hale and comely, he was in existence before the foundation of the world. The name of the younger is Human Knowledge; and as his birthplace was this earth, so he partakes of the infirmity and imperfection of all earthly things. Hence you see that he is much more wrinkled and broken down with age than his elder brother.

"The Father Almighty," continued Piety, "sent Divine Knowledge from his dwelling-place on high, to be a guide and comfort to fallen man; and Human Knowledge was charged never to lose sight of this his elder brother, nor ever to engage in any undertaking, except in conjunction with Divine Knowledge. But," continued Piety, "notwithstanding the strict injunctions laid upon these brethren by the Most High, mankind have, in almost every age of the world, prevailed in their attempts to separate them. And even now," continued she, "the sons of men may be divided into two classes; those who, like Mr. *Worldly-Prudence*, pay Divine honours to the younger brother; and those who, utterly despising the younger, pretend the highest esteem for the elder. But they that judge wisely, give the highest honour to the elder without despising the younger, and take delight in seeing them labour hand-in-hand, each occupying his proper place, in the blessed work of instructing the ignorant."

Now I saw in my dream that, when the damsel Piety had thus spoken, she led the children up to the ancient brothers, introducing them as little ones who were humble, and willing to be instructed. So after laying their hands upon them, and blessing them, the sages caused them to occupy places at their feet.

On that very day therefore they began to study under the direction of these venerable teachers: and from thenceforward, while they remained in the palace Beautiful, they went daily at a certain hour into the library, there to receive such instruction as was adapted to their age and condition. And now Humble Mind was made to understand wherein Mr. *Worldly-Prudence's* system of education was defective, to wit, in that he did not make the Book of God the basis and groundwork of his plan, using heathen authors only as auxiliary lights, and their works as books of reference. And thus he not only bewildered and lost himself amid the mazes of heathen darkness and heathen morality, but became the means of misleading multitudes of others.

In receiving the instructions of these venerable men, the little pilgrims spent many hours every day; and whenever they had discovered extraordinary assiduity, I saw that they were allowed by the damsels of the palace to enjoy the fields or gardens of Innocent Pleasure. These gardens are the peculiar gift of the Lord of lords to the damsels the Virtues, and by him rendered inexpressively delightful; in order that the saints upon earth, being sometimes permitted to take the air in them, may have some little foretaste of those joys which are reserved for them in heaven, through the merits of Him in whom is their trust. These gardens are near adjoining to the palace Beautiful, and the damsels of that house have the sole charge of them, with express command from the Most High, that none enter therein, or eat of their fruit, but such as love him and seek to do his will.

Now I looked, and behold, there was nothing wanting in these gardens that could render them desirable, such as mossy fountains and curious waterfalls, blooming parterres and fragrant groves, verdant uplands and shadowy glens, with every variety that could delight the eye or ravish the fancy. Here were specimens of certain lovely flowers of Paradise, which had escaped the general destruction made by sin. Here were young lambs sporting without fear, and little fawns bounding over the hills. And here also I beheld many birds of exquisite plumage and extraordinary note, such as certain ancient pilgrims are reported to have listened to with peculiar transport when travelling through these parts. These birds were heard answering each other from the high woodlands in sweet song, and their voices were wonderfully ravishing to such as silently walked in the shadowy dells beneath. I saw too, among these fields, many lovely cottages and quiet resting-places, which God had prepared for certain aged pilgrims who loved and trusted in him. These were under the charge of Charity, who had the care of providing them with such things as were necessary: and there "the poor among men rejoiced in the Holy One of Israel." Isaiah xxix. 19. Here were also a variety of pleasing arbours, to which, in the cool of the day, the two venerable brothers, Divine and Human Knowledge, were accustomed to retire, together with Prudence, Piety, Charity, and the other damsels of the palace, for the purpose of taking their evening repast. Here while they temperately feasted upon the milk of the flock and the fruits of the garden, they held profitable discourse on subjects of high importance, to wit, how they might best fulfil the will of God, in relieving the wants of the poor, and in turning the simple to the wisdom of the just. And sometimes, in these hours of quiet leisure, Divine Knowledge would unfold the interesting secrets of prophecy, together with the mighty plans of Providence for bringing about the restoration of lost mankind, and the final glory of Christ's kingdom upon earth—and blessed were they who heard the gracious words that proceeded from his lips. There was, moreover, present in these assemblies an aged matron called *Experience*, whose tales of ancient times were at once very profitable and pleasant; and I perceived that all her discourse continually tended to prove one thing, namely, that, like King David, she had been young, and then was old, but had never seen the righteous forsaken, nor their seed begging their bread. Psalm xxxvii. 25.

The little children were permitted at these seasons to sit upon the moss at the feet of Charity, where, while they listened with delight to that which was spoken, they thankfully partook of the food provided for them. After which they either played together upon the hills and lawns, rivalling the young fawns and lambs in their innocent gambols; or they walked with Piety in the solemn grove, where they were regaled with the music of its sacred songsters; or they performed some kind offices for the aged pilgrims, whose little cottages were scattered over these delightful regions. And at these times the gladness of their young hearts not only shone through their eyes, but very frequently expressed itself in such songs as these—

"These are the joys he makes us know
In fields and villages below;
Gives us a relish of his love,
But keeps his noblest feast above."

CHAPTER XIII.

Now I saw in my dream that the King of kings permitted the children to remain in the palace Beautiful for a considerable length of time; where as they increased in stature, they grew in favour both with God and man. Two young damsels, called *Decency* and *Order*, had the special charge of them, and led them sweetly through the duties of every day. They were called up early every morning, and taught to devote the early part of the day to God; after breakfast, they spent a few hours with their tutors; at noon they were fed by Temperance; and in the afternoon they were taught by Prudence such useful works as are necessary to the economy of human life: after which they were directed by Charity to apply those works to such uses as shall be approved in that day when the Lord shall say to those on his right hand, "Come, ye blessed of my Father, inherit the kingdom prepared for you from the foundation of the world: for I was an hungered and ye gave me meat: I was thirsty, and ye gave me drink: I was a stranger, and ye took me in: naked, and ye clothed me: I was sick, and ye visited me: I was in prison, and ye came unto me." Matt. xxv. 34–36. Here also the children learned from Piety to perform the sweet work of praise; putting music to its best and highest use, namely, the setting forth the glory of God.

During the whole of this season which passed so pleasantly with the little pilgrims, *Inbred-Sin*, aware that all the inhabitants of the palace would rise up against him if he should once dare to show his face among them, kept himself carefully in the back-ground; where it was his object to persuade the little ones that he was in a very weak and languishing state, and never likely to be in a condition to torment them again as he had formerly done. Yet at this very time, while he affected such extreme languor, he was scarcely less busy with his mischievous suggestions than in seasons of more apparent liveliness and vigour. It was now his way, when he could get at the children's ear unobserved, to flatter them upon their great attainments in virtue, and even to speak in high terms of their victory over himself, as well as of the esteem in which they were held throughout the palace. Thus he went on, secretly introducing poison into their hearts, and making even their good works the means of their transgressing: nevertheless, as his work was silently carried on, so its effects, for a season, were not discoverable.

I perceived then that, after a while, it was signified to the children that they must continue their pilgrimage. Upon which Prudence, Piety, and Charity took them apart, and kissed them, and prayed with them, and shed over them many tears. "O my little sweet ones!" said Charity, "over whom we have so tenderly watched for these many months, guarding you from the assaults of that 'roaring lion who goeth about seeking whom he may devour' (1 Pet. v. 8.), think of the sorrow you will occasion us, if ever we should hear of your turning away from the paths of truth and holiness. Always remember, my children, the happy days you have enjoyed in the palace of the Virtues, with the blissful hours which you have spent in the fields of innocent pleasure; and know assuredly that, on becoming the slaves of sin, you will taste of such happiness no more. For the ways of the wicked are full of trouble, their torment beginning even in this world: 'but the work of righteousness is peace: and the effect of righteousness, quietness and assurance for ever.'" Isa. xxxii. 17.

Then I saw that Piety would needs pray with them; so making the little ones to kneel by her, she thus breathed out her requests: "O holy Father, we pray for these little ones, whom thou gavest us for a season. *We* are not in the world, but *these* must go into the world—O holy Father, keep them through thy name, that they may be one with thee. While we were with them, we kept them in thy name, and none of them is lost. We have given them thy word; and the world will hate them, because they are not of the world, even as we are not of the world. We pray not that thou shouldest take them out of the world, but that thou shouldest keep them from the evil. They are not of the world, even as we are not of the world. Sanctify them through thy truth: thy word is truth. Father, we pray thee that these, the redeemed of thy blessed Son, may be with thee, where he is, that they may behold his glory which thou hast given him; for thou lovedst him before the foundation of the world: and, finally, we pray that the glory which thou gavest him, he may give also to them, that they may be one with thee, and with him." John xvii.

After this, Prudence informed the children that, as they advanced in their pilgrimage, they would come to a mighty city, which is the metropolis or royal city belonging to the prince of this world, the determined enemy of pilgrims. "That city," said she, "is called Vanity, and its inhabitants are the men of this world. There," added she, "pilgrims, ever since the beginning of the world, have been exercised with various trials, in order, if possible, to make them weary of the Way of Salvation. In former days many were there tortured with fire and sword; and even to this day there are some parts of the city in which the servants of Christ are in danger of losing their lives for his name's sake. But," continued she, "in the more civilized part of that city, these barbarous customs have fallen into disrepute, the fury of the enemy being mercifully restrained by the Lord of pilgrims. Nevertheless the profession of a pilgrim is held in the greatest contempt throughout the whole City of Vanity, and the traveller to Mount Zion is exposed to every species of contumely and reproach in its *streets*, through which he must yet necessarily pass, or go entirely out of his way. For the town is full of those who mock at religion, according to the words of Scripture—'Know ye not, in the last days there shall come scoffers, walking after their own lusts, saying, Where is the promise of his coming? for since the fathers fell asleep, all things continue as they were from the beginning of the creation.' 2 Pet. iii. 3, 4. Ye therefore, my beloved," proceeded the damsel Prudence, "'seeing ye know these things before, beware lest ye also, being led away with the error of the wicked, fall from your own steadfastness. But grow in grace, and in the knowledge of our Lord and Saviour Jesus Christ.'" 2 Peter iii. 17, 18.

I heard then that the damsels explained to the children that, from the beginning of the world, the Lord had always preserved to himself a little remnant of chosen ones. "Of whose salvation," said they, "the ark is a standing type: for as in the ark Noah and his family were preserved during the destruction of the world by water; so, amid the abounding wickedness of the world, a pure and holy seed has still been maintained in the earth, from generation to generation."

Upon this Prudence represented to the little pilgrims that their safety in the town of Vanity would much depend on their finding out the abodes of these true Christians, and familiarly associating with their families.

I heard then that Piety gave the children certain marks or signs by which they might, under the divine direction, distinguish these true children of God from those who through worldly motives assume their garb and adopt their language. And among these tokens, the following were especially to be noted—first, whether they, as members, hold the Head, which is Christ, "from which all the body by joints and bands having nourishment ministered, and knit together, increaseth with the increase of God" (Col. ii. 19.); secondly, whether they have love one towards another—for it is written, "By this shall all men know that ye are my disciples, if ye have love one to another" (John xiii. 35.); and thirdly, whether they bring forth the peaceable fruits of righteousness—for the tree is known by its fruits—" A good tree bringeth not forth evil fruit, nor an evil tree good fruit." Matt. vii. 18. Moreover, the damsels gave the children a note to a certain venerable clergyman, named *Orthodox*, who dwelt as a stranger and pilgrim in the town of Vanity, waiting, like Abraham, till he should be called to a better inheritance. To which Prudence added many directions, by which she hoped that the little ones would be enabled to find the dwelling of this venerable man: neither did she omit to admonish them continually to seek counsel by prayer.

Being thus duly prepared for their journey, I perceived that the children were led forth by the damsels of the palace till they reached the brow of the hill Difficulty, on that side which looketh towards the Celestial City; where they kissed each other, and affectionately separated, with many tears on both sides. So the fair damsels having gone back, the young pilgrims remained for some time weeping on the brow of the hill: and *Inbred-Sin* was with them.

Now I remarked that the descent before them was exceedingly steep, insomuch that it seemed impossible to go down into the valley beneath, without the hazard of many dangerous slips and falls. The deep valley into which they looked was called the Valley of Humiliation—but of this we shall have occasion to speak more hereafter. The damsels had charged the children to move warily on their way, and to use all possible caution in going down the hill: nevertheless, when the little ones began to centemplate the valley which was spread at their feet, and the precipitous path by which they were to reach it, they not only expressed great dread of this hazardous undertaking, but presently broke out into murmurings, very bitterly lamenting the necessity of making such a descent. And I perceived that *Inbred-Sin* mingled very eagerly in the conversation that took place among them, and gave his opinion with surprising freedom, looking as brisk and as pert as I had ever at any time seen him: whereat I much wondered, on considering the very weak and low condition in which he had appeared at the palace Beautiful. I also much marvelled to find that the children did not remark this sudden change in him; neither reproving nor checking him, but listening to all he said with apparent complacency.

Upon which *Inbred-Sin* spoke much in favour of the extraordinary elevation of the hill Difficulty, the towering summits of which, he remarked, afforded a most glorious prospect on all sides: whereas the valley spread at their feet, he said, was so despicable a place, that he could not conceive why the Lord of pilgrims had caused the way to Zion to pass through it. I heard, then, that he proceeded to flatter the little pilgrims upon their uncommon perseverance, and the wonderful exertions they had made, in attaining the glorious height on which they then stood, and which had happily introduced them to the palace of the Virtues—and I perceived that he ascribed to their own efforts all the glory of what they had done, referring nothing to God, nor even adverting to the rod of *Discipline*.

I saw, however, that after listening for awhile to *Inbred-Sin*, the children bethought themselves, that, as they must needs descend the side of the mountain (the Lord having signified his will that they should continue their pilgrimage), it would be better to do so before night came on. So, having no time to lose, they began their descent; yet it was with a very ill will, since they had nothing before them but the Valley of Humiliation, whose gloomy appearance has alarmed many a traveller who afterward found such consolations therein as were not to be met with in any other part of his pilgrimage.

And now, although I was heartily vexed, yet I could not but smile to observe the strange pranks and manœuvres of *Inbred-Sin*, with the various tricks he played the little pilgrims as they were going down the hill, thereby rendering their difficult path a hundred times more difficult. First, he would have it, as I before said, that they should not go down at all, but tarry where they were; because the top of the hill was, as he said, nearer heaven than the valley. Then, upon Humble Mind's arguing with him, and pleading that they had no choice, but must go down, he became petulant, and would have them to proceed in haste, that so desperate an adventure might speedily be concluded. So they ran down the side of the mountain till each of them got a very sore tumble, in which they bruised themselves severely against the stones. Whereupon *Inbred-Sin*, while they lay groaning half-way down the mountain, insultingly laughed them to scorn, crying out, "See now what you have gained by all this eagerness to obey the orders of your King!"—thus impiously charging upon the Prince of princes those wounds which the little pilgrims owed entirely to their own impatience. For, although it was the pleasure of the Lord of pilgrims that Humble Mind and his sisters should descend into the Valley of Humiliation, yet he never required them to lay aside all prudence and caution in making that descent.

Here I was sorry to observe that the little pilgrims, being thus sorely bruised and wounded, did not reprove *Inbred-Sin* on his suggesting these false and blasphemous accusations against the King of kings; but that, as they rose from the ground, they sighed and mourned like persons delivered over to despair. The steepness and danger, however, of the place where they then lay not permitting them to take any rest, they resolved to go forward, though in a more wary and careful manner. Then I saw that *Inbred-Sin* stepped before them; but while he pretended to remove stones and stumbling-blocks out of their way, he contrived so to entangle himself in their steps, that he first pulled down one, and then another of them, at short intervals, through the whole of their way. And in this manner did he so vex and bewilder the poor children, that on reaching the foot of the mountain, they found themselves in a most forlorn and miserable condition.

Now I have heard it said by many an old pilgrim, that there is not in all the Way of Salvation, from the gate which is at the head of that way even to the very land of Beulah, a more delightful place of sojourn than the Valley of Humiliation, although it be held in universal contempt by the men of this world. This valley was the favourite dwelling-place of the Lord of pilgrims, when residing upon earth. Yea, so exceedingly soft and balmy is the air of this valley, that, though few descend into it willingly, yet many have confessed, as is intimated above, that the happiest hours of their pilgrimage were passed in its peaceful retirement. This valley is shaded with all manner of trees which are agreeable to the sight or good for food. A clear stream of the water of the fountain of life winds its gentle and untroubled course through its whole extent; and daily, before sunrise, manna is found thickly scattered over every part of it; moreover, the voice of the heavenly dove is often heard from the clefts of the rocks which enclose the valley on either side.

It was nearly dusk when the little pilgrims reached the bottom of the hill; where, on account of their present pain and vexation, they could neither enjoy the balmy air of the valley, nor find rest on the soft green turf which it spread beneath their feet. They, however, sat themselves down for a time; and, being greatly exhausted, they ate of the dried fruits with which the damsels of the palace Beautiful had supplied them. But their repast afforded them very little refreshment, because it was received with a discontented mind; so greatly did they regret losing the pleasures they had enjoyed in the palace Beautiful, and so deeply did they lament the meanness of their new situation;—for *Inbred-Sin* had taught them to consider the palace Beautiful as a more honourable station in society than the valley they were now entering. Then I looked again at these little pilgrims, and found them still sitting at the foot of the hill as the darkness began to cover them: and I marvelled to find how familiarly they allowed *Inbred-Sin* to converse with them, after appearing to keep him at such a distance in the palace Beautiful. But I considered not how exceedingly powerful an effect pious company produces upon the minds of young pilgrims, in restraining them from sin: neither did I then recollect how commonly our more gross inbred corruptions lie still and quiet, and seem, as it were, dead or extinguished, when they have no opportunity of working to any effect. Nor did it strike me at the moment, that this very *Inbred-Sin*, though he had not broken forth into any openly disgraceful act in the palace Beautiful, had nevertheless been effectually at work, to the injury of the little pilgrims, in filling them with spiritual pride and high thoughts of themselves, as now indeed too clearly appeared from their extreme abhorrence of the Valley of Humiliation. For they who are really humble love this valley, and would be thankful if it extended from one end to the other of their pilgrim's course.

So the little pilgrims sat hearkening to *Inbred-Sin*, till, being overcome with weariness, they fell asleep. Then gazing on these sinful little ones, I seriously considered the state of man upon earth; how utterly lost he is to all that is good, and how apt to fall, even after having known the way of righteousness! And as I mused on these things, I felt a deep conviction that the salvation of man is all of grace; insomuch that he is unable in his own strength to take one effectual step towards it. Nay, I clearly perceived that, even when considerably advanced in the Way of Salvation, the saint is as entirely dependant on his heavenly Parent, and as much in need of the daily supplies of his grace, as the tenderest babe in Christ. I now also comprehended many of those dark and mysterious providences which had beforetime so often tried my own weak faith; plainly discerning that it was necessary for the Lord occasionally to withdraw his support from his people, in order to make them sensible of their own nothingness and insufficiency, as well as to lead them to the exercise of a more absolute reliance upon himself. Moreover, I recollected having sometimes remarked, that great humiliations generally follow states of high prosperity or singular exaltation among the saints on earth; just as the present state of darkness and dejection among these little pilgrims, with their stupid submission to the will of *Inbred-Sin*, had followed the prosperous and happy days lately spent in the palace Beautiful.

Now it came to pass, while I was lost in these meditations, that I suddenly perceived a light in the sky towards the east, whence presently a very bright form, yet clothed with a cloud in order to conceal a part of its dazzling glory, descended from the heavens, and drew near to the little pilgrims. On the appearance of this heavenly vision, I saw that *Inbred-Sin* concealed himself; but the little ones remained in a deep sleep, while the heavenly visitant addressed himself to Humble Mind, saying, " Lovest thou me, my son ?"

I perceived then that Humble Mind started from his sleep, and looking up, said, " Who art thou, Lord ?"

The other replied, "I am He that 'was wounded for thy transgressions, and bruised for thy iniquities.' Isaiah liii. 5. For thy sake 'I gave my back to the smiters, and my cheeks to them that plucked off the hair: I hid not my face from shame and spitting.'" Isaiah l. 6.

Then I saw that Humble Mind fell upon his knees, and lifting up his hands, cried, " My Lord and my God!"

Upon which the Holy One replied, "'He that taketh not his cross, and followeth after me, is not worthy of me.'" Matt. x. 38.

With that I perceived that the glorious vision faded from the view of the little pilgrim; and behold, the child lay awhile prostrate on the ground, bitterly weeping; for his heart smote him on account of his ingratitude to his Saviour; and he felt utterly unworthy of that special condescension which had led the Prince of princes a second time to reveal himself to him, and plead with him, as it were, face to face. He lay, therefore, weeping and lamenting till dawn of day; when, rising from the ground and awaking his sisters, he reported to them what he had seen, and how he had thereby been made sensible of the pride and ingratitude of his heart.

Now I saw in my dream that these little ones were much affected when they heard the words of their brother; for it pleased the Lord to bless his report to their profit. And they said one to another, "We have indeed sinned grievously in hearkening to *Inbred-Sin*, and in presuming to murmur against the commands of our Lord."

So, when they had wept over each other for awhile, they arose from the ground; and having drunk of the water which flowed in a pure clear stream by the wayside, and also washed themselves therewith, they filled their golden pots with the manna which, a little before sunrise, appeared thickly scattered around them on the grass: then, earnestly asking the Lord's blessing on their journey, they began to set forward along the Valley of Humiliation. And behold, *Inbred-Sin* followed upon their steps; for he would in no case suffer himself to be left behind, although the little pilgrims would most gladly have been quit of his company.

CHAPTER XIV.

I SAW then in my dream that, although the children began their day's journey in considerable sadness of heart (being cast down by a strong sense of their late sin and ingratitude towards the Prince of princes), yet as they advanced along the Valley of Humiliation they became more easy, till at length the expression of peace was entirely restored to their countenances. And I remarked that their eyes were directed more continually towards the splendid prospect before them, namely, the glories of Mount Zion rising faintly and indistinctly above the eastern horizon, than they had at any time been during the former part of their pilgrimage. Moreover, I marked that *Inbred-Sin* was as quiet in this valley as ever I had seen him; although I observed that he sometimes uttered a low whining cry, which no doubt would have broken out into loud murmurs against the King of kings, if Humble Mind, who kept his late vision continually in remembrance, had not sharply rebuked him, pressing him closely with the following words of our Lord, to which he could offer no reply—"Then said Jesus unto his disciples, If any man will come after me, let him deny himself, and take up his cross, and follow me. For whosoever will save his life shall lose it: and whosoever will lose his life for my sake shall find it." Matt. xvi. 24, 25.

Now after advancing a little way in the Valley of Humiliation, the young pilgrims were enabled to discover that the place abounded with beauties, such as they had never seen in all their travels. The brook of water, of which we have spoken before as for the most part winding its course near to the Way of Salvation, seemed, as it were, to linger among these delightful meadows, and to show itself more full and clear than in any other part of the pilgrim's path. Many flowers grew in these fields, and especially on the margin of the brook. These were, for the most part, flowers of humble growth and delicate appearance—flowers of the valley, which could not live on higher grounds, being unable to endure the rough winds to which such situations are generally exposed.

I heard then that the little pilgrims began to discourse with each other as they walked along. And thus spake Humble Mind: "Dear sisters, though yesterday I came down the hill with such an ill will, yet I am now inclined to think that the Valley of Humiliation is the safest, and perhaps the happiest place upon earth, for a poor sinner to sojourn in. I am ashamed when I think of the high thoughts I once had of myself; and *that* not only before I became a pilgrim, but since. Even yesterday how was my heart filled and puffed up with spiritual pride! I call it *spiritual pride*," continued he, "because I was not proud of any thing external, but rather of what I thought the good and prosperous state of my soul. Now indeed I see my folly; and I thank God for opening my mind, and showing me that he who has by his sins brought the Son of God to the cross, can never have any cause of glorying, except in that cross itself."

"But, brother," said Playful, "there is one thing which I wish to understand—I observe that every holy person, when talking on the subject of man's salvation, is accustomed to speak of the death of Christ our Lord as if he had died for him or her only, and not for the whole church."

To this Humble Mind answered, "It is very proper that each one should do so; because, if you, or I, or any other person had been the only trangressor of all the sons of Adam, the Lord must have died for that one person, if that one person was to be saved. Therefore, as far as you, or I, or any other individual of the sons of Adam is concerned, every sinner is guilty of the death of Christ our Lord, and must lay to his own account every trial which he endured."

Here Playful began to look grave; while Peace answered, "Brother, I now see my heavy guilt in having put to shame and to death that Holy and Blessed One, who is the chief among ten thousand; and I feel how becoming humility is to such a wretch as I am."

I saw then that Humble Mind drew his book from his bosom, and read these words—"'When men are cast down, then thou shalt say, There is lifting up; and he shall save the humble person.' Job xxii. 29. 'He forgetteth not the cry of the humble.' Psalm ix. 12.

'Humble yourselves in the sight of the Lord, and he shall lift you up.' James iv. 10. 'For whosoever exalteth himself shall be abased; and he that humbleth himself shall be exalted.'" Luke xiv. 11.

Thus the little pilgrims went on their way, entertaining themselves with holy discourse and divine meditation till noon-day, when they came to a garden or plantation of nuts, where the ripe fruit hung invitingly upon the trees. Then said Humble Mind, "See what the Lord has provided for us!" So after gathering, they sat down and ate of the nuts. Moreover, they drank of the water of the brook; and being refreshed, they again went on their way.

Then looking for *Inbred-Sin*, I saw him skulking behind, and appearing like one meditating mischief: nevertheless he kept himself quiet, and, for the present, said not a word. For, as I before observed, the skill of this *Inbred-Sin* often discovers itself in keeping altogether quiet and out of sight, until some favourable opportunity offers for making an attack with advantage. And on the other hand the wisdom of the saints lies in standing continually upon their watch-tower, ready armed for the battle; according to that which is written, "Watch and pray, lest ye enter into temptation." Mark xiv. 38. But these little pilgrims, like too many others even of superior age and larger experience, seldom feared *Inbred-Sin* when he was quiet: and, therefore, as he did not particularly inconvenience or trouble them at this time, they were glad enough to let him alone.

Now I saw in my dream that the little ones having slept peacefully that same night in the Valley of Humiliation, continued their journey in the morning. But I perceived that, after journeying all day, towards nightfall the valley seemed to sink lower and lower, and to become more and more narrow. It appeared also in this place less verdant, there were fewer flowers, and the brook no longer wound its course near the pilgrim's path. Then said Humble Mind, "Methinks we are leaving the pleasanter part of this valley behind us, while that which lies before seems even more gloomy than the spot on which we now stand."

"Let us then," said Playful, "go back a little way into the more lightsome part of the valley, just to find a night's lodging; since the country which lies before us has so very dismal an appearance."

To which Humble Mind replied, "Know you not, sister, that it is unlawful for a Christian to go back on any occasion? because his safety depends on having his face always turned Zion-wards." Nevertheless, though Humble Mind spake so wisely on occasion; yet, at the entreaties of Playful and *Inbred-Sin*, he consented to go back a little way: where, when the children had found such a place as they deemed convenient for their night's lodging, they sat down on the grass by the way-side, and began to converse with each other.

And first spake *Inbred-Sin*, "This Valley of Humiliation," said he, "after all that has been said in its favour, with respect to its suitableness to man's state as a sinner upon earth, is, methinks, at best but a place very little desirable: and surely, if the Lord loved his servants, he would not appoint them to spend so many hours of their pilgrimage in so dreary a solitude."

But when *Inbred-Sin* proceeded to murmur against the King of kings on account of his dealings with his people, I observed that Humble Mind rebuked him; at the same time reading from his book these encouraging sentences—"The Lord will not cast off for ever: but though he cause grief, yet will he have compassion according to the multitude of his mercies. For he doth not afflict willingly, nor grieve the children of men." Lament. iii. 31–33.

I perceived then that *Inbred-Sin* shifted his ground, saying that he did not mean to charge the King of kings with inflicting unnecessary chastisements upon his people, and upon *them* in particular; "For," said he, "your King is just and good. But then, of what manner of spirit must you be, if such afflictions have become necessary for you?" I heard then that he proceeded to lay all their sins and all their troubles in order before them; charging them especially with having so often listened to him, although, in their esteem, an undoubted child of hell.

And behold, while I wondered greatly, and said to myself, "What will come of all this? Is *Inbred-Sin* himself become a preacher? and 'is Saul also among the prophets?'" 1 Sam. x. 12. Even while I wondered at this, it became evident to me, that he was no less engaged in performing his master's work, when he seemed to be pleading for the Lord, than when he spoke without disguise the language of hell. For after having affirmed the afflictions of the little pilgrims to be without precedent, he proceeded to prove from thence that their trangressions had likewise been without example, and that their sins were beyond the measure even of Christ's mercy—designing thereby to excite in their minds the dreadful apprehension, that they were already lost beyond the hope of salvation. Moreover, when Humble Mind turned to his book to find there some comfortable words wherewith to assure himself that, however grievous his transgressions had been, they were not beyond the reach of redeeming mercy, *Inbred-Sin*, looking over his shoulder, directed him to such passages as served only to perplex and trouble him the more. And thus it sometimes happens, that the sin of a man's heart may perversely wrest even the Holy Book of God to his own destruction.

The text which at this time *Inbred-Sin* pointed out and applied to the case of Humble Mind and his sisters was this—"For it is impossible for those who were once enlightened, and have tasted of the heavenly gift, and were made partakers of the Holy Ghost, and have tasted the good Word of God, and the powers of the world to come, if they shall fall away, to renew them again unto repentance; seeing they crucify to themselves the Son of God afresh, and put him to an open shame. For the earth which drinketh in the rain that cometh oft upon it, and bringeth forth herbs meet for them by whom it is dressed, receiveth blessing from God: but that which beareth thorns and briers is rejected, and is nigh unto cursing; whose end is to be burned." Heb. vi. 4–8.

I perceived then that, as Humble Mind and his sisters continued to listen to *Inbred-Sin*, they became more and more troubled. And now night coming on, a hollow whistling wind arose, which sweeping violently up the valley, benumbed all their limbs with cold; insomuch that they could not stretch themselves out separately upon the grass with any hope of comfortable repose. They therefore gathered close together, and sat up all night, bemoaning themselves; sometimes listening to *Inbred-Sin*, sometimes reproaching him, and often exclaiming, that he would surely bring them to destruction, if indeed he had not already fashioned them into vessels of wrath.

Now I understood that what these little pilgrims then suffered, arose from their own faint-heartedness and want of faith, as well as from their taking alarm at the prospect before them, and turning back to what they thought a better and safer spot of ground for their night's repose. For it hath been agreed among all pilgrims from the time of Abraham, who was himself a stranger and pilgrim upon earth, down to this present day, that whatever station the Lord appoints as a temporary resting-place for his servants, must needs be more safe and easy than any place of their own providing; and that it is neither lawful nor by any means safe to go back in the Way of Salvation, though it should be ever so short a step. Moreover, by this error of the little pilgrims in going back to seek a commodious night's lodging, they gave great advantage to the enemy, and thereby wholly deprived themselves of that night's repose. For their minds becoming greatly discomposed through sorrow for the past, as well as through fear of the future, they found it utterly impossible once to close their eyes. Neither did their comfort return with the returning day: for the prospect before them still appeared exceedingly dreary. They were almost at the mouth of the Valley of the Shadow of Death—a place of dragons, as described by David the king: and, indeed, a fearful place it was. But they must needs pass through it, or give up all thoughts of the kingdom of heaven.

This valley is a place where the pilgrim is cut off from all spiritual comfort,—where his sins are set before him in order, and where the face of the Saviour is hidden from his view. Moreover, in this place the torments of the damned are often brought before the mind of the pilgrim, while his path is haunted by appearances of the most appalling description. In this valley, the day is as darkness; God regards it not from above, neither doth the light of heaven shine upon it. Job iii. 4. Nevertheless, they that trust in the Lord shall be brought through it: "The Lord will bring them by a way that they knew not; he will lead them in paths that they have not known: he will make darkness light before them, and crooked things straight. These things will he do unto them, and not forsake them." Isaiah xlii. 16.

Now when *Inbred Sin* beheld this valley by the morning light, he was very urgent with the young pilgrims not to venture forward. But notwithstanding all the terrors they felt, the Lord afforded them such secret help as enabled them to proceed, though with much fear and trembling, and under great dejection of spirits.

Thus therefore they went on till they came to the entrance of the valley itself; and behold, as they advanced, the way became darker and more frightful. Their path also was here so extremely narrow, that they could scarcely keep their footing, but were in danger every moment of slipping off from the sound ground into the bogs and quagmires which were on either hand. And now as the darkness became greater, the air seemed to be filled with whisperings; which whisperings were so full of dreadful blasphemies, and so exceedingly terrifying, that the little pilgrims were ready to faint at the sound. But the children could not discover the whisperer; not knowing whether it was *Inbred-Sin*, or some evil spirit close at their ears. Then said Playful, "Surely we shall be lost in this place, and never see the Celestial Kingdom!"

"Nay, but," said Peace, "have we not now the promises of our Lord to support us, as heretofore? and hath he not said, 'I will never leave thee nor forsake thee?'" Heb. xiii. 5.

The little pilgrims then endeavoured to proceed, finding it as painful to stand still as to go forward. And behold, as they advanced, the place became still more dark and dismal; neither was there one cheering ray of light afforded them through the whole of that awful passage. So they began to pray aloud, making earnest supplication unto God: and behold, while they prayed, they found assistance, which enabled them to go on all that day, and indeed all that night, though scarcely knowing whither they went. Towards morning, however, they saw a faint light before them, which grew stronger as they advanced, gradually enabling them to pick their steps. Whereupon they hastened forward, till, to their unutterable joy, they found themselves quite clear of the valley. And no sooner did they see again the light of day, and begin to breathe a purer air, than they broke into loud songs of praise, magnifying and adoring the name of their great Deliverer.

Then said Humble Mind, "I have often heard of the Valley of the Shadow of Death, but never could have supposed it to be so dreadful a place."

"Let us give glory to our God," returned Peace,

"who has brought us out of those doleful regions, into the way of light and salvation!"

So the little pilgrims sat down and refreshed themselves with such things as they had; after which they continued their journey.

CHAPTER XV.

On leaving the Valley of the Shadow of Death, the children speedily reached the caves of giants *Pagan* and *Pope*. Now these giants, by reason of their age and infirmities, were incapable of doing so much mischief as they had formerly done: but they sat at the entrance of their caves, the one on *this* side of the road and the other on *that*, from whence they called to the little pilgrims as they passed, inviting them to their several places. Whereupon the children hastened away as fast as their feet could carry them. And it was well they did so; for the giants became so enraged when they found their persuasions disregarded, that they began to abuse both them and their King, and to use such language as Christian children ought not to hear.

Now I saw in my dream that the children had scarcely passed a bow-shot from the giants, when they entered into a grove of dark and gloomy trees, on the branches of which sat a number of owls and bats; creatures which, not being able to endure the light, kept their eyes constantly closed through the day. These are strange doctrines, doubts, errors, and vile conceits. Then said *Inbred-Sin*, "What are these?"

"Let them alone," replied Humble Mind, "while we pass forward; for if we disturb them, they will only be flapping about our eyes and ears."

"Nay, but," said *Inbred-Sin*, "I should like to know what they are."

"They are best let alone," said Humble Mind again.

Inbred-Sin, however, could not be persuaded to let the little party go quietly on without disturbing these creatures; but he would have it, that one or other of the children should throw a stone at them. So Playful, allowing herself to be over-persuaded, took up a handful of pebbles and threw them into the trees, although Humble Mind and Peace called aloud to her to forbear; whereupon such a cloud of these evil birds rose from the trees and descended upon the children, as nearly overwhelmed them. At this unexpected onset, little Peace was suddenly thrown flat upon her face; and it was as much as Humble Mind and Playful could do, to stand their ground: for the creatures kept beating upon them with their wings in every direction, uttering, at the same time, such doleful shrieks as added greatly to the children's perplexity. As to *Inbred-Sin*, who had been the prime cause of all this trouble, he stood by laughing heartily, and calling out first to one of the little pilgrims, then to another, in such a manner as bewildered them more and more.

I was in hopes that these obscene creatures would immediately take again to the trees: and so they would, no doubt, had the little pilgrims kept themselves quiet. But *Inbred-Sin* advised them to maintain the conflict, and to put forth all their strength in contending with and buffeting their winged enemies: by which means they were only rendered the more troublesome. Humble Mind, however, having contrived to raise little Peace from the ground, they at length made shift to disengage themselves from these unclean creatures, when they ran off with all speed, and thus escaped further harm.

Then I wondered for a time what this could mean, till the matter was made plain to me: and behold, it was this—that when young Christians are so unfortunate as to fall in the way of those who hold strange doctrines, or entertain errors and filthy conceits, their only security is to hasten forward, shutting their eyes and their ears, yea, and their lips too; not allowing themselves to be induced, by pride and conceit, to suppose themselves powerful enough to contend with and conquer their subtile enemies.

Now I perceived that, after the little pilgrims had got clear of their enemies, they ran for a time as though it were for their lives, while *Inbred-Sin* kept close on their steps: and behold, he amused himself and kept up their alarm by repeating the hoarse croakings and shrieks of the obscene birds by which the little pilgrims had been lately attacked. However, after awhile Humble Mind recovered himself sufficiently to distinguish between the cries of the birds and *Inbred-Sin's* imitation of them;

when he reproved *Inbred-Sin* for thus mimicking the hideous noises by which they had been so much terrified. So *Inbred-Sin* held his peace, and the little pilgrims went quietly forward.

I perceived then in my dream, that, as the pilgrims journeyed on, they came to a place where was a very wide wilderness, an exceedingly solitary place, and promising very little comfort. Nevertheless, they found more satisfaction in this part of their pilgrimage than they at first expected; and especially, because the manna lay thick on the ground in many parts of their way. And there being in these countries no inns or places of refreshment for pilgrims, the little travellers to Mount Zion were, I saw, particularly careful in gathering the manna betimes every morning, and filling their golden pots for every day's consumption. Moreover, although the brook did not here flow along by the wayside as in other parts of the children's path, yet even in this dry and parched wilderness there were not wanting certain wells, here and there, by the way-side, from which the little people were enabled to draw water for their refreshment. So that upon the whole, their passage through this wilderness was made with much comfort. Not that they were free all this time from the interruptions of *Inbred-Sin;* for, as I have often before observed, it is the nature of this our bosom inmate never to rest, but to be always either openly or covertly employed in some mischief. They were however enabled, through the divine help, without which nothing good can be effected, to check and repress him whenever he would be putting in his word: and it really did me good to see how manfully these little ones were enabled to contend with him in this place.

If he attempted to give his opinion on any occasion, one would say to him, "When your advice is not asked, why do you put in your word? We will, with God's help, serve the Lord, and not hearken to any of your opinions." And another would say to him, "Hold your peace: we will have no fellowship with you." And thus he was rebuked on all sides; for the little pilgrims, during their passage through this desert, being strengthened by the manna on which they subsisted from day to day, and not having their stomachs loaded with grosser aliments, became very brisk and lively, and were continually on their guard against all the attempts of this their inbred tormentor to draw them to evil. Nevertheless I marvelled greatly at the unblushing effrontery and indefatigable perseverance of *Inbred-Sin* in pursuing his purpose, which was to turn the little pilgrims from the way of life into the paths of destruction. Sometimes he would be as smooth as oil, and put on all the meekness of a dove, walking by the side of the pilgrims with his eyes turned Zion-wards, and his hands joined in prayer. Then, when he thought they began to look on him with a favourable eye, he would talk of religion, and quote Scripture: and it is surprising how glibly he would run off the language of Mount Zion. Moreover, if not checked, he would join them in their devotions, yea, and lead those devotions too, and that in as fervent a manner, and with as audible a voice as any one of the company—and yet, before any one was aware, he would suddenly turn all these religious exercises into ridicule, suggesting some vain or foul thought, by which all was at once polluted and spoiled. If detected or reproved at this hypocritical work, he was not abashed or confounded, but was ready in an instant with some other contrivance for advancing his master's cause. And it was marvellous what expertness he showed in suiting his temptations to the age and state of those with whom he associated: so that it would require a large volume to report the half of his tricks and contrivances—"for the heart is deceitful above all things, and desperately wicked: who can know it?" Jer. xvii. 9.

Now I saw that, when the little pilgrims had arrived at the end of this wilderness, they came to a little rising ground covered with tall trees; and on reaching the top of this hill, behold, they saw before them, at no great distance, the mighty town of Vanity. Here therefore they remembered that the damsels of the palace Beautiful had spoken to them of this city, informing them that they must needs pass through it, and that it was a place of more than ordinary danger for pilgrims.

The children stood all amazed on beholding this mighty city, which extended itself towards the east, the west, the north, and the south, much farther than the eye could reach, adorned with all manner of gay and magnificent buildings; such as theatres, castles, towers, halls, palaces, and various kinds of places of worship. The noise and din of the city reached even to the hill on which the children stood; and its smoke, which rose up to the very heavens, entirely concealed the bright light on the eastern horizon, which had been pointed out to the little pilgrims by Evangelist. Then said Humble Mind, "My heart faints within me at the sight of that great and wicked city: would to God, my dear sisters, that the whole of our journey lay through wildernesses and solitary places, and that we might be spared a passage through the town of Vanity!"

"Brother," replied Peace, "does it become us to wish things otherwise than our Lord has ordered them? Did not the Son of God himself, when on earth, spend many days in this town of Vanity? and have we not been informed that in its streets he was crucified? If, therefore, it pleases him that we should walk through it in our way to the city, let us not murmur, but rather pray that we may not be drawn aside by the vanities of the place."

"Beloved sister," said Humble Mind, "you are quite right, and I have spoken amiss: but shall not we stop here awhile and take a little rest, since the day is very far spent? Let us, I pray, have some sweet discourse together in this verdant shade, before we proceed on our journey: for I love not the thought of yonder vain and tumultuous city; and I fear lest we should not readily succeed in discovering there the abode of the true Christians."

Then spoke Playful, "Methinks, brother, that you are fearful without cause. Did not the damsels give us tokens by which we might know the true servants of God from the other inhabitants of Vanity Fair? And where must our wits be, if we allow ourselves to be misled?"

Wondering much at these words of Playful, I looked, and behold, *Inbred-Sin* was seated close at her ear; and there he had been whispering unreproved for some minutes. Now I saw, in my dream, that the children sat down upon the grass, and refreshed themselves with manna from their golden vessels: but the eyes of Playful were frequently drawn towards the city of Vanity, which, as the shades of night advanced, was lighted up with many lights. So Humble Mind and Peace held sweet discourse together for some time. After which I heard the little party, according to their evening custom, repeating to each other certain portions of their Holy Book.

Now behold, while they were thus employed, there arose a gentle rustling among the trees, of which there were many in this place. After which a fragrant and refreshing breeze passed over the little pilgrims; and in the breeze was heard a sound (and indeed a most ravishing sound it was), as of angels hymning the high praises of God. So the children looked one at another, while the tears came into their eyes; moreover, they smiled for joy: but, until the music had ceased, they spake not to each other. Then said Humble Mind, "Did I not say but now, that I should be glad if the whole of my course lay through such solitary places as these? And at this moment I recollect the damsels of the palace Beautiful giving us an account of certain holy persons, who, being driven out from the presence of mankind, and condemned to dwell in deserts and caves of the earth, were there often consoled by such heavenly music as we have just heard."

Peace. I remember it also; and perhaps this music has been sent for the purpose of encouraging us to stand firm during our sojourn in the town of Vanity.

Humble Mind. My heart fails me, by reason of the trials to which we shall probably be exposed in the wicked city before us.

I saw then that Peace began to weep; and presently she broke out in these words—"O my sweet brother and sister! how pleasant it is to sit apart from all the world, thinking and speaking of holy things as we now do! Ah, beloved companions! what pleasant hours have we spent together in these days of our pilgrimage! —in the fields of the shepherd Sincerity; in the house of Mr. Interpreter; at the foot of the holy cross; in the fields of Innocent Pleasure; in the palace Beautiful; in the Valley of Humiliation; and lastly, in this wilderness—happy hours, in which we have communed with our Saviour and our God! while weak, poor, sinful, and utterly vile as we are, we have been brought, step by step, on our way towards his heavenly kingdom. Let us earnestly pray that the dear Saviour who has hitherto led and supported us, may never leave nor forsake us, till the glorious work of our salvation be finished: and then shall we spend a happy eternity together in praising God and the Lamb for ever and ever."

Now I wondered greatly to hear such words proceeding from the mouth of such a babe, though I had for some time past observed her greatly outgrowing her elder sister in grace. Upon which I recollected that God is no respecter of persons; but that he giveth much to one and less to another, according to his own free will and pleasure.

After awhile I looked again at the little pilgrims, when they were engaged in prayer; which being concluded, they laid themselves down upon the grass and fell asleep. Now in this part of the wilderness, which lies near to the City of Vanity, were many wolves and dogs prowling about, creatures which find subsistence among the the burying-grounds on the skirts of the city. And I became alarmed for the sleeping children, when I saw these animals approaching their resting-place, and skulking around them among the brakes and bushes.

But, while I wondered wherefore they did not spring upon them and tear them limb from limb, I looked, and behold, there sat beside the little sleepers a certain shepherd, clothed in white, with a crook in his hand; and the face of this shepherd was all glorious and beautiful, such as I could not steadfastly look upon. Then I recollected the words of the holy psalmist—"The Lord is my shepherd; I shall not want. He maketh me to lie down in green pastures." Psalm xxiii. 1, 2.

CHAPTER XVI.

Now I saw in my dream that, when the children awoke in the morning, they beheld the great city before them all resplendent with the rays of the rising sun. And behold its golden domes, palaces, temples, pagodas, mosques, pantheons, theatres, walls, gates, towers, and bulwarks, filled them with amazement; and while they stood gazing upon them, *Inbred-Sin* broke into loud expressions of admiration. I heard then that Humble Mind reproved him: but Playful was pleased with his remarks. So, being encouraged by Playful he took upon him to say that the City of Vanity was by no means such a place as the damsels of the palace Beautiful and many other over-much righteous persons had represented; that the city itself was an exceedingly fair city to look upon, and indeed the prime glory of the world; moreover, he added, that they were very uncharitable who asserted that there were not many good persons in that city. In this manner he ran on, to the great perplexity of Humble Mind and Peace; who while they thought it their duty to reprove him, performed that duty in too timid and trembling a manner. Whereupon this bold one became still more bold, as I shall have occasion to show by-and-by. For he that reproveth sin, and doeth it not courageously and effectually, gives an advantage to the Evil One of which he will not fail to avail himself. The little pilgrims then, having looked awhile on the city, betook themselves to their journey.

Now it was not long before they approached the outer wall of the city. And behold, many of the inhabitants were walking forth to take the air; and as they brushed by the little pilgrims, they looked upon them just as men look upon a person whom they despise. Nevertheless they suffered the strangers to pass on: for, as hath been before remarked, it is not now usual in the town of Vanity to imprison pilgrims and put them to violent deaths, as in former times. In ancient days, pilgrims passing through the town of Vanity had trial of cruel mockings and scourgings, and of sundry other bitter persecutions; of which an account is given in the eleventh chapter of the Epistle to the Hebrews. But the influence of the better part of the inhabitants of the town having now become greater, the enemies of the Lord are not able to carry it towards Christians as in former times. So the little pilgrims might have passed on in perfect peace to the gate of the city, if *Inbred-Sin* would have suffered them: but as soon as he observed the scornful looks of those who passed by, he failed not to point them out to the pilgrims. And though Humble Mind reproved him, saying, "We are servants of him who was crucified in this town—Is the servant greater than his Lord? If they persecuted him, will they not also persecute us?" John xv. 20. —yet this inbred tormentor would not remain quiet, but kept continually observing how the inhabitants discovered their scorn, shooting out their lips and shaking their heads. I perceived also that even Peace and Humble Mind, who had, as I thought, made up their minds to expect nothing better than contempt and ridicule in the town of Vanity, became much discomposed, as their glowing cheeks testified; while Playful was thrown into such a state of confusion, that she seemed hardly to know what she was doing.

In this manner they proceeded till they came to the city gate, which they found wide open; for the gate of Vanity is never shut. So passing through the gate they entered into a wide street, which stretched away before them as far as they could see. Now there were such a bustle and noise in the street, such passing to and fro of carriages, horsemen, and foot-passengers, that the little children were jolted and hustled at every step. Moreover, their eyes were continually turned towards the fine things which they saw displayed in the windows of the shops on every side: so that, instead of hastening over this dangerous ground, they made little or no progress forward. Now this was *Inbred-Sin's* time; and never did I see him more active, more insolent, or more unreasonable, than he was in these streets of Vanity. He had twenty conceits in a single minute, his humour changing as fast as the colours on the back of the chameleon. He would one minute assert that the town of Vanity was a very good place, its customs honourable, and its people worthy of esteem; the next minute he would be filling the hearts of the little pilgrims with the dread of persecution and ridicule; then again he would have them put off their pilgrims' garments, and put on some of the gaudy dresses which were exposed in the shop-windows—and thus he went on, not giving the little pilgrims a moment for collecting their thoughts or lifting up their hearts in prayer.

Now I perceived, in my dream, that, as the pilgrims advanced, the children of Vanity, who were playing in the streets, began to gather after them, and to use such by-words and terms of reproach as are there generally applied to pilgrims. At first they did but whisper and mutter; but soon becoming bolder, as the multitude gathered about them, they grew quite loud and scurrilous in their abuse, raising such a commotion that the whole street was disturbed, while the inhabitants came crowding to their doors and windows.

Then said *Inbred-Sin*, "Did I not tell you it would be so? Why, then, did you not listen to my advice, and pull off these outward garments, which are peculiar to pilgrims, and put on such as accord a little with the fashions of the place? In so doing, you might have passed quietly through the town; after which, at a more convenient time and place, you might readily have put on your white garments again."

"But," replied little Peace, "our Lord hath solemnly said, 'Whosoever shall be ashamed of me and of my words in this adulterous and sinful generation; of him also shall the Son of man be ashamed, when he cometh in the glory of his Father with the holy angels.'" Mark viii. 38.

Inbred-Sin answered, "But who can feel otherwise than ashamed on such an occasion? And who can help fearing such a generation of men as these, even more than they fear him who will hereafter come in the clouds of heaven with all his holy angels?"

Then did Peace rebuke *Inbred-Sin;* but Humble Mind and Playful kept silence.

Now the crowd pressed more and more upon the little pilgrims, terrifying them exceedingly with their bold and blasphemous language; neither did they refrain from casting mud and mire at them, in order to defile their beautiful garments which had been made white in the blood of the Lamb.

Then was *Inbred-Sin* very earnest with the little ones to turn into some of those convenient houses on the side of the street, which are opened by the prince of Vanity for the use of passengers, and provided by him with all such accommodations as are agreeable to the flesh: in return for which accommodations, however, no less is required than the whole of a man's estate, both body and soul, to be delivered up for ever to the prince himself.

Meanwhile the insults and threatenings of the mob continued so to alarm the little pilgrims, that they looked this way, and that way, like persons beside themselves, not knowing what course to take. Playful was for following *Inbred-Sin's* advice without hesitation; while Humble Mind looked as white as a sheet; but little Peace notwithstanding the perplexing whisperings of *Inbred-Sin,* continued instant in prayer—for the Lord was with her—and as she held the hand of Playful, she restrained her from turning into any of those houses of entertainment in which *Inbred-Sin* would have had them take refuge from the insults of the mob. All this while the ungodly multitude ceased not to press upon the little pilgrims, still pelting them with mire and dirt; insomuch that, with the heat of their onset and the violence of their clamour, the discouraged travellers were nearly overcome; and little Peace especially, being young and of a tender constitution, though strong in the power of the Lord, actually fainted and fell. At this, certain persons in the crowd, who were less hard-hearted than the rest, cried out shame! Whereupon the throng giving way, the child was lifted up and placed at the door of a house near at hand; where her brother and sister stood by her, chafing her temples and moistening her lips with cold water, which some charitable person had brought in a cup. And behold *Inbred-Sin* shrunk back at the sight.

Now, as she lay fainting, I observed her sweet pale face to change, as for death, while the cold sweats stood upon her brow. Then I looked up and called for help, being exceedingly afflicted at the situation of little Peace. But ere I could frame my lips to a prayer, behold, two shining ones appeared in the east: whence they approached with an exceedingly swift motion, and rested in the heavens over where the dying infant lay, waiting to receive her spirit—but they who were below perceived them not. Presently, the paleness left her face for a moment, when she looked affectionately at her brother and sister, saying, "Sweet companions of my pilgrimage, I am about to leave you: but I go to him who died for me—to him who shed his blood for me upon the cross—to him who loved me more than his own life—and he will present me to himself without spot or stain of sin." Then suddenly lifting up her eyes, she saw the pitying angels, as messengers waiting to convey her home, and holding in their hands the crown of glory which was prepared for her, through the free grace and mercy of her Lord. Then did all earthly scenes pass for ever from her view wrapped together as a scroll—and at that moment an internal struggle took place between heavenly joy and mortal anguish. She smiled in the agony of death, continuing to look steadfastly at the angels till her eyes became fixed and motionless; when she breathed more and more slowly, till at length her fair spirit, made pure through her Redeemer's blood, and holy by his imputed righteousness, quitted her little languid body, resigning it to corruption and the worm until that day when the trumpet shall sound, and when that which was sown in corruption shall be raised in incorruption—that which was sown in dishonour shall be raised in glory—that which was sown in weakness shall be raised in power—and that which was sown a natural body shall be raised a spiritual body. "O death, where is thy sting? O grave, where is thy victory? The sting of death is sin. But thanks be to God, which giveth us the victory through our Lord Jesus Christ." 1 Cor. xv. 42–44, 55–57.

Then the holy angels who were waiting above, received her spirit in their arms, and bore her away to the gates of heaven—and I saw her no more. Thus she was delivered from *Inbred-Sin*, and from the devil, that adversary of mankind, who, "as a roaring lion, walketh about seeking whom he may devour." 1 Pet. v. 8. And now she walks with God, high in salvation and the climes of bliss; where she sees the King in his beauty, and beholds the land which is very far off. Isaiah xxxiii. 17.

So for awhile I could look no longer, by reason of the tears which filled my eyes and obscured my sight: nevertheless, I blessed God for delivering this little fair one from all her spiritual enemies, as well as from all the troubles and mischances of this present life. Then perceiving that Peace could not dwell with vanity, I applied to the little departing pilgrim these words of the wise man—"She pleased God and was beloved of him; so that living among sinners she was translated. For her soul pleased the Lord: therefore hasted he to take her away from among the wicked." Wisdom iv. 10, 14.

CHAPTER XVII.

As soon as I could wipe away my tears, I looked after poor Humble Mind and Playful; and behold, they had fallen down by the body of their sister, each holding one of her pale cold hands; and there they lay like persons more dead than alive. And behold the noisy multitude had fled, terrified at the sight of death—for "the wicked flee when no man pursueth: but the righteous are bold as a lion." Prov. xxviii. 1.

Now, about this time, good Mr. *Orthodox*, of whom mention hath been made before, received a letter from the damsels of the palace Beautiful, entreating him to have regard to certain little pilgrims, Humble Mind, Playful, and Peace, who about that time were to pass through the town of Vanity. For after the little ones had left the palace Beautiful, Prudence said to her sisters, "I am much afraid lest those little ones should miss of the house of Mr. *Orthodox*, and carry our letters to some other person; since there are several individuals, it is said, in the town of Vanity, who assume the name of that worthy and discreet pastor. I therefore advise that we write another letter to Mr. *Orthodox*, and send it by some trusty person, entreating him to look after the young pilgrims." So, the damsels approving what Prudence suggested, the letter was written in haste, and Mr. *Watchful*, the porter, charged with providing a fit person to carry it.

On the receipt of this letter, good old Mr. *Orthodox* lost no time in making diligent search after the little ones: when he shortly found Humble Mind and Playful, as I before described them, lying beside the body of Peace. After being much affected at the sight of so pitiable a spectacle, Mr. *Orthodox* caused Humble Mind and Playful to be lifted up and carried to his wife, whose name was *Bountiful*, and who he well knew would spare no pains to administer unto them every consolation of which their situation was capable. He ordered also the body of little Peace to be raised from the ground, and conveyed to his house; where it was placed in a fair chamber, from whence it was removed at a convenient time, and buried according to the custom of Christians in those parts. Mr. *Orthodox* likewise caused a fair white monument to be placed over the body of the little pilgrim, in order that such young persons as should in future visit her grave might be encouraged, by the example of Peace, to trust in the same adorable Saviour who enabled that little saint to stand fast unto the end.

Upon this monument was the following inscription:—

REMEMBER

PEACE,

WHO DIED IN THE SEVENTH YEAR OF HER AGE;

Choosing rather to suffer affliction with the people of God than to enjoy the pleasures of sin for a season.
Hebrews xi. 25.

Thou didst make me hope when I was upon my mother's breasts.
Psalm xxii. 9.

Now I saw in my dream, that Mr. *Orthodox* and his wife, Mrs. *Bountiful*, used their utmost endeavours to comfort Humble Mind and his sister; for which purpose they kept them in their own house, and used them very tenderly; so that, after a while they were enabled calmly to listen to such words of consolation as Mr. *Orthodox* thought suitable to their state.

I perceived then that this pious man arranged his motives of comfort under two heads: first, the gain accruing to little Peace herself from her death; and secondly, the benefit which her brother and sister might reap from their present affliction. And first, he spoke of the gain which little Peace herself had made. "She was," said he, "a poor and helpless orphan, wandering in the wide wilderness of this wicked world, as a hart upon the Mountains of Leopards. Her body was liable to sickness, pain, and death; while *Inbred-Sin* was the close, the intimate, though I trust the abhorred, companion of her steps. He was inseparable from her. And as she found it impossible to escape him; so you well know that she could have no solid rest or ease, by reason of this internal tormentor. Her blessed Saviour had indeed called her, and separated her from those who are the willing slaves of *Inbred-Sin:* nevertheless, though her only hope was in the merits of her Saviour's death, yet *Inbred-Sin* was continually interrupting her intercourse with that dear Redeemer. But now!" continued Mr. *Orthodox*, "being set free from sin, her union with the Saviour is rendered complete!—she dwells for ever with him!—yea, she is built up as a polished corner-stone in the church triumphant, of which he is the foundation!

"Happy Peace! her warfare is finished, and she is made more than conqueror. She mixes with that rejoicing multitude who stand before the throne and before the Lamb, clothed in white raiment, and having palms in their hands; of whom it is said, 'These are they which came out of great tribulation, and have washed their robes and made them white in the blood of the Lamb. Therefore are they before the throne of God, and serve him day and night in his temple; and he that sitteth on the throne shall dwell among them.'" Rev. vii. 14, 15. Thus Mr. *Orthodox* described the happiness of little Peace in the ears of her brother and sister. In the next place, he proceeded to point out the benefit which Humble Mind and Playful might receive from their present affliction. He remarked that the human race, having fallen from their first estate of innocence and glory, in which they appeared as the children and companions of God, it had become necessary, in order to their salvation, to deal with them in a manner totally different from that which their heavenly Father would have used, had they preserved their original innocence. "You are thoroughly impressed," said Mr. *Orthodox*, "I trust, with this one mighty leading truth, which unless a man has received, he is no better than a heathen; namely, that 'there is no salvation in any other' but the Lord Jesus Christ; and that 'there is none other name under heaven given among men whereby we must be saved.' Acts iv. 12. You are, I trust, also convinced, that all who are brought to Christ, and united with him, will certainly be saved: because such persons become one with Christ and he with them; he is the head, and they are the members. In these views the humble Christian has everlasting happiness and eternal glory ensured to him: for if one member suffer, all the members of the same body must suffer; and if one member be honoured, all the members of the same body must be honoured. 1 Cor. xii. 26.

"Now," continued Mr. *Orthodox*, "although there is but one name by which sinners can be saved, and but one Holy Spirit whose office it is to bring sinners unto Christ; yet that Spirit is found to work with different individuals in different ways. Among which different methods this is one—that as the earth is generally prepared for the seed which is afterward to produce fruit by the plough, the spade, and the harrow, which tear up its rugged bosom, making it soft and tender; so the stony heart of man is often broken up by affliction, and rendered soft by sorrow, in order, with the divine blessing, to fit it for the reception of the divine Word. Therefore, my children, 'despise not ye the chastening of the Lord, nor faint when ye are rebuked of him; for whom the Lord loveth he chasteneth, and scourgeth every son whom he receiveth. If ye endure chastening God dealeth with you as with sons; for what son is he whom the father chasteneth not? But if ye be without chastisement, whereof all are partakers, then are ye bastards, and not sons. Furthermore, we have had fathers of our flesh, which corrected us; and we gave them reverence: shall we not much rather be in subjection unto the Father of spirits and live? For they verily for a few days chastened us after their own pleasure; but he for our profit, that we might be partakers of his holiness. Now no chastening for the present seemeth to be joyous, but grievous: nevertheless, afterward it yieldeth the peaceable fruit of righteousness unto them which are exercised thereby. Wherefore lift up the hands which hang down, and the feeble knees."' Heb. xii. 5–12.

In this manner did Mr. *Orthodox* reason with and comfort the little pilgrims: till, by God's blessing upon his pious endeavours, their grief became greatly mitigated. Nevertheless, Humble Mind received comfort sooner than Playful, and for this reason, because his heart was more in heaven than the heart of his sister. On this account, as well as from the consideration that the present world is not our resting-place, he became gradually reconciled to the idea of a temporary separation from his beloved Peace. But Playful seemed inclined, for a considerable time, to murmur and complain, on being deprived of her lovely little sister; while she allowed *Inbred-Sin* to suggest many impatient, and evil thoughts to her mind on that occasion. Not daring, however, to make an open discovery of her feelings, she kept *Inbred-Sin's* communications on this subject as secret as possible from Mr. *Orthodox.*

Now I saw, in my dream, that while the little pilgrims remained in the house of Mr. *Orthodox*, this worthy gentleman took Humble Mind under his special care and tuition. He also requested his wife, Mrs. *Bountiful*, to do the same by Playful, and to take the child with her whenever she went to visit and teach the poor: for Mrs. *Bountiful*, as became the wife of the minister *Orthodox*, was ever mindful of the poor, being, like Dorcas, "full of good works." Acts ix. 36.

So Playful began to help Mrs. *Bountiful* in these labours of love; in which she shortly became so engaged that she had less time and inclination to listen to the evil suggestions of *Inbred-Sin.* Moreover, Mrs. *Bountiful* gave her many lessons concerning those duties which especially belong to females; on which occasions she was accustomed to catechise her after this manner.

Mrs. Bountiful. In a few years, my daughter, you will be no longer a child, but will exchange that condition for woman's estate. Now, whereas it is appointed unto all persons once to die, and after that the judgment, it is of great consequence to us to know what manner of life God willeth us to lead in the different states unto which he hath called us: tell me, therefore, my child, are there any points in which the duties of men and women differ?

After some consideration, Playful answered; "Men are commanded to preach, and women to be silent, in the churches—'Let the woman learn in silence with all subjection. But I suffer not a woman to teach, nor to usurp authority over the man, but to be in silence.'" 1 Tim. ii. 11, 12.

Mrs. Bountiful. How should wives behave to their husbands?

Playful. "Wives, submit yourselves unto your own husbands, as it is fit in the Lord." Col. iii. 18.

Mrs. Bountiful. If it be the duty of a woman to obey her husband, how careful should a believing woman be, not to join herself with an unbelieving man! But supposing that a woman be already unfortunately married to such a one, in what way must she try to bring him over to the solid profession of Christianity?

Playful. "Likewise, ye wives, be in subjection to your own husbands; that if any obey not the Word, they also may without the Word be won by the conversation of the wives; while they behold your chaste conversation coupled with fear." 1 Pet. iii. 1, 2.

Mrs. Bountiful. What is said of those women who love pleasure?

Playful. "She that liveth in pleasure is dead while she liveth." 1 Tim. v. 6.

Mrs. Bountiful. When women forget Christ, what kind of habits do they commonly fall into?

Playful. "They learn to be idle, wandering about from house to house; and not only idle, but tattlers also, and busybodies, speaking things which they ought not." 1 Tim. v. 13.

Mrs. Bountiful. In what manner should women adorn themselves?

Playful. "In like manner also, that women adorn themselves in modest apparel, with shamefacedness and sobriety; not with broidered hair, or gold, or pearls, or costly array: but (which becometh women professing godliness) with good works." 1 Tim. ii. 9, 10.

Mrs. Bountiful. You have answered well, my child.

"I learned these things," said Playful, "of the holy ladies in the palace Beautiful: but when I should afterward have called them to mind (sinner that I was!) I totally forgot them." Then I saw that Playful wept.

Mrs. Bountiful. Come, my child, "forget those things which are behind, and reach forth unto those things which are before." Phil. iii. 13.

Playful. I remember part of a sweet psalm, which we used to sing in the palace Beautiful, of which my sad miscarriages now remind me—

> "Happy are they, and only they,
> Who from thy presence fear to stray;
> Who know what's right, not only so,
> But seek to practise what they know."

Mrs. Bountiful. Well, my dear child, if the faults you have committed serve to make you humble, it is well. With this view it was, no doubt, that the Lord left you to yourself for a little while; as it is written—"That thou mayst remember, and be confounded, and never open thy mouth any more because of thy shame, when I am pacified towards thee for all that thou hast done, saith the Lord God." Ezek. xvi. 63.

I saw then that Mrs. *Bountiful* asked Playful if she could mention some of those good works, which seem to be particularly required of women?

"I think," said Playful, "I could tell some few of them; yet would I rather hear them from you."

Mrs. Bountiful. There are two duties which more especially lie upon women; first, that of bringing up children, and secondly, that of relieving the afflicted. And whereas the necessities of infants and those of the sick are twofold, a woman should learn to administer to both, otherwise she does but half her duty towards such persons.

Playful. Dear madam, I do not understand you exactly.

Mrs. Bountiful. To explain my meaning more fully—Every infant is formed of two parts; the immortal soul and the little tender body. If either of these is neglected, injury, if not ruin, must be the consequence of such neglect. A woman, therefore, who takes the charge of an infant, should not only know how to make its clothes, to administer its proper food, to comfort and cherish it, and, under God, to preserve its health; but, since we are all born in sin, she should also know how, as its sense increases, to correct its evil tempers, and lead it into that knowledge of God which is eternal life. Sick and afflicted persons likewise often require the same attention as infants: nourishing food and comfortable clothing must be provided for their bodies, while their poor weak minds should be drawn towards God by holy conversation, prayer, and pious reading. I would, therefore," added good Mrs. *Bountiful*, "have young females, from their tender youth, to store their minds with such chosen portions of Scripture, together with such pleasant and profitable histories of pious persons, as are calculated to excite the attention of children and sick persons of all ages and all degrees, to the great work of their own salvation. They should also learn to sing such sweet psalms and hymns as may sooth infants to sleep, or compose the uneasy minds of the sick. They should moreover labour to become patient, self-denying, long-suffering, kind, gentle, and courteous; since all these qualities are necessary to form a good and tender nurse. Females should also early be taught to make cheap and convenient clothing for the needy, as well as to prepare wholesome, simple, and economical dishes for their occasional support and comfort. And, lastly, they should learn to dress themselves in a decent, cleanly, and modest manner, with as little expense as possible of that precious time and those other talents which must hereafter be accounted for at the judgment-seat of Christ."

Now the conversation of Mrs. *Bountiful* was very pleasant to Playful, who endeavoured to store up in her heart the instructions of that excellent woman.

I saw also, in my dream, that, when the minds of the children became more composed, and their grief a little abated, Mr. *Orthodox* showed them, from time to time, such things as were worthy of notice about his house and his church.

One day in particular, I observed that he took them into a large room adjoining to his church, where many persons were engaged in printing; and the types which they used were those of every language under the sun. Now at the door of this room there stood many persons, who received the books as soon as they were printed, and ran off with them, in order to disperse them through the different districts of the city. Then inquired the children, "What are those books?"

Mr. Orthodox. They are all copies of the one great Book of Life; even that same book by the reading of which you found your way hither, and by which I trust you will also find your way to a better home. And I have orders from my Master to distribute these books through every street of the city.

Then I saw that Mr. *Orthodox* took one of the books in his hand, and said, "This holy volume, my dear children, containeth all things the knowledge of which is necessary to salvation: so that whatsoever is not read therein, or may be proved thereby, ought not to be required of any man to be believed as an article of the faith, or be thought requisite or necessary to salvation. And here you must carefully note that by the term Holy Scriptures we understand those canonical books of the Old and New Testament of whose authority there was never any doubt in the church." (*See 6th Article of the Church.*)

Now the young pilgrims remained many days with good Mr. *Orthodox* and Mrs. *Bountiful;* where they increased in stature and in favour with God and man. At length the period approached, at which they were to proceed on their pilgrimage. But before they departed Mr. *Orthodox* led them into his church, and caused them there to receive the holy sacrament of the body and blood of Christ; explaining unto them how "that the Lord Jesus, the same night in which he was betrayed, took bread: and when he had given thanks, he brake it, and said, Take, eat; this is my body, which is broken for you; this do in remembrance of me. After the same manner also he took the cup, when he had supped, saying, This cup is the new testament in my blood: this do ye, as oft as ye drink it, in remembrance of me. For as often as ye eat this bread, and drink this cup, ye do show the Lord's death till he come." 1 Cor. xi. 23–26. Moreover, before they departed, he would have them to visit the grave of Peace: for "it is better to go to the house of mourning than to go to the house of feasting; for that is the end of all men; and the living will lay it to his heart." Eccles. vii. 2. So Mr. *Orthodox* and Mrs. *Bountiful* led the way, and the children followed.

Now, when they came to the grave, and read the name of Peace upon the fair white monument, and the verses, which Mr. *Orthodox* had caused to be graven underneath, Humble Mind looked very pale, and Playful began to weep. Upon which Mr. *Orthodox* said, "Wherefore are you sorrowful? If you loved your sister Peace, you ought to rejoice; because she is gone to her heavenly Father."

So Playful wiped away her tears.

Then spake Mr. *Orthodox*, as he stood by the grave, "Hearken unto me, my children. You have been often taught, and I hope have many times sensibly felt, that having received forgiveness of sins through the Lord Jesus Christ, you have become one with him, as he is one with the Father; according as it is written—'At that day ye shall know that I am in my Father, and you in me, and I in you.' John xiv. 20. This mystical union," continued Mr. *Orthodox*, "between Christ and his children, is a doctrine not only held altogether in contempt by the world, but it is a doctrine which even many who are constant comers to my church cannot receive; and for this reason, because they love the world, and cleave to it, though it be a stranger and an enemy to the Spirit of truth.

"Now this mystical union," added the good man, "is neither a fancied nor a figurative thing, but a sacred reality. When you were joined to Christ, my children, sin lost its absolute power over you; the Holy Spirit at that time entered your hearts, and you became temples of the living God. 1 Cor. iii. 16. Christ is the head of all believers, and believers are his members; so that a Christian hath no power to do any one good thing, but through the help of the Holy Spirit, which he receives as a member of Christ. Through faith the believer is enabled to bring forth the fruits of righteousness; by faith he is strengthened in the inner man: and when he fails to seek the help of the Spirit, he becomes weak and faint as other men, and perhaps falls into grievous sins, as was the case with King David.

"Our little sister," continued Mr. *Orthodox*, "whose body lies in this grave, was, through the grace of God, born again in Christ, and made a new creature, many months before her death, as we have abundant reason to believe from her orderly and even course, as well as from the delight she took in communing with her God.

She must then have been a true member of Christ—for 'the branch cannot bear fruit of itself, except it abide in the vine' (John xv. 4); and therefore is her salvation sure."

"Now understand, my children," continued he, "that our mystical union with our great Head is not destroyed by death; but we are as near to Christ, and as much a part of him, when lying in the grave and in the dust, as when living on the earth. For it is written, 'Whether we live, we live unto the Lord; and whether we die, we die unto the Lord: whether we live, therefore, or die, we are the Lord's. For to this end Christ both died, and rose, and revived, that he might be Lord both of the dead and living.' Rom. xiv. 8, 9. In this grave, therefore, and under this little white stone, lies a part of the mystical body of Christ,—a member belonging to the Divine Head. All that remained of sin and corruption in this mortal body is now destroyed—for 'except a corn of wheat fall into the ground and die, it abideth alone; but if it die, it bringeth forth much fruit.' John xii. 24. But the better part of this your dear sister still remains; and at the last day, when the trumpet shall sound, she will be raised up, and joined for ever to her glorious Head. 'When Christ, who is her life, shall appear, then shall she also appear with him in glory.' Col. iii. 4. For while in the flesh, she received forgiveness of sins through the Redeemer; and having been justified by him, she will be also glorified (Rom. viii. 30), and shall stand with him to judge the world. 1 Cor. vi. 2. Therefore, my dear children, grieve no more for your beloved Peace, but rejoice that she was enabled to fight the good fight of faith; and 'abide ye in the Lord Jesus Christ, that, when he shall appear, ye may have confidence, and not be ashamed before him at his coming (1 John ii. 28): but that ye may have boldness in the day of judgment: because as he is, so are his children.'" 1 John iv. 17.

Now the time was come for the children to depart. So Mrs. *Bountiful* prepared for them such things as she thought might serve for their refreshment by the way; while Mr. *Orthodox*, taking them aside, knelt down with them and prayed, saying, "Plead thou the cause of these little ones, O Lord, with those that oppose them, and fight thou against them that fight against these. For the eyes of these pilgrims are unto thee, O God the

Lord, and in thee is their trust. Let the souls of these thy servants be precious in thy sight. Leave them not, neither forsake them, O God of our salvation! Many are the afflictions of the righteous: but thou deliverest them out of all. The Lord conduct these youthful travellers safely on their way, and bring them at length to his holy hill of Zion, even to the place which he loveth. Praies the Lord!"

Thus prayed the holy Mr. *Orthodox*: after which he rose up and kissed the children. Then Humble Mind and his sister being fully prepared for their journey, Mr. *Orthodox* and his wife thought it proper to see them safe out of the town. So having passed the populous parts of the city, and reached the skirts of the town, Mr. *Orthodox* and Mrs. *Bountiful* again kissed the young pilgrims, and returned to their house.

CHAPTER XVIII.

Now it came to pass, when Mr. *Orthodox* and Mrs. *Bountiful* had taken their leave of the little pilgrims at the gates of Vanity (for it suited not the convenience of these excellent persons to accompany them farther on their journey), that Humble Mind and Playful proceeded along the suburbs for some time, weeping as they went: and *Inbred-Sin* was with them.

I had remarked that *Inbred-Sin* kept himself very quiet in the house of Mr. *Orthodox*. Not that he refrained from his secret whisperings and evil suggestions; but only that he took unusual care to avoid every open breach of decency or good manners: insomuch that, notwithstanding their former experience of his deceit on like occasions, the young pilgrims were inclined to hope, and almost to believe, that he had really become so much weaker that they should never again be so harassed by him as in former days. And thus many persons, far more experienced and advanced than these little pilgrims, have frequently been deceived with respect to their victory over sin; when, by certain outward circumstances, such as the failure of health, the influence of holy society, or some other restraining consideration, they have experienced a temporary relief from the tormentings of their inbred corruptions: till, being thrown off their guard, by vainly supposing themselves no longer liable to the baneful influence of their sinful tendencies, they have presently fallen again into the snares of the enemy. So great is the deceptive power of sin; and on this account it is that the Lord of pilgrims exhorts his people to watch continually.

But to return to the little pilgrims.

I hoped to see them presently freed from the suburbs of Vanity. But I perceived, much to my surprise, that those suburbs extended along the Way of Salvation to a great distance, and that, like the city itself, they were set forth with all manner of enticing delights; especially with summer-houses and pleasure-gardens, abounding with fruit of various kinds—not such as grew in the Interpreter's garden, or in the fields of innocent pleasure; but fruits of an intoxicating and poisonous tendency, and partaking of the nature of that tree whereby our first parents acquired the knowledge of evil.

Now the odour of the fruits and flowers which grew in these gardens seemed to be particularly sweet and exhilarating to *Inbred-Sin;* for he no sooner began to snuff it, than he stepped forward, and walking in a line with the little pilgrims (a liberty which I had not observed him to take during the whole time of their residence in the house of Mr. *Orthodox*), he began to give his opinion in a very free and familiar manner. And this he did without asking permission, well knowing that such a request would only put the little pilgrims upon their guard; whereas it was probable that, on taking them by surprise, he might carry his point, as many an unhappy point is carried in the world. So, stepping forward, he began to speak with an impudent and unblushing face; for *Inbred-Sin* cannot blush, neither can he be disconcerted or diverted from his purpose: and hence it is said, that they who are ruled by him, to wit, "the children of this world, are wiser than the children of light." Luke xvi. 8. First, he began to compliment and congratulate the little pilgrims upon their escape from the dangers of Vanity. And this he did through deceit; that, lulling their fears to sleep, he might the more easily succeed in beguiling their minds. For, although they had passed safely through the high places and chief streets of the city, he was well aware that many snares and dangers awaited them in the suburbs and outskirts of Vanity "You have," said he, addressing himself to them both, "fought a good fight, and obtained a great victory; nothing therefore now remains but to give thanks for this victory."

To this Humble Mind replied, "Let us at least wait till we are wholly clear of this City of Vanity, before we sing the song of triumph."

"But," said *Inbred-Sin*, "are you not already clear of the city? We see nothing here but gardens and summer-houses—places to which the inhabitants of the town retire to refresh themselves in the summer-season with innocent pleasures and rural sports. Surely here can be no snares laid for pilgrims, nor any employments or pleasures of which they may not innocently partake."

"I desire to know no pleasures," returned Humble Mind, "except such as are to be found in the presence and service of Him who was nailed to the cross for my salvation; but as for the pleasures of the world, I will have nothing to do with them. These are the pleasures for which thousands and tens of thousands of immortal creatures, being ensnared by such as thou art, thou child of hell, have given up the favour of their heavenly Father, and the love of their Redeemer. For these they have renounced the joys of heaven; eternal youth, immortal health, everlasting peace, the society of saints and angels, together with a crown that fadeth not away: in exchange for which they have received nothing but pain, and death, and everlasting destruction from the presence of the Lord." Then Humble Mind read these words from his book—"The heart of the sons of men is full of evil; madness is in their heart while they live, and after that they go to the dead." Eccles. ix. 3.

I perceived that about this time the little pilgrims had come to a place where was a house of entertainment, which projected its sign quite across the Way of Salvation, bearing the emblem of a youth crowned with rose-buds. And behold, in the court of this house a number of young people were gathered together, dancing, singing, and quaffing wine from golden cups. Then did *Inbred-Sin* direct the eyes of the pilgrims towards the young persons within the court. Moreover, he made them observe the emblem upon the sign, saying, "Come on, therefore, let us enjoy the good things that are present; and let us speedily use the creatures like as in youth. Let us fill ourselves with costly wine and ointments; and let no flower of the spring pass by us: let us crown ourselves with rosebuds, before they be withered: let none of us go without his part of our voluptuousness: let us leave tokens of our joyfulness in every place: for this is our portion, and our lot is this." Wisdom ii. 6–9.

Now I heard that Humble Mind did a second time rebuke *Inbred-Sin;* but Playful sighed. Upon which *Inbred-Sin* spake again; and being somewhat encouraged by Playful, he ventured to arraign the Most High in the ears of the little pilgrims, saying, that he was a hard master, and that he required more from his young servants than ought in reason to be expected from them. Moreover, he spake of the happiness of the men of this world, "whose bellies," said he, "are filled with hid treasure: they are full of children, and leave the rest of their substance to their babes." Psalm xvii. 14.

To this Humble Mind answered, "'I will not fret myself because of the ungodly, neither will I be envious because of the workers of iniquity.' Psalm xxxvii. 1. I desire 'rather to suffer affliction with the people of God, than to enjoy the pleasures of sin for a season.'" Heb. xi. 25.

I saw then that *Inbred-Sin* grew extremely wroth at being thus opposed. Whereupon he cried out, with more than usual audacity, "I love the pleasures of this world: and you, Humble Mind, being my property and my slave, shall love them also, even though you renounce heaven itself for their sake." So he stepped round, and set himself in defiance before Humble Mind, saying, "You shall proceed no farther till you have solaced yourself in these courts of pleasure, drinking of their costly wines, and eating of their delicious fruits. For this once, on so trivial an affair, I will not be refused; and especially since, on more important occasions, you have already proved yourself a traitor to the King whom you pretend to love."

Then did Humble Mind tremble exceedingly. I also felt some alarm on his account, when I perceived a certain evil spirit, whom I knew to be the prince of the power of the air, approaching with an eye of malice fixed upon Humble Mind (though the boy knew it not), and beginning to raise enchantments, for the purpose of inthralling the spirits and senses of the young pilgrim. And my alarm was increased on observing that the youth began to feel the effects of those enchantments; for his colour came and went. Nevertheless, he was not wanting to himself on this trying occasion; for he fell on his knees, and lifted up his hands in prayer: and his earnest supplication was immediately answered, according to the words of the promise—"Then shalt thou call, and the Lord shall answer; thou shalt cry, and he shall say, Here I am." Isaiah lviii. 9. And behold a bright and glorious spirit descended from on high, which, drawing near to the young pilgrim, shed a part of its heavenly glory and vigour upon him. Whereupon the youth sprang up, and seizing *Inbred-Sin* with an irresistible force, he cast him to the ground; where, after trampling him beneath his feet till he lay like one dead, the intrepid pilgrim passed on his way, drawing his sister along with him.

So they went on till they had got clear of the suburbs of Vanity, Humble Mind still drawing Playful forward, who seemed to move heavily along, as though she hankered after the pleasures of Vanity. Nevertheless, her brother had power given him to persuade and prevail with her to choose the better part. And behold, *Inbred-Sin* had not only risen from the ground, but was by this time close upon their heels again; although, for the present, he judged it best to let Humble Mind alone. The young pilgrims therefore proceeded on their way till the approach of night; when they came to a little hill, thrown up in the King's highway by his enemy the prince of Vanity. This hill is called the Hill of Regrets, and it is scattered over with little sharp stones, which prove very uneasy to such pilgrims as ascend it. Now about half-way up the hill was a covered arbour, built at the suggestion of the prince of Vanity, placed with its back to Mount Zion, and its face towards the town. Here *Inbred-Sin* persuaded Playful to solicit her brother that they might turn aside and spend the night in that arbour; to which Humble Mind consented, as the evening was far advanced, not considering that a house whose aspect was not towards Mount Zion could never afford suitable accommodation to pilgrims. Nevertheless Humble Mind consented; and they went into the arbour, where they reclined themselves on certain soft and commodious couches, with which the prince of

Vanity had furnished the place, in order to tempt travellers to seek repose there.

So the young pilgrims, being seated at their ease, began to converse; and *Inbred-Sin*, notwithstanding his late defeat, placed himself by their side and entered into discourse with them.

Now it is the peculiar property of *Inbred-Sin*, as I think I have elsewhere remarked, to turn every event in the life of a Christian, however apparently unpropitious to himself, to the advancement of his own purposes; and it is marvellous with what address he does this, and how exactly he suits his discourse and his temptations at such seasons to the tempers and circumstances of those he has to deal with. On the present occasion he began with bitter self-bemoanings, as one who had been beaten almost out of heart; after which he went on to compliment Humble Mind upon the spirit and valour he had evidenced in their late contest. "Upon my word, Humble Mind," said he, "you did play the man indeed, and brought me, as it were, to the very last gasp; and that without human assistance."

"But, undoubtedly," replied Humble Mind, "I was helped from on high; for I well know that no man can deal with *Inbred-Sin* without Divine help."

"True," said *Inbred-Sin;* "it is certain that no man can conquer me without special help from on high. What an evidence then is this of your being highly favoured and peculiarly gifted from above!" He then spake many words tending to fill the youth with spiritual pride: and I was sorry to observe that Humble Mind listened to him with much self-complacency.

And behold, as the night came on, the city which was spread out before them was lighted up with many lights. Now the City of Vanity is so contrived as to present a very fair show towards the Hill of Regrets, where stood the arbour in which the young pilgrims were then sitting. And it has often happened that young pilgrims, ay, and aged ones too, after having withstood all the allurements of the city, and advanced to this hill—it has often happened, I say, that by looking back from this arbour, they have been tempted to return unto Vanity, to the destruction both of soul and body.

I saw then in my dream that *Inbred-Sin*, having obtained some advantage over Humble Mind, thought he might advance a step farther, and even venture to propose to the young pilgrims an immediate return to the City of Vanity; "for," said he, "our life is short and tedious, and in the death of a man there is no remedy: neither was there any man known to have returned from the grave. For we are born at all adventure: and we shall be hereafter as though we had never been: for the breath in our nostrils is as smoke, and a little spark in the moving of our heart: which being extinguished, our body shall be turned into ashes, and our spirit shall vanish as the soft air, and our name shall be forgotten in time, and no man shall have our works in remembrance; and our life shall pass away as the trace of a cloud, and shall be dispersed as a mist that is driven away with the beams of the sun, and overcome with the heat thereof." Wisdom ii. 1–4.

Much as I had known of this *Inbred-Sin*, I could not but here marvel at his assurance in thus addressing Humble Mind. I wondered, in the first place, at his presuming to make any such a proposal; and I marvelled still more at his addressing him as though he had been a downright unbeliever, and destitute of all religious feeling: but my amazement was still greater to find that Humble Mind, who had been enabled to contend so victoriously with him in the morning, should now sit quietly listening to his dangerous suggestions. Neither do I know what might have been the result of this weakness on the part of Humble Mind, had not the Prince of pilgrims very unexpectedly provided for his assistance.

CHAPTER XIX.

Now it had pleased the Lord to occupy the thoughts of Mr. *Orthodox*, as he was walking back to his own house, with the dangers which awaited the young pilgrims in the suburbs of Vanity: in consequence of which, on his arrival at home, he directed one of his most trusty servants to follow them on the way as far as to the hill before described. And behold, this worthy man came up to them just as *Inbred-Sin* was delivering his opinion in the manner above mentioned. Whereupon he addressed the young pilgrims by name, asking them what they did in that place.

I saw then that Humble Mind and Playful, at the sound of his voice, sprang up from the place whereon they sat; when Humble Mind replied, "We turned in hither for a single night's lodging, and hope that we have not sinned in so doing."

"Do you not see," said the servant of Mr. *Orthodox*, "that the back of this arbour is placed towards Mount Zion, and its face towards Vanity? And do you not remember Lot's wife, who was turned into a pillar of salt for looking back upon Sodom when commanded to flee from that city? My master and his servants are under orders to abide awhile in the City of Vanity; not indeed to partake of its pleasures, but to execute the work allotted them by the King of kings in that place. But for you it is ordained otherwise; you are commanded to hasten forwards, and you will find it written in your book, 'Turn away mine eyes from beholding vanity; and quicken thou me in thy way.'" Psalm cxix. 37.

The young pilgrims then thanked him for his rebuke, while they expressed their gratitude to Mr. *Orthodox* for his attention in sending after them so trusty a messenger. Upon which they arose and followed the man; who led them along the Way of Salvation till they came to a very deep valley: into which they had not descended many paces before they entirely lost sight of the town of Vanity, notwithstanding all the blazing lights with which it was illuminated.

Now I perceived that a sort of shuddering came over Humble Mind and his sister, as they entered this valley; for the air of it was sharp and cold, a solemn silence reigned through it, and the rocks on each side shot up, as it were, to the clouds. Many yews and cypress trees grew also thereabouts, through which the wind whistled in an exceedingly melancholy manner. Then said Humble Mind to the servant of Mr. *Orthodox*, "What is this valley? for I have not seen in all my pilgrimage a more dismal place, excepting the Valley of the Shadow of Death."

"This valley," replied the servant of Mr. *Orthodox*, "is no more to be compared to the Valley of the Shadow of Death, than the vestibule of heaven is to be compared to the gates of hell. The Valley of the Shadow of Death is a place in which the soul is bereaved of all divine consolation, where the Lord hideth his face, and causeth the believer to pass through a state of painful separation from himself. Yea, in that valley are sometimes felt, in a degree, the very torments of hell itself, which consist, we believe, in an eternal separation from God. So that, could a man in the Valley of the Shadow of Death be surrounded by earthly pleasures of every description, he would still find it a hell; because God being the fountain of all true happiness, not even a single drop of real comfort can be tasted where he is absent. But the valley into which we are now entering is called the Valley of Adversity; and it hath been sunk in this place by the express command of the King himself, that pilgrims, in travelling through it, may utterly lose sight of Vanity. This valley, moreover," continued he, "though stripped of every earthly comfort, abounds in such pure and spiritual delights, that many experienced pilgrims, after passing through it in a right frame of mind, have been constrained to say, *It is well for us that we have been in trouble.* Notwithstanding which," added the messenger, "I never knew any one descend into the Valley of Adversity, without shuddering and trembling as you now do."

"Indeed, sir," said Playful, "I cannot wonder that any one should tremble in descending into this valley; for never, indeed, did I see so gloomy a place. Here too I find that all the afflictions of past days are brought to my recollection; and especially the loss of my little Peace, which is as present with me at this moment as if it had happened but yesterday. Neither is there any thing at hand to divert my thoughts from these sad remembrances: but wherever I turn my eyes, they encounter only emblems of sorrow and mourning."

Then said the servant, "The evening is now far advanced, and you must needs be much fatigued; let us therefore sit down in this place, and endeavour to take some repose."

So sitting down by the way-side, they there produced some of the refreshments given them by Mrs. *Bountiful.* But when they sought water, they could find only an exceedingly bitter stream, which flowed from a neighbouring rock.

I heard then that the messenger began to reason with

them on this disappointment, and to declare the salutary effects which sometimes flow from the bitterest dispensations of Providence; when being deprived of other comforts, the soul is led to seek those consolations for which it had not the slightest desire in more prosperous circumstances. "By these means," continued he, "do pilgrims in the Valley of Adversity acquire the habit of communing with God, and fixing their affections on things above; while their spirits are refined and sanctified, through the blessing of God upon their earthly affections: thus 'tribulation worketh patience; and patience, experience; and experience, hope.'" Rom. v. 3, 4.

"But do you think, sir," said Humble Mind, "that afflictions must necessarily be endured in order to salvation?"

"Affliction," replied the messenger, "may be used as an outward means to bring us into closer union with Christ: but, without the Divine help, it can profit us nothing. For unless the blessing of God be upon our trouble, it will rather harden and irritate, than fit us for the reception of truth. In proof of which, as you travel along this valley, you will see the graves of many who, having refused comfort where alone it could be found, at length despairingly put an end to their own lives, and were buried by the way-side as a warning to others."

After this, the servant of Mr. *Orthodox* proposed that they should all go to prayer, in order that, before they slept, they might seek consolation from above. They addressed themselves therefore to prayer, and continued for some time calling upon their Saviour, earnestly supplicating him to undertake their cause, and appear as their Advocate with the Father—when behold, while they yet called upon their Redeemer, a "light rose in obscurity, and the darkness was as the noon-day." Isaiah lviii. 10. Then looking up to the heavens, they were favoured with the same kind of glorious vision which caused the martyr Stephen to exult even in the agonies of death. So they gazed till the tears gushed from their eyes; and as they gazed they exclaimed, "It is good for us to be here; and here we could remain with thee for ever, O Lord, our refuge in time of affliction (Jer. xvi. 19): 'for thou hast lifted up the light of thy countenance upon us;' yea, 'thou hast put gladness in our hearts.'" Psalm iv. 6, 7.

Then said the messenger, "Did I not tell you what things were to be expected in this valley? and how blessed those times often prove in which we enjoy the fewest earthly comforts ?"

Thus the young pilgrims continued looking upwards, and talking with the messenger, till their hearts becoming warm with the love of God, they rejoiced with joy unspeakable and full of glory. And now they were enabled to speak even of the death of Peace in the language of cheerful hope, though not indeed without shedding tears of tenderness. "Our little Peace," said Humble Mind, "was everywhere my sweet companion and my friend. She lay in my bosom through all the nights of our pilgrimage; and as she slept her little arms embraced me. Nevertheless I am now enabled to give her up without a murmur; inasmuch as I know that she is at home and at rest in the presence of her heavenly Father." "Where," added Playful, "we shall shortly meet her again, never more to be separated; and where she, and we, and our beloved parents shall dwell together, rejoicing before the throne of our adorable Saviour."

Then I heard that Humble Mind broke into a transport of praise, saying, "Our beloved Saviour 'is white and ruddy, the chiefest among ten thousand. His eyes are as the eyes of doves by the rivers of waters, washed with milk, and fitly set. His countenance is as Lebanon, excellent as the cedars. His mouth is most sweet: yea, he is altogether lovely.'" Sol. Song v. 10, 12, 15, 16.

In this manner they continued conversing together, and occasionally meditating upon the glorious vision they had enjoyed, till sleep overcame them; for they had travelled far that day, and their repose was sweet unto them.

They remained asleep till day-dawn: and no sooner did they awake, than they began to relate their dreams to each other, and behold, they were the same. In their sleep they thought that Peace came and stood immediately before them: and she was all fair; there was no spot in her. Sol. Song iv. 7. And she called to them, and spake to them; and her words were like "a very lovely song of one that hath a pleasant voice." Ezek. xxxiii. 32. "Weep not for me, nor bemoan me, sweet brother and sister," she said; "but watch over yourselves, lest you should by any means dishonour your holy profession. When the Lord took away my breath, my mortal part went down into the dust, but my spirit was carried by the angels into my Father's bosom. I have received the crown of righteousness—all tears are wiped from my eyes—I am 'arrayed in fine linen, clean and white' (Rev. xix. 8.); and the Lamb hath presented me to himself without spot or stain of sin. Mourn not for me, beloved companions of my pilgrimage on earth; but mourn for your sins, lest by them we should be separated for ever. 'For godly sorrow worketh repentance to salvation not to be repented of: but the sorrow of the world worketh death.'" 2 Cor. vii. 10.

Now, while Humble Mind and Playful yet rejoiced in their sweet dream, behold, the messenger of Mr. *Orthodox* called upon them to rise and gather the manna, which then lay thick upon the ground—thicker indeed than the little pilgrims had seen it in any part of their journey, saving under the cross and in the Valley of Humiliation: so the children presently filled their golden pots, and betook themselves to their journey. But, before they set out, the messenger took his leave, saying that he had already staid beyond his appointed time, and that his master's business required his speedy return.

"What!" said Humble Mind, "must you go and leave us in this valley?" The messenger, however, having convinced them that his return was absolutely necessary, they opposed it no further, but allowed him to depart without another word.

I saw then, in my dream, that the young pilgrims continued to descend deeper into the valley during the whole day. But although their way was indeed very dismal, I observed that they were so refreshed by the manna which they had gathered in the morning, and with which they continued to regale themselves through all the hours of the day, as well as with the remembrance of their cheering dream, that they no longer heeded the doleful objects which were everywhere presented to their view. Now through all the valley were scattered cypress-groves, tombs, open graves, decayed and gloomy edifices, sandy and salt wastes, black and fetid pools, precipices, and pitfalls; and on a certain spot in the very bottom of the valley there was a flock of vultures, with other unclean birds, feeding on the corpse of one who, not being able to endure the gloomy scene around him, had endeavoured to put an end to his misery by rushing uncommanded into the presence of his Maker. The only plants which grew in this valley were such as wormwood and rue, with a few other bitter herbs. Nevertheless, amid all the disheartening appearances with which they were surrounded, the little pilgrims proceeded on their way, from morning to night, not only without uttering a single complaint, but "blessing God, even the Father of our Lord Jesus Christ, the Father of mercies, and the God of all comfort; who comforteth *pilgrims* in all their tribulation." 2 Cor. i. 3, 4.

Thus they continued their journey till night; when they quietly laid themselves on the ground, and soon fell fast asleep. So I observed the young pilgrims as they slept: and behold, *Inbred-Sin* was busy as aforetime at their ears, and his whisperings seemed greatly to disturb them, for they often started in their sleep. Nevertheless, their sleep was heavy, so that they did not awake till the sun was high. And behold, on opening their eyes and looking around, they perceived that the manna, which had lain thick about them at the dawn, was now melted away; upon which they began bitterly to lament their slothfulness. Moreover, they endeavoured to refresh themselves with some of the preserved fruits and other good things which they had brought from Mr. *Orthodox*. But this food, being now dry and stale, did not afford them such nourishment as they used to derive from the bread which cometh down from heaven, to wit, that sacred manna which has been the appointed food of pilgrims from time immemorial.

The young pilgrims then arose to prosecute their journey; and *Inbred-Sin*, being in high spirits, ay, and much at his ease (as he generally is with such persons as rise too late in the day to have leisure for their usual devotions), walked side by side with the pilgrims, and soon entered into discourse with them. And first, he found fault with the length of the valley, with its dismal appearance, its extreme solitariness, and the bleakness of the air which blew through it; and not being rebuked by his companions, he ventured even to speak certain words of dissatisfaction against the Most High, for directing the path of his servants through such dreary scenes.

I perceived then that the spirit of cheerfulness and holy resignation which had supported the young travellers during the past day, forsook them entirely while they sinfully hearkened to the words of *Inbred-Sin.* Whereupon they began not only to loiter in the way, but, after a while, to stand perfectly still; when *Inbred-Sin* ventured to propose that they should turn back immediately to the town of Vanity. But although Humble Mind dreaded to proceed any further in that dismal valley; yet he foresaw the danger of turning back. He therefore stood demurring, while *Inbred-Sin* pressed and urged him to return without delay; Playful all the while weeping, and hanging about him, wishing in her heart that he would consent to do so, though not presuming to solicit him.

Now, having always observed that whenever *Inbred-Sin* could bring the young pilgrims to hesitate, or to parley with them on any point, he was sure to carry the day; so I now expected every moment to see them turn their backs on Mount Zion. And this, no doubt, would have been the case, had not the Lord sent them timely assistance. For behold, while Humble Mind and his sister stood thus sinfully demurring with *Inbred-Sin*, a company of pilgrims came along the way from the town of Vanity, with their faces towards Mount Zion. And as they walked, they beguiled the solitary way with songs of praise.

This party consisted of a middle-aged matron, of a comely and decent appearance, with two little damsels of very tender age. And behold, the elder pilgrim led the younger ones by the hand, supporting their steps lest they should stumble: for the way in this place was as rough and uneven to the foot as it was unpleasant and forbidding to the eye. Nevertheless, there was nothing of discontent or dissatisfaction in the countenances of these pilgrims. They had happily learned in whatever situation they were, therewith to be content; and could therefore travel through the Valley of Adversity with cheerful countenances; because their affections, especially those of the elder pilgrim, were set upon things above, and not upon things on the earth.

Now I saw in my dream that when these pilgrims, the elder of whom was called Martha, and the two young ones Grace and Truth, came near to Humble Mind and his sister, they stood still, while the matron thus addressed them:—"Wherefore, my young pilgrims," said she, "for pilgrims I see you are by your white garments, and the impress of our Lord's signet upon your forehead,—wherefore do you stand still, with your faces, as it were, turned from Mount Zion? Having come thus far on your journey to the blessed country, surely you cannot have a thought of turning back! Or perhaps you are offended, as many have been before you, with this Valley of Adversity; supposing, though falsely indeed, that they only who are Christians are liable to affliction in the flesh. Whereas, 'man is born unto trouble, as the sparks fly upward' (Job v. 7); insomuch that he who would escape it must needs leave the world itself."

I saw then that Humble Mind and Playful looked ashamed on being thus addressed by the stranger pilgrim; when *Inbred-Sin* whispered to them that they should deny having had any thoughts of returning. So they replied to the pilgrim Martha, "We have had no thoughts of returning; but are only standing a while to rest ourselves, before we proceed on our journey."

"My children," said Martha, "I am unable to look into your hearts, and, being but a stranger, I have no right to question you upon your delay. There is One, who is a Discerner of the thoughts and intents of the heart, to whom you must be accountable: nevertheless, as it is not yet noon-day, be advised by me, and proceed on your journey without further delay. Wherefore should you linger in this valley? is it so agreeable a place that you should desire to abide in it? 'Look at the generations of old, and see: did ever any trust in the Lord and was confounded? or did any abide in his fear, and was forsaken? or whom did he ever despise that called upon him?'" Eccles. ii. 10.

The pilgrim Martha then proposed that they should join company, and go on together; to which she was the more inclined, as she was a lover of little children, and had great delight in leading them along the way of holiness.

Now Humble Mind and Playful in some respects liked this proposal, perceiving that the stranger was a person of an agreeable countenance; for although she appeared grave, as it becometh a pilgrim to be, yet her manner withal was very pleasant. Moreover, they liked the aspect of little Grace and Truth; and especially as the features of Truth somewhat resembled the well-remembered features of little Peace. Nevertheless, *Inbred-Sin* supposing that the company of these pilgrims would not be favourable to his cause, endeavoured as much as possible to put Humble Mind upon rejecting Martha's invitation. She, however, would take no denial, fully persuaded that her company might be advantageous to the young pilgrims; on this account she pleaded hard, and at length prevailed. So Humble Mind and his sister consented to go on with the unknown pilgrims.

I saw then, in my dream, that Humble Mind soon found himself peculiarly refreshed with the society of the pilgrim Martha. I hearkened therefore to their discourse as they walked on; and behold, they beguiled the time by relating to each other the events of their pilgrimage, and the dealings of the Lord with them. Humble Mind and Playful first related what had befallen them in the way: after which Martha thus began:—

"I am," said she, "in common with all others of the children of Adam, a native of the Valley of Destruction, and my heart was 'in bondage under the elements of the world.' Gal. iv. 3. Even those dear friends whom I had received from the Lord, my husband and children, proved but so many ties binding me down closer to the world. I was truly dead in sin, and even pleaded my earthly comforts as excuses for my worldly mind. Nevertheless, the Lord in his infinite mercy called me to himself; and *that* in as peculiar and tender a manner as the mother adopts towards her sucking child; neither was this call used only once or twice, but many and many times repeated, while I remained deaf to its importunity."

I heard then that Playful interrupted Martha, in order to put this question, to wit, What she meant by the calls of the Almighty? whether she was to understand by them a voice from heaven, or any other miraculous interference?

To which Martha replied, that she presumed not to say, that, even in these days, none were called in a somewhat extraordinary manner; but with respect to herself, no means had been used which could be called miraculous or out of the usual course of God's dealings with his servants.

"Nevertheless," said she, "this is certain—not only that every event of my life has been ordered by the

Almighty Ruler of all things for the advancement of my spiritual good; but that, after being once awakened from the death of sin, I was made to hear the voice of God in every event that befell me. Still, however, I felt a strong attachment to the world; and more especially to my husband and my two sweet babies, from whom my chief domestic comforts flowed. My home was then my gourd, under the shade of which I delighted to dwell; but when it pleased the Lord to prepare a worm to smite my gourd, I became distressed above measure. My husband was first removed from me. He became a pilgrim, and, like little Peace, in a short time fulfilled a long time; when being made white in the blood of his Saviour, he passed through the river of death, and is now rejoicing in the house of his Father above.

"Being deprived of this my beloved companion," said Martha, "I clung more fondly to my children. But the Lord was pleased shortly to remove these also; thus bereaving me totally of my dearest earthly comforts, and causing me to forget the days of my prosperity. And now, in this season of adversity, the Lord revealed himself to my soul in such a manner as effectually to overcome all resistance. He drew me towards himself with the cords of love, compelling me to seek rest in his presence, 'to the praise of the glory of his grace, wherein he made me,' the chief of sinners, 'accepted in the Beloved.' Ephes. i. 6.

"Hereupon I quitted my native place, even the Valley of Destruction; and having entered in at the gate which is at the head of the way, I have come thus far on my journey towards my heavenly Father's house."

CHAPTER XX.

Now it came to pass, that when the pilgrims had travelled for some days through the Valley of Adversity, the country became more open and pleasant; soon after which they came out from the valley upon a pleasant plain, scattered over with clumps of trees, affording a delightful shade. The air on this plain, though fresh, was not so piercing as in the Valley of Adversity, while all the surrounding objects wore a cheerful and lightsome appearance. Then I looked after the pilgrims, and saw that Humble Mind walked first with little Truth; for Humble Mind loved the little girl exceedingly, fancying that he discovered in her some resemblance to his beloved Peace: and I heard that he endeavoured to instruct her, as he had been accustomed to instruct his departed little sister.

After proceeding thus for a while, *Inbred-Sin* crept softly up to the ear of Playful; when I immediately became alarmed for the consequence, though unable to imagine what kind of mischief could be brought out of their present circumstances—not considering that *Inbred-Sin* is never at a loss how to produce evil, and that he is a workman capable of effecting great things with few or no apparent materials. So *Inbred-Sin*, as I said, drew up close to Playful, and whispered something in her ear; upon which, she fell back behind the other pilgrims, for the purpose of meditating at leisure upon the whisperings of the tempter. Then said *Inbred-Sin*, fetching a course about, as his manner often was before he came to the point at which he aimed, "Tell me, Playful, do you not love your brother above all the world besides?"

"Certainly I do," said Playful.

"But do you imagine," replied the other, "that he has an equal regard for you?"

"I always thought so," said Playful.

"You thought so, because your heart is good, and free from suspicion," returned *Inbred-Sin:* "but cannot you recollect that he generally showed a preference for your sister Peace, and that he more frequently conversed with her than with you?"

"If he loved Peace more than he loved me, he did but what was right, and I cannot blame him," said Playful; "for my beloved little Peace was more lovely than I am, and more worthy the regard of those who are taught to prefer that which is excellent."

"That may have been so far true," said *Inbred-Sin*, "as to form some excuse for your brother's loving Peace better than he loved you. But what excuse can be made for his preferring the company of Truth to that of his only sister?"

"I have no reason to think that he does so," said Playful.

"Do you not perceive then," said *Inbred-Sin*, "how he seeks her company at all times, and how frequently he shares his morsel with her? And even now," continued he, "see how he leads her by the hand, and bends his ear to her prattle."

Here I perceived that the poison began to work Playful's cheek grew flushed, and her eye began to kindle with anger: nevertheless she stood her ground a little longer, and made this reply—"If my brother prefers the company of yonder little stranger to that of his only remaining sister, does it not become me, as a follower of our meek and lowly Master, to bear this seeming neglect without murmuring? nay, and even to return love for hatred?"

"Assuredly," said *Inbred-Sin*, who could talk religion whenever it suited his purpose, even while he was seeking to undermine it, "assuredly it is your duty, if need be, to forgive your offending brother, not only seven times, but seventy times seven: nevertheless I see no occasion why you should bear every affront he chooses to put upon you, when perhaps, by a single word, you might bring him back to a more attentive behaviour." I heard then that *Inbred-Sin* proceeded to place the conduct of Humble Mind in a still stronger light, till he had gradually wrought Playful into such a humour as prepared her for the commission of any kind of folly that could be proposed to her.

Inbred-Sin then, perceiving his advantage, was not long before he actually proposed what at another time she would have started from with abhorrence, but which now, by reason of the ill state of her mind, she closed with immediately: this proposal was, that she should turn her back upon the whole company, ay, and upon Mount Zion itself, directly setting her face as if she intended to return. This indignity she was to put upon her King, by way of testifying, as *Inbred-Sin* expressed it, the great displeasure she felt at her brother's marked neglect. Without therefore considering the consequences of so unreasonable an action, she turned herself about, and began to measure her steps back again.

Now Playful meant nothing more, when she turned about, than to recall the attention of her brother, and to exercise her power of tormenting him: but when *Inbred-Sin* had influenced her thus far, it was not in his nature to stop there. No sooner therefore did he see her with her back towards Mount Zion, than he began to whisper in her ears expressions of contempt for the religion of Jesus; outrageously railing at a pilgrim's life, and setting before her the advantage she would derive from an immediate return to the town of Vanity. And to such lengths did he proceed that I could hardly believe my own ears; never supposing it possible that he could exercise such power over the heart of a regenerate person, as now appeared evident. So Playful hearkened to *Inbred-Sin:* and how long or how far he might have misled her cannot easily be determined, had not the other pilgrims who had gone forward about a stone's throw before they perceived her defection, disturbed her communications with the tempter by calling to her aloud. Whereupon she came to a sudden stand: yet would she not make any movement towards them.

I heard then that the pilgrims called earnestly to her to come on; and Humble Mind was on the point of running back to her in order to persuade her to reconsider her ways. But the pilgrim Martha would not allow him so to do, saying that not even to save a brother was it lawful for a pilgrim to turn his back on Mount Zion. Humble Mind, therefore, having nothing in his power but prayer, I saw that he prostrated himself on the ground in earnest intercession for his sister. And while he made his request known to God in the name of his Saviour, behold, the pilgrim Martha and the two little ones joined in his importunate supplication.

Now I saw in my dream that, while the pilgrims were engaged in prayer, behold, the Evil One, who is ever going about seeking whom he may devour, having discovered the advantage which *Inbred-Sin* had obtained over Playful, judged this a suitable time for the successful exertion of his own superior influence. So drawing near to the young pilgrim, without her perceiving it (because, being a spirit, he is invisible to eyes of flesh), he began, as aforetime, to practise his enchantments. And first, by a process which I could not understand, but by which it is well known one spirit can act upon another, he began to entice and entangle the affections of Playful, setting before her the many pleasures which she might enjoy in the City of Vanity, could she be prevailed upon to give up a pilgrim's life and return thither. And behold, when he had in some measure excited her affections and inflamed her imagination with the delusive pleasures of sense, he caused his servants (for he was accompanied by several of his ministering spirits) to throw certain invisible bands around the limbs of the young pilgrim; by which he directed them to draw her back with a gentle force. And behold, the young pilgrim gave way as the enemies applied their strength; insomuch that, unless assistance were given from on high, it appeared to me that she would assuredly be lost; there seeming to be no power of resistance left in her, nor indeed even so much as the will to resist, or to call out for help.

But while I looked on, I perceived one coming along the King's highway, who held in his hand a whip of small cords. And behold, he came up close to Playful, whom he first sharply rebuked, and then sorely chastised. Whereupon, starting up as from a deep sleep or trance, she suddenly broke all the ligatures with which the enemy had bound her. And behold, as she continued to feel the lash which was appointed to correct her wanderings, she hastily turned her back on the City of Vanity, and fled forward till she reached the place where the other pilgrims were anxiously tarrying for her. So she happily escaped for that time.

Then did Humble Mind and Martha receive her joyfully. Nevertheless Martha reproved her, but with maternal tenderness; taking occasion, from her late apostacy, to point out to her the exceeding weakness and frailty even of regenerate persons—that even the best are continually liable to fall into gross and grievous sins; that whosoever is saved is saved by grace alone; and that no man can in his own strength do any thing towards the advancement of his own salvation. "For the condition of man," said she, "after the fall of Adam is such, that he cannot turn and prepare himself by his own natural strength and good works to faith and calling upon God; wherefore we have no power to do good works pleasant and acceptable to God without the grace of God by Christ going before us, that we may have a good will, and working with us, when we have that good will." (*See 10th Article of the Church.*)

"According to this view of things," said Humble Mind, "it is marvellous how any man can be saved."

"Marvellous, indeed!" returned Martha: "but what

is impossible with man is possible with God. And hence it is written—'Let us hold fast the profession of our faith without wavering; for he is faithful that promised.'" Heb. x. 23.

Now I saw in my dream that Playful remained for a while much dejected after her heinous transgression, and greatly humbled. Moreover, through the painful views she had of her own exceeding sinfulness, she was led to look more to her Saviour than she had done in the former part of her pilgrimage, and thereby to make a more rapid growth in grace. Thus was the malice of the enemy defeated, through the infinite mercy and wisdom of God, who by his overruling providence brought good out of evil, in the same manner as honey was once produced from the carcass of the lion.

After this, I saw that the company of pilgrims went on their way till they came to a pleasant river, called the River of the Water of Life, by which their road lay, and where grew many green and shady trees, producing a rich variety of sacred fruits. And as the pilgrims passed along, they took of the fruits and drank of the water; upon which their hearts were filled with joy and peace unspeakable. In this place also the elder pilgrims held much sweet discourse together, while the little ones enjoyed their innocent play in the meadows: neither would any of the pilgrims, at this time, allow *Inbred-Sin* to disturb their minds. For though he was as busy as usual, whispering in the ear of one and another, yet they were all enabled by the Holy Spirit to watch against his wiles, and to say, "The Lord rebuke thee." Jude 9. So *Inbred-Sin* here obtained no advantage against them, though he was unwearied in his attempts to prevail. As night drew on the pilgrims arrived at a place in which many lilies grew; where laying themselves down to rest, they slept as sweetly as they had done in any part of their pilgrimage.

For several days they travelled through these pleasant meadows; where I observed that the pilgrim Martha continually laboured with the young ones, in order, as much as in her lay, to bring them into a nearer acquaintance with their Saviour. And she took great delight in speaking of this dear Saviour, describing the manner of his birth, his life, his death, and pointing out some of the most remarkable passages of his pilgrimage upon earth. She spoke much also of his tender love to pilgrims, weeping often over those wounds of his by which sinners are healed, and that voluntary death of his by which the dead are restored to life. Martha was indeed as a mother to all the younger pilgrims, and they were to her as so many sons and daughters.

At length they reached a place where the way separated itself from the pleasant meadows and trees. At this the children complained; but Martha admonished them contentedly to go straight forward, although the way might not appear inviting. So they went on without murmuring; while, in order to pass the time profitably, they had recourse to their books. And so deeply were they engaged in this employment, that they passed by the stile and path leading to the ruined castle of giant *Despair* without even perceiving them.

Now, towards sunset, Humble Mind, looking up, said, "Behold, I see far away certain beautiful blue hills directly before us."

Martha. Those are the Delectable Mountains, upon which our Lord's shepherds dwell. We have made a considerable progress to-day; and if we do as well to-morrow, we shall reach those mountains before night comes on.

Then were the little pilgrims pleased; for they had heard much of the Delectable Mountains, and had letters of recommendation with them from Mr. *Orthodox* to the shepherds who dwell there. So they continued their journey till it was dark, without heeding their weariness: and they were up the next morning before sunrise to proceed on their way, so impatient were they to reach the Delectable Mountains.

Now early in the morning it was pleasant to feel the breezes, fraught with all manner of fragrant odours, which descended from the flowery sides of the mountains. At length the pilgrims saw the sun rising behind the lofty range of hills which lay eastward of them; and as it ascended above them, the pilgrims could distinguish the little dwellings of the shepherds scattered here and there among the hills, with their hanging gardens and their sheep-cotes: they could also hear at intervals the pipes of the shepherds, and the bells of the flock. Then Humble Mind looked into a map of the road, which Mr. *Orthodox* had given him, in order to find the names of the hills; by which he soon distinguished Mount Marvel, Mount Caution, and Mount Error (the latter of which lieth to the left, somewhat out of the direction of the Way of Salvation), together with Mount Sabbath, which rose beyond the rest of the hills towards the Celestial City, rendering itself observable by its extraordinary elevation.

Now Humble Mind was in better spirits here than ever I saw him in all the course of his pilgrimage. So the pilgrims hastened forwards: for though they were exceedingly foot-sore, yet their spirits sustained them. And as they approached the mountains, they could distinguish orchards, olive-yards, vineyards, and gardens abounding with every kind of vegetation: crystal fountains, where the flocks were washed and watered; and shepherds feeding their sheep. But the way was so steep that they were minded to rest themselves a few minutes before they began to ascend the hills.

Now the shepherds Knowledge, Experience, Watchful, and Sincere had been informed by one who watched his flock on the side of Mount Clear, that a company of pilgrims were on the road, and that the party consisted chiefly of little children. In consequence of which information, the good shepherds lost no time in ordering a wagon to the foot of the hills, furnished with every suitable accommodation, and well stored with provisions, there to wait the arrival of the pilgrims for their easier conveyance to the shepherds' houses.

This wagon therefore was waiting at the foot of the mountains when the pilgrims came up, intending there to halt for very weariness. Then came the wagoner, a careful old man, to Martha, whom he thus bespake:—

"Welcome, worthy pilgrim, to the Delectable Mountains! and welcome, all ye, my sweet babes! By my masters' orders I have brought this wagon to assist you up these hills to the abodes of the shepherds. And as you will find in this carriage all manner of accommodations, there is no occasion for a moment's delay in this place."

Upon which they all got into the wagon, the old man lifting in little Grace and Truth: and it proved a very seasonable assistance to these almost exhausted travellers. And as they moved, the bells of the horses began to ring; for the horses had bells, and on those bells was written, "Holiness unto the Lord." Zech. xiv. 20. So they proceeded up the hills, eating of the fruits and bread which the good shepherds had sent them, as they went along.

Playful then spake: "Well, this is very pleasant; this exceeds all that we have before met with in our pilgrimage. Had we been so much discouraged in the Valley of Adversity as not to advance to this place, how ill we should have done!"

Martha. We should have done as all those do who trust not in God—very foolishly and very wickedly.

Then cried Humble Mind, "O! what lovely cottages, what fair pastures, and quiet resting-places do I see! How very delightful is this place!"

"Look at those lambs feeding near the waterfalls!" cried little Grace.

"And behold that flock of sheep which is going up from the washing!" said Playful.

"Those sheep," said Martha, "are fed in a good pasture, and their folds are upon the high mountains of Israel: for the Lord hath sought them out and 'delivered them out of all places where they were scattered in the cloudy and dark day.' Ezek. xxxiv. 12. In like manner," said she, "has the Lord sought us out, and brought us to this place, showing himself our guide and protector through every part of our pilgrimage." Then sang the pilgrim, for her heart was full of holy joy and gratitude: and the children also joined in the song:—

"Then let our songs abound,
And every tear be dry,
We're travelling through Immanuel's ground
To fairer worlds on high."

By this time they drew near the shepherds' houses; when behold, Watchful, Experience, and Sincere were coming forth to meet them. And the shepherd Watchful saluted them with these words:—"Peace be unto you, ye children of the King."

Then said the shepherd Experience, "'Fear not, little flock; for it is your Father's good pleasure to give you the kingdom.'" Luke xii. 32.

The shepherd Sincere next spake, "Welcome, thrice welcome are you, O ye redeemed of the Lord, to the Delectable Mountains!"

I saw then that Martha, having alighted from the wagon, bowed low before the shepherds, and said, "'How beautiful upon the mountains are the feet of them that bring good tidings, that publish peace; that bring good tidings of good, that publish salvation; that say unto Zion, Thy God reigneth!'" Isaiah lvii. 7.

When the whole party had descended from the wagon, the shepherds said to the little ones, "Welcome, welcome, pretty babes! you have made a prosperous journey, and are far on your way to the Celestial City. Of the thousands that set out on pilgrimage, there are but few who reach this place."

Then I saw that Watchful and his companions conducted them into the house, and led them into a fair large hall, where a long table was preparing for their evening repast. Now from the windows of this hall much of the neighbouring country was to be seen, presenting so beautiful and charming a prospect as could scarcely be equalled in the whole world. Here, therefore, while the pilgrims stood feasting their eyes, the shepherds went abroad to see their flocks safely folded for the night. After which, supper was immediately served up, when they all sat down to meat, giving thanks to their great Benefactor.

On finishing their evening meal, the children became heavy with sleep; whereupon the shepherds said, "Since the little ones are beginning to look towards their beds, we will have prayers without delay, and then show them to their chambers. And on the morrow, when their spirits and strength are recruited, we hope to have some conversation with them—for we long to know what they have met with in their pilgrimage." The shepherds then called an old female servant, of whom they were very fond, named *Hospitality*, who forthwith conducted the pilgrims to their several chambers, consisting of two comfortable rooms adjoining each other; the larger one for Martha and the little girls, and the lesser one for Humble Mind. So they retired to rest, and were presently fast asleep.

Now at break of day, after listening for a while to the bleatings of the sheep upon the hills, they got up refreshed and cheerful: and having thanked God for bringing them to so desirable a place, they went down into the hall.

Being all met at breakfast, I heard that the shepherds entered into discourse with the pilgrims concerning their pilgrimage. On this subject the shepherds had many interesting questions to propose; to all of which when the pilgrims had satisfactorily replied, the shepherds spake thus—"Happy indeed are you in having come so far on your journey; since this is not the lot of all who look with some desire towards the Hill of Zion: for 'strait is the gate, and narrow is the way, which leadeth unto life; and few there be that find it.' Matt. vii. 14. There are even many that shall seek to enter therein, and shall not be able. Let us therefore," said the shepherds one to another, "offer thanks unto God on account of these pilgrims, for that he has assisted them by his grace to reach Immanuel's Land—this happy land, from which the Celestial City may be seen —and these unwithering pastures, where the flocks of our Lord do securely feed, and where we his shepherds dwell in peace and joy."

I saw then that the shepherd Experience, addressing himself to the pilgrims, and more especially to Martha, said, "My beloved children, had you not met with those afflictions which you have just reported to us, and of which you cannot speak without letting fall the tears of human weakness—you perhaps had not now been thus far on your journey; nay, in prosperity you might have utterly forgotten the Lord, as many others have done. But resolving to make you his own, he mercifully took your treasures from you, and laid them up in heaven; that where those treasures were, there your hearts might be also. Matt. vi. 21. 'For whom the Lord loveth he chasteneth. Wherefore lift up the hands which hang down, and the feeble knees: and make straight paths for your feet. For you shall assuredly come unto Mount Zion, and unto the city of the living God, the heavenly Jerusalem, and to an innumerable company of angels, to the general assembly and church of the first-born, which are written in heaven, and to God the judge of all, and to the spirits of just men made perfect, and to Jesus the mediator of the new covenant.'" Heb. xii. 6, 12, 13, 22–24.

After this the shepherds spake of the shepherd Sincerity, the Interpreter, and Mr. *Orthodox*, saying, "We are all brethren, the servants of one common Master, and are all employed, in our different stations, about the same great work, namely, feeding the flock, for which our Redeemer was contented to be betrayed, given up into the hands of wicked men, and to suffer death upon the cross. We are constituted a universal, spiritual, and living priesthood, having the sheep of the flock committed to our care from generation to generation. Moreover, we continue our priestly office without ceasing; and shall continue it until the time when the universal church shall ascribe dominion, and reverence, and thanksgiving to the Lord of all lords, raised from the dead, who dieth no more, and whose kingdom is an everlasting kingdom. Then shall the borders of the church be enlarged; the same church which you saw in the City of Vanity, of which Mr. *Orthodox* is minister;—she 'shall break forth on the right-hand and on the left; and all her children shall be taught of the Lord; and great shall be the peace of her children. In righteousness shall she be established, and shall be far from oppression.' For this church, although now but little, is the espoused of the Lord—'Her Maker is her husband; and her Redeemer, the Holy One of Israel. He will lay her stones with fair colours, and her foundations with sapphires: he will make her windows of agates, and her gates of carbuncles, and all her borders of pleasant stones.' Isaiah liv. 3, 5, 11–14. Yea, the time shall come, and is near at hand, when her God shall be called 'The God of the whole earth.' Isaiah liv. 5. And then will all the earth be like these happy mountains, every man living in peace and contentment 'under his own vine and his own fig-tree.'" Zech. iii. 10.

Martha then exclaimed, "O happy prospect! how my soul longs for the time when all the kingdoms of the world shall become like the pleasant hills on which we now stand!"

Shepherds. They who understand the signs of the times, have reason to think that happy period not very far off.

Martha. Blessed, indeed, will that season be to those who watch and wait for it!

Shepherds. Pray ye, therefore, that ye also may be found watching.

Martha. I thank God, who by the chastisements of his rod has in some measure compelled me to watch.

"And I too may thank God," said Playful, "who caused me to feel the loving corrections of his hand, when I was like to be lost."

Watchful. I exhort you still to persevere, watching unto prayer: the danger is not past; the enemy is still abroad. Inbred or original sin may be quiet a while; but when occasion offers, he will certainly rouse himself again, and entice you to that which is evil. Labour therefore to "work out your salvation with fear and trembling." Phil. ii. 12.

Then said Martha, "We know that while we are at home in the body we must be absent from the Lord. O that we could be absent from these vile bodies, and present with the Lord!" 2 Cor. v. 8.

"The Lord in his good time will grant you your heart's desire," said the shepherds.

Breakfast being finished, the shepherds called the pilgrims out to walk upon the hills, that they might show them some of the wonders of the place. So they pointed out to them all those things which they were wont to show their guests. They led them first to a place whence they had a clear view of Mount Error, whose sides are so steep that in attempting to climb to the top of it many have fallen and been dashed to pieces. The shepherds also informed the pilgrims that, if any of their sheep by chance strayed to that hill, it was ten to one but they came to some evil end.

Now while they were looking thereon, there came a company of brisk lads from the town of Vanity: and being led on by one *Conceit*, they began to climb the hill on the most dangerous side. Upon which the shepherds called aloud to them, in order to warn them of their danger. But, instead of heeding their cautions, the strangers began to mock, calling the shepherds old fools, with other like reproachful names: and then following their guide towards the top of the hill—suddenly they lost their standing and fell, and were dashed in pieces. Whereupon *Conceit* returned the way he came: but the pilgrims were much grieved.

I saw then that the shepherds took the pilgrims to the top of Mount Marvel; where they showed them a beautiful hall, the walls of which were hung with numerous pictures, exhibiting the marvellous works of Christ, and describing the most extraordinary events of his life upon earth, from his miraculous birth to his resurrection and ascension into heaven. And as the pilgrims gazed upon these pleasant pictures, their hearts were filled with love, while their eyes overflowed with tears.

The shepherds next led them to the top of Mount Clear; and bidding them look eastward, they asked the pilgrims what they saw; who answered thus—"Far, very far away, we see a bright light, even the same light which has guided us through all our pilgrimage: but we can distinguish no particular object in the light."

I saw then that the shepherd Experience drew a glass from his pocket, to wit, the glass of Faith; and putting it to his eye, he said, "By the help of this glass I have sometimes discovered such things as cannot be described. But this happens not every day; nay, I must confess that it rarely happens, and that those are precious seasons indeed when I can use this glass to the best advantage. The fault, however, I know well, is never in the glass, but in my own eye." So the shepherd, having looked through the glass and seen that it was properly set, he offered it first to Martha, and then to the younger pilgrims, saying, "After what you have just now seen, my beloved children, on Mount Marvel, your eyes, I trust, are well prepared for the use of this instrument."

The pilgrims then tried the glass. But what they saw I know not: though they must assuredly have seen something unutterable and exceedingly glorious; for while their eyes were fixed, the fashion of their countenances changed, and shone, like that of Moses when he descended from the mountain; but they knew it not: Exod. xxxiv. 29.

The shepherds therefore, observing how delighted the pilgrims were with the glass, and that they were able to use it rightly, very cordially presented them with it, to their unspeakable joy. And thus the morning being nearly worn away, the shepherd Watchful proposed that they should return to the house.

Now, whereas it was ordained that the pilgrims should remain a while on the Delectable Mountains, the shepherds appointed to each of them some suitable employment, having received a command from their King not to permit any of the pilgrims who should visit them to pass their time in unprofitable idleness. So they allotted to Martha and the little girls the care of the dairy, with such of the lambs as had lost their mothers; while Humble Mind went out daily with the shepherds, to learn of them the proper management of pastoral concerns. Among other things, Humble Mind was taught to know what herbs were useful for the healing of such wounds or bruises as the sheep might chance to meet with—in which pastures the finest herbage grew—and where the purest springs were to be found. Very speedily also he learned the names of the sheep, with so much exactness as easily to discover whether any of them were wanting. In short, I perceived that the boy was wonderfully taken with a shepherd's life; insomuch that he resolved, if spared to man's estate, that he would by God's good pleasure become a shepherd. Moreover the pilgrims here learned many of the shepherds' songs; and it was most pleasant to hear them repeating those songs as they walked among the hills in the cool of the day.

After the pilgrims had spent six days with the shepherds, early on the following morning there was a cry among the shepherds of great joy—"This is the day which the Lord hath made; we will rejoice and be glad in it!" Psalm cxviii. 24.

When the children heard these words they were delighted, and ran to tell Martha: so they hastened to eat their breakfasts and feed the lambs; after which they went with the shepherds to Mount Sabbath.

Then I looked, and lo, the shepherds led the pilgrims to a certain very high hill, around the foot of which was a wall, within which wall no unholy thing was allowed to come. Now the hill, even at a distance, looked wonderfully green and pleasant, fresh and beautiful: and under the shadow of the wall, on the outside thereof, lay many beasts of burden, enjoying the day of rest. The summit of the hill was bright and glorious as the sun; and within the walls, towards the lower part of the hill, were many little dwellings with gardens among groves of trees, pleasant lawns, flowery fields, and sunny banks. Certain streams of water also, which took their rise from the top of the hill, ran down among these groves and gardens; which streams, as the shepherds informed the pilgrims, were never dry, even in the hottest season. These waters, which are the waters of mercy, after visiting every little habitation upon the hill, afforded refreshment to the poor beasts which lay under the wall.

Now I listened, and heard the sound of harpers harping with their harps from the higher parts of the hill, with the voice of multitudes continually crying out, "Glory, glory, glory to the Lord Jehovah!"

Then said the shepherds to the children, "Hear ye those sacred songs which call us up unto the house of the Lord, 'with the voice of joy and praise, among the multitude that keep holy day' (Psalm xlii. 4); inviting us 'to behold the beauty of the Lord, and to inquire in his temple?'" Psalm xxvii. 4.

The pilgrims therefore gladly hastened forwards, while the shepherds repeated, at intervals, their joyful invitation, "Let us go into the house of the Lord." Psalm cxxii. 1.

Now I saw that Playful and the two little girls, Grace and Truth, were frightened when they came among the beasts, and began to shrink back; which the shepherds perceiving, spake thus, "Little ones, what do you fear? Know you not that those poor beasts, having drunk of the waters of mercy, are at peace with all mankind?" Then the children blushed, and came forward.

When the pilgrims had accompanied the shepherds through the gate of admission to Mount Sabbath, their eyes were delighted with a near view of the pleasant lawns and woodlands, with the many peaceful dwellings scattered among them. Each cottage had its garden, in which grew pinks and violets, little bushes of fragrant southern-wood, marjoram, and wholesome rue, with other such humble and harmless plants as the Lord hath prepared to adorn the dwellings of the poor; the sweet odour of which was diffused through all the air. Every house looked clean; while the inhabitants, who at the sound of the bells were then stepping forth, old and young, to visit the house of God, appeared cheerful and healthy.

Now, as the pilgrims and shepherds walked along, they met an aged couple coming out from a little garden to go up the hill. The head of the old man was hoary, and his wife wore a white veil. So the shepherds saluted the aged pair; and as they walked up the hill together, while their hearts burned within them, they fell into sweet discourse about the mountain, and the happiness of those who dwell thereon.

This old man's name was *Christian-Cheerfulness;* and as he looked upon the pilgrims, he saluted them thus—"Right welcome are you, my children, to this holy mountain! for blessed are they which call the Sabbath a delight, the holy of the Lord, and honourable; not doing their own ways, nor finding their own pleasure, nor speaking their own words, but delighting themselves in the Lord." Isaiah lviii. 13, 14. Then addressing himself to the shepherds, I heard him say, "I am now an old man, and have lived from my youth upon this hill, where I never yet saw any of its inhabitants forsaken. Peace and plenty are still found in the dwellings of the righteous; for while they remember the Sabbath to keep it holy, the Lord of the Sabbath remembers them for good."

Now the voice of praise was heard more sweet and loud, as the pilgrims ascended the hill: and as I looked after them, my eyes were ravished with the lovely scenes which presented themselves on every side. For the Lord had planted on this mountain the cedar, and the myrtle, and the oil-tree: he had set there the fir-tree, and the pine, and the box together: on this mountain also grew the rose of Sharon, and the voice of the turtle never ceased from this peaceful land.

Thus the whole company went up as friends to the top of Mount Sabbath, where they employed themselves for a season in public prayer and praise in the temple of God. And while they were thus engaged, my ear was charmed with the sweet psalms and hymns which occasionally animated their sacred services, and which might be heard at a considerable distance. So, having spent a few hours in the heavenly exercise of prayer and praise, behold, the gates of the temple of God were again thrown open, when all the worshippers came out in order to return to their respective habitations. And I could not but remark what satisfaction and joy appeared in every countenance, while the little ones, in their holyday garb, ran innocently sporting among the flowers.

Now, as each family returned to its cottage, behold, *Christian-Cheerfulness* would have the shepherds and the pilgrims to turn in with him, and to partake of that which was provided. So they turned in with him.

I saw then, that a table being spread under a cedar-tree in the old man's garden, his wife set on dinner. First, she brought forth a dish of all manner of wholesome vegetables: upon which the old man remarked, "A dinner of herbs where love is, is better than a stalled ox and hatred therewith." Prov. xv. 17. After that, she produced a dish of meat; together with milk and honey for the little ones. So, when she had set the dishes on the table, the shepherds would make her sit down; "And let the children," said they, "fetch what is wanted, as is becoming."

The good woman therefore sat down, while the children ran for what was required; and surely I never saw a happier party. For *Christian-Cheerfulness* was a man of so pleasant conversation, that he entertained the company in a very agreeable manner; and particularly he amused the little ones, who were wonderfully taken with his pleasant discourse. But I perceived that the company never once forgot that they were conversing together on Mount Sabbath.

Dinner being over, the elder part of the company sat talking, while the little ones walked into the woods to gather flowers. Playful went with the young ones; but Humble Mind staid with the elder ones, although he took no part in their conversation, well aware that it became him not to speak before his elders, unless first spoken to. So as the evening came on they all returned home to the shepherds' house.

Humble Mind and Playful remained many days with the shepherds; where Martha was as a mother to them, while little Grace and Truth were as their sisters. Every seventh day they went with the shepherds to Mount Sabbath, always spending a part of the day with *Christian-Cheerfulness;* who generally in the course of the week returned the friendly visit, accompanied by his wife.

Thus many weeks passed happily away at this place: nevertheless, when it was signified to the pilgrims that they must continue their journey, they murmured not—"for they desired a better country, that is, an heavenly: God having prepared for them a city." Heb. xi. 16. But, before the pilgrims departed, the shepherds gave them a map of the road, bidding them particularly to beware of the Enchanted Ground.

Then asked the pilgrims, "What is the Enchanted Ground?"

"It is that state," answered the shepherds, "in which the flesh, that is, the unrenewed part, frequently prevails so far as to make the pilgrim slothful and secure, neglecting for a season the exercise of grace. In some cases the renewed part strives vehemently against this stupifying distemper, applying at the same time for that assistance which is promised in temptation—but," continued the shepherds, "there have been instances, and those terrifying ones too, in which the flesh has prevailed to the destruction of both body and soul, and *that* at a very advanced period of the Christian profession."

I heard then that the shepherds related several awful instances of pilgrims, who had apparently held a prosperous course as far as the Delectable Mountains on their way to Mount Zion, but, nevertheless, were finally lost on the Enchanted Ground, upon the very confines of the promised land—thus affording an awful example to Christians how dangerous it is to confide in their own strength.

"Awful, indeed!" said Martha: "and earnestly do I pray that we, profiting by the failure of these miserable persons, may walk in the strength of the Lord, and not in our *own!*"

Then said the shepherds, "A wise man feareth, and departeth from evil: but the fool is confident." Prov. xiv. 16.

After which, the shepherd Watchful added this caution—"Exhort one another daily, while it is called today; lest any of you be hardened through the deceitfulness of sin. For we are made partakers of Christ, if we hold the beginning of our confidence steadfast unto the end." Heb. iii. 13, 14.

So the shepherds, having kissed and blessed the little company, after conducting them a few steps on their journey, returned to the hills to take care of the flocks over which the Holy Ghost had made them overseers; while the pilgrims went on their way.

CHAPTER XXI.

THEN looking after the pilgrims, I saw that *Inbred-Sin* was with them; and he walked as one planning mischief. But the pilgrims held pleasant discourse one with another, from time to time looking upon their books, and meditating upon the contents of them.

Now I observed, in my dream, that, after a while, the pilgrims came to a place where a certain way put itself into the King's highway, which was to all appearance as straight and even as the highway itself. This was the place where certain pilgrims of old time had been turned aside by the flatterer. And here, just at the junction of the two roads, sat a company of persons dressed in pilgrims' habits, who were talking aloud and corrupting each other with flatteries: nevertheless, as they spoke a language nearly resembling that commonly used by pilgrims, Humble Mind and his sister, at the private suggestion of *Inbred-Sin*, felt an inclination to acknowledge them as brethren. Now these persons were of the number of those who love greetings in the market-place, and who make their prayers in the corners of the streets. So they called to the pilgrims, inviting them to join their company, and partake of such refreshments as they had.

But Martha said, "We are going for our lives to Mount Zion; and as we do not just now stand in need either of refreshment or rest, and as the sun is still high in the heavens, we are unwilling to be delayed."

"But," said they who were sitting by the way-side, "deny us not your company, which we believe will prove exceedingly edifying to us, and profitable to our salvation. For we know that you are persons highly favoured of the Lord: and because your fame has reached us from far, we have come hither on purpose to meet with you."

"Well," said *Inbred-Sin* in the ear of the younger pilgrims, "this appears to be a goodly company, and their words are full of wisdom." But Martha said, "Meddle not with them that flatter with their lips." Prov. xx. 19. So the children, being influenced at that time by the Holy Spirit of God, hearkened to the voice of Martha and passed on.

I heard then that those who sat by the way called after them aloud, uttering such cruel taunts and reproaches as brought up the blood into the faces of the pilgrims. Upon which Humble Mind and Playful thanked Martha for her advice: "For," said they, "we being children, and foolishness being bound in our hearts, we should surely have entered into the society of those ensnaring strangers, had you not given us a caution."

"Hence," said Martha, "the folly and sin of those who flatter young children: for if neither strength nor wisdom is to be found in the heart of the most advanced and venerable pilgrim, how much less in that of a child!"

The pilgrims then went on till night, when they came to a grove of cedar-trees beside a pool of water. This place appeared so exceedingly agreeable, that the travellers sat down upon the grass, and partook of that which they had with them: after which they looked upwards and gave thanks.

Now I saw in my dream that, while they sat on the grass enjoying the sweet solitude of the place, behold, two pilgrims advanced towards them along the King's highway: of whom one was an aged woman, and the other a boy about the age of Humble Mind. So they sat still till the pilgrims came up, when they addressed them thus: "If you come in the name of the Saviour, we cordially bid you welcome."

Whereupon the pilgrims modestly saluted Martha, meekly speaking of themselves as unprofitable servants, yea, the chief of sinners. But Martha, observing their white robes and the mark on their foreheads, was satisfied that they were true pilgrims: so pressing them to join their company, the strangers thankfully accepted the invitation. The name of the old woman was Ruth, and that of the boy, her son, was Plain Sense.

I saw then that the younger pilgrims presently fell asleep: but while they slept, Ruth and Martha conversed with each other for a considerable time after sunset. Ruth informed Martha that she was an inhabitant of a certain country called Darkland, lying to the north of the village of Family-Love, in the Valley of Destruction, where she had lived in total ignorance of her Saviour till within a few months past. "And there," said she, "I should still have lived in the same miserable state, had it not pleased the Lord to make my little son, who is my only child, the means of persuading me to leave my all for the Saviour's sake. But now," continued she, "I humbly trust, although I came not into the vineyard till the last hour of the day, that through the free grace and unsearchable merits of the Redeemer, I shall be counted worthy, though utterly worthless in myself, to enter the kingdom of heaven."

To this Martha returned, "Through faith only are we counted worthy, and not on account of our own works or deservings. Abraham 'believed in the Lord, and it was counted to him for righteousness.' Gen. xv. 6. And unless the righteousness of Christ be imputed to us by faith, we must all utterly perish."

I heard then that Ruth informed Martha how her little son was brought to the knowledge of the truth by reading the Holy Book of God, which had been delivered to him by one of those servants of the Lord who now go to and fro into the dark corners of the earth to publish his Word. Moreover, she told her how unwilling she had been to receive the Gospel at first, and that she had even obstinately shut her ears against it. "Nevertheless," continued she, "I was at length brought to the knowledge of my sin and my need of a Saviour: and now having advanced thus far on my way, behold here I stand before you this day, a miracle of grace."

"Let us then," said Martha, "give glory to God for all that we have received at his hand; and let us humbly confess that it is of his own superabounding grace and goodness, manifested through the Son of his love, that we are not now enduring the punishment due to our transgressions." I heard then that the two pilgrims broke forth with one voice in praise of their Redeemer; after which, they betook themselves to rest.

The repose of that night was sweet to the whole company, and on the morrow they were ready, by dawn of day, to pursue their journey. And now, whereas for some time past nothing has been said of *Inbred-Sin*, I think it necessary here to state, although I did not interrupt my pleasant account of the Delectable Mountains by speaking of this evil one, that he was nevertheless continually with the pilgrims during their stay in those mountains, causing them frequent uneasiness, though not breaking out into any very open or glaring act of violence. His apparent quietness, however, during that season is to be attributed to the vigilance of the shepherds, who, knowing him well, and keeping an eye continually towards him, put a check upon his actions at every turn; so that he could gain no ground whatever. But now being set free from the watchful eyes of the shepherds, he began to entertain better hopes of success among the pilgrims, who were at this time, he well knew, approaching their journey's end. He knew perfectly well that his time was *now* or *never*—of which his master Beelzebub, the great enemy of pilgrims, was equally sensible—he therefore determined without delay to exert himself to the utmost for the destruction of the pilgrims. Nevertheless, as they were now more experienced, and better acquainted with all his turnings and windings than they formerly had been, he judged it necessary to act with more caution than he had done in the former part of their course. It was not now his wish to bring any one of the pilgrims, in this advanced stage of their journey, to commit any very open and flagrant act of sin; since such a circumstance, he believed, however it might hurt the individual, would but put the rest more upon their guard. But having privately taken counsel with his master, he resolved, by plausible blandishment and flatteries, to lull them, if possible, into that sleepy and secure state in which many promising Christians have perished everlastingly. With this diabolical purpose therefore in his mind, as soon as he was well clear of the Delectable Mountains, he began to deal with the pilgrims, working cautiously and without noise, like the silent mole beneath the surface of the ground. In this unsuspected manner, he adapted his temptations and flatteries to each individual with all the art of Satan: and though his mode of going to work was different with each individual, yet his object with all was one and the same, namely, to draw them into a state of carnal security, causing them to believe that in this last stage of their pilgrimage all danger had completely passed away, and that the kingdom of heaven was, as it were, already in their possession.

In order to bring this about, I perceived that he was incessantly whispering in the ears of the pilgrims, and exerting all his influence to abate the fervour of their minds, by suggesting vainglorious thoughts of their own attainments. And though repulsed by one, and reproved by another, he returned again and again to the charge, till he had persuaded some of the party to listen to him with complacency. Oh! who is able to deal with this *Inbred-Sin!* for he knoweth how to render every feeling and every affection of our nature serviceable unto himself. Who can count up all the treacheries and deceits that lie concealed in the heart of this our enemy? or who can tell when our war with him is at an end? We have not only the old work to do over and over again with this unwearied foe; but new devices are continually to be prepared for. The place of his habitation is unsearchable, even the most secret recesses of our hearts: and he is most, perhaps, to be feared after we have gained some notable advantage over him. It was in the advanced age of David that *Inbred-Sin* obtained so great a victory over him. And thus it very frequently happens that pilgrims are overcome by this insidious enemy towards the latter end of their course, after having been enabled to contend successfully with him in their early days—and this, chiefly, on account of their ceasing too soon from the mortification of sin, or contending no longer in the strength of the Lord.

Now *Inbred-Sin* employed every opportunity of privately carrying on his work. I saw also, that the prince of this world, on observing that the pilgrims were now drawing near to the end of their journey, became greatly incensed at the prospect of losing such a company. And behold, he called his servants about him, for the purpose of consulting together concerning the surest means of ravishing these his purchased ones, out of the hand of their King, the Lord of glory. Wherefore, after consultation had, they took their several stations on that part of the King's territory which lieth nearest to the land of Beulah, through which rolls the black River of Death: and there they began to prepare their enchantments. So the pilgrims passed on till they came to the Enchanted Ground.

Now the Enchanted Ground was one flat and even plain; and it was covered with grass, short and smooth as velvet; insomuch that here were no rough ways, no stumbling-stones, no rocks of offence. This part of the way is visited by none save experienced Christians, who, having urged their way to this advanced point through a host of enemies, and finding themselves here no longer beset by those temptations which assaulted them in the earlier part of their pilgrimage—are apt to suppose that every difficulty is now overcome, and that a few more easy steps will introduce them to the high reward of all their labours.

Before the pilgrims entered upon this ground, their subtle enemy had completed his enchantments—for he had covered the whole plain with a hot and heavy vapour, which served entirely to obscure all the glories of Mount Zion, now not far away; drawing over that part of the horizon which used to reflect those glories a deep and dense cloud, on whose dark surface certain gloomy and sepulchral figures were indistinctly portrayed. There was also a deep stillness spread over all this Enchanted Ground; so that the voice of the speaker returned to his ear in a deep and hollow echo.

Now I perceived, that when the pilgrims entered upon this ground, they immediately became sensible of the weakening effects of the hot vapour; while the gloomy prospect before them seemed to impress every one with a degree of terror, which he had not the power of describing to his companions. Thus being deprived of the exhilarating view of Mount Zion, which had been more or less visible to them during the greater part of their pilgrimage; and being at the same time weakened by the hot and damp vapour which overspread the plain; they not only lost all desire of proceeding, but even the power of supplicating assistance. They now required rest and quietness above all things: and, indeed, they seemed to find it no easy matter to keep their eyes open.

I saw then that *Inbred-Sin* pointed out to them certain arbours built in that place, a little out of the highway, furnished with couches and pillows, together with every other desirable accommodation for the ease of the flesh; and he was exceedingly urgent with the pilgrims, especially the younger ones, that they should turn into these commodious arbours, and take some rest. So the thing was proposed to Martha; who was enabled, by divine grace, to oppose this counsel of the enemy.

"This," said Martha, "is the last device of our ensnaring enemy. When he sees that pilgrims have almost reached the end of their journey, he causes a deep heaviness and a deadly security to fall upon them: so that here many have stopped short of the kingdom, without manifesting the least inclination to go farther."

Humble Mind. Alas! alas! How dreadful a thing must it be, to fall short of happiness, when it is almost within our grasp!

Martha. Now is the time for us to befriend each other, by keeping a strict watch upon each other's motions.

Then said Ruth, "I have heard much of this place, and have been told that on coming hither, the wiser pilgrims have had recourse to the exercise of praise, 'speaking to each other in psalms, and hymns, and spiritual songs, singing and making melody in their hearts unto the Lord.' Eph. v. 19. Sing us therefore one of the shepherds' songs; for I know you have learned many of them; and I and my son will join you as well as we can."

So they began to sing lustily and with a good courage. And these were the words of their song—

"Jesus our all to heaven is gone,
He whom we fix our hopes upon;
His track we see, and we'll pursue
The narrow way till him we view.

"The way the holy prophets went,
The road that leads from banishment,
The King's highway to holiness,
We'll choose, for all his paths are peace."

I saw, too, that the children supported one another when any of them appeared likely to fall; while Humble Mind and Plain Sense watched over each other with a friendly solicitude.

They went on therefore tolerably well till towards night; when it became very foggy, attended with a drizzling rain. The two little ones now began to cry for very weariness; and the old pilgrim also complained much of dulness, declaring that her limbs had become like the limbs of one afflicted with the palsy. Then Martha, taking from her bag some wheaten cakes of the shepherds' preparing, gave a cake to each: but instead of sitting down to eat thereof, they ate them as the children of Israel did the passover—with their loins girt, and their staves in their hands. So, after moistening their lips with the wine which the shepherds had given them, they found themselves greatly refreshed. Whereupon they marshalled themselves in the best order they could; resolving, whatever might befall, to march all the night, without allowing themselves to sleep on the Enchanted Ground: such strength the Lord gave them to resist this last effort of Satan. And this was the manner in which they arranged themselves: Plain Sense, being a stout boy, had the charge of little Grace, while Humble Mind took Truth under his care, sometimes carrying these little ones, and sometimes leading them by the hand, as suited best. Playful walked in the midst, while Martha, supporting the old pilgrim, came up behind. So they continued going straight forward all night, having nothing to guide them but a faint light towards the east.

Now about midnight the enemy caused a wind to blow towards the pilgrims, which brought with it a deadly putrid smell from the banks of the River of Death; at which the pilgrims, particularly the elder ones, started, and became much affected. Then said Ruth, "Are we not approaching the regions of death? Although I have long thought upon death, and hoped that I could meet it in the strength of my God; yet now that it approaches and stares me, as it were, in the face, I feel myself unable to encounter it."

"Alas, my sister," said Martha, "this is because you depend upon your own strength, rather than upon the strength of your Lord. And what is equally to be lamented, when death approaches we are apt to seek for something in ourselves that may make us acceptable to our Lord. We like not to go quite empty-handed into the presence of our Redeemer; but, like Jacob, are searching for the best fruits of the land to carry with us to the King—not considering that our barren natures are unable to supply us even with the smallest portion of balm or honey, spices or myrrh, to sanctify the vessels which must be presented to our God. And yet, what does the whole purport and tendency of our religion teach, from first to last, except this—that in ourselves we are miserable, and poor, and blind, and naked; while we possess all things in Christ Jesus?" Then sang Martha, and all the pilgrims joined her—

"O for an overcoming faith,
To cheer our dying hours,
To triumph o'er the tyrant Death,
And all his frightful powers!"

Now I perceived that the pilgrims, being no longer affected by the deadly smell of the river, continued singing and praying aloud, notwithstanding their fatigue; while Martha occasionally animated them with words like these—"Sing unto the Lord, O ye saints of his, and give thanks at the remembrance of his holiness. For his anger endureth but a moment; in his favour is life: weeping may endure for a night, but joy cometh in the morning." Psalm xxx. 4, 5.

Towards morning the rain abated, the road improved, and the air became as sweet and pleasant as that which sweeps over fields of flowers. And behold, when the sun arose upon the pilgrims, they saw before them the lovely land of Beulah, perhaps at the distance of a short day's journey. That land is never forsaken of the Lord; yea, the Lord delighteth in it; and they that dwell in that land are called, "The holy people, The redeemed of the Lord." Isaiah lxii. 12.

No mortal tongue can describe the beauty of the land

of Beulah; nor hath any one seen that land but the well-beloved of the Lord. It is there that the Lord allows his people a foretaste of the joys of heaven. In that land the more perfect happiness of the Christian begins, even that which is to continue and increase for ever. There "perfect love casteth out fear." 1 John iv. 18. There is "the banqueting-house" of the King, in which "the banner of his love" is displayed. Sol. Song ii. 4. There he rejoiceth over his redeemed, and "feedeth them among the lilies." Sol. Song ii. 16. There grow "the rose of Sharon, and the lily of the valleys; the fig-tree putteth forth her green figs, and the vines with the tender grape give a good smell." Sol. Song ii. 1, 13. There the living plants of the King's gardens "are as an orchard of pomegranates, with pleasant fruits; camphire, with spikenard; spikenard and saffron; calamus and cinnamon, with all trees of frankincense; myrrh and aloes, with all the chief spices." Sol. Song iv. 13, 14.

I saw then, as the pilgrims drew near to this lovely land, that, on looking at their garments, they said one to another, "We once imagined our garments to be white; but in this goodly place they appear black and defiled." Sol. Song v. 3.

"Yes," said *Inbred-Sin* (for he still kept close to the pilgrims), "you must not presume to appear before the King of the country thus vilely clad. Turning aside therefore while you have time, first wash your garments with soap and nitre, that they may be clean." But the pilgrims were aware that this suggestion was from the Evil One.

"We are black, indeed," they answered. "We had white garments given unto us at the gate which is at the head of the way; but we have not kept them unspotted. We will therefore go humbly to him who alone can make them white; for soap and nitre cannot wash out their stains." Then I saw that they hastened forward, thus inquiring of all whom they met in the way, "Tell us where the chief Shepherd feedeth, even the King whom our soul loveth; where he maketh his flock to rest at noon: for why should we be as those who turn aside to the fold of the stranger?" Sol. Song i. 7.

Then I saw that the people of the land pointed out to them the footsteps of the King's flock; and bidding the pilgrims to follow them, behold, they speedily brought them to the Shepherd's tent. There they were joyfully received and bountifully entertained in the royal banqueting-house; where also their garments were rendered as pure as at the beginning. Moreover, they were there adorned "with rows of jewels, and their necks with chains of gold;" while their garments were enriched with "borders of gold and studs of silver." Sol. Song i. 10, 11. Thence also they were taken into the garden of their Lord to taste his pleasant fruits: and there, being weary, they slept—though their hearts still waked, and their thoughts were still engaged with ineffable delights. So they slept among the myrrh and spices of the King's garden. Sol. Song v. 1.

Now there was music and rejoicing through all the land of Beulah on account of the pilgrims' safe arrival; the inhabitants of the land also showed them all manner of kindness; and nothing was wanting to gratify their wishes. Nevertheless their hearts burned to be at the end of their journey: for they could see the Celestial City itself, although only indistinctly, because of its dazzling brightness. And they longed to be at home with their Lord, their Redeemer, and their King, their Almighty Maker, and the Maker of those parents, sisters, and children, whom they had loved upon earth, and who were passed on before. But there lay between them and the Celestial City a deep black river, through which all the children of mortality must pass—even the River of Death.

The pilgrims were at this time so eager to reach the farther shore, that they almost longed to plunge themselves into this river. But secretly struggling with their own impatience, they submissively waited their appointed time. So they pitched their tents in the happy land of Beulah, contented to tarry till the expected messenger should summon them away.

Now the first of the pilgrims thus summoned away, was the mother of Plain Sense. The old woman received the message joyfully, for her heart was with her King; and she cheerfully requested all her fellow-pilgrims to accompany her to the edge of the water. I saw then that, as she approached the river-side, the opposite banks appeared so clear, so bright, and so lovely, that she could not forbear crying out in a transport—

"Sweet fields, beyond the swelling flood,
Stand dress'd in lively green—
So to the Jews old Canaan stood,
While Jordan roll'd between."

She then took leave of all the pilgrims, one by one. But when her son came to her, "O my child! my son!" she said, "when thou comest to this hour, with what joy wilt thou recollect that thy persuasions and example were made the means of sweetening these bitter waters to thy aged mother! I lived in sin, a slave of the world, and in bondage to its lusts; when, by the grace of God, my only child became the instrument of leading me from darkness to light, and from the power of Satan unto God. Blessed therefore be the Lord, who in his tender mercy hath saved both mother and son!" Then stepping into the water, she said, "My foot standeth firm upon the Rock of Ages." After which the black waves rolling over her head, they for a season lost sight of her. But presently, with the help of the glass which the shepherds had given them, they distinguished her again: and behold, certain shining ones had received her, and were bearing her through the clouds to the gates of heaven. So she vanished from their sight, and they returned to their tents.

Now I saw that after many days had passed, a messenger came, inquiring for Humble Mind and Martha. Then Playful wept, while little Grace and Truth were sorely distressed. But Martha, embracing and kissing them, said, "Do ye sorrow, my children, even as others who have no hope? 'Who shall separate us from the love of Christ? I am persuaded that neither death, nor life, nor angels, nor principalities, nor powers, nor things present, nor things to come, nor height, nor depth, nor any other creature, shall be able to separate us from the love of God, which is in Christ Jesus our Lord.'" Rom. viii. 35, 38, 39.

The messenger however not being very hasty or urgent, Martha and Humble Mind had time to make known to their friends what they wished them to do after their passage through the river. And first, Humble Mind requested his sister to hold herself in readiness to follow him; "For," said he, "you know neither the day nor the hour wherein the Son of man cometh." Matt. xxv. 13.

I saw also that Martha besought Playful to take

charge of little Grace and Truth; very earnestly entreating, that as her age and experience were greater than theirs, she would bring them up in the nurture and admonition of the Lord.

Now Humble Mind's last request was, that his friend Plain Sense would take his sister to wife, that they might remain affectionate fellow-helpers to each other through the remainder of their pilgrimage. He also earnestly commended the two children to their care; for he greatly loved little Grace and Truth.

When therefore the appointed day was come, they went down to the River of Death together. So having come to the river-side, the departing pilgrims there knelt down in the midst of their kneeling friends: and I saw, that they who were going to pass the river wept not, but that their friends wept sorely. Then they prayed earnestly, in the following words: "O Almighty God, with whom do live the spirits of just men made perfect, after they are delivered from their earthly prisons, we humbly commend our souls into thy hands, as into the hands of a faithful Creator and most merciful Saviour; most humbly beseeching thee that they may be precious in thy sight. Wash them, we pray thee, in the blood of that immaculate Lamb that was slain to take away the sins of the world; that whatsoever defilements they may have contracted in the midst of this miserable and naughty world, through the lust of the flesh or the wiles of Satan, being purged and done away, they may be presented pure and without spot before thee. And teach those who survive, in this and other like daily spectacles of mortality, to see how frail and uncertain their own condition is; and so to number their days, that they may seriously apply their hearts to that holy and heavenly wisdom while they live here, which may in the end bring them to everlasting life, through the merits of Jesus Christ thine only Son our Lord." (*See Visitation of the Sick.*)

Thus having prayed, they arose and kissed their weeping friends; when Martha, crying, "Lord Jesus, receive my spirit," stepped down into the water, Humble Mind immediately following. But, no sooner had the soles of their feet touched the cold stream, than *Inbred-Sin* shrieked aloud, and attempted to pull them back. Whereupon they turned deadly white, while the cold sweat stood upon their brows. Then did the gasping pilgrims appear to be sinking under the agonies of temporal death: insomuch that their earthly friends could commune with them no longer.

Now as they struggled in the water, like persons nearly overcome and ready to perish, their groans and cries for deliverance became exceedingly distressing to those who stood by. When, in the midst of their extremity, behold one, whose beauty was without blemish, advanced to meet them. They who stood upon the shore beheld him through the glass of Faith, and knew him, by his form, to be the sinner's Saviour, full of grace and truth. And behold, the waters of death fled back at the touch of his feet. Joshua iii. 13. So approaching the pilgrims, who had now fainted—by a sudden exertion of his omnipotence, and in virtue of his own all-sufficient merits, he separated *Inbred-Sin* from their inmost souls, and annihilated him for ever. Upon which I perceived that the bitterness of death passed away from them; for the sting of death is sin. Then speaking tenderly unto the pilgrims, and bearing them up in his arms, their gracious Lord triumphantly conveyed them to the further side.

Here, even they who used the glass of Faith could scarcely discern any thing farther, by reason of their tears. But I continued to look after the pilgrims; and behold, a multitude of the heavenly host were waiting on the other side of the water, ascribing glory to Him who was more than conqueror over death. And they received the pilgrims with acclamations of joy—crying out, "Glory, glory, glory to the Lamb! Death is swallowed up in victory! Hallelujah! hallelujah! hallelujah!" Then casting their crowns at the feet of Him who had brought up the pilgrims from the River of Death, they fell down before him and worshipped.

Now as the pilgrims went up from the River of Death, they became bright and shining, being transformed into the image of Him that redeemed them. And behold, they were surrounded by thousands and tens of thousands of glorified saints and angels, who placed crowns on their heads, and golden harps in their hands; with which they instantly joined the heavenly host in their triumphant songs.

So the glorious multitude, accompanying their Almighty Lord, began to ascend through the region of the air towards the gates of heaven which were opened wide to receive them. And as they ascended they cried out, " Hallelujah! for the Lord God omnipotent reigneth!" And again they said, " Hallelujah to God and the Lamb!" Thus the glorious company of these blessed ones reached the regions of ethereal light, whither my eyes could follow them no more.

Upon which I awoke from my dream, and hastened to write it in a book.

" Let me die the death of the righteous, and let my last end be like his!" Numbers xxiii. 10.

END OF THE INFANT'S PROGRESS.

THE
FLOWERS OF THE FOREST.

THE

FLOWERS OF THE FOREST.

CHAPTER I.

I SHALL commence my narrative by stating that I am a native of France, and a very old man. More than forty years since I was a minister of a small parish situated in the beautiful province of Normandy, in France; that province which gave her conquerors and her princes for many generations to the country in which I have now taken up my abode.

I was educated for the pastoral office; the parish which was appointed me lies upon the Seine; it extends along the left bank of that beautiful river, which, as is well known, rises near Saint Seine, in Burgundy, and mingles itself with the sea below the city of Rouen.

It is a region rich in orchards and vineyards, in fragrant meadow-lands and thymy downs.—To the north thereof lies a forest, extending itself for several leagues over a space most beautifully diversified with hill and dale, and affording within its deep recesses such a great variety of cool grottoes, waterfalls, and natural bowers as I have seldom seen in any other part of the world. There is the sweet village, each little dwelling of which has its thatched roof, its rural porch, and its gay flower-garden. We had our chateau also, which being built of gray stone, and having a commanding site, afforded a pleasing object to the road which runs from Paris to Rouen on the other side of the Seine; its fanes and turrets at that time being exalted above the neighbouring woods, though, as I now understand, they are levelled to the dust; and near the chateau was the Tour de Tourterelle, which gave the title to the family,—a huge old tower coeval with the first dukes of Normandy.

While residing in Normandy, I was a Papist, though now, through the influence of a clearer light shining upon my soul, I am a Protestant: and 1 humbly pray that my mind may never again be brought under the dark delusions in which it was involved in my younger days.

It is possible that my youthful reader may not precisely understand the points on which the Protestant and the Papist are at variance. These particulars are numerous, and many of them are not easily ascertained, because the Papists do not present the doctrines of their church in a simple or well-defined form. When a Protestant refers to the works which are held in authority among the Papists, and points out the errors contained therein, they shift their ground, and in all possible ways evade a straight-forward line of argument. Their most authenticated modern forms of worship are from the decrees of the Council of Trent, which commenced its sittings in 1545, and continued, though a long interval intervened, until 1563. That council was held by the command of the pope at Trent, a city in the north of Italy, and many decrees were issued by it, both as to matters of faith and ceremonies. These were sanctioned by the highest authority of the Church of Rome, and have never been in any way repealed or modified; they may therefore be referred to as the authorized statement of popish doctrines, and Protestants may reason respecting them as the rule of faith of the Romish Church. It is true that they were not received with the same degree of implicit submission by all the countries which continued to profess themselves followers of the Church of Rome; and in Protestant countries at the present day, the Papists are unwilling to admit fully, that they, as such, are bound by the decrees of the Council of Trent; their policy appears to consist in continually shifting their position, and presenting new forms of defence, which being of a shadowy and mysterious nature, are incapable of being overturned by plain reason, or other means which might be used against their errors if advanced in a more substantial form. The Protestant, on the other hand, uses no subterfuge whereby he may confound his enemies, and escape the consequences to which the principles he recognises must lead, but simply maintains his belief in Scripture, and asserts that whatsoever is not read therein, nor may be proved thereby, is not to be required of any man that it should be believed as an article of faith, or be thought requisite or necessary to salvation.

But I forget that I am writing for such as cannot be supposed to enter fully into discussions of this nature. I shall therefore avoid going more deeply into them, simply requesting my youthful reader to bear these things in mind, namely, that of the two principal orders of persons calling themselves Christians, the first, namely, the Protestants, profess to take the Bible as their rule of life and of belief; the second, the Papists, bind themselves to obey the commandments of their church, of which the pope is, as they pretend, the father, the spiritual head, the absolute and infallible ruler: and the priests of that church assume to themselves a power and authority far beyond that of any mortal being, in all matters connected with religion.

When first admitted to my cure, the family at the chateau consisted of many individuals, but one and another of these being removed by death or marriage, Madame la Baronne only was left to us after a few years, and such were the kindness and amiable deportment of this lady, that it was commonly said of her, that all the virtues of the long and illustrious line of ancestry, of which she was the last in that part of the country, had centered in her. In fact, her conduct merited our sincere affection and gratitude; but when we are made acquainted, through the divine teaching, with the fallen and corrupt state of human nature, we dare not to use or admit that high strain of panegyric which more presumptuous individuals employ without apprehension.

Between the village and the chateau stood our church, built also of gray stone, in the Norman Gothic style, and near to the church was a large dark timbered house, with two gable-ends pointed with wooden crosses, where lived a decayed gentlewoman, a widow, whom I shall call Madame Bulé.

This lady being an accomplished woman for that day, and much reduced in her fortune, received young ladies into her house for their education, and was, I believe, as far as the dark state of her mind would admit, a faithful and laborious guide to her young people.

Near to Madame Bulé's seminary was my own little mansion, nay, so near, that the window of my study, which was an upper room, projected over the garden wall of the seminary, and I used often to amuse myself by showering sugar-plums from thence upon the little ones who were assembled on the lawn beneath.

From the period of my entering upon my charge until I was more than forty years of age, I enjoyed a long interval of comparative peace. I was fond of a retired life. I had a particular delight in the study of nature, and in that part of it especially which refers to the formation and beautiful variety of the vegetable world. I made a collection of all the plants in the neighbourhood, and would walk miles for the chance of obtaining a new specimen. I had other pursuits of the same kind, which filled up the intervals of my professional duties, and, through the divine goodness, kept me from worse things during those years of my life in which I certainly had not that sense of religion which would have upheld me in situations of stronger excitement. Thus I was carried on in a comparatively blameless course through a long period of my life, for which I humbly thank my God, and take no manner of credit to myself; though I feel that it is a mercy for which an individual cannot be too grateful, when he is brought to a sense of sin and to a knowledge of his own weakness, to find that in the days of his spiritual darkness he has been guarded on the right-hand and on the left, from shoals and rocks and whirlpools, in which wiser persons than himself have made terrible shipwrecks. But, as I said above, I was led on from year to year in a sort of harmless course; and whereas I enjoyed much peace, so was the same bestowed upon my neighbours in general, in a larger proportion than could have been expected, when the agitated state of our country, as it regarded religion and politics, is brought under consideration. In the mean time, the little establishment of Madame Bulé was carried on in a manner so peaceful and tranquil, that it can hardly be questioned but that the protecting hand of Providence was extended over this academy, although undoubtedly the instructions there received partook of the spiritual darkness at that period spread over the whole country.

At length, however, as madame became less able to exert herself, and as new modes of instruction and more fashionable accomplishments became requisite, in order to satisfy the parents of her scholars, she thought it right to procure an assistant, and Mademoiselle Victoire, a young lady who had been educated in Paris, was appointed to the situation. Thus the wolf was admitted into the fold; for this young person, being exceedingly vain and worldly minded, no sooner found herself established in the family of Madame Bulé, then she began to disturb the peace of its inmates.

All those accomplishments which delight the senses were what were chiefly held in esteem by mademoiselle; she had no value for the qualities of the heart, and no discernment of retiring and humble merit; hence her favours were ever lavished on the vain and frivolous, provided they were possessed of such qualities as she admired; while some of the most amiable young people in the seminary were continually exposed either to her ridicule or her reproaches.

In consequence of this unjust conduct she presently raised a very unamiable feeling among the young people, many of whom began to form false estimates of each other's merits, and to hate and envy those individuals among their companions who possessed any of those qualities or distinctions, whether mental, personal, or accidental, which were calculated to ensure the favour of mademoiselle. And then it was that I first observed a change in the air and appearance of the young people when they came out to amuse themselves in their garden during the intervals of their studies; then it was that the voice of anger first arose towards my window, and my ear was then first saluted with the tones of discord, disturbing the beautiful harmony of the scene. I observed also, after a while, that there was an entire cessation of those games and diversions in which the young people formerly seemed to take such interest; neither did I hear those cries of joy proceeding from the playground which were in former periods so delightful to my ear as I sat in my study—for worldly purposes and feelings had crept into this little society, and I, as if aware that these symptoms, observed among these young people, were only the beginnings of misfortunes, frequently at that time looked back on the days of innocent (comparatively innocent) pleasure which were fast passing away, with a sort of regret which seemed even more bitter than the occasion warranted.

The time had been, nay, it was hardly gone, when it had been the chief delight of the pupils of Madame Bulé to cultivate flowers in all attainable varieties, and madame had given a small piece of ground to each little girl for this purpose.

I had often busied myself in procuring rare seeds and fine specimens of flowers for these little people, by which small services I had obtained the name of Le Bon Pere,* Le Bon Pere Raffré, and was saluted with cries of joy whenever I appeared in the garden. Then with what eager delight did the little rebels gather round me, and some indeed were daring enough to thrust their hands into my pockets, to rob me of the small packets of seeds or bulbous roots which had been deposited therein to attract the pretty little thieves. More than once I have seized a dimpled hand in the very act of felony, and then have taken out my large clasp knife, to open it wide, to whet it on the nearest stone, and to pretend that I was about to take instant and cruel revenge; while the sparkling and blooming delinquents shrieked and danced around me, now receding now advancing, now approaching now retiring, till every avenue of the garden re-echoed with the merry notes of innocent delight. Oh joyous days of happy and unapprehensive youth, when the light heart never wearies with the same jest, however often reacted or repeated, nor yawns at the oft-told tale!

Often too was I invited to the collation at four o'clock, when the weather would permit the little party to enjoy that simple meal in the open air; and when Father Raffré promised his company, most happy was that little fair one who could contribute the most elegant decorations for the feast, or supply the most beautiful baskets of reeds or osiers to stand in lieu of the china or plate which adorn the tables of more magnificent orders.

As I before said, I was then a Roman Catholic; it was the religion to which I had been brought up, and although I will not say that from time to time some faint apprehensions might not have crossed my mind even then, respecting the soundness of the principles in which I had been nurtured, yet these gleams of light had hitherto been transitory as the rays which fall upon the earth when the morning is spread upon the mountains and the clouds are driven forward along the path

* The good father.

of the sun. But this I trust that I may say of myself, and of many of my brethren at that time, that, as far as our knowledge went, we were sincere; and that if we sometimes appeared to be otherwise, it was because we were not always assured that our faith had that foundation in truth, which it must needs have in order to be effective. Notwithstanding which, I think I may add, that I did endeavour, when thus familiarly associated with these little people, to press upon them the importance of spiritual things, and with this view directed them often to raise up their hearts to God when employed in their most ordinary actions. To this piece of excellent advice I added, as might be expected, certain admonitions respecting forms, of a nature which I now see to have been decidedly prejudicial, inasmuch as outward forms so frivolous as those which are commanded by the church to which I then belonged, have a direct tendency to lead the mind from seeking that inward and spiritual grace, of which outward forms are but the types. Among those forms which I particularly enforced, I well remember one, which was that of making the sign of the cross many times during the day; I also insisted that these young people should repeat the Ave Maria, and certain other prayers which I taught them in the Latin tongue, as often as they could make it convenient so to do; assuring them that by their obedience or disobedience in these particulars, they would rise or fall in favour with God and with the church. Thus I endeavoured, though on false principles, to shed the odour of sanctity on our little assemblies, and for some years I had no strong reason to perceive that the weapons of warfare which I had placed in the hands of my little pupils, were not sufficiently powerful to enable them to resist the snares of Satan and the dangers of the world. For, as I remarked above, while Madame Bulé alone presided over her school, and while her pupils were small, the ill effects of the heartless and formal system inculcated by me did not appear; neither did the evil break out till the general agitation of the country was in some degree extended to this little society, by the arrival of Mademoiselle Victoire, who, according to the prevailing spirit of the age, no sooner found herself established in the seminary than she took the lead, before her superior, and commenced that work of disorganization which was already advancing in the capital.

CHAPTER II.

At the time of which I am about to speak, there were in Madame Bulé's seminary three young ladies, whom I shall have particular occasion to mention by-and-by, and shall therefore proceed to describe in this place. The eldest of these was named Susette, and was, in point of external perfection, the rose of the parterre—a blooming, lovely young person, but of a high and haughty spirit when opposed; yet one, I think, which might have been led to any thing by a kind and gentle hand.

Susette was a chief favourite of Mademoiselle Victoire, and had her warm partisans, her open admirers, and secret enemies in the little establishment. Neither was she without her rival; for what favourite is so happy as not to have sometimes reason to dread the influence of another. Mademoiselle was capricious, and whereas at one time she caressed Susette, at another time she was all complacency to Fanchon, the only young lady among the pupils of Madame Bulé whose pretensions could be brought in comparison with those of Susette—but whereas I have called Susette a rose, Fanchon, whose hair was of a bright and rich auburn, might best have been compared to the golden lily, the pride and glory of the oriental gardens.

But I must confess that the character of Fanchon never pleased me, she had none of that candour and openness of temper so agreeable in youth, and which I would rather see in its excess than its deficiency, although that excess may border on imprudence; for age assuredly must add prudence to the character, whereas it seldom deducts from a spirit of cold and selfish caution.

The third among the pupils of Madame Bulé whom I must particularly describe was an English girl and an orphan. I never knew by what chance this child had been consigned to the care of Madame Bulé, neither do I recollect her real name; but she was called Aimée by her preceptress, and by that name she went among us. Neither do I know more of her age, than that she was thought too young for confession till she had been in the house more than two years, and therefore I judge that she was between eleven and twelve years of age at the time of which I am speaking. This little girl was small for her years, and was one who would generally have passed unnoticed in a group of children, yet when closely examined, she had one of the sweetest countenances I ever beheld; her hair and complexion marked her Saxon origin, and the tender innocence and dimpled beauty of her sweet face brought her frequently in comparison, in my imagination, with some such figure as I have often seen of an infant Jesus, whom the artist has represented in the arms of his mother, looking down from some high altar with love and compassion on the multitude kneeling before him. Such were the high comparisons which I made for the lovely little Aimée—yet why do I call the comparison high? Are not images, however beautiful, however exalted, however held in honour, but blocks of wood and stone, carved into the similitude of man by the hand of man? and is not the body of man the work of God himself, and in every instance wonderful and past imitation, and even past comprehension! for what doth David say on this subject? Psalm cxxxix. 14, "I am fearfully and wonderfully made, marvellous are thy works, and that my soul knoweth right well."

Nevertheless, I own that the time has been when I bowed with religious awe before the graven image, and poured forth my soul thereunto in solemn prayer, without considering any of those subtle distinctions which the learned of the papal church pretend to make respecting relative and inferior honour: for the Roman Catholic church, when making its comments on the first commandment, uses the following expressions, which I shall give in the form of question and answer, as I found it in the authorized catechism published in this country:—

Question.—Does the first commandment forbid us to give any kind of honour to the saints and angels?

Answer.—No; it only forbids us to give them supreme or divine honour, which belongs to God alone; but it does not forbid us to give them that inferior honour, which is due to them as the faithful servants and special friends of God.

Q.—And is it allowable to honour relics, crucifixes, and holy pictures?

A.—Yes, with an inferior and relative honour, as they relate to Christ and his saints, and are memorials of them.

But as I have already remarked, when kneeling before these crucifixes and images, I fear that I too often retained but very imperfect ideas of these distinctions; and in the visible type or representation too often lost the recollection of the antetype.

To return to little Aimée: she was a child exactly formed to be the delight and joy of some venerable grandmother, or of some widowed and bereaved wife and mother. One who in retirement would have been the sweetest friend and companion which sadness or sorrow could ever know, being no doubt divinely endowed with that holy peace of mind and tranquillity of spirit which the world can never disturb, because the world can have no intercourse therewith. Yet at the same time, being a character which was so entirely overlooked in scenes of bustle and worldly commotion, that her companions seemed seldom to take any farther notice of her than to push her aside when she crossed their paths; still, however, she possessed in so large a degree the spirit of harmlessness so truly congenial with the Christian character, that it would have been impossible (one should have thought) to hate this little girl. Nevertheless she did incur the active hatred of Mademoiselle Victoire, and this in a way which such as are not somewhat skilled in the nature of the human heart will not easily comprehend, but which will be evident enough to those to whom the secret recesses of that fountain of all that is impure are in some degree revealed—some fault had been committed in the house soon after the arrival of mademoiselle, the blame was laid on Aimée, and on the bare suspicion mademoiselle punished her severely, neither would she remit her punishment till madame interfered; it was found afterward that Aimée was innocent, but mademoiselle never pardoned her

I had observed, as I have before remarked, that since the arrival of Mademoiselle Victoire the simple, cheerful spirit which had formerly animated the family of Madame Bulé had disappeared; and instead of the lively games in which the pupils of all ages had hitherto engaged, I could see from my window that there were parties formed in the young society. It was very evident that there was an open rivalry established between the rose and the fleur-de-lis* (by-the-by, a rivalry of old and renowned establishment); also I could perceive that there were few of the young people who did not enlist themselves under one or other of these banners, and I could sometimes hear words running very high between individuals of the different parties, though I could not exactly understand the precise subject of these controversies.

At length, however, it happened as I was sitting one afternoon with my window open, it being two days before the feast of Easter, that I saw the young people proceeding in a body from the porch; Mademoiselle Victoire was in the midst of them, and she was talking with great vivacity on a subject which seemed to interest every one. They advanced in a direction which brought them nearly under my window, and then mademoiselle sat down on a garden chair in the centre of the grass-plat, while her two favourites stationed themselves on each side of her, and one by one she called each of the other young people to the footstool of her throne, for she sat in much state, and after having looked into the palm of every hand with the grimaces used by a fortune-teller, for so I understood the scene, she dismissed each individual, with some prognostic or witticism, which, as I perceived, excited peals of laughter, but not such laughter as I felt agreeable to me. It appears that the young people had at that moment forgotten that it was possible I might be so near them, for although I could see them well, and distinguish every gesture, yet I was myself so concealed by a jasmine just bursting into leaf, which I had trained over a part of my window, that it would not have been easy for the most penetrating eye to have detected me behind this natural screen, and thus as I was not within their view, neither was I in their thoughts at that period.

This pastime, of whatever tendency it might have been, had proceeded for some time, and each of the little people then present had presented her palm, and heard the prognostics of her future fate from the self-elected

* The lily.

prophetess, when suddenly a sort of demur arose among the party, and I saw every one turn to look around her; at length I heard the voice of mademoiselle calling Aimée, and at the same time I perceived that the little girl had not been present. The next minute all the young party began to scatter themselves over the garden, as if in quest of the child, and the name of this little one proceeding from the various parts of the pleasure ground, was returned by an echo, caused by an angle formed by the tower and the body of the church. Some minutes elapsed, it seems, before the little lost one was discovered; she was (as I afterward learned) at last detected in an arbour formed of flowering shrubs, at the very bottom of the garden, cowering down under the shade of a laurustinus, and deeply engaged in reading a very small book. She was instantly seized upon by Susette and Fanchon, who both sprang upon her at the same instant, and dragged her between them into the awful presence of Mademoiselle Victoire.

The little captive uttered no sound, and used but little resistance; but when brought directly before Mademoiselle Victoire, she fell on her knees, and, pointing to Susette, seemed to be earnestly imploring some favour of the utmost importance. What this favour was I could not discover; but I was made to understand that, so far from having obtained it, she had only incurred more violent displeasure by the strength of her pleadings, for I saw mademoiselle push her away several times, and then I heard my own name repeated, with an assurance that something, I knew not what, should not be concealed from me.

Being thus, as I considered, called upon, I arose, and putting my head out at the window, I called to mademoiselle, and asked her what had happened, and wherefore my name was mentioned.

Mademoiselle, who had stood up to correct the child, turned hastily at the sound of my voice, and approaching as near to me as possible, "My good father," she said, "we have need of your advice and counsel, and we hope that you will insist that this child shall endure a severe penance"—here she stopped to recover breath, of which her passion had deprived her, and then proceeded. "This wicked little heretic," she said, "whom madame has always upheld as a sort of saint among us, has it seems, retained in her possession, ever since she came into this place, a volume of the Holy Scriptures in her native language, though she knows that children like herself are not competent to use these holy books to any advantage. She has actually been discovered in an arbour of this garden, deep in the study of this volume, using such art in so doing as shows the blackness and depravity of her heart." Thus speaking, she gave the child a push from her, with that sort of expression of abhorrence which one would use to a loathed animal.

"And where is this book?" I asked. It was immediately held up to my view by Susette, and I perceived that it was an abridgment only of the sacred Scriptures, being an exceedingly small volume, not above four inches square; it looked old and much worn: and it struck me that there was a malicious feeling shown towards the child in making so much of this insignificant matter, and not, as I thought, much policy in it, as it related to the interests of the church to which I was then attached. I therefore said, "Let the book be given to madame, and to-morrow I will come over and speak to her on the subject."

I hoped by this that I should satisfy all parties; but in this I was mistaken. No sooner did little Aimée understand that the tiny volume in question was to be given to madame, than she dropped on her knees upon the grass, and looking up to me with streaming eyes and united hands—"O dear father, kind Father Raffré," she said, "order me the severest penance, let me live on bread and water for a year to come, but do not take away my book—my lovely little book: do not take my poor little book."

"Dear child," I replied, "dear child, wipe away your tears; to-morrow I will meet you in the church; you shall confess all to me about your little book; and do not fear, you shall have justice done to you." And thus I dismissed the whole party, though I felt that I had not given satisfaction to either side by the manner in which I had answered the appeal. Neither was I mistaken in this my opinion, for mademoiselle returned in a very ill humour to the house; and though Aimée and the affair of the book were spoken of no more that evening, yet the young ladies began to quarrel with each other upon these grounds,—namely, that Mademoiselle Victoire had promised to one a prince and a coach-and-six, a duke to another, a barouche-and-four and a marquis to another, a simple baron to another, a rich burgher to another, and to a less favoured one a mere coachman. As I had suspected, and I afterward learned, mademoiselle had been telling her pupils their fortunes, or rather had taken this way of giving them some idea of their several pretensions, and by this means had excited in their minds every sort of idea which ought to have been held back from them; and, indeed, so high did the rancour of the several parties rise on this occasion, that Madame Bulé was obliged to exert her authority, and very severe was the reproof she gave when she understood the cause of this uproar which had disturbed her peace. "Do you not know," said she, "that the day after tomorrow is Easter, and that to-morrow you are to meet Father Raffré for confession; and in what spirit or temper will you be for this sacrament if you retire to rest in the indulgence of such angry passions? For shame, young ladies; do not thus convert an innocent jest into a subject of discontent and rancour."

It is needless surely here to remark, that in this reproof of Madame Bulé, which was faithfully reported to me, there were two important errors; in the first instance, confession is no sacrament, neither a part of a sacrament, there being but two sacraments appointed by our blessed Saviour, namely, baptism and the supper of the Lord;* and the jest of Mademoiselle Victoire was every thing but innocent, therefore madame should not have so designated it.

CHAPTER III.

Early the next morning, it was signified to me that Madame Bulé desired to speak with me; and when I had obeyed her summons, the amiable woman opened her mind to me to the following effect: "My dear Father Raffré," she said, "my mind has lately been much troubled respecting my pupils; the time was, as

* The Church of Rome considers that there are seven sacraments; adding to the two mentioned in the New Testament five others, namely, penance, confession, orders, matrimony, and extreme unction.

you well know, when we enjoyed a degree of peace which is now utterly foreign to our household. I was then," she added, and the tear was in her eye when she spoke, " more alert and active than I now am, and better able to endure the fatigues of my situation. It was then," she continued, " that every hour brought its pleasures, and every change its delights; my children came with cheerfulness to their lessons, and left them with glee to enjoy their sports; if one did amiss, all were humbled; if one was praised, all were pleased; if one received a present, all were to have a share in it; if one was unwell, all partook in her pain. Now the case is entirely altered, I hear of nothing but of rivalries and of ill-will: if I praise one individual I offend twenty, and if I find fault with one offender I give cause of triumph to twenty more. It is not now a question who can do best, but who is most accomplished or most genteel; and instead of joy and peace, my household is one continued scene of dissatisfaction."

" And cannot you account, madame," I said, " for this change in the character of your household? are you sure that the person whom you employ to assist you is exactly suited to your purpose?"

" Mademoiselle Victoire," she replied, " is diligent and accomplished; I might not get a better were I to dismiss her: but you, my good father, shall hear my children's confession, and I am sure that they will find in you a faithful and pious counsellor."

After this conversation, I took the earliest opportunity of calling the young people to confession. The church was set aside for that duty; and Madame Bulé made a point of being in the church with us, although she did not remain within hearing.

As a confessor, I have, through the course of a long ministry, heard many awful secrets, and though I am now no longer of the Romish church, I still would make it a point of honour not to betray any confidence which was placed in me under the character which I formerly held of a father confessor. The confessions, however, which were made to me by the pupils of Madame Bulé were not of such a nature as to render it of the smallest consequence whether they are or are not divulged; neither, even if they were more important, can they possibly now affect the penitents in the smallest point. I shall therefore venture to inform my readers of what passed that morning in the church between me and those of the young ladies of the establishment with whose names and descriptions I have made them acquainted. Susette was the first who was brought to me, and when she appeared, the traces of tears were upon her cheeks.

"Daughter," I said, "you are sad; what has afflicted you? Open your whole heart to me, and be assured that the counsel I shall give you shall be to your advantage." She immediately burst into tears, and speaking passionately, made it appear that injustice was done to her by her companions, especially by Fanchon.

"Fanchon," she added, "who was once my dearest friend, is turned against me, and that because she is jealous of me. Some persons think me handsomer than she is, and she cannot endure a rival, and she bears herself maliciously and spitefully towards me; and if she can find a flaw in my conduct, she is pleased and makes it a rule to exhibit it, and to make little errors appear in the light of serious offences."

I shall not repeat all I said to her on this subject. No doubt my advice, though in some points good, was mingled with error, for I remember well that, after having pointed out to her the beauty of charity, and recommended the exercise of it towards her companions, I added, "for know you not, my daughter, that 'charity remits sin, and gives spiritual life to the soul.'" By which assertion I set charity in the place of our Saviour, and gave our good deeds the power of redeeming us from the consequence of our evil ones; whereby I denied the words of Holy Scripture, for are we not taught that a man is not justified by the works of the law, but by the faith of Jesus Christ? Galatians ii. 16.

In reply to what I had said, Susette answered with a frankness which was natural to her. She acknowledged that she had a considerable portion of pride, and that she could neither bear a rival among her school-fellows, nor refrain from despising those whom she thought her inferiors. She spoke again of Fanchon as of one whom she looked upon with envy and jealousy; and among others whom she heartily despised she mentioned Aimée. In reply to all which I told her "that pride was counted by the church among the seven deadly sins. Pride," I said, "is an inordinate love and esteem of our own worth and excellence—it is a mortal sin, and can only be remitted by hearty contrition and the sacraments of baptism and penance."

At the word penance Susette started, as under fear; on which I spoke soothingly to her, and added, that she need not be afraid, that I would not be severe.

"The sacrament of penance, my daughter," I remarked, "consists of three parts, contrition, confession, and satisfaction. The tears of contrition I have seen on your features; you have performed the duty of confession; and what now remains to be done is satisfaction."

"And in what," asked Susette hastily, "does this duty of satisfaction consist?"

"In what I shall require of you to do," I replied.

"Then, dear Father Raffré," she answered, "you surely will not make me ask pardon of little Aimée, or seek a reconciliation with Fanchon"—and she looked imploringly at me.

"I shall exact of you," I replied, "before I can venture to give you absolution, that satisfaction which the church requires. 'For satisfaction, which is the third part of the sacrament of penance, is a faithful performance of the prayers or good works enjoined by the priest to whom the penitent confesses.'"

"I am willing, father," she replied, "to repeat as many prayers as you could desire."

"Be it so my daughter," I answered: and I know not how many Ave Marias and Pater Nosters I enjoined, to be repeated before the image of the Virgin in the closet of Madame Bulé before the hour of mass on the following day; and thus having slightly healed the wound of my penitent, or rather administered fresh subject for future self-satisfaction to one who was already but too well pleased with herself, and as it were added fuel to the fire I should have sought to quench, I dismissed Susette, and proceeded to confess her rival, who soon afterward entered the church and approached the confessional.

The confession of Fanchon was but a repetition of that of Susette, with this difference only, that this second penitent was more reserved and guarded in her acknowledgment of error than the former had been. I was in consequence less satisfied with her, and doubled her portion of Ave Marias and Pater Nosters, giving her also, for the performance of her service the gloom of evening, instead of the bright morning hours; and this young lady having withdrawn, I requested that Aimée might be brought to me.

There was some interval between the departure of Fanchon (with whom Madame Bulé had gone out) and the entrance of Aimée. I was left alone, and the scene was an impressive one. The church was an ancient Gothic edifice, richly decorated with carved figures and ornaments; I was in a chapel of the Virgin, which was situated at the end of a long arched aisle; all was motionless around me, and no sound was heard but the soft low murmuring of the wind among the towers and battlements; my mind was full of what had just passed, and the anxious inquiry of Susette respecting what satisfaction I should require of her recurred to my thoughts. It was very natural, I perceived, that she should expect me to insist on her seeking a reconciliation with those whom she had offended, common sense dictated such a satisfaction, and common justice required it; but the church to which I then belonged had demanded no such hard service—to put its votaries out of humour with themselves was no part of its policy. In the case in question I had acted as a faithful son of the church, I had regarded its interests; and the question was suggested to my mind, "Had I or had I not applied a remedy which would have the smallest efficacy in humbling a haughty spirit? Is then the policy of my church calculated merely to promote the pleasure and present comfort of its votaries, and to quiet and sooth the conscience, or to remedy the real evil of our fallen nature?"

I endeavoured to repress and banish these thoughts, which appeared to me almost blasphemous. I crossed myself, and looking up to the image of the Virgin, repeated the angel's salutation, "Hail thou that art highly favoured, the Lord is with thee, blessed art thou among women:" to which I added in Latin, "Hail, Mary, full of grace, the Lord is with thee; blessed art thou among women. Holy Mary, mother of God, pray for us sinners now and at the hour of our death.—Amen."

I had scarcely concluded this prayer, when a soft footfall sounded along the aisle, and turning round, I saw a small figure just entering through the narrow side door of the church. It was Aimée; she was dressed in white, and the air from without agitated her flaxen ringlets and snowy drapery as she advanced towards me, giving an almost ethereal lightness to her appearance. At one moment, as she passed under each archway, a deep shade was cast on her figure, and again a golden light was shed upon it, as she traversed those portions of the pavement on which the rays of the sun descended through the richly decorated windows above. The purity and beauty of this infant figure, together with the innocent expression of her gentle eye, as she ascended the steps of the little chapel at the door of which I was standing, and looked up to me half timidly, yet as it were in the noble consciousness of having nothing to conceal, suggested to my mind the idea of some blessed spirit just restored to its glorified body, and ascending from the grave to mount to that place of happiness which is prepared for the redeemed. The ideal resemblance was presently heightened in my imagination by the beautiful smile which illuminated every feature, and sparkled in her eye, as I extended my hand to her, and said solemnly, "The Saviour of men, and the Lord of angels bless my little girl, and as she is called the beloved on earth, may she be truly the beloved in heaven!" I then took my usual place, and invited her to confession, by asking her to account to me for the scene of the past night. This question led to many others, and in the end I obtained from the lovely child the following narrative of her short but till then comparatively perfect course, for indeed the words of the wise man could never have been more justly applied than to this blameless infant; "He being made perfect in a short time, fulfilled for a long time, for his soul pleased the Lord; therefore hasted he to take him away from among the wicked."

"I was born in England," said the sweet child; "I remember well my native place, it was a white house, and there were woods near it, and a garden full of flowers; the house stood on the side of a hill, and from the windows we saw flocks feeding in green fields, and blue hills at a distance, and villages and groves of trees, and the woods were so near us, that when the windows were open in the summer, we heard the wind rustling among the trees, and blackbirds and linnets singing in the branches, and waters rushing, and bees humming. My father used to bid me hearken to these sounds, and now I never hear sounds like these without thinking of my home. My parents were alive then, my dear father," continued the little girl, "and my mother, my kind mother, I remember her dressing-room, and her guitar and her cabinet. And I had a brother too, he was two years older than myself; he had golden hair, and soft bright eyes: and I had a very little sister too, and when she was asleep she looked like an angel; but she died first, and then, father (and the poor little girl burst into tears), then grief came; my little sister died, and my brother died—it was of a fever; and I was taken away and was never sent home again; and my parents are dead too, and I am here. I was brought to this place I know not wherefore, and I have no home in England to return to:" and the child wiped away a few tears, and then looked up again, as if awaiting my further questions.

"And are you happy here, Aimée?" I asked.

"Yes, father," she replied; "madame is very kind to me."

"And have you nothing to complain of?" I asked.

"None, father," she replied, "if I might have my book again."

"Why do you love that book so much?" I asked.

"It was my brother's," she replied; and she wept again. "May I not have it?"

"But it is not a proper book, Aimée," I said; "and I think you know that it is not proper, otherwise why did you go into a retired place to read it?"

"I always do," she answered.

"And why do you," I asked, "if you do not think you are doing wrong when reading that book?"

"Because nobody here cares for the things that are in that book," she answered, mildly; "and those are the things which make me happy."

"What things?" I asked.

"The things I learned when I was a baby. I cannot forget them;" she replied.

I again asked, "What things?"

"The things papa and mamma taught me, father," she answered.

"Please to explain yourself, Aimée," I said; "What things did your parents teach you?"

"They taught me that my heart is bad, sir, and that I can do nothing good without God's help."

"Go on," I said.

"And that God had sent his Son to die for me, and his Holy Spirit to make me good; and they taught me to read—and told me that I was to love my Bible, and follow all that is written in it."

"But how," I asked, "can a child like you understand the Bible?"

"I don't know, father," she meekly answered.

"Do you pretend to say that you do understand it?" I asked, and drew her near to me as I sat.

"I have not got a large Bible," she answered; "there are only small parts of the Bible in my little book; but even my little Bible tells me many pleasant things."

"What pleasant things, Aimée?" I asked.

"It tells me," she replied, "what my Saviour has done for me, and I find in it the promises of that happy world where I shall enjoy a home more pleasant than that which I have lost, and see my papa and my mamma, and my brother and sister again. And sometimes, when I have been reading that little book all alone in the garden, or wherever I can get unseen by any but the eye of God, I have had such sweet dreams and such delightful thoughts; I fancy I see the world in that time when Christ shall be King over all the earth. And then I fancy I see places like what I remember of my happy home, and my papa and my mamma, and brother and sister, all glorious like angels, and the Lord Jesus Christ in company with them, and I am so glad to see them happy, and every thing that is pleasant in this place brings these things fresher into my mind: and there is a valley, sir, in the forest, which I often visited last summer, which reminds me, too, of these things. And when I hear music, or the bells ringing, or the organ at mass, all these things fill my heart with pleasure, and make me wish that the time would come when I might go to my dear parents; but I know that I ought not to be impatient to leave this world, where you and madame and so many people are kind to me."

"You talk of much kindness, Aimèe," I said; "have you no unkindness to complain of? have you no feelings of malice or envy in your heart? you know that if you have such feelings it is your duty to confess them."

She looked very earnestly at me, and repeated the word malice, as if she did not understand its meaning, or at any rate as if she did not take in the purport of my question.

"To be plain with you, Aimée," I said, "are the young ladies your companions so kind to you that you never feel any thing like anger or ill-will towards them? are you in charity with every one?"

"They were cross with me last night, my father," she answered.

"And are they not so often?" I asked.

"I don't think they are," she replied.

"That is, you do not think much about them," I said.

"I do," she replied; "I love them, yes, I hope I love them."

"Then you have not perceived that they are unkind to you?" I added.

"Not to me particularly," she answered; "they sometimes quarrel a little among themselves; but is not that what we must expect? Are not our hearts bad, father, and do we not all do wrong at times? but when they are cross I think of my happy home, and then I do not mind it; and I have such delight sometimes when I am alone in my room and see the sun set, and think of that distant time when I shall be with my beloved Saviour, as I could not describe."

"Then it is because your mind is fixed on the world which is to come, that you do not enter into the quarrels of your companions. My little Aimée," I said, "if this be the true state of the case, you are a happy child indeed, happy and blessed beyond all the children I have ever known; and tell me, my little girl, how long your mind has been thus devoted to heavenly things?"

"I do not think that I am devoted to heavenly things," she replied; "for I am not good, and people who are devoted are good, I have heard madame say so; but it is now many months since my parents died, and since I lost my brother and sister, and from that time I have never had so much pleasure in any thing as in thinking of the time when I shall see my relations again; and I know that I never shall see them unless I love my Saviour, and am enabled to obey him; and these thoughts are always coming to my mind, and I cannot get rid of them."

"And why, my little fair one," I answered, "should you wish to get rid of them? Do they not make your happiness, and do they not mark your call to a holy life? But think you not, my daughter, that if you were to intercede with the holy Virgin and the blessed saints that they would join their prayers with yours, and that you might in this manner more easily obtain all that you desire?" and I pointed to the image above the altar, and directed the child to observe the mild and beautiful expression of the countenance of her whom I then called my Lady.

"That image cannot hear me," she replied.

"But she whom it represents, namely, the holy Mary, can and will hear you, Aimée," I answered: "she will unite her prayers with yours, in order that all you ask may be granted you."

"Was not she a woman?" said the little girl doubtingly.

"She was," I replied: "but as our Lord was truly God, so she, his mother, was the mother of God, and therefore is worthy that we should address our prayers to her."

The little girl looked down upon the pavement, but did not speak till I had repeated some part of what I had before said; she then lifted up her gentle eyes, and asked, "Do you pray to the saints, my father? Is it right to pray to them? My mamma told me that there is no other name under heaven by which we can be saved but that of our Lord Jesus Christ."

CHAPTER IV.

I HAVE before hinted that I had already had some little misgivings respecting the foundation of my faith; and at that instant such a gleam of light shot through my hitherto darkened soul, that I could not answer the child. I remained silent and confused, while the little one stood meekly before me, being wholly unconscious of my embarrassment. The tolling of the clock was at that moment heard from the tower of the church; I availed myself of it to say that I had an engagement which demanded my immediate attention, and bestowing a rapidly pronounced blessing on the little girl, I hastened from the church, assuring her that I would not only procure the little book for her, but obtain permission for her to study it whenever she pleased. I spent the remainder of that day in the solitude of my study. This little girl is a *heretic*, I said to myself; what our church indeed calls such; but there is no malice or bitterness in her heresy; she has not yet even discovered how widely our religion differs from her own, there is therefore no prejudice mingled in her mind with her prepossessions. She takes her faith entirely from the Bible, as she has been taught to do by her excellent parents; and surely, if the fruit is to prove the nature of the tree, we cannot doubt, from the beauty of the fruit which this dear child is able to produce, that the root is excellent. While meditating on these subjects, I took a dusty Latin Bible, which had once belonged to a priest of the church of Geneva from its shelf in my study, and began to compare its contents with the received doctrines of our church, and was struck with the comparison of Matthew xv. 19,—"Out of the heart proceed evil thoughts, murders, adulteries, fornications, thefts, false witness, blasphemies,"—with the following clause in our catechism, namely, "Is it possible to keep them all? (speaking of the commandments.) *Answer.* It is, by God's grace; Zacharias and Elisabeth were both just before God, walking in all the commandments of God without reproof." I felt more and more confounded while meditating on these things; and the result of these reflections was, that I resolved not to speak even to Madame Bulé of the heretical state, as I then apprehended it to be, of the little Aimée.

Under this embarassment of mind I remained in my study several days, or walked in the most solitary places I could find, meditating on many things. In the mean time, Susette and Fanchon having wiped away their offences, as they thought, by the repetition of the prescribed modicum of Ave Marias and Paternosters, returned, not in the least humbled thereby, to their usual situations in the school-room, where presently they failed not to administer fresh cause of dissatisfaction to each other, which being taken up by the parties on either side, the whole household was shortly again all in flames; and Madame Bulé found it more difficult than ever to set things in order. After various admonitions, all of which she found inefficient, the worthy lady sent a second time for me, and I undertook to admonish the young people in a discourse, which, accordingly, I delivered in an apartment of the house set aside for purposes of this kind, where I had formerly given many lectures on different subjects to the young people.

I took the text or motto of my discourse from the various beauties exhibited in a highly cultivated garden. "I understand, my daughters," I said, "that your minds have lately been painfully, and I may say sinfully agitated by envious feelings respecting each other, and by the vain desire of outshining and surpassing each other in those qualities which you esteem admirable in a human creature. Of the sinfulness of these feelings, my dear daughters," I continued, "I need not speak; but on their folly I will enlarge, inasmuch as it seems that you are not aware of this folly. The Almighty is not so partial a parent that he has not bestowed some beautiful and excellent quality on each of his children. Look at the flowers in that blooming parterre which extends itself beneath the window. Among these some attract the eye from a distance, some shed powerful odours in the air, some are endowed with healing qualities, some retire from the view and are only admirable when closely inspected; some excel in only one point; some in several, some in every quality attributable to the vegetable creation: but all are so exquisite in their way, so perfect in their conformation and their internal construction, that the utmost art of man would endeavour in vain to imitate the simplest, the most humble flower among them. Go forth into the forest and observe the leaves of the trees; compare them one with another; remark the delicacy of their texture, the infinite variety of their forms, and make a comparison, if it lies in your power, of the beauty of one with that of another; say, if you can, that one is worthy of admiration and another of contempt; that one is surpassingly fair and another despicably ugly. And such are each and all of you, my fair daughters; all and each of you have some beauty, some perfection, some lovely quality, external or internal, which sets you more on a par with each other than an inconsiderate observer would at first suppose: thus the rose of this parterre has no cause to triumph over the violet, neither has the tulip any occasion to envy the whiteness of the lily."

Having finished my exordium much to my own satisfaction, though I believe with little effect upon my audience, I withdrew, and that very evening met Madame Bulé at the chateau, where Madame la Baronne happening to mention that she intended to give an entertainment to the young ladies on the day of her fete (her birthday), Madame Bulé thought it necessary to tell her the state of her family as it regarded the jealousies and rivalries which subsist among her pupils.

Madame la Baronne smiled at this state of affairs, and after some reflection said, "Make my compliments to your young ladies, Madame Bulé, and invite them on my part to the chateau. Tell them that my fete this year is to be called the *Feast of the Flowers*, and that I shall expect each young lady to appear adorned with a garland or wreath of her favourite flower;" adding, "I shall bestow a crown on that young lady whose ornaments please me best; and lest," she added, "my taste should be disputed, there shall be a motto woven with the myrtle of which my crown is to be composed, which shall signify the rule by which I am to make my selection."

Madame Bulé assured Madame la Baronne that her message should be faithfully delivered; and I was very solicitous to know of the lady what was to be the import of her motto.

"I assure you, father," she replied, "that it shall be one you shall not dare to disapprove; but lest you should give a hint to some little favourite you may have, I cannot tell you." I was therefore obliged, after having shrugged up my shoulders several times, to acquiesce in my ignorance.

Madame Bulé did not fail to inform the young ladies of the kind invitation of the Baronne; and the next day, when these young people had concluded their morning exercises, an envoy was sent to request my company at the collation, in order that I might be consulted respecting preparations for the *Feast of the Flowers*.

As soon as I arrived, various questions were put to me by one and by another, to many of which I was not able to answer.

"To whom," said one, "does Madame la Baronne mean to give the crown; to the one who has the fairest garland, or to the one whom otherwise she likes best?"

"With respect to the beauty of the garland," I answered, "it might perhaps be hard to judge; tastes may differ; one person may think that no wreath can be compared to that which is formed of roses, while another perhaps might prefer a garland of jasmine as being more elegant."

"Then you do not suppose," said another of my inquirers, "that she will bestow the crown on her who has the fairest wreath?"

"Indeed I cannot tell," I replied.

"You are in the secret, we know, Father Raffré," said Mademoiselle Victoire; "we are sure of it."

"Well, it may be so," I answered; "but you shall none of you be the better for my knowledge. I will for once keep what I know to myself."

Mademoiselle would have been angry at this, had I cared for her anger; but as I did not, she proceeded to discuss the choice of the garlands with her favourite pupils.

Each one was, it was understood, to select a different flower, and the eldest chose first; Susette chose the rose; Fanchon would, she said, be royal, and adorn herself with the lily; a third selected the jasmine; a fourth the white thorn. The laurel, the honeysuckle, the sweet scented clematis, the convolvulus, and the orange-flower, were none of them forgotten; and as there was a fortnight to elapse before the day of the fete, great pains were taken to nourish and preserve such flowers as might then be required to add beauty and fragrance to the festival.

It was on the eve of the fete, as I was walking with Madame Bulé in one of the avenues of her garden, being deep in conversation on subjects which at that time exercised our minds, in common with many others —subjects which had indeed some tendencies to what our church would have deemed heretical; for my opinions on many of our doctrines were beginning to be more and more confused—when we suddenly heard several angry voices, proceeding from an arbour, in the centre of which was a circular range of seats where the young people often assembled during the hours of leisure. Standing still and looking through the openings of the trees, we saw several of the lesser children gathered round Aimée, who had formed a small wreath for her waxen baby from an azure flowering creeper which hung in festoons from an archway of lattice-work at the entrance of the arbour. The exclamations of rapture uttered by the lesser children had, it seems, attracted the attention of Susette, Fanchon, and several others of the larger girls; and Susette had expressed so much admiration of the wreath, as to declare that after all, Aimée had made the best choice, and that there was no wreath hitherto thought of that would prove so light and beautiful as that she had chosen. It was just at the moment she had uttered this opinion when madame and I stood to listen to what was passing.

"The little sly thing!" said Fanchon. "I doubt not but that she had a wreath of this kind always in her mind, and that she would not mention it, lest any of her elders should insist on taking it from her."

"If she had such an intention, she would have done well to wait a little longer," said Susette; "for it is not now too late for us her elders to change our minds. I am out of humour with the idea of wearing red roses; I have been thinking this very day that I should prefer another colour for my wreath; I like that beautiful azure, and I will wear it; and therefore, my little lady, you must please to look for some other ornament for yourself."

"I am content," replied Aimée, meekly: adding, "if you approve it, mademoiselle, I will help you to make your garland."

"And what will you wear yourself?" said Susette: "you shall, if you please, adopt the rose I have relinquished."

"I beg your pardon, Susette," said Fanchon; "there is no one who can come before me but yourself; you have given up the rose, and I claim it. I here give notice, that to-morrow I shall wear a garland of roses; and, as we are all to be different, no one else is to dare to assume even a rose-bud."

So violent an altercation then ensued between the rivals, that Madame Bulé thought it necessary to interfere; and requiring each of the rival ladies to declare the name of the flower she meant to adopt, she desired that no change of plans might henceforth be resorted to. She did not, however, insist upon the blue wreath being relinquished to Aimée, as I should have thought but just: it was evident that she was under some dread of Susette and Fanchon, and was afraid of provoking them too far; and it certainly was not my business to interfere, neither did I think the matter of sufficient consequence to induce me so to do.

Susette accordingly declared again for her wreath of roses, while Fanchon adopted that of the azure creeper, which was, in fact, a most elegant ornament. Madame and I then withdrew; but I had scarcely reached the garden gate on my way home, when I was overtaken by Aimée, who, placing her little hand within mine, said, "My father, you walk out, I think, every morning before breakfast."

"I do, my child," I answered.

"Will you permit me to accompany you to-morrow?" said the little girl. "I have obtained permission from madame. Will you take me to the forest?"

"Most willingly," I replied. "But for what purpose, my child?"

She smiled, and with a sweet innocent air, repeated these words of an ancient ballad of her own province:—

"The garden is gay with the gaudy weed,
And attired like the jewell'd queen;
But the flowers of the forest are fair indeed,
Though ofttimes doom'd to blow unseen."

The words, Charming little creature! what innocent device has that gentle bosom now conceived? were upon my lips; but I did not utter my thoughts, and simply answered, "I will be at the garden gate before six o'clock to-morrow morning, my little fair one; be sure that you are punctual."

The dew was still upon the herbage, and glistened on every leaf, as I knocked at the garden gate; it was opened to me at the first signal by the little maiden, and she ran out to me, all prepared for her appointment, with a neat basket in her hand.

"Good-morning, fair one," I said; "a blessing from above be upon my little girl! But whither are we to bend our steps?"

"To the forest, my father," she replied, "where I know of certain deep shades in which those flowers grow of which I wish to make my garland. I only feared that some other person might think of these flowers of the forest, which are my delight, and claim a first right to them, but they have not entered into the mind of any one; and now no one can take them from me."

"Oh! oh!" I said, smilingly, "you have, I see, been acting a cunning part, my little one."

"Cunning!" she repeated: "ah, Father Raffré, that is an ugly word; do not call me cunning. I would rather wear a wreath of asphodel than be called a cunning girl."

"And why not wear a wreath of asphodel?" I asked.

"Because it is bitter, very bitter," she replied; "but," continued she, "was there any harm in my thinking of a flower and not mentioning it, lest it should be chosen? I would not be cunning, indeed I would not, for the whole world; and I have no pretensions to that crown of myrtle which the lady is to bestow, indeed I have not; but I wished for my favourite flower for a very particular reason."

"What may be that very particular reason?" I asked.

"I will give you my reason, father," she answered, "when you have seen my favourite flower: but I must tell you that the discourse you made to us about a fortnight since was what led me to think of these things; and then I remembered a hymn which I had learned when I lived at my happy home, and some things which my dear papa taught me when I was a very little child; and I put all these things together, and when I heard of 'the feast of the flowers,' I then fixed upon the garland I should like to wear, though I did not suppose it would be left for me."

"Indeed, my Aimée," I answered, "you must be a little plainer before I can understand you; please to explain yourself; of what things did my discourse lead you to think? and how was what I said connected with what your father had taught you, and with the hymn you had learned? Please to explain all these matters to me."

"You compared us, sir," replied the little girl, "to so many flowers growing in the garden; and what my dear papa taught me when I was a little child was this, that the church of God in this world is compared in the Bible to a garden, in which grow all sorts of beautiful plants and flowers: he taught me the very verses, and I have not forgotten them."

"Repeat them, if you please, my dear child," I said: for, although I confessed it not, I knew so little of Scripture as to be utterly ignorant of that beautiful passage to which the child alluded. She immediately obeyed, and repeated what follows.

"'A garden enclosed is my sister, my spouse; a spring shut up, a fountain sealed. Thy plants are an orchard of pomegranates, with pleasant fruits; camphire, with spikenard; spikenard and saffron; calamus and cinnamon, with all trees of frankincense; myrrh and aloes, with all the chief spices; a fountain of gardens, a well of living waters, and streams from Lebanon.'" Song of Solomon iv. 12–15.

"Very beautiful," I replied, "and well remembered; but tell me who is it that is supposed to repeat this passage?"

She answered, "Our Saviour, sir; and he speaks it of his church."

"Then you imagine," I replied, "that the garden enclosed is the true church, and all the plants therein are the people."

"Yes, sir," she said; "those who love God are the plants growing in this garden, and some of them are tall and noble, like the cedar-tree, and others are small and of less beauty, others supply pleasant fruit, others are good only for shade, others are very lovely to look at, and others fill the air with sweet odours, but altogether they make the garden very beautiful, and none are to be despised."

"And do you suppose, Aimée," I asked, "that you yourself are one of the members of this garden?"

She hesitated a little, and at length said, "I desire to be one, and I hope I am; but I know that my place, if I have a place in this happy garden, is a very low one, down in some very deep valley, and under shade and out of sight. I think I should not do so well if I were to be removed to the higher parts of the garden, and clothed with many colours, and made to be an object of admiration; for when I am praised I become vain, and take less delight in holy things than when I am not noticed."

I was on the very point of commending the ideas of this little girl, when her last remark gave me a timely check, and I simply said, "Apparently, your parents took much pains to give you instruction."

"It was the Bible they used to make me understand," she answered; "and when they taught me any thing in the Bible they showed me something out of doors by which I was to remember it; and by this means, now that they are gone away, every thing almost which I see when I walk abroad reminds me of something I learned when I was a baby."

"That is," I said, "they took pains to associate natural with spiritual things, and by this beautiful mode of instruction they have succeeded in impressing their holy lessons so strongly upon your mind that you never can forget them. Let me tell you, my daughter, that you have reason to bless God for having given you such parents."

Two gentle tears dropped from her eyes as I spoke: and at the same moment my conscience reproved me for having bidden a child to thank God for having given her parents who were heretics! and then again such doubts arose in my mind respecting my own principles, and their foundation in truth, that I walked on a considerable way in silence.

CHAPTER V.

We had left the village and the chateau behind us, and were entering on the borders of the forest, before I extricated myself from the perplexing thoughts in which I was involved. At length, as we passed under the shade of the trees which skirted the wood, I recollected myself, and said, "Aimée, where are you leading me? How far are we to go?"

"Are you tired, father?" she said. "If you wish it, I will go no farther; I can make a wreath of any flower I see in the hedges."

"Tired, my dear child," I said, "tired in your company! No, little sweet one, I could take you by the hand and travel the world over with you! but you have raised some anxious thoughts in my mind. I have been considering what place I occupy in that garden of which we have been speaking." She made no answer. I know not what she thought, but she took my hand, and kissed it with a courtesy and tenderness which in one so young were peculiarly beautiful. I think she had a religious dread of flattering me on a subject so important, yet was anxious to show her gratitude and affection.

We passed on, and for the space of a quarter of a mile, pursued a beautiful path which leads through the centre of the wood. At length, coming to a spot where the shade was exceedingly thick, she pointed to a very narrow pathway which put itself into the road, and asked me if I should object to follow her. I knew the path, it led to a small but deep valley, at the bottom of which ran a pure cold stream; but I was surprised at its being so well known to the child, and asked her how she came to be so well acquainted with the windings of the forest.

"Last summer," she replied, "I was sent after an illness, for change of air, to a cottage in these woods, and then I learned to know where beautiful flowers grow, and sweet birds sing; and I have not forgotten these places," she added, smiling, and tripping lightly before me.

But my little guide in her glee had forgotten that where she could pass with ease, I, being taller and larger, would find a thousand obstacles. Accordingly, when she told me that she had but a very little way to go for the accomplishment of her object, I bade her hasten forward, while I followed at my leisure, and in consequence I soon lost sight of her; but still pursuing the same wild and tangled path into which she had led me, I presently arrived at a more open part of the forest, from whence I looked down upon a dingle, in the bottom of which was a pool, and on the side of the pool a sward, which, from its smooth deep green, intimated the moisture of the place. A ruined cottage, of which the gable-end and doorway alone remained entire, peeped out from amid the trees and underwood. The rays of the morning sun shot slantingly over the forest, and shed a flickering, trembling light on the whole scene, presenting the most beautiful varieties of light and shadow. This also was a place for the sweet singing of birds, and for balmy zephyrs, which, as they passed, produced that agitation of the leaves which, together with the rushing of a waterfall, heard but not seen, filled my senses with a degree of delight I had not often experienced. At the moment when I had reached the brow of the dell, my little guide appeared near the bottom, springing, like the gazelle, from one rude steep to another, and anon I beheld her stooping down to gather certain flowers which grew here and there on the greensward. The rude trunk of a tree near which I stood formed a convenient seat; I placed myself upon it, and quietly awaited the return of the little fair one. A quarter of an hour had hardly elapsed, when I saw her re-ascending the rocky side of the glen, and presently she stood before me, glowing with delight. At my feet she set her basket, which was filled with that lovely flower we call the muguet, better known by its more appropriate name the "lily of the valley."

"There, my father," she said, "there are the flowers which are to compose my garland; and those are the flowers I would choose for my device. The rose," added the little girl in high glee, "is the emblem of beauty, the laurel of glory, the heart's-ease of content, and the jasmine of innocence—but what are all these without my lily of the valley? Tell me, dear father, what is any good quality without humility?"

"Aimée," I said, in amazement and admiration, not only of the sentiments of this charming child, but of the elegant manner in which she expressed them,—"Aimée, my little one, who taught you all this?"

She looked innocently upon me, and said, "Papa and mamma used to instruct me in these things; it was poor papa who taught me that the lily of the valley was the type of humility, and sometimes when I pleased him he called me his lily. Ah, sir, I wish I were really like the lily; for the lily loves the cool valley and shadowy places by the streams of living waters."

"Sweet child," I answered, "you are indeed a lily of the valley. Would to God," and I crossed myself as I spoke, "would to God I were a lily too!"

"No, sir, no," she replied, "you shall not be a lily, but you shall be a noble tree, planted by the water-side, and I will dwell under your shade."

I was affected—I could not help it; the tear trembled in my eye; which the little girl observing, she stooped down and kissed my hand, at the same time taking up her basket. Having obtained what we wanted, we turned our steps towards our home, and as we went along we remarked other flowers growing in the forest; among these the wood anemone and the party-coloured vetch particularly attracted our attention, and we wondered that things so beautiful should have been formed in places where none saw and none admired; and this led me to speak of the infinite goodness of God, and of his bounty towards the children of men.

At length we reached our village, and parting at the garden gate, I retired to my study to examine the Holy Bible respecting those passages to which my little companion had alluded. And in that long quiet day, a day never to be forgotten by me, such convictions flashed upon my mind respecting the errors of my church, that before the evening hour I was almost, if not entirely, as much what my people would have called a heretic as I now am, although I had not yet made up my mind to acknowledge my belief, and give all up for the truth.

Scarcely had the ardent heat of the day subsided, when, according to appointment, I repaired to the chateau; where, having passed the avenue of linden-trees, which then extended from the gate of the domain to the lawn in front of the mansion, I entered upon a scene which chased away, for a time, the perplexing thoughts by which I had been agitated during the greater part of the morning. Figure to yourselves, my gentle readers, an ancient many-windowed stone mansion, whose fashion spoke of at least two centuries past, in the almost perpendicular roof of which were three tiers of windows, peeping out from the moss-covered tiles, closed with wooden shutters instead of casements. In the front of this ancient and in some respects dilapidated mansion extended the lawn, in the centre of which was a square marble basin, where a huge Triton spouted water from a cone to the height of many feet, affording rather the idea than the reality of freshness. On each side of the lawn, yet answering exactly to each other, a statue, an arbour, and an archway of trellis-work opening into certain gardens beyond, alternated with each other, according to the formal taste then prevalent in my country. The lawn was set forth with several long tables, covered with fruit, cakes, cream, and other refreshments; while on an elevated scaffolding near the centre of the open space was a band of musicians, who from time to time gave us a national air, while waiting the commencement of the dancing, which was to take place towards the end of the evening.

The company for whom this fete was prepared were, without exception, every inhabitant of the village who was able either to walk or be carried to the chateau, together with some superior persons from the neighbourhood, who had come by special invitation.—These, the superiors of the party, were, with the Baronne, grouped at the upper end of the lawn, sitting, standing, or moving about, as it suited them; the inferior persons being at the lower end, or in the centre, according to their stations in society, but all seemed equally gay and happy; I saw not a solemn countenance as I made my progress round the circle. I had almost omitted to describe a very important part of the show, whereat I much wonder, considering that it is the feast of the flowers to which I am endeavouring to bring my readers in imagination, and this was a statue on a pedestal which stood exactly in a line with the front of the house, at the bottom of the lawn. This statue was a female one, and therefore suited very well to serve as a representation of the goddess Flora; she was richly decorated with garlands and wreaths, and on her head was placed the crown of myrtle, through which was twisted an azure riband, on which a motto was wrought in threads of gold. The crown on the statue was pointed out to me by the persons who stood near it, and I attempted to decipher the motto, if such there might be, but I was not able, for the riband was so curiously and artificially twisted that I could only make out part of a word here and there, and was therefore obliged to rest in my ignorance.

The party were all assembled when I arrived on the lawn, with the exception of the family of Madame Bulé, but while I was paying my compliments to the Baronne on the arrangement of the scene, the excellent instructress and her numerous train appeared at the end of the avenue.

"There come our queens of the May," said the Baronne; and she ordered a beautiful and lively air to be struck up, while she advanced with the ladies and gentlemen of the party to meet the elegant procession. And elegant indeed it was; elegant, and gay, and various, and fragrant. First came Susette and Fanchon, the rival queens, all attired in white, and decorated, the one with rose-buds, the other with the azure creeper before mentioned; ribands of rose colour and of blue were mingled with the several garlands; the next pair were the acanthus and the laurel, with scarfs of green and purple; then came the fragrant hyacinth, and the auricula, the woodbine and the columbine adorned another smiling pair; and as each lovely couple passed by the group of ladies and gentlemen, they greeted and were greeted by smiles and courtesies, as gracefully bestowed and received as if the lawn had been a royal presence-chamber, and the Baronne a crowned head. As each lovely pair passed the Baronne the parties separated, and formed a variety of blooming and lovely groups around the company, meriting and receiving that admiration which was due to their smiling and charming figures, and the taste which each had displayed in the arrangement of her fragrant ornaments. The last of the procession was Madame Bulé herself, leading the youngest of her pupils and little Aimée by the hand: the exercise and excitement of the scene had given an extraordinary lustre to the complexion of my little favourite, yet her eyes retained their usually placid and gentle expression. She seemed to be attentive to what passed, and also pleased; but there was not that restless anxiety in her countenance which was remarkable in all those among her companions who thought they had any chance of obtaining the crown; her enjoyment of the scene was therefore as unmixed as it had been when she was gathering her favourite flowers in the depths of the forest. She, like the rest of her companions, was attired in white, and with no other head-dress than those clustering ringlets which, together with the delicate tincture of her skin, marked her Saxon ancestry. She had formed a lovely garland of her lilies, having woven them together with a band of light-green ribands, tied on her right shoulder with a knot, and falling under her left arm. I saw the eyes of the Baronne rest upon this lovely child for a moment; but as soon as Madame Bulé dropped her hand, she receded into the background, and her elegant form was soon wholly shrouded by the more splendid figures of her companions.

Our nation are remarkable for being able to pay a compliment with grace and delicacy; and what occasion, I would ask, could have administered fairer opportunities of doing this with truth than the present? Neither were the gentlemen, or even the ladies, then present, slow in availing themselves of these opportunities; every comparison or simile in which flowers have any concern was called forth on the occasion, and the exhilaration of the moment enabled even the most dull to do this with effect. But did I say dull? What Frenchwoman was ever dull in a scene such as the lawn then presented?

"Your Feast of the Flowers, Madame la Baronne," said the Viscomtesse de T——, "is splendid, is superb—it surpasses all I could have conceived of a thing of the kind. Yet I cannot say that these elegant garlands add beauty to these charming young ladies; I would rather say that these flowers derive new splendour from the beauty of those who wear them." And she appealed for the confirmation of her assertion to the Comte de S——, one of the few specimens then remaining of the court of Louis XVI.

Being thus called upon, the old courtier endeavoured to produce some compliment of a superior nature to that of the lady, and asserted, that the roses were grown pale, and the jasmines yellow, for envy, to find that their bloom and sweetness were entirely surpassed by those who had chosen them for ornaments.

This species of light and trifling conversation had proceeded for some time, when the Baronne took her place beneath the statue, and, having commanded the band to cease their strain, caused the crown to be handed to her; while, by the direction of Madame Bulé, the young ladies formed a half-circle around her, the rest of the company, of whatever degree they might be, gathering close in the back-ground.

There was a momentary pause and dead silence in the company, while a servant climbed upon the high pedestal of the statue and carefully lifted the crown from the head. It was then delivered into the hands of the Baronne, and as I stood next to her, I saw that it was a beautiful thing; it was not of real myrtle, which would presently have faded, but was an imitation of myrtle, the leaves being formed of foil, the flowers of gold and mother-of-pearl, and the berries of coral; it was beautifully executed, and the motto, in letters of gold wrought on a blue riband, twisted into the wreath. The Viscomtesse de T——, who stood on the right-hand of the Baronne, as I did at the left, would have taken it for a moment into her own hands, exclaiming, "Permit me, madame; ah, how beautiful! it is perfectly captivating!" But the Baronne would not part with it from her hand, nor suffer the golden letters on the blue riband to be read.

"I am, I feel," she said, "in a perilous situation; I am about to make a choice amid so many beauties, that I shall be in danger of incurring the odium of possessing a bad taste in still rejecting the most worthy, let my choice fall where it will; and I therefore have nothing but my motto to depend upon to extricate me from this difficulty: therefore none must see my motto till I choose to show it myself."

The Baronne then paused and looked around her, and as her eye ran along the lovely circle, I saw that several of the young ladies changed colour, especially the two at the head, namely, Susette and Fanchon; and such was indeed the charming bloom of one of these young ladies, and the elegance of the other, that I never doubted but that the crown would be adjudged to one of them.

"You are at a loss, madame, I see," said the Comte de S——, "and I cannot wonder at your embarrassment; there are so many beautiful figures in this circle, that it would be very difficult to say to whom the golden apple ought to be given."

"Pardon me," replied the lady, in a voice which, though low, was so distinct as to be heard by all present, "but you have mistaken my intention.—It is not to the most beautiful or the most accomplished, the fairest or the ruddiest, the most witty or the most discreet, that my crown is to be given; but to her who, in my opinion, understands how to select the most becoming ornament."

"So far we understand madame," said the Abbé, "nor would we be so impolite as to question your taste. Madame la Baronne can never be supposed to judge amiss in the eyes of persons of discernment, but perhaps we may not all here present be persons of discernment, and madame has undertaken to render every person in this company satisfied with her decision, and she depends upon her motto to stop the mouths of every one. Indeed, madame, unless your motto is a very extraordinary one, I do declare" (and he shrugged up his shoulders and smiled) "you are in great peril. I am, I confess, in great pain for you, madame."

"Well, then, my friend," replied the Baronne, "I will hasten to place you at ease. Ladies and gentlemen, you shall hear my motto, and I am assured that no one here present will dispute its authority when I assure them that it is divine, and that it is taken from the Holy Scriptures." So saying, she untwisted the riband from the myrtle crown; and stating that the passage was addressed by St. Peter to his female converts, she proceeded to read it in a soft, yet clear and distinct voice: it was to the following effect:—"Whose adorning let it not be that outward adorning of plaiting the hair, and of wearing of gold, or putting on of apparel; but let it be the ornament of a meek and quiet spirit, which is in the sight of God of great price." 1 Peter iii. 3.

CHAPTER VI.

When the Baronne had ceased to read, she looked up, and her eyes were directed to Aimée. "The lily of the valley," she said, "is the acknowledged emblem of humility; this sweet flower conceals its beauties within its verdant covering; it is spotless, pure, and fragrant; its leaves have a cooling and healing influence; it loves retirement and shade, yet when brought to view is exquisitely lovely. The lily, therefore, I must consider as the best chosen ornament for a youthful female, and therefore I must adjudge my crown to her that wears the lily."

There was a murmur of applause throughout the assembly on this decision, and every eye was fixed on the little girl, who came blushing forward at the command of the lady.

"Aimée," said the Baronne, as the lovely child bowed humbly before her, "I rejoice that I can, with a sincere feeling of love and esteem, bestow on you this simple preference; your character has long been known to me, and the purity, humility, and harmlessness of your conduct, since you entered the family of Madame Bulé, have not only been noticed by me, but have filled me with admiration. In those talents and external qualities which are pleasing in our sex you have many equals now present, and you will thoroughly understand, that the regard I now express has no reference to these qualities; it is your humility and your holy harmlessness, your exemption from envy, and your freedom from bad passions, which constitute your chief and crowning ornament, even that ornament which is above all price."

So saying, she raised the myrtle crown above the head of Aimée, and was about to place it there, when the little girl, bending low and falling on one knee, in a manner which I thought exceedingly graceful, raised her lovely eyes to the lady and said, "Ah, madame, could I wear that crown I should prove to all here assembled what is but too true, that I have not deserved it. I desire, indeed, to be like the lily; but I am not so. I know my own heart; I know that it is full of evil passions, and if I do not betray these evil passions so often as I feel them, it is not to my own strength I dare to give the glory. My dear lady, do not put the crown upon my head."

There was a dead silence in the assembly, every one was impressed with a solemn feeling: at length it was broken by the lady, who said, while holding the myrtle wreath over the head of the kneeling child, "Aimée, my beloved, indeed you must not resist our united entreaties, you must submit to wear the honour you have so justly merited."

"Ah, no, lady, dear lady!" she replied, lifting up her face as she knelt, with a sweet and unaffected earnestness; "no, no! it cannot be;" and at the same time gently removing the garland of lilies from her shoulders and laying it on the grass at the Baroness's feet. "I am neither worthy to wear the lily nor the crown; sweet lady, place the crown upon the garland, and then I will endeavour to merit both; at least," she added, "if not in life, yet perhaps in death, for then—then I shall be——." But we could not catch the last part of the sentence, for the little girl was unable to speak clearly, by reason of her tears.

"Aimée! lovely Aimée! sweet, sweet child! you have conquered," exclaimed the Baronne, laying the crown at her feet upon the garland, and then coming forward, she embraced the child, and wept as she pressed her to her heart.

It was an awful feeling that impressed the company at that moment; the tear was in every eye. The Abbe whispered to me, "Heaven have mercy upon me a sinner! If that child thinks herself impure in the eyes even of her fellow-creatures, what am I in the sight of God!" and he crossed himself. I heard expressions of the same nature from many mouths; and Susette pleased me much, by assuring me that she now felt ashamed of herself and of her own vainglorious opinions of her merits.

It is hardly necessary that I should assure my reader that the conduct of Aimée on this and on all other occasions evidently showed that there was no art or affectation in her conduct—no pretence of humility which she did not actually feel, but really a deep and heartfelt sense of her own unworthiness, and an utter disregard of what effect might result from her conduct, or what impression it might make on those who were present. I mention this, for although it is a lovely thing to see *true* humility in a child; nothing is more displeasing to God, or more offensive to those of our fellow-creatures whose minds are well regulated, than to perceive attempts to display a humility which is not really felt.

In the mean time the Baronne ordered the garland and crown to be carried to the church, and to be placed in the Lady chapel there; and it was some time before the assembly could so far divest themselves of their serious feelings as to enter into the amusements of the evening. As to myself, I must confess that it was during that evening that I for the first time made any serious reflections on the violence which the mind suffers in being drawn from solemn feelings into those which are merely earthly, and the contrary; and I was led to think that human wisdom consisted in avoiding those excitements of earthly pleasure by which the feelings more suited to our state as dying creatures are rendered distasteful and uncongenial to our minds.

After the Feast of the Flowers, several months passed during which nothing particular took place in our private circle worthy of record.

During this period our minds were much agitated by public affairs; that dreadful revolution, so awful in its progress and so wonderful in its effects, had commenced. The capital was already in confusion, but we in the provinces still only heard the thunder rolling in the distance.

In the mean time, the remainder of the summer and the whole of the autumn and winter passed away. In the middle of the winter I was seized with a rheumatic complaint, which confined me to my bed till towards the end of spring. During this period a friend undertook my duty, and I saw little of my people; my Bible was, I thank God, my constant companion at that time, and the reading thereof, I have reason to think, was blessed to me in a degree which can hardly be conceived. It was thought, however, necessary when I left my bed that I should change the air, and accordingly I was carried from my bed to the chaise which was to convey me to the house of a married sister, who lived not very far from Rouen; there I remained two months, but at the end of that period was much distressed by letters from the Baronne, who informed me that a contagious disorder had broken out with violence in the house of Madame Bulé; that many of the children were very ill, and that our little Aimée was in peril of her life.

It was very late in the spring when I received this news, and as my health was nearly re-established, I lost no time, but hastened back to my flock—that flock which I was destined soon to quit under the most painful circumstances, and to quit for life; for the door of my restoration to my former place is for ever shut against me—my principles would now be held in abhorrence by those who loved me formerly—nor could I, even if permitted, now take a part in services of whose idolatry I have been long assured. But no more of this: it has no doubt been good for me and for others of my countrymen, that their ancient ties have been dissolved—ties which bound us to the world and to a false religion, and which we should never have had strength to break by our own efforts.

It was a glorious evening in the end of May when I arrived within view of my own village, from which I had been absent many weeks. I had quitted the public vehicle in which I had travelled, on the opposite bank of the Seine, and having crossed the river in a small boat, I proceeded on foot the short remainder of my journey. As soon as I left the boat I was in my own parish, I was in fact at home, and I was making my way along an embowered pathway towards the village, when I overtook a decent peasant in her best apparel going the same way. To my inquiry, "How is it with you, neighbour Mourque? How are all our friends?" she replied, "Ah! Father Raffré, we have lost one of our fairest flowers, and I am now going to see the last duties paid to her blessed remains."

"Our flowers," I repeated; "not my lily, I trust; is it Aimée who is no more?"

"It is, sir," she replied; "and when I last saw her at the chateau I thought the little angel would never live to enjoy another fete; such as she, father, are not for this world—nay, her own very words, when she refused the crown and spoke of what she should be, proved to me how it would be, and others said the same. But the crown and the garland, are to be placed on her coffin, sir; the garland indeed is withered and shrunk, but the crown is not made of such things as can fade, they tell me; but it will be a touching spectacle, and surely, sir, there will not be many absent from the church this evening who were at the lady's feast of flowers."

I was so affected that I could not speak: so the good woman proceeded without interruption.

She informed me of many things concerning the sickness and death of the dear child; and of the grief of the Baronne and of Madame Bulé, who both together, as she said, waited on the dear child day after day and night after night; and she told me how she had prayed while her senses had been continued to her, and how she had again and again called upon her Saviour, and spoken of her hope of being speedily taken to him who had died for her—and how she had expressed her love for her instructress and the lady of the chateau, and her tender regard for her school-fellows—"but," added the peasant, with some emotion of manner and some expression of regret, "it is a grief to me to think that the poor child was so insensible when the priest attempted to administer the last sacrament, that she knew nothing of what passed; she was as insensible to the holy anointing as a lifeless babe; neither did she take the smallest notice of the holy cross which was held before her—the Lord, have mercy on her soul! I am thinking, father, could she have been a heretic? Was she not from England?"

"Ah!" I said, "was it so? 'tis true, she was from England."

The woman started at the manner in which I spoke, and looked anxiously at me, saying, "Do you doubt, sir? do you doubt of her final happiness?"

I interrupted her, "Ah! would to God," I answered, "that I were as blessed and happy as that dear child now is! On whom did she call in her dying hours, whom did she live only to please, to whom did she give all the glory, but unto the only true Saviour—He who is above all saints and angels, the God incarnate, He by whom alone the sinner can be saved."

The poor woman crossed herself as I spoke, and assented to my assertion.

"Blessed little lamb!" I exclaimed, "and art thou gathered to the fold of the only true Shepherd? Sweet lily of the valley! and art thou removed to a more congenial soil? but who shall fill the place which thou hast left?"

At that instant the tower of the church broke upon my view as we turned an angle of the road, and a distant sound of choral harmony burst upon my ear. I was ashamed of it, but I could not help it; I burst into tears and wept like a child. I did not know till that moment how dear the orphan Aimée was to my heart. I roused myself, however, and walked on, and a few steps brought me to the entrance of the village street, and in full view of the western front of the church, the great door of which being open, I could distinguish the crowd within, and hear the soft melody of the human voice attuned with the full-toned organ within, in such a chant, so solemn, so touching, so sublime, as seemed to raise my mind above all earthly feelings, and make me (I was about to say) desire to be with my Aimée, absent from the body and present with my Lord. As I advanced I perceived that all the houses in the street were deserted, and the deep silence which reigned amid these dwellings enabled me to hear the requiem more clearly and more distinctly.

At length, as I passed under the doorway of the church, I found myself in a crowd, not only of my own parishioners, but of persons from the neighbouring villages who had assembled on this solemn occasion; however, way was immediately made for me, and I advanced towards the high altar, before which was the coffin of my beloved Aimée, covered with a white pall, and beyond it, in a semicircle, stood all her former companions. But there, in that sad hour—sad for us who remained, yet most blessed for her who was gone—were no garlands of roses, no flaunting ribands, no gaudy attire; each fair young creature wore a long white veil; and even the once blooming cheeks of Susette were pale with grief and moist with tears—nay, the very levity of Mademoiselle Victoire had given way on this affecting occasion, and she stood a monument of silent wo. Ah! did she not remember then all her cruel behaviour towards the gentle child whose cold remains were stretched before her?

On the white pall lay the faded garland of the lily of the valley; an affecting emblem of her who had plucked those flowers and woven that garland, affecting to all, yet how much more so to me, who so well remembered the gay delight of the holy little fair one when she had obtained the object of her innocent and elegant desires—an emblem consecrated by holy writ, which says, "As for man, his days are as grass; as a flower of the field, so he flourisheth; for the wind passeth over it and it is gone, and the place thereof knoweth it no more." Psalm ciii. 15, 16. No eye looked up when I approached the altar, though all, as I afterward found, had been aware of my presence. I came up near to the coffin at the moment when the last note of the requiem was dying away along the vaulted aisles, and at the same instant Madame la Baronne came forward with the myrtle crown in her hand. The garland had been formed of perishable materials, but not so the crown—as compared with the garland of lilies, at least, it was imperishable—it was fresh and fair as it had first appeared; it thus formed a beautiful emblem of that "crown of glory which fadeth not away;" and it was an emblem which all present understood, though no one spoke to point it out. It was laid upon the coffin over the faded garland by the Baronne herself, and when she had stopped to kiss the pall, Madame Bulé and all her pupils stepped forward to follow her example; after which the service proceeded, and the remains of our little beloved one were consigned to the dust in the vault of the family of the chateau.

I remained alone in the church when all the congregation had withdrawn, and it was then that I solemnly resolved to renounce the vanities in which I had been educated, and, with the Divine help, to quit all earthly considerations to follow the truth as it is stated in the Holy Scriptures, unto all extremities to which my abandonment of the Church of Rome might reduce me.

I was speedily strengthened in this resolution by the afflictions of my country, and forced by persecution to fly from that land in which under more prosperous circumstances I might have been again involved in the mazes of error and of death.

And here I close my little narrative, leaving my Aimée to rest in her cold grave in a distant land.

This lily of the valley was indeed nipped ere yet it had attained its perfect growth; its stem was cut down to the earth while yet its flower was in the bud; but the root has not perished; it lives still beneath the sod, and in the morning of the resurrection it shall be translated from the wild forest of this world to the garden of our Lord, where it will bloom with a celestial lustre, and enjoy a never-fading verdure. The grass withereth, the flower fadeth; but the word of our God shall stand for ever: and blessed are the dead that die in the Lord.

The lilies of the field,
  That quickly fade away,
May well to us a lesson yield,
  Who die as soon as they.

Then let us think of death,
  Though we are young and gay;
For God, who gave us life and breath,
  Can take them both away.

THE END OF THE FLOWERS OF THE FOREST.

JULIANA OAKLEY.

JULIANA OAKLEY.

CHAPTER I.

Some account of her Parents and Family—Her Father goes abroad, and she is sent for by her Grandmother—Her Journey with Mrs. Bridget to Hartley Hall—Arrival there; and introduction to the old lady, Uncle Barnaby, and Cousin Cicely.

Although it has pleased my heavenly Father to protract my life to an advanced age, and although, during that period, among a thousand experiences of his tender love and paternal care, I have been made to pass through many scenes of trial, in the various characters of wife and mother; yet there are certain scenes of my childhood, of which I retain so affecting a recollection that I cannot think of them even to this day without tears. But inasmuch as that I would willingly caution others from falling into such errors as those which to this moment imbitter some of the remembrances of my girlish days, I shall enter into a detail of the particulars to which I allude, and for this purpose must make my reader acquainted with many of the circumstances of my early life.

The person who will fill up one of the most important places in my history is my grandmother. She was an heiress, and was in her bloom so far back as the reign of George I. She married early, and was left a widow with two children soon after her marriage. I know not what sort of a person her husband was, nor am I acquainted with any particulars respecting him, excepting that he wore, on occasion, a full-bottomed wig, and a coat and waistcoat richly trimmed with gold lace, in which costume he was painted at three-quarters length, and made no despicable figure in his gilt frame, over the fireplace in the great drawing-room at Hartley Hall.

I never could perceive that my grandmother suffered

much from the loss of her husband. She was a woman of too high and independent a spirit to be very happy in a married state, and therefore, though often solicited to change her situation by a second marriage, could never be brought to listen to any overtures of the kind; but, after her husband's death, devoted the remainder of her youth, and her more mature years, in performing the office of her own steward, seeing that her maids did not neglect their spinning-wheels, and putting out her savings on the best securities.

In the mean time, though counted one of the most prudent women of her time, and held up as a pattern of good management, it appears that it never entered into her head, that there could be any means of promoting the well-being of her children more effectual than that of increasing their future properties. This being the case, my uncle and mother were left wholly without education, excepting what my grandmother's maid and the butler could supply; with the occasional assistance of the curate of the village, who sometimes gave my uncle a few lessons in the rudiments of Latin; and assisted my mother in certain rude attempts, which she now and then made, to write joining-hand in such a manner as should be legible.

In the mean time, these young people, being perpetually left to themselves, made the servants their constant companions: and while my poor mother was romping with the maids in the housekeeper's room and the kitchen, my uncle found store of amusement in the stable and dog-kennel. It may be asked how it was possible for a clever woman like my grandmother, and one who was so particularly attentive to some of her duties, to be thus careless of her children, and thus blind to their real interest; but the state of the case is this, that, independent of the blindness with respect to their children, too commonly seen in parents in these days of comparative light, education was not then understood as it is now; added to which consideration, children were at that time kept at so great a distance by parents, that the latter had not the opportunities which they now have, of studying and examining their characters: and hence were liable to be deceived by them in a degree which can hardly be believed in the present state of things.

But not to dwell any longer on this subject, which is

not altogether to my present purpose, I shall shortly state that this education, such as I have described it, failed not to produce the effects which might be expected: my uncle, when grown up, was fit only to be the companion of his own gamekeeper or coachman: and my mother married, early in life, so very imprudently that my grandmother would never forgive her, and, indeed, could never be prevailed upon to see her again. What my father's situation was when he married my mother, I know not; but a commission in a marching regiment was bought for him by my mother's family, immediately after his marriage: and when I can first recollect any thing, I was living with my parents in that unsettled state to which persons are liable who make the army their profession.

I have an exceedingly confused idea of the years that passed before I was twelve years old. The number of scenes which I went through—the number of persons I became acquainted with—the multiplicity of faces which passed before me—the extraordinary variety of shabby lodgings, apartments in barracks, tents, and inns, in which I lived with my parents, for days, weeks, or months, as it might happen—the perpetual interchanges and successions of soldiers' wives, wearing felt hats, and gilt earrings, who performed the parts of my mother's waiting-maids and my governesses, during this period, have left such a medley of ideas in my mind, that it would be almost an Herculean labour to attempt to reduce them to any thing like order or regularity. Suffice it to say, that, during this time, the regiment in which I was born was stationed, for the most part, in some of the most remote and wild districts of the Highlands of Scotland; and in those parts of western Ireland whose shores are for ever invaded by the waves of the stormy Atlantic; and where the shrieks of the sea-gull among the rocks convey to the superstitious natives such ideas as fill the gossips' tale with images of horror and amazement.

Sometimes, indeed, we were removed, for a season, from the solitary forts and garrisons which are found in these situations, to certain little country towns, in different parts of the United Kingdom; and then, though quartered in small, inconvenient, and often sordid lodgings, these situations were commonly so abundant in opportunities of amusement to my mother, and the ohter ladies of the regiment, that I was commonly more neglected than usual when in stations of this kind.

At length the regiment was ordered to Gibraltar; on which occasion my grandmother sent over her own maid to Dublin, where we were then stationed, with a handsome present to my mother, together with a request that I should be delivered to her charge.

I do not recollect that any objection was made by either of my parents to this arrangement of my grandmother's; but, as I had been hitherto allowed to run almost wild, a great bustle was made in order to prepare me for a decent appearance in the presence of the old lady, who was known to be very eagle-eyed, with respect to such matters as affect externals.

On this occasion I was taken from the hands of the sergeant's wife, who happened at that period to be my mother's confidential servant, and was fitted with a pair of stiff stays, directed to hold up my head and drop my shoulders; and was provided with a brocade slip, a hoop petticoat, and other suitable ornaments.

These things being prepared, I was led by my parents to the bay, and there embarked in a packet with Mrs. Bridget, my grandmother's maid; who, by-the-by, appeared to me to be the finest lady I had ever seen in my life. I have no recollection of what I felt when I parted from my parents, nor can I distinctly call even their persons to mind; this probably arose from my having been less intimately associated with them than with their servants. For although I have so faint a recollection of the authors of my being, the figure of the sergeant's wife, as she stood upon the pier looking after us, while the sailors put off with me to the packet, is still as present with me as if I had seen it only yesterday. She was an Irish woman, from the province of Connaught, and might have been tolerably good-looking had she not had hair of a carroty red, with abundance of freckles. She was dressed in a man's beaver hat, and man's shoes and stockings, having no cap, and her hair in part turned up with a comb, the rest hanging about her ears. She wore a short blue petticoat and jacket, with a woollen apron, the corner of which she held up to her eyes, as she called after me with a piercing voice, to bid me adieu, denominating me her jewel, her darling, and precious life.

I remember, that I looked upon her with tears in my

eyes, till I was lifted out of the boat, and put up tne side of the packet, where such a variety of novel objects presented themselves that I probably soon forgot my sorrow. Thus closed my military career, and the first period of my childhood. A favourable wind soon wafted the packet over to the shores of England, and, in a few hours after my separation from my parents, I found myself in a post-chaise with Mrs. Bridget, on my way to Hartley Hall.

I do not precisely remember how I first opened a conversation with Mrs. Bridget, for whom I had conceived a very high respect; but I well recollect, that before we had advanced far on our road, in the manner I have described, she began to hint to me that it would be necessary for me to lay aside many practices in which I had hitherto allowed myself. "For instance, miss," she said, "you must not pick your teeth with your fingers, as you have seen those wild Irish do; nor stoop your head till your ears and shoulders salute each other; nor sit as you now do, kicking your feet and scratching your head; but you must behave like a pretty miss and a young lady, and hold yourself proper; and be sure never cool your tea in your saucer, and then blow it, as you did this morning at the inn." Much more, to the same purpose, did Mrs. Bridget say to me; but it so happens that the memory, which of all our faculties is the most capricious, will not assist me to detail any more of her injunctions; and, indeed, it is almost marvellous that I should have recollected so many, inasmuch as my reader will see that they were not delivered with any manner of attention to system or order; but that small and monstrous offences against propriety were weighed in the same balance, and placed together in the same forcible point of view.

But to go on with my history: this, my first lecture, continued till we were arrived at the place where we were to sleep. We travelled the whole of the next day, and expected to reach Hartley Hall before six o'clock on the following evening.

When, on the last day of our journey, we stopped at the town which was only one stage from my grandmother's, Mrs. Bridget took me apart, dressed me in the clothes which had been prepared by my mother, for my appearance before the old lady, and repeated all her injunctions respecting my behaviour; taking this occasion to impress upon my mind that which she had repeatedly said to me during my journey, viz. that my grandmother was a lady of high respectability—that my family was of more consequence than any untitled family in the country—that although I had hitherto lived in an humble way, I was a young lady by birth, and would probably inherit a large fortune—that she had been ashamed to see me in the hands of such a low person as my late servant—that a waiting-woman was not fit to serve a lady, unless she had something smart and polite in her deportment, and had received the education of a gentlewoman; and that henceforth she hoped I would be above familiarity with low persons, but would behave myself genteel, and with suitable dignity, according to my rank.

In this manner I was tutored by the waiting-maid, and, inasmuch as feelings of pride are by no means incompatible with the grossest ignorance, and the utmost habitual coarseness of mind, I was by no means backward in inhaling the ideas which Mrs. Bridget desired to convey to my mind; and thus I soon found in myself every disposition to become as fine a lady as my new friends could wish me to be.

The waiting-lady's lecture and my toilet were scarcely concluded, before the arrival of my grandmother's coach-and-four at the inn; and I, who but a few days before had been glad of the attendance of an Irish sergeant's wife, was handed into this handsome carriage by a smart footman.

We made the last stage of our journey with such rapidity that I was quite surprised when Mrs. Bridget pointed out to me the family seat, as seen at a distance. It stood on a slight elevation, in the centre of a plain, and was surrounded by woods, the approach being through a long avenue. The house itself was of brick, and extended itself in two large wings, conveying the idea of that kind of splendour which proceeds from magnitude.

When we came to the porter's lodge, at the entrance of the avenue, and began to approach through the grounds towards the house, I remember that I could not contain myself any longer, but broke out into some expression of admiration; whereby I again brought upon myself the reproaches of Mrs. Bridget, who told me that nothing in the world was so vulgar as to seem full of wonder and amazement. "It looks just," said she, "as if a person came out of a wood, or had never seen any thing decent or genteel in their lives before. Do, dear miss," she added, "do, I pray, keep your wonder to yourself, let what will happen, or the very footman will be sneering and making a jest of you."

I promised my tutoress that I would endeavour to obey her; nevertheless, I found so much to gape at when I alighted from the coach, that I imagine I gave but a bad specimen of my tractability in this particular.

The approach to the door of the hall was by a very high and wide flight of steps, and the hall itself was an immense room, having a staircase at each end; the walls being set forth on all sides with paintings, all of which had some reference to rural sports. Among these was a specimen of that exquisitely elegant and touching design so often exhibited in old collections, to wit, that of a dead hare, hanging up by the heels, and a number of pheasants and partridges lying, without life, in the fore-ground. There, also, were the figures of certain favourite dogs and horses, which had belonged in times past to some of my ancestors; and an immense family picture, in which my grandmother herself, in her younger days, was represented in a laced joseph and jockey-cap, leading a fox-hunt, accompanied by all her male relations, each of them mounted on some favourite horse, and cutting and spurring over hill and dale, moss and moor, like the heroes of Chevy Chase. The chimney ornaments of this large apartment, for there was an immense fireplace at one end of it, consisted of bucks' horns, foxes' heads, and old fowling-pieces. Such were the curiosities of this apartment; but I was not allowed to examine them at that time, but was led forward by Mrs. Bridget to a large parlour at the farther end of this hall, where I was introduced into the august presence of my grandmother.

The parlour itself was boarded and wainscoated with oak, which was considerably imbrowned with age, and embellished with a cornice of the same, curiously and richly carved, representing buds, flowers, and ears of corn, whimsically grouped together in a kind of running pattern. The floor of this room was bright as a looking-glass, and the windows, though large, were casements in stone frames; the grate was highly polished, and filled with boughs of yew-tree, although the weather was sufficiently cold; for my grandmother never allowed a fire to be lighted in any other part of her house than the kitchen before a certain specified day of the year, and until that period arrived, it was dangerous for any one to complain of being chilly under her roof, as the old lady was exceedingly tenacious of her own ways and opinions, and never failed to take such complaints, however delicately expressed, as censures of her management.

But to return to my story. At a small table, in the centre of this large, cold, and comfortless room (for such it appeared to me, as I was led into it by Mrs. Bridget) sat my grandmother. She was richly dressed in a laced headdress, a large hoop, a rich silk gown, and long ruffles; having before her on the table a large gold snuff-box, and a pair of spectacles; opposite to her, at the same table, sat a thin, tall, starched figure, whom I afterward found to be a poor cousin, who filled up the complicated parts of companion, flatterer, and tea-maker to my grandmother, being one who would bear any thing, by which she might obtain the privilege of eating a good dinner every day, and now and then taking an airing in a coach-and-four.

My grandmother appeared to be holding forth, with no small vehemence, on some subject by which she was strongly interested, at the moment when I entered; but on my cousin calling out, " Oh, madam, here comes pretty little miss," she ceased to speak, put on her spectacles, and, holding her hand out to me, encouraged me to come up to her, saying, "And so, Bridget, you are earlier than I expected. Come, my dear, give me a kiss—you are welcome to Hartley Hall."

I had by this time conceived so high an opinion of my grandmother, that I was considerably frightened when she drew me to her to kiss me, and failed not to avail myself of the first opportunity which offered itself of making my retreat to the other side of the table, where Mrs. Bridget was still standing, and waiting to answer such questions as her lady might choose to put to her.

And now, my reader, you may picture us all, as we were assembled around the table. My grandmother, in the first place, seated in her arm-chair, dressed as I have before described her, and retaining such spirit, and even dignity of countenance, as proved that she had long been in a situation of command. My cousin Cicely sitting at her right-hand, being a tall, thin, elderly maiden, dressed in my grandmother's cast clothes, and plying her needle with much diligence, while she from time to time stole a look at me, and then at my grandmother, uttering exclamations in confirmation of every opinion expressed in her presence. In addition to these, you may fancy Mrs. Bridget, who, in the presence of my grandmother, was all obsequiousness, and in consequence fell much in my opinion. And to finish the group, picture to yourself my figure, richly dressed in my new suit, which was standing on end with large flowers, and from terror and amazement bringing into one point of view almost every awkward trick I had ever learned during the course of my life; at the same time gazing on my grandmother, with eyes and mouth extended to their utmost capability.

Of the conversation which took place at this time I remember a little, but in a very confused and disjointed state. Such, however, as I recollect, I shall deliver to my reader, who is, I trust, not altogether uninterested in my concerns; although I must acknowledge that I have not yet appeared to him in the most attractive point of view which it is possible to imagine: for I was in fact, at that period, as disagreeable and as impertinent a child as could well be imagined; being full of defects myself, and at the same time possessing much of that spirit of detraction so frequently met with in ordinary minds.

Agreeably with this spirit, I had scarcely received the salutations of my relations, before I began to make my private observations upon their appearances, characters, and conversation; and first, I remarked that my grandmother had put her spectacles on, and was looking intently at me, at the same time that she addressed Mrs. Bridget to this effect:—"Did I hear you right, child? like my daughter did you say? No, no, it's the father's face altogether."

"Miss is like her father, to be sure," said my cousin; "exceedingly like him—the very picture of him."

"How can you go for to say any such thing, Miss Cicely?" said Mrs. Bridget; "Miss Juliana is the very counterpart of her mother, I would venture to assert it in any company, and to any one's face. She only wants a little education, and then it will be seen which of us is right. Why, look you, Miss Cicely, she has the very fine black eye of the Hartleys."

"And," said my grandmother, with an expression which I could not make out, "what a discoverer of wonders you are, Bridget. And I suppose," she added, "that you have also discerned in the child the same long neck and falling shoulders for which I was remarked in my younger days."

"Madam is pleased to be merry," said Mrs. Bridget, smiling, "I said nothing about the shoulders;" and at the same time she tapped me on the neck, and gave me a signal to pull up.

"Miss is, certainly, not very upright," said my cousin Cicely, stitching away, and drawing herself into a more erect form than usual. "But you will try to do better to please grandmamma—won't you, miss?" addressing me, and at the same time directing a side-glance of her eye towards my grandmother.

I could have answered, that I did not know what I should choose to do, not having yet made up my mind whether I might think it worth my while to please my grandmother or otherwise; but I thought it best to be silent, being anxious to catch every word that fell from the old lady's lips; who, after having looked some time longer upon me, deliberately took off her spectacles, and while she put them into their case, uttered a kind of groan, exclaiming, at the same time, "I do not know what is to be done—I doubt whether it will ever be possible to make her fit to be seen."

"Oh! madam," said Mrs. Bridget, "did ever any one hear the like! When we have had the dancing-master, and the French master, and when I have altered the trimming of her slip, and taught miss to do open work and scalloping, she will be quite another thing; and you will say so, I am sure, madam."

"Well, well," said my grandmother, taking a pinch of snuff, "I hope your predictions will come true, Bridget, and I have the more confidence that they will do so, because I know that you have a tolerable taste and judgment for one of your condition."

Mrs. Bridget received this compliment with a courtesy, and left the room.

I remember no more of the conversation which then took place, and probably should not have remembered so much had it not affected me so nearly, and kept me in a state of such doubt and suspense about my appearance; sometimes leading me to think that I was an absolute monster; and again filling me with the idea, that, if I chose, I might become a lady, like my grandmother.

All further discussions respecting me, at this time, were, however, as I well recollect, interrupted by the servants with the tea-equipage. Soon after which our ears were saluted with a whoop and halloo, such as persons commonly use when calling dogs, and in a few minutes a great big figure, in a shooting-jacket and jockey cap, entered the room, accompanied by five or six dogs. This person was no other than my uncle Barnaby, who, at the sight of me, fixed his hands on his sides, and laughed till he made the whole room ring again, calling me a little droll figure, a pug dog, and a Dutch doll, and advising his mother to have my picture taken at full length: however, when his fit of merriment had somewhat subsided, he gave me a hearty kiss, and said, "You and I shall be good friends by-and-by," and began a kind of boisterous play with me, which was commonly renewed whenever we met, from that time for some years to come.

Thus have I given my reader a considerably detailed account of my first introduction into my grandmother's family; and shall proceed to say that every thing I afterward saw and heard was of a piece with this first introduction. I was presently made to despise my former modes of life and manners, and aspire to something more genteel. Mere worldly motives were given to me for exertion. I was taught to think myself a person of great consequence, and to dread vulgarity and low life above all things: but at the same time, entirely false notions were given me of the nature of true gentility, and I was led to confound poverty with coarseness, humility with meanness, and simplicity with awkwardness. I had no criterion given me by which I might distinguish true greatness from that which is false, or the fine polish of truly elegant manners from the false glare of fashion.

There is a certain good taste and discernment of what is really lovely, which true religion only can bestow; but at that period of my life of which I speak, I had not the least knowledge of religion, nor do I know that any attempt was ever made, during my childhood, by any of my own family, to communicate to me any opinions on this subject. No time, however, was lost, I well recollect, after my arrival in England, in modelling my exterior into something more tolerable than what it first presented. I was placed in the hands of the best dancing-master the neighbourhood would afford—was taught to enter a room with a skimming courtesy, such as was then in fashion—to manage my hoop with dexterity, when I stepped into a carriage—and to smile without displaying every tooth in my head, as I had been accustomed to do. I also learned to speak a little French, and to play on the harpsichord: also, to do open work and net purses, with certain other accomplishments of the same description, which I acquired from my friend Mrs. Bridget, who, while she taught me the exercise of my needle, failed not to amuse me with such discourses as at once fed my pride and exalted my self-love.

CHAPTER II.

Goes to Boarding-school—Her Journey thither, in company with her Grandmother—Description of her Governess.

THREE years had now elapsed since I had been brought to England, and those who saw me on my first arrival scarcely could recognise the little wild Irish girl in the haughty miss into which she was then converted.

About this time my uncle Barnaby went to London, why or wherefore I know not; but this I remember, that he went with some reluctance, and staid a long time; so long, indeed, that my grandmother, who never trusted him long out of her sight, thought it expedient to go up to town in search of him; and on this occasion, as I was not thought old enough to be introduced into the world, and as she had no one with whom she could conveniently leave me at Hartley Hall, as I was known to have a high spirit, she began to look about for a school in the neighbourhood, in which she might place me for a few months.

The old lady had some difficulty in making me submit to this arrangement, for my heart beat for a journey to

London; but my grandmother was tolerably peremptory when she had once decided upon any point; and as I happened to know this feature in her character, I was compelled to acquiesce.

My grandmother, after having brought me to consent, had some difficulty to decide upon a school suitable to her purpose; but, after some deliberation, her choice was fixed by the lady of the rector of the parish, who mentioned a little seminary in a neighbouring village where a niece of hers had been placed for two years, and had done great honour to her teacher, by a peacock which she had worked in chenilles, and which was said to be even more beautiful than the creature itself, in its greatest perfection. This was enough, my grandmother fixed on the school in question without further hesitation; and, the governess having been duly apprized of our intentions, we set out one fine afternoon, in the month of July, in my grandmother's coach-and-four, in quest of this seminary.

A few months before these events had taken place, a young lady from a boarding-school in the neighbouring town had been spending the holydays at Hartley Hall, and as she was my bed-fellow when there, I had been amused, I will not say profited, during many a long night, with details of her school frolics, of tricks played to the masters, of tarts purloined, of governesses deceived and teachers insulted.

The hope of being enabled to have a part in exploits like these had done more to reconcile me to the prospect of going to school than all the arguments of my grandmother, and her auxiliaries, Mrs. Cicely and Mrs. Bridget, brought together in one point of view.

Accordingly, when my grandmother and I got into the coach, I was presently lost in the anticipation of these frolics, and scarcely observed the direction in which we were moving, till we had left the Hall considerably behind us, and were advanced upon a road which led through the most intricate and solitary parts of the park.

I remember that it had been an exceedingly hot day, and therefore the deep shade of the trees was particularly grateful to us. It was also amusing to see the deer start and fly away at the unusual sound of wheels in this solitude, and even the birds seemed to be disturbed as the coach brushed between the trees.

"And where are we going, madam?" I said, as I addressed my grandmother; "there is no town, that I know of, in this direction."

My grandmother then informed me, that the place we were going to was retired, that I should have few companions, but that I should be perfectly safe, and might be very happy till her return. This description of the place of my destination did not by any means coincide with the expectations which I had conceived, and in a moment destroyed all the plans of amusement which I had formed. I in consequence became sullen, and remained silent till the carriage emerged from the shadowy scenes which I have described, and passing through a gate of the park, which was seldom required to be opened, entered upon a common, skirted with many trees, towards the west: from which arose, in the very face of the setting sun, a slender white spire, which belonged to the village church. Many cottages and other humble habitations were seen here and there, partially covered by the trees. A number of sheep were feeding on this common, where the wild thyme and heather blossoms afforded many a fragrant banquet for the bees.

As soon as we entered on this heath, we were aware of the freshness and balmy sweetness of the evening breeze; and any one but a person agitated as I then was, with high and angry passions, would have been touched and interested by the soothing tranquillity and charming simplicity of this scene.

Although the common was more than a mile across, we soon reached the entrance of the village, which I have before described as being situated among trees; and passing immediately under the church, and along a kind of rural street, we presently came to a stop before a small house, which, for its neatness, simplicity, and the romantic beauty of its situation, was seldom equalled, and perhaps never excelled. The house itself was old and irregularly built, presenting to the front two gable ends, with a porch between; the roof was high and slanting, being covered with thatch, and having several windows projecting from the thatch. The building was incrusted with a kind of rough-cast, washed white, and it seemed as if nature had been peculiarly fanciful in the formation of the grounds around this dwelling, forming, in a small compass, such a variety of hill and dale as is rarely to be met with in a space of many miles. Neither was there wanting, to complete this fairy landscape, the utmost variety of fragrant flowers, whether wild or cultivated by the hand of man; which, together with the richest verdure, and the sparkling of a little brook, that came tumbling down from the higher grounds, formed altogether such a delicious retreat as monarchs might envy. Near this house a milk-white cow was feeding in a small field, and as soon as the carriage stopped, our ears were saluted with the joyful exclamations of children at play. The notes were not loud or harsh, but indicative of well-educated sprightliness and chastened merriment. My grandmother was gratified, and expressed her pleasure at this scene.

We alighted, and walked up the garden-walk to the house-door; there, having knocked, the door was opened to us by a neat female servant, and we were introduced into the best parlour, or room kept for visiters, where, while we waited the appearance of the mistress of the house, I had the opportunity of making such comments on all I saw as served to feed my pride and increase my ill-humour.

The apartment was of a tolerable size, and had been handsomely fitted up in its day; but its ornaments were old-fashioned, and bore the marks of the ravages of time; and though the utmost attention had evidently been paid to neatness through every part of it, yet there were certain circumstances relative to its furniture, and even its walls, which proved to me that its inhabitants were such as found it necessary to be attentive to economy. The old-fashioned hangings had been repaired, and eked out in several places; the furniture of the chairs was of patchwork, and several pieces of needlework, which hung upon the wall, wanted those frames of gilt-work, and that glazing, which I thought they deserved. Being occupied in discerning these blemishes, I had no eye for a wilderness of sweets and beauties which was spread before the open window, till my attention was called to it by my grandmother, who hinted that I could not be otherwise than happy in a situation abounding with so many delicious circumstances.

Before the pert reply which hung upon my lips had time to form itself into words, the door of the room opened, and the mistress of the house, whom I shall henceforward call my governess, entered the room, and paid her compliments to us, with such an air of Christian humility, unfeigned charity, and undesigning simplicity, as for a moment awed me into something like respect. She was a little woman, considerably advanced in years, and habited as a widow. She had in her younger days been handsome, as was very evident from the regularity of her features, and the remaining delicacy of her complexion; but that which was most remarkable in her appearance was the expression of that grace which enables us to bear afflictions and calamities with constancy and calmness of mind, and with a ready and cheerful submission to the will of God. Even to one blinded by pride as I was, these characteristics were sufficiently legible, and seemed to demand my esteem, as it were, in spite of myself; and, probably, I should have been more ready to bestow it, had I not perceived, in the dress of this excellent and amiable person, certain little circumstances which marked a degree of frugality, which I, as the pupil of the elegant and accomplished Mrs. Bridget, had learned to look upon with the most sovereign contempt. What these circumstances were I now forget, but, probably, some symptoms of repairs in her well-saved gown.

CHAPTER III.

Her Grandmother's departure—She is introduced to Anna and her companions—Their conversation with the Governess.

I REMEMBER little of what passed between my grandmother and my new governess, and can only recollect that when my grandmother arose, I followed her to the door, and burst into tears. My grandmother failed not to chide me for what she considered as a symptom of a want of submission to her will, and, hastening to her carriage, left me with my governess, who, addressing me kindly, entreated that I would be comforted, and in order, probably, to divert my thoughts, asked me if I would accompany her into the garden, whither she was going to call her children.

So saying, she offered her hand, that hand which, as I afterward found, was so continually employed in softening the bed of sickness, and conveying relief to the distressed; but I pretended not to observe the motion, and drawing back with affected humility, to permit her to go first, followed her through a back-door of the small hall or vestibule, into a garden, where I presently seemed lost in a kind of flowery labyrinth. Through this, however, I soon made my way, being led by my governess, who at length brought me out on a green terrace, terminated by an alcove, in which several children were busily engaged in play; a little table stood before them in the centre of the alcove, on which lay several dolls, which I rather wondered at, as three of the young people appeared to be nearly my own age. This little party consisted of six, and I could, at this moment, give my reader not only each of their names, but the exact description of all their persons. I shall, however, content myself with the minute description of one only, who, being the eldest of the party, and the niece of my governess, seemed to exert a gentle authority over the rest.

The name of this little girl was Anna, and at the time I knew her, she was thirteen years of age, though, from her appearance, she might have passed for much younger; while the constant prudence and equanimity of her deportment would have done credit to one a great deal older.

The appearance of youth, which I mentioned, proceeded from her extraordinary delicacy of complexion, the mildness of her eyes, and the thousand dimples which played around her coral lips, together with a simplicity as charming as it is uncommon.

At the moment when we were first seen approaching the bower, she was forming a wreath of eglantine, and fastening it on the hat of the youngest of the little group, a pretty child of about five years old, whose name was Ermina, and whom I afterward found to be an orphan; while the others were all calling upon her to take some office in their gambols, which could not be agreeable without their beloved Anna.

At sight of us, however, the sports immediately ceased; but not the gay expression of the happy party, who, after having paid their compliments to me, with that kind of politeness which proceeds from real good-will, gathered round their governess, and silently, yet eagerly, strove to obtain one of those hands which I, but now, had so insolently rejected. The old lady looked round upon her little people with a kind of maternal tenderness, and reminding them that it was getting late, moved in the midst of them towards the house.

When arrived there, we were taken into the school-room, the simple furniture of which again afforded matter for my comments. Here the cloth was laid on the oak table, and a little supper set out, which I afterward found had been done in compliment to me, as a new comer, as no meal at this hour ever afterward appeared.

This plain and homely repast, excellent as it was of its kind, consisting of strawberries and cream, and small white loaves, brought with it no satisfaction to me, because I was resolved not to be pleased; but I found that this unexpected treat was a matter of high delight to the blooming and smiling young creatures with whom I was now associated. On this occasion the gentle Anna displayed all her dimples, and the little Ermina, who was commonly called Minny by those who loved her, absolutely broke out into such an intemperance of mirth that her governess was compelled to look somewhat seriously upon her; but this cloud being past away, sunshine was presently restored to every countenance, for I speak not of my own. And now I witnessed that which I had never before seen, namely, that innocent play of spirits and of wit which can only proceed from those who feel their minds at peace with respect to their most important concerns. It is written, "For as the crackling of thorns under the pot, so is the laughter of fools." Eccles. vi. 6. And again, "Even in laughter the heart is sorrowful, and the end of that mirth is heaviness." Prov. xiv. 13. But, "The Lord will bless his people with peace." Psalm xxix. 11. And it was, indeed, such a peaceful, such a tranquil state of enjoyment, which I now witnessed, as I never before had formed a conception of; and now could by no means understand. I remember, however (for my memory is particularly tenacious of the events of these days), many remarks that were made while this little assembly were regaling themselves with the simple fare which was spread before them. And first, our governess observed, that "she could not conceive any delicacy whatever, which labour or money could procure, more exquisite than the present feast which was spread before them, and hence," said she, " we may infer the goodness of the Almighty, who prepares such dainties for humble and simple persons, as the tables of kings could not excel."

She then remarked, that " fruit was the food of sinless man in Paradise," and proceeded to point it out as the Scripture emblem of all manner of spiritual good things.

She then proceeded to speak of Eden, and the manner of man's life in that ancient seat of glory, hinting that " there were many assurances in Scripture of the restoration of that same blessed order of things, which prevailed before the fall, in the last days of the world."

Her young people, I observed, answered her as if well acquainted with the subjects she was speaking of; and expressed a wish that they might be enabled to conform to that simplicity of habits and behaviour which their Saviour loved.

" And here," said Anna, on whom my eyes had been almost constantly fixed, ever since I had sat down at table, being, as it were, fascinated by the extraordinary simplicity and beauty of her expression, " if it were possible to form a Paradise in this present state of things, we have every thing here which might be needful: trees, and flowers, and brooks, and breezy lawns, and shadowy bowers, and leisure to receive instruction, without any worldly people to come in and destroy our peace."

" My dear child," replied her aunt, " that retreat must be deep indeed into which sin and the world do not enter. Remember, that the seat of sin is in the heart, and whoever knows his own heart must be assured that a very great change must pass in that heart before he is fit to become an inhabitant of Eden."

" Oh! my aunt," replied Anna, while such a lovely blush rose in her cheeks as I had never before seen, and a tear trembled in her gentle eye, " I was far from presuming to say, that although this place is like a Paradise to me, we are, any of us, fit to live in Eden. I know that we are all desperately wicked by nature, and that 'there is none good, no, not one.' "

Had not pride sealed my lips, I should have spoken on hearing this remark; but as I believed it was more for my dignity to remain perfectly silent, I failed not so to do, contenting myself with fixing my eyes, with an unmoved gaze, upon my young school-fellow. She, however, either did not, or would not, notice my rudeness; but looked attentively at her aunt, who thus addressed her :—"I believe you, my dear; I am sure you have too much humility to question your own natural depravity, or that of any of your fellow-creatures. You have not so read your Bible, I trust, my child: and this being premised, I cordially agree with you in what you have further said respecting this place, and our little society here. If there is a set of persons on earth who are happy in each other, and surrounded by blessings, it is ourselves; and though we have the sin of our nature still to contend with, and shall have until death, nevertheless, we have often such sweet experience of the tender love of our God and our Saviour, that we find as much of Eden in this our humble retreat as was ever found on earth since the fall of man."

CHAPTER IV.

She retires to rest, for the first time, at School—The apartment—Its furniture and Ornaments—Overhears the morning hymn of her School-fellows—The course of Instruction pursued in this Boarding-school.

The conversation then took a less serious turn. Little Minny made some remark which made all the little ones laugh; and my governess told us some curious anecdotes of her childhood, exhibiting before us curious pictures of the manners of those times, contrasting them with those of the present day.

When the hour of separation arrived, our governess knelt down in the midst of us, and prayed; after which I was led up-stairs into a small room, where I was made to understand that I was to sleep alone; an arrangement which did not please me, for I had seen a young lady at supper who was called by her school-fellows Olivia, whom I had fixed upon as my bed-fellow, having conceived some hope that she was a character which might be worked upon, and which might be won over to my own ways of thinking. There was however, as I thought, no use in expostulating; I therefore wished my governess, who had attended me to my room, a good night, with no small ceremony; and when she was gone, turned round to contemplate every circumstance about my little apartment.

The bed was small, and hung with blue and white check; the walls were covered with common blue paper. An old-fashioned glass stood on a toilet, at one end of the room, and two old upright rush-bottomed chairs stood on each side of the bed. On the antiquated mantel-piece stood two lambs of wood or wire, clothed in cotton wool, and having eyes made of black beads; and above, upon the wall, was a small red and white oil painting, representing two little children, which, like the babes in the wood, stood hand in hand, the one being the similitude of a little boy, as I judged by his robings, and a small whip which he held in the hand which was unoccupied, and the other, undoubtedly, a little girl, as her cap was adorned with a bunch of roses.

Although the painting was but an ordinary one, there was not wanting, in the expression of these little ones, in their delicate features, their coral lips, and soft blue eyes, a certain something which would have induced the spectator to believe that they might once have been some tender mother's pride, and would have induced him to ask, whose are these little ones? where are they now? what has been their fate? has any mother mourned their early deaths? But no tender inquiries of this kind suggested themselves to my mind. On the contrary, I turned away disgusted from all I saw, and throwing myself on a chair, burst into a flood of tears, proceeding from pride, passion, and selfishness. However, when I had bewailed my fancied afflictions for a sufficient length of time, I bethought myself of going to bed, where I soon fell into a much more profound, refreshing sleep than a person in my afflicted case could be expected to enjoy.

It was morning when I awoke, and the red beams of the early sun rested on the walls of my room. I got up in haste, and opened my window; the air was balmy and fragrant, and the dew still glistened on the grass and flowers, on the bank opposite my window, for the ground of the garden arose with considerable precipitancy from the house to the higher parts of the garden. There, while I stood for a moment, I suddenly heard a chorus of soft and melodious voices rising up towards my open window, as from the room below, and could distinctly make out the following verses:—

"To thee, our Father and our God,
Our joyful songs we'll raise;
Be all our pleasure and delight,
To celebrate thy praise.

To worship and to serve thee, Lord,
Give us no work but this;
Employments such as angels love,
We ask no other bliss."

I can give you little idea of what my feelings were on hearing this strain, but I recollect that I stood at the window till it ceased, and then lifting up my eyes towards a grove of oak-trees, which was situated at the top of the hill, beyond the bounds of the garden, and presented beneath its branches many shadowy and inviting recesses, I began to compare in my own mind those pleasures of religion and retirement spoken of the day before by my governess, with those of scenes of pomp and worldly pleasure which I had often heard my grandmother describe. At length, recollecting myself, I hastened to dress, and to make my appearance at the breakfast-table, where the little family were by this time assembled. After breakfast my governess appointed me a place in the school-room, and every one presently engaged in her usual employment. Education at that period was, in some respects, not so well understood as it now is; in others, perhaps, much better: fewer accomplishments were then taught,—the French language even was little studied, and not taught at all by our governess, but she took great pains to teach her pupils to read and write their own language with propriety. She understood history and geography well,—was an excellent Bible scholar, and few persons had such skill with their needle. She accordingly arranged her day in such a way as to give proper attention to each of these branches of instruction.—The mornings were always devoted by her to making us learn our lessons and write; at one we dined, after which we took some exercise for an hour, and then assembled again till five o'clock, which period was devoted to our needles, while one of the party, by turns, read the Bible aloud, or sometimes one or other of those few little volumes which were at that time prepared for children.

CHAPTER V.

Dissatisfied during her first evening at School—Olivia inquires the cause—Their conversation; and the Story of the little Chuckoor.

The first evening which I spent at the school turned out, as it happened, very rainy; accordingly, having spent our time till five o'clock in the way I have mentioned, we then drank tea, after which we were allowed to play, and the dolls were produced, at the sight of which my pride again took alarm; and though Anna explained to me that it was partly in accommodation to the taste of the little ones that the elder children submitted to this kind of amusement, yet I could by no means bring my mind to a participation in these puerile entertainments, and in consequence sat down in the window-seat determined not to make myself agreeable.

In the mean time the dolls were dressed, and I observed that Anna (who but now had pleaded her desire to please the little ones as a kind of apology for playing with dolls) was to the full as deeply engaged in the amusement as Minny herself: and now, if it will not be deemed out of place, I must pause to make this remark, which has often occurred to me, though I cannot recollect having heard it made by any other person, viz. That uneducated and unsubdued children are as unfit for play as for work; and that the same qualities are requisite to make a child agreeable in the play-room, as successful in the school-room. The generality of children are aptly described by almost the very words of our Saviour (Matt. xi. 16, 17), " We may pipe unto them and they will not dance, we may mourn unto them and they will not weep."

Perhaps some persons may feel themselves inclined to doubt the accuracy of this remark, and for this reason: that it is commonly supposed that there are in all societies of children certain popular characters which are more agreeable to their companions than to their masters. I answer,—that there are characters who have a natural influence over their fellow-creatures, and that such will always have a party, and a number of adherents in every society; but let these characters be closely examined, and it will be found that they form no exception to my proposition, viz. "That the same qualities which make a child agreeable and successful in the school-room are equally necessary to make him acceptable upon the play-ground."

But to return to my former self, whom I left sulking on the window-seat. I had remained for some time utterly neglected by the happy party, when Olivia, of whom I before spoke, during a pause of the play, sidled up to me, and, after some hesitation, addressed me with a request to join in the amusement.—I answered, in a low voice, "that I was too unhappy to play."

"Unhappy, miss!" replied the other, "I am sorry for it; what has made you unhappy?" and at the same time she took a place on a corner of the same window-seat on which I had enthroned myself in all the dignity of my fancied importance.

As the rest of the party were now again engaged in high festivity, having made houses with benches in the two farther corners of the room, and divided themselves into families, I had full leisure to answer Olivia's question, and I failed not to make the best of it, by representing my case in a very doleful point of view.

I first described my happiness at home, the splendour of my grandmother's establishment, the habits to which I had been accustomed, the silver mug out of which I drank, and the superb teacup from which I daily sipped my breakfast; and then I proceeded to draw the dreadful reverse of my situation, the comparatively small room in which I sat, the closet in which I slept, the exchange of damask curtains for hangings of blue check, together with sundry other afflictions of the same nature, which I described as being altogether more than I could bear.

In reply to this Olivia looked at me with an expression indeed of some compassion, for I was crying bitterly, but with more wonder, and at length she said, "But we are very happy here. Every thing is quite clean; and what signify those things you talk of?"

"What signify those things, miss!" I said: "why nothing at all to those people who know nothing better."

"Oh! but," said Olivia, "I do know better things, for our tea-room at home, miss, is hung with pea-green cut velvet paper; and our best bed-room is of red damask."

I have a look of contempt, as much as to say, Who

cares for your tea-room and your best bed-chamber—what are you compared with me? For I had learned that she was the daughter of an attorney in a neighbouring town. However, as I felt the need of some person to fill up the place of Mrs. Bridget in my confidence, I thought it best to answer her with some politeness, and accordingly replied, that "pea-green was as pretty a colour as could well be imagined for a tea-room," and expressed my astonishment that she, who had been used to so handsome an apartment, should be perfectly happy in such a house as that in which she then resided.

"Oh! but," said Olivia, "we do not sit in the tea-room every day, only when there is company; and I am always glad to get out of it, for I am so afraid of soiling the carpet, or some other such mischief."

Our conversation then took another turn, and I told her how many suits I had—how they were trimmed—what jewels my grandmother had in her jewel-box, and how many headdresses of lace she bought during the year, with other matters of equal moment, by which vanities I so far worked upon the mind of my little companion, that when she was at length called to join the play, she answered fretfully that "she was tired, and did not love dolls."

Thus had the poison begun to work, and the worldly discourse which I had introduced in this seat of peace had already begun to produce its never-failing effect, namely, the exchange of cheerfulness for gloom, and peace for discontent, in the mind of that person who had been exposed to the temptation.

It was getting dusk, and the hour of retirement was near at hand, when our governess appeared at the door. At the sight of her, all the younger part of the company ran up to her, and leading her to a chair, begged her to sit down and tell them a story. She smiled, but suffered herself to be prevailed upon: and taking little Minny on her lap, told us the following story, every word of which I remember as well as if I heard it but yesterday.

THE LITTLE CHUCKOOR.

"The chuckoor was a handsome brown bird, about the size of a small fowl; he was hatched in a hollow tree, among some of those ranges of hills at the back of the English settlements in the East Indies. When he was a young bird he was taken by one of the hill-men, and shut up in a cage of wicker-work, which was without a door, and in this plight was made a present of to the wife of a certain chief, who lived in a little fort among the hills.

"It came to pass, after a while, that this chief went out with his men and plundered the English, who had possessions of lands not far from them. Whereupon, the English attacked them and took their fort from them. Immediately after this fort was taken, a certain English gentleman, belonging to the army, went into the fort, and while he was looking about him, he heard a noise under his feet like the clucking of a hen, and he looked to that side from whence the noise came, and there was the poor chuckoor in his cage, nearly covered over with dead men and fragments of the demolished walls of the fort. Had not this gentleman seen this poor bird, he would probably have been there till he had died of hunger.

"Then the gentleman pitied the poor bird, and took up the cage and brought the little creature to his tent, and set bread and water before it; but the Hindoos, who knew the nature of this bird, said that he did not want water in the cold season of the year, and that some kind of grain would be more acceptable to him than bread: so the gentleman kept the chuckoor in his tent, till he had an opportunity of sending it to his children, who were with their mother at an English station at some distance from the hills.

"Now I leave you to imagine how pleased these little children were, when they saw the little prisoner which had been taken in the fort: they begged their mamma to buy a new cage for it, and covered it over with a green baize cloth every night, because this little creature could not bear the sharp and fresh air of the night in the cold season. They also appointed a servant to take care of him.

"This servant, who was a black man, was very fond of the little chuckoor, and he took out his cage every day and set it in the sun; and sometimes he allowed the bird to go out of its cage, and amuse itself with going about in his sight; but this was not till the little creature knew his master, and would obey his call.

"And now I must tell you a wonderful quality of this

bird; he would take bits of burning wood and sparks of fire in his mouth without being hurt; hence he was called the fire-eater, and it was a great amusement to the children to see this little bird eat fire.

"So the little chuckoor led a very happy life with these children, though he met with two great alarms, the one was from a cat, and the other from a rat, who came near his cage one night, but both his enemies were driven away immediately, and it was quite affecting to hear how the little creature afterward tried to talk, and express his fears to his servant, and the rest of the family.

"At length the time came when the good gentleman and his family must go to Europe, and for this purpose they must needs go on board ship, and experience many hardships, and suffer much from cold; and on this occasion they began to feel anxious about their little bird, because they could not take him with them, on account of the cold, for this little bird could not bear cold.

"The good gentleman and his family had been living up the country, many miles distant from the sea, and, in order to prosecute their journey, it became necessary for them to go down to Calcutta, which is near the sea. They made the first part of their journey in boats, upon the river Ganges, and when they arrived in Calcutta, and began to prepare to go on board ship, they became more anxious about their bird, and were entirely at a loss what to do for him.

"Now, while things were in this state, the gentleman went out one day to visit an acquaintance, and when he was introduced into his parlour, he found that one side of it opened into a large aviary formed of wire-work, and, behold, in this aviary were all manner of tame and beautiful birds; and while he looked into this aviary, the person who was employed to take care of them came in at an opposite door, and having swept the floor of the aviary, he set forth the daily food and drink of its inhabitants in twelve shallow pans. In these pans were plantains and brown sugar, boiled rice and dry rice, and all kinds of grain, besides clear water. In short, every thing which the most fastidious bird could desire, and all these arranged with the neatness and order which one might expect at a royal table.

"And now, my dear children," continued our governess, "I think it will not be needful to tell you, that the good gentleman, on seeing this, thought of his little chuckoor, and begged that this, his feathered favourite, might be admitted into this happy society of birds. Thus, after his many adventures and many difficulties, the little chuckoor found rest at last, and the good gentleman's children, to this very day, tell the history of the hill captive, and of the happy termination of his sufferings."

CHAPTER VI.

The Story of the little Chuckoor explained—Juliana acquires religious knowledge, but still cherishes the idea of her own superiority—The cause of her intimacy with Olivia discovered by Anna.

"But, my dear governess," said little Minny, "is this story true, quite true?"

"Yes," replied the old lady, "very, very true, for I knew the gentleman who found the bird, and all his dear children. But, my young people, before we dismiss this story, shall we not try to draw some profitable moral from it? Who is this chuckoor story like, and what lesson of wisdom does it contain?"

"I know, my dear aunt," said Anna, rising hastily, and drawing near to the old lady, "it is like mine—like your poor niece's, my dear aunt. I was left destitute and helpless when a very little baby—without a father, without a mother, and surrounded with the ruins of our domestic happiness, and you became my dear honoured mother—you took me into your bosom—you guarded and protected me from those who would have injured me—you supported me during my tender infancy, and now, in this sweet retirement, I am daily enjoying every temporal comfort, and every spiritual advantage which can be partaken on earth. The little chuckoor is not capable of thanking his Maker for all that he has done for him; but I, with the Divine help, will thank him—I will praise him—I will bless him, and that for ever, for all his unspeakable mercies." So saying, she laid her sweet face upon the bosom of her aunt, and burst into tears; while the good lady, half chidingly, half caressingly, replied, "Oh! my Anna, what have I done for you which is not daily repaid to me a thousand-fold, by your tender love and sweet affection."

Thus closed our evening. And as I have now given my reader a view of one twenty-four hours in my new situation, I now content myself with saying, that as this first day passed, so passed many more days, and in fact some weeks, with little variety, excepting that whenever the evenings were fine, we walked out and explored many exquisite scenes, of which I should despair to give an adequate description; for, after all, when even the finest writer has assembled every beautiful object which our rocks and hills, our forests and our brawling brooks, and transparent lakes, can possibly afford, together with every charm of fragrant flower, breezy lawn, azure sky, &c., it must depend on the imagination of the reader to group them with taste, and represent them to himself with accuracy. But enough of this, and too much, perhaps, considering that it is for very young persons I am now writing, and that these, commonly, consider all matters impertinent, in a narrative of this kind, which do not immediately promote the progress of the story.

These walks of which I speak had generally some act of charity for their end and object; and not unseldom when these little works of love were accomplished, and some poor creature relieved by a present of a garment, or a cordial, or some other small matter, would we sit down under the shade of some spreading tree, or on the side of a hill, or near some brook, or bank of flowers,—and there, while the little ones played around her, our governess would take occasion to tell her elder children some profitable story, or pleasant anecdote, for which she not unseldom took the hint from some natural object within her view, elucidating many parts of Scripture from these, and teaching us, as it were, to read in the book of nature, and compare visible with invisible, and natural with spiritual things.

It was on certain occasions of this kind that I formed my first ideas of some of the most important doctrines of our blessed religion, namely, the doctrine of man's depravity—of his utter helplessness—of the nature of the Holy Trinity, that is, as far as man can be said to comprehend it—of the love of the Father—the work of redemption finished by the Son—and the various operations of the Holy Spirit. It is very true that I was not led at these times to admit the love of Christ into my heart, although my head was furnished with much knowledge; neither did the world lose any of its hold upon me; and though sometimes almost surprised out of my cold insolence by the sweetness and gentleness of my instructress and companions, the world, nevertheless, retained its full power; and while I remained at school I never lost sight of my first object, which was, if possible, to make those about me feel their own littleness and my superiority.

In this view I was, however, strangely baffled for a length of time, by the uncommon simplicity, and what I called ignorance, of those about me. With the exception of Olivia, no one seemed to be in the least aware of my importance, and yet I could not complain of the slightest want of respect; in vain did I talk of my grandmother's coach-and-four, and produced one piece of finery after another; my school-fellows seemed to want that faculty by which things of this kind could be appreciated, and if they were polite to me, they were equally so to the curate's wife, who now and then came to drink tea with our governess. Thus I had the mortification to see that I had no influence over any one in the house but Olivia, who, after a while, withdrew herself almost entirely from Anna and the rest of the little party, and associated herself on every convenient occasion with me.

I have given my reader a specimen of the manner in which our conversation began, but I would not deceive him so far as to lead him to suppose that, in the course of its progress, it continued to touch upon topics equally harmless with the description of the pea-green hangings.

Olivia, after a few weeks, used to come into my room at night, in order to help me to undress, as I had pathetically stated my difficulties in being without a waiting-maid: and on these occasions it would be much more easy to point out what we did not speak of, than what we did. I, for instance, told the whole history, as far as I knew, of my own family; and took off all the singularities of my grandmother, my cousin Cicely, and my uncle Barnaby, being at the same time very careful to let my young companion see that we were people of no small consequence, and that our very singularities showed our importance. And in return for these communications, my school-fellow told me all she knew of our governess and school-fellows, and joining with me in ridiculing the humble modes of life of the former, and trying to fasten upon her the imputation of meanness.

Thus I led on this little girl from one fault to another, till the simplicity and cheerfulness at first remarkable in her deportment entirely disappeared, and gloom and sullenness succeeded. And oh! I would it were in my power to suppose that Olivia was a solitary instance of this kind of corruption, practised by one school-fellow upon another.

But to proceed with my story. Upon reflection on my governess's character, it appears to me, that lovely and excellent as she was, she had neither the spirit to contend with such a character as mine, nor, perhaps, the discernment to penetrate its deep corruption. She was without guile herself, and without suspicion of evil in others; a woman of a gentle and tender disposition, and one than whom no one could be more fit to manage humble and well-disposed children, and to lead them forward in the heavenly way.

Things had passed on in the manner I have described for some weeks, and I believed that the change in Olivia had not been observed, nor the nature of our conversations understood by any one; but it seems that I was mistaken, as I shall presently make appear.

It was the first day in August, and it had been the custom for some years in our little school to bestow some annual prizes on the second of that month, which was Anna's birth-day. Many pretty presents, consisting of embroidered pincushions and work-bags, were ready for the occasion; and if the evening was fine, the children were to have a treat in the alcove on the terrace, which on that occasion was always decorated by them with wreaths and garlands of flowers.

On the eve of this day, at the hour of retirement, Olivia came as usual into my room, and I thus addressed her, using less caution, and speaking louder than I had formerly done: "And so to-morrow is the great day," I said, "the day of days, and I suppose, Olivia, that you mean to be as gay as Minny herself." Before Olivia could reply, Anna came in behind her, and called her school-fellow by name, as soon as I ceased to speak

We both started at the sound of her voice, and reddened to our very eyes.

Anna came forward with a calm dignity, such as I have never since seen in one of her age, and addressing Olivia, she said, "I am come to say that it would be better for you to withdraw to your own room; henceforward I will assist Miss Oakley, if help is needful for her."

"And why must Olivia go to her room, Miss Anna?" I asked.

"Because," said she calmly, "you are doing each other the greatest mischief by your conversation, and setting each other against your best friends."—"And how do you know all this, miss?" I said; "you have been listening at the door."—"No," said Anna, "I never listened in the way you hint at; but I have long seen that Olivia is entirely changed,—she is no more the pleasant and cheerful companion she once was—she is not full of love and joy as she was in past days. I could not account for this change, because I did not suspect you, Miss Juliana; but what I heard this moment, as I was coming into the room on an errand from my aunt, has opened my eyes, and led me to understand the cause of the change in my Olivia."—"And what did you hear?" said I, swelling with passion.

"An expression of contempt uttered by you, and unreproved by Olivia, that Olivia, too," continued the sweet girl, "whom I once so tenderly loved. And what was it, Olivia," she asked, "that you were speaking of with contempt? Why of an effort about to be made by your kind, your gentle governess, to make you happy. Oh! pride, pride," she added, clasping her hands in a manner indescribably pathetic, "to what cruelties does this passion lead us." Then bursting into tears, and sinking on a chair which stood near, "Olivia! Olivia!" she said, "I thought you really loved and honoured my aunt —you who are so well acquainted with her history—who have heard the detail of all her sorrows—who have seen her gentle tears flowing at the memory of her husband and children dead,—those sweet children," added Anna, directing us, by a glance of her streaming eyes to the painting before mentioned, over the chimney-piece, "who were once her treasures, her only earthly comforts—you who have for months past had occasion to witness her self-denial, her charity, her extraordinary liberality—you, who have experienced her indulgence so long, and have professed so much filial affection for her. Olivia, Olivia, I could not have believed this of you."

So saying, she was so entirely overcome by her feelings, as to sob aloud. Olivia looked at her with every expression of guilt and shame, and uttered not a single word; but I, who had less feeling and less modesty than my fellow-offender, was able to speak, and asked, with much pertness, "what it was we were suspected of?"

By this time she had, in a great measure, recovered her composure. She had risen from her chair, and again coming close to us, kissed Olivia, and approaching her sweet face to me, as if to invite me to the same token of reconciliation, which I, however, thought right not to notice; and then making a kind of apology for the agitation which she had betrayed, she proceeded to plead the interests of religion to us in a manner at once so forcible and so simple, and to state, in a style so emphatic and so striking, the loveliness of a peaceful, modest, and grateful behaviour in young people such as we then were, that Olivia appeared to be very much overcome, and it was with difficulty that I could restrain my emotions.

"It is true, Miss Oakley," said she, "that you have been accustomed to live in a very different way to what we do; but, since it has been your grandmother's good pleasure to place you here, it has become a duty in you to submit as entirely to your governess's pleasure as the youngest child in this house. Remember the example of our Saviour, who, though God in human flesh, submitted himself to the will of his mother, not only till he was of our age, but until he was thirty years old, working with his reputed father at his trade, and submitting to the humble circumstances of his situation. Remember the sweet words of the hymn:—

"'What bless'd examples do we find
Writ in the word of truth,
Of children that began to mind
Religion in their youth.

"'Jesus, who reigns above the sky,
And keeps the world in awe,
Was once a child as young as I
And kept his father's law.

"At twelve years old he talked with men,
The Jews all wondering stand;
Yet he obeyed his mother then,
And came at her command.'"

When the sweet Anna (for lovely and precious she is, indeed, in my recollection, little as I prized her at that time) had finished these verses, she took Olivia by the hand and led her out of the room, having wished me a good night, in a manner very little varied from her usual graciousness.

CHAPTER VII.

Olivia's stolen interview with Juliana, who would not accept the invitation of Anna—The distribution of the Prizes—Juliana's ungenerous conduct to her Governess, and the sudden arrival of Mrs. Bridget.

I HAVE no recollection of what passed in my mind when Anna left me; but I well remember that I slept till the next morning, when I was awakened by the voices of my school-fellows under my window, busily speculating upon the weather, and deciding, from the very heavy dew upon the grass, and the cloudless azure of the sky, that it would be a charming day. Soon after these awakening calls, I got up, and going to my window, saw the children, busy in their preparations in the alcove, which, as I have said, was in the very highest part of the garden.

"I hope," said I to myself, as I opened the window, "that Olivia is not with them, but perhaps the poor girl cannot help herself, she is overawed by her companions. Well, to-day I shall have an opportunity of letting them see how little I care for them."

I stood, however, at the window, looking on what was passing, till the bell rang to call us to prayers, at the sound of which the young people all came running in, every face being radiant with happiness, and with that true kind of happiness too with which the duties of religion appeared to form no kind of discordance.

There was more talking than usual at breakfast among

the young people; each of whom had some little scheme for rendering the day more delightful, to impart to her governess: and even Olivia looked as if she could have thoroughly enjoyed herself, had not I been present to sustain, by my significant and stolen glances, that influence which I had so lately obtained.

After breakfast, the young ones again hastened to their arbour, and my governess went into a little light closet, which opened from the parlour, and where she kept her stores, as it was supposed, to prepare some little feast, and perhaps to wrap up the presents which were prepared, and to direct them according to their several designations. This breaking up of the breakfast party occasioned a little bustle, during which I got to the side of Olivia, and whispered to her, "Watch your opportunity, and come to me in my room, I have something to say." The little girl turned hastily to me, and nodding her head as a sign of assent she ran out into the garden with her schoolfellows, while I went up to my room, and endeavoured to amuse myself with the examination of my clothes.

I had passed some little time in this way, when I heard my name repeated by some one standing under my window; and looking out, I saw Anna standing, and looking up.

Never shall I forget her figure, as it there presented itself; she was dressed in the simplest manner imaginable, in a slip of dove-coloured stuff, with a muslin apron and bib, the corner of her apron being tucked up to her waist. She had taken off her cap, and round-eared little flat straw hat, which were then in fashion, and her fair hair, in consequence, fell in a thousand charming ringlets over her face and neck, and on her head she was balancing a basket full of roses, which the old man who cultivated the garden had just bestowed on her, in order to adorn her bower.

As soon as she saw me at the window, she raised one hand to support her basket, and courtesying low, with a smile full of sweetness, "I am come," she said, "an unworthy messenger, indeed, from the Lady Ermina, whom we have chosen to be our queen, to solicit the honour of your company, Miss Oakley. Permit me," she added, "to lead you to our palace, where we promise you that which is not always to be met with in the bowers of queens, namely, a hearty welcome, and much good faith."

It might seem to be almost impossible to reject such an invitation, thus sweetly tendered; nevertheless, I did reject it, for I had resolved not to be pleased with any thing I saw or heard in this place, and coldly thanking the person who had been sent to invite me, I sat down to repair a necklace of garnets, which I had broken the day before.

It was not till after we had met to dinner, and were again dispersed, that Olivia found her way to my room. She then came, apparently in a great hurry, and asked me what I wanted.

I repeated her last words with some astonishment, and asked her why she had not come before.

"I could not very well," she said; "I could not without being observed."

"I can scarcely believe that, Olivia," I said; "no, the truth is this, you are amused with these child's plays, and are anxious for some of those sixpenny gewgaws which are to be given away this evening. And after all, why should I wonder, when I consider that you have seen nothing of the world yet?—nothing beyond your own pea-green tea-room and this place."

On hearing this, Olivia reddened, as well she might, at my rudeness, and I was instantly made aware that I had said too much, and that I should entirely lose my ally, if I did not alter my tone. I accordingly began immediately to hint at an invitation which I intended some time or other to give her to Hartley Hall, and at certain little presents which I intended for her, when I could go home and look after my things; and when by this means I had got her into some good-humour, I said, "I am sure, Olivia, when we are all met together this evening, and the parson's children are come, and the prizes are given—I am sure you won't think of playing?"

She hesitated a little, on which I pressed the point, and she had just given me a hesitating promise that she would acquiesce in my wishes, when one of the other children came to the door, and told her that "Miss Anna inquired for her, and begged she would come immediately." She blushed on receiving this summons, and ran away with such haste, that I half suspected she was not quite so sincere in my cause as I had hoped.

Now it may be asked what motive I could possibly have had for endeavouring to make a disturbance in this little family? I answer that my motive was a mixture of pride and envy; and I fear that there are few societies on earth which have not suffered, more or less, from characters of this kind.

After Olivia had left me, I remained for some time alone, busy with my garnets, till about four in the evening, when I was summoned to join the rest of the family and a few visiters, who were come to see the little festival, and the distribution of the prizes. When arrived on the terrace, I found the company consisted only of one or two of our nearest neighbours, and the wife of the curate, and these were seated on chairs opposite the alcove, in which were placed two small tables, the one covered with a little repast of fruit and sweetmeats, and the other with the prizes and presents which were to be distributed. The children stood in a half-circle round these tables, and being dressed in flowers, as well as the alcove itself, they presented a very pleasing spectacle to the eye. As I had no reason to expect any present, I made no attempt to join this smiling group, but placed myself in a situation from whence I could observe all that passed.

Sundry little ceremonies now took place, and the governess took occasion to commend some of the little girls for certain excellences, and to thank others for certain proofs of affection, honour, good-manners, &c. which they had given during the past year. By what she said to Olivia, I perceived that Anna had not explained the scene of the past night to her aunt, and I was obliged to confess that there was much, very much of kindness in this forbearance, at the period, when she would have brought her little friend to public disgrace by a contrary conduct. Olivia blushed violently when she heard the commendations of her governess, and seemed as if it were absolutely out of her power to lift her eyes from the ground.

Our governess having finished her addresses to her pupils, the prizes were delivered. After which some of the little ones left their places in the alcove, and came forward to speak to their friends, and to examine their little presents, every eye at the same time sparkling with pleasure, and every heart beating with rapture. In the confusion which ensued in consequence of these removals of the young party, I contrived to get near

Olivia, and interrupting her in the midst of certain exclamations of delight, on account of a blue satin housewife which she had just received, "Olivia," I said, "I am glad to see you so happy; but why do I wonder that babes should be delighted with playthings?"

I forget what answer she made; but we conversed for some minutes, during which I succeeded in making her very uneasy. All her gayety left her, and she was on the point of bursting into tears. While struggling with these feelings, our governess and Anna had begun to hand about the fruit and cakes; and the kind old lady coming smiling up to us, held to us a little basket of all sorts of cakes, at the same time calling us her dear children, and inviting us to partake of her treat.

There was in the countenance of this excellent woman, at that moment, an expression of mingled love and joy—joy to see her children so happy, without the smallest idea that there could be one of the party less pleased than she meant them to be. Thus she approached us, and offered her basket.—I was almost subdued by her unsuspicious and gentle expression of countenance, but Olivia was observing me, and I was at that moment more ashamed of the incipient desire which I felt of doing better, than I had before been of long and stubborn rebellion. In compliance, therefore, with this feeling of shame, I rejected the treat my governess offered with considerable scorn,—on which the old lady seemed hurt; and having again offered and been again refused, she presented her basket to Olivia, who stood half turned from her, and kindly inviting her to partake of what she offered, but was again subjected to a refusal. Surprised at these rare circumstances, for it is uncommon indeed for school-girls to refuse tarts and cakes, a sudden light seemed to strike upon her mind, and she gave me such a penetrating look as I had never before received from her; then stooping down, and looking hard in the flushed and sullen falling face of Olivia, a tear suddenly trembled in her eye; she attempted to speak, but her voice faltered, and she looked round for her niece, as if she required her assistance to explain this mystery.

Being drawn by her aunt's eye, Anna presently came up to us, and was asked by her if she understood what was the matter with us? "You see, Anna," she said, "how dissatisfied they appear to be: I fear they are not well,—do speak to them, my dear Anna, and press them to tell me if they are unwell, or indisposed?"

"They are perfectly well, my dear aunt," said Anna, looking at us with more displeasure than I had ever seen in her countenance before.

"Then entreat them, I beg you, my dear," said our governess, "to tell us what grieves them, tell them that it is my greatest pleasure to see my children happy; and this evening," added the old lady, wiping away a tear, "this evening I had hoped to enjoy that pleasure without alloy." So saying, she turned to us, and offering a hand to each, for she had set down her basket on the grass, she entreated us to lay aside our sadness, adding, "if any thing has vexed you, my dear children, try to forget it, and be cheerful."

I scarcely know how I should have acted on this occasion, had leisure been afforded me for an instant's deliberation, but before one second had intervened, I heard my governess's name, as well as my own, repeated loud from the house, and at the same moment, saw my governess's maid-servant appear at the hall-door, accompanied by Mrs. Bridget: at sight of this last, I deliberated not a moment, but ran down the slope to meet her.

CHAPTER VIII.

Her Grandmother being taken ill sends for her to London—Her Governess's parting kindness—Juliana receives intelligence of the death of her parents—Goes to reside in Bath—Her Uncle's marriage; and her narrow escape from sudden death the means of producing a beneficial change to her character.

Without repeating all that passed between me and Mrs. Bridget, I shall inform my reader of the events which caused her sudden appearance in this place, at a time when I was thinking of nothing less than of herself.

It appeared that my grandmother, who was still in London, having had some uneasiness respecting my Uncle Barnaby, had been seized, a few days before, with a kind of paralytic attack, which threatened her life, and which, at first, rendered her quite insensible. Her senses, however, returned, after some hours, and she became so exceedingly impatient to see me, of whom she had lately become more fond than ever she had been of my mother, that it was thought advisable to humour her; and as travelling at that time was by no means so convenient as in these days of mail-coaches and steam-packets, it was thought expedient to send Mrs. Bridget down with all speed, to bring me up to town. Mrs. Bridget came charged with a letter from my cousin Cicely, and which enclosed a handsome present to my governess, and a request that I should be allowed to set off at a moment's warning, my governess being desired to send up my clothes after me to town. I had scarcely gathered the principal parts of her errand from Mrs. Bridget, when my governess joined us, and I have no recollection, such was the hurry of that moment, of what passed between my governess and my grandmother's maid. As soon, however, as I was made to understand that we were to depart, that very minute I ran up stairs, threw my clothes together into my drawers, put on my cloak and hat, and gave one look through the window on the terrace, the alcove, and the happy little party there; and strange to say, it was not without regret that I felt I was now going from them.

Who is there who, having parted, during the course of life, from some dear friends, or interesting companions, does not possess such a power of abstraction from present scenes, as sometimes to be able to close his eyes, and represent to himself, as in a picture, those objects and persons once so loved. On these occasions, in what lively colours does fancy sometimes paint a tender parent, now no more; a child cut off in the bloom of youth; a husband, brother, wife, or sister; and how naturally does it paint the scenes in which we have been wont to see them. Thus, at this moment,—though so many years have since passed—though so many events have intervened, I can still close my eyes, and behold this charming scene. The high bank enamelled with flowers,—the solemn grove in the back-ground,—the alcove decked with garlands of roses, and the lovely Anna presenting her baskets of fruit to her guests and her companions.

It was the shrill voice of Mrs. Bridget which called me from the contemplation of this scene, and it was the same notable body who hurried me from the presence of my governess, whose last look to her rebel pupil was that of love, and whose last action, as it respected me, was to place in my lap a paper containing some of those very cakes which I had lately rejected with so much insolence.

It is not my purport to fatigue my readers with a full history of my life, which has been long, and much varied; I shall therefore satisfy myself with passing hastily over every event which is not immediately necessary to the promotion of the object which I had in view when I began these memoirs.

When I left my governess's house, I was put into a post-chaise with Mrs. Bridget, and proceeded to town, where I found my grandmother better, but still so much indisposed that it was thought necessary for her to take a journey to Bath, where she was induced to take a house, the waters being thought necessary even to the preservation of her life. There we remained some years, and returned not at all during that time to Hartley Hall. In the mean time, I heard of the death of both my parents by fevers abroad, but remembered too little of them, and was too thoroughly selfish, to grieve for them, as all children ought to do for the authors of their being. During this period I had grown up, and was become one of the gayest in that gay and dissipated city. I spent all my mornings in visiting, and all my evenings in public, leaving my cousin Cicely to attend my infirm grandmother, who was indeed my only parent.

In the mean time my uncle Barnaby, who generally resided at Hartley Hall, used frequently to come to see us; and here, being persuaded by his mother, he selected a wife, and was led by Providence, I doubt not, to make a very good choice. The lady was not a young woman, and possessed little or no fortune; but she was a remarkably pleasant companion, and, in some respects, displayed more sense than commonly falls to the share of our sex. As my grandmother was in a very feeble state when this marriage took place, my aunt and uncle resolved not to leave her, in consequence of which, we became one family for several months.

At this period, there arrived a very celebrated preacher in Bath; this gentleman preached for many weeks in the abbey, through the favour of the rector, and there the mind of my aunt was opened to divine subjects in such a manner, as it never was before. She would willingly have engaged me to attend this preacher, and indeed succeeded in one or two instances; but my mind being filled with other matters, it was with little or no effect that I heard the words of truth from this minister.

Thus I proceeded in my career of folly and sin, without interruption, for some time after my uncle's marriage; till one evening, being dressed for a ball, and wearing a headdress of an immense height, such as were then in fashion; while I waited for a chair, I sat down to read a play which I intended to see the next day, and bringing my head (by accident as I then thought) in contact with the candle, my lappets took fire, and before the flames could be extinguished, one side of my face, and the back of my neck, were cruelly burnt. I can give you little idea of what I suffered from these burns; but the anguish was such, and the consequent depression of my spirits, that I almost could have wished to die, had I not a dread of exchanging the pains of time for those of eternity: for, Oh! who can dwell with everlasting burnings?

During my confinement with these wounds, I was attended by my aunt in such a manner as ever afterward endeared her to me beyond measure. It was this kind friend who daily dressed my burns; and it was this dear friend who availed herself of this suitable moment to lead me to my Saviour, to call my attention to my own natural depravity, and to other important truths inculcated by our blessed religion; and so successfully did she labour with me, or rather, so greatly were her labours blessed with regard to me, that I arose from my bed with new feelings; and though there remained but small marks of my wounds, I experienced no desire to return to the world, or to enter again into my former pursuits; my views of things were wholly changed, and I now began to see my former character in an entirely new and different view. Neither can it be doubted, but that I now recollected, with sorrow, my former ill behaviour to my governess and my little school-fellows, and my many impertinences to my grandmother.

CHAPTER IX.

The death of her Grandmother, and Juliana's return to reside at Hartley Hall—Her desire to revisit her amiable Governess, and to apologize for her misconduct—Her Aunt accompanies her to the School—Juliana's deep compunction upon learning the decease of her Governess.

I HAD not left my room many months after the accident I have recounted above, before I lost my grandmother. I rejoice to say, that through the instrumentality of my aunt, the poor lady's mind was considerably opened on the subject of religion. By her last will she provided handsomely for me; neither were Bridget nor my cousin Cicely forgotten. We left them behind us in Bath, where they had determined to live together, and I returned with my aunt and uncle to Hartley Hall, where we had resolved to reside in future, having given up the house in Bath. The first few days after our arrival in the country were, as you may suppose, fully occupied in settling ourselves in our habitation; but before one week had elapsed, we had so far arranged things within the house as to have leisure to look abroad, and it being the early part of summer, I accompanied my aunt one afternoon in an airing in the park. Our coachman having accidentally driven us into that part of the park through which we had formerly passed with my grandmother to the school, it was natural for me to recur to those days and scenes and persons I had witnessed and seen at that time, and I petitioned my aunt to gratify my impatience to see my dear old governess again, by ordering the coachman to proceed to the school.

My aunt, who was always willing to oblige me, instantly gave orders such as I desired, and we proceeded rapidly to the remote gate of the park before mentioned, and in a short time found ourselves upon the same breezy common formerly described.

During this our progress, I was busied in describing to my aunt my governess, her house, her garden, her lovely niece, her simple habits, and the pious tendency of her whole life and conversation. Neither was I by any means backward in speaking of my own very improper conduct, or in expressing my anxiety for an opportunity of making every apology. As I proceeded with my narrative, I recollect that I became considerably animated—my heart seemed to warm towards my old companions—I called each by their name, and began to conjecture in what manner they would be changed, and to ask myself, "Whether my governess would be much altered by age, or Anna much improved, through the lapse of time?"

My aunt asked me, "How many years had passed since I had left this spot?" to which I answered, "It will be four, when the time of year shall be come round again."

"Ah! my dear," she replied with a sigh, "and during this interval, may there not have occurred many changes, which you do not now calculate upon?"

This remark seemed to sink cold upon my heart; however, I made no reply: but, as we were now drawing near the village, I employed myself in tracing our old rambles among the neighbouring fields, and in such directions over the country as my eye could reach from the window of the coach.

At length we entered the village, and I called to the coachman to drive on to a white house at the very extremity of it. "My dear," said my aunt, "shall we not stop and inquire?" but as I did not second her motion, the coachman drove onwards, and presently we found ourselves in that part of the road directly opposite the gate of the school-garden.

And now, every well-known object was again before me; the thatched roof, the gable ends, the little porch, the casement window, the white rough-cast coat on the wall, the high bank of the garden, partly visible over the roof of the house, and the grove of oak-trees formerly mentioned, on the summit of the hill. I saw also, the waterfall, pouring down its mossy channel, and the little meadow, in which our quiet cow was accustomed to feed. Here also were the lilies, the laburnums, and the rose-trees, which used to be so highly cherished by our governess, and a low garden-seat, under the shade of a spreading chestnut, on which I had often seen her sit to read, while her family were amusing themselves in another part of the little domain.

But, although every natural and artificial object answered thus accurately to the impression left on my memory, there was shed around, and on every object, a certain air of solitude and neglect, which could not have escaped the eye of the most inaccurate observer. The garden-walks were overgrown with grass, and the flower-beds with weeds; the window-shutters of both the parlour-windows, and some of the bed-chambers, were closed: and instead of the jocund sound of happy infant voices, such as had saluted us when I first visited that place with my grandmother, we heard only the cawings of certain ravens, which had built their nests in the tops of the oak-trees above-mentioned, and the bleating of some sheep in a field on the other side of the road.

While I looked with dismay on this scene, I felt that sudden sinking of the spirits, which every person must feel when any bright and joyous feelings, which they may have experienced, meet with a sudden check.

My aunt had directed one of the servants to go up to the door of the house, and knock. He accordingly obeyed, and I waited with much anxiety the answer. It was some time, however, before the door was opened, by a feeble old woman, who in answer to my inquiries (for by this time I had alighted with my aunt, and entered the garden), informed me, that the lady I inquired after had been dead some time!

"Dead," I repeated, while the tears gushed into my eyes, "and shall I never see her more—never be able to tell her how much I now love her, and how glad I should be to repair the injuries I have done her?"

"My love," said my aunt, taking my hand and drawing me into the little vestibule, in order to screen me from the observation of the servants, "the good old lady is happy, we cannot doubt it. Why, then, should you grieve as one without hope?"

"And where," I said, "where is the lovely Anna—where is little Minna—where is Olivia?" and, as I mentioned each name, I burst into fresh agonies of tears.

"Ah! miss," said the old woman, whom I then recollected as being one who had formerly resided in the village, "ah! miss, I know not—I cannot answer you. It was, indeed a sad day when the dear old lady died, and all those sweet children were scattered abroad as lambs without a shepherd. Miss Anna grew up to be a bright example of piety in early youth. She was, indeed, as one of the polished corners of the temple; but when her aunt died she was left a second time without a home, 'a waif upon the world's wide wilderness.' And the poor little miss, the least of all, where was she to find a home, at least such a home, and such a mother, as she had lost?"

I wept with increased violence as the old woman proceeded. I could not help it, and the recollection of my former pride and hardness of heart struck like a dagger to my breast.

My aunt came near to me; she pressed my head against her gentle bosom, and pleaded every argument for comfort which our blessed religion can supply. She represented to me, that such a woman as my former governess, that is, one who had so long and so entirely relied upon her Saviour, as she appeared to have done, could not but have changed for the better, in leaving this world; for although "when a wicked man dieth, his expectation shall perish,"—nevertheless "the righteous is delivered out of trouble." Prov. xi. 7, 8. "And who, my dear niece," proceeded my aunt, "are those who are counted righteous in the sight of God, but those humble, and meek, and unpresuming characters, such as you have described the dear lady in question to have been, who, having through the divine mercy, been led to cast away all self-righteousness, desire only to be clothed in the righteousness of their Saviour, and in this garment to be presented unto him without spot or blemish?"

"I have no doubt of the happiness of my dear governess," I replied; "I could, indeed, have wished to have seen her once again, and to have confessed my faults and offences to her, and to have begged her pardon and blessing: but oh! my dear aunt, I cannot bear to think of the deserted and afflicted state of the lovely Anna—that sweet young creature, whom I once so wickedly insulted, though I never could truly despise one in whom I saw so many excellences."

"Make yourself easy, my dear," said my kind aunt, "we will seek her out, and if she is in distress, we will help her,—she shall not be left destitute—she shall not want a friend—Hartley Hall shall be her home." This kindness of my aunt seemed at that moment perfectly to overcome me, and I dropped my face on her bosom, as she sat by me.

In the mean time, the old woman gave us an account of the death of my governess, which she represented as having been very sudden. "Ah! madam," she added, addressing my aunt, "unless you had seen it, I could give you no notion of the very happy way in which the old lady lived with her little people. Every morning in summer, and every afternoon when the windows were open, I used to hear the sweet sounds of these children's voices lifted up to heaven in songs of praise; and then they were so kind to the poor, so smiling, so gentle, so polite, so fond of each other, and of their governess. Ah! ladies, it was a sore day when this little family was broken up, and their tender mother and faithful friend laid low in the dust. And now, miss," she said, "now I never more hear those songs of praise issuing from the windows, and no sweet infant faces are ready to smile upon me as I enter these garden gates."

"Oh! my aunt, my aunt," I said, "I could bear all this, if it were not for the recollection of my ill-behaviour and ingratitude when residing under this roof."

I then rose up with the intention of revisiting our school-room, my little bed-room, the terrace, and the alcove, but my heart failed me: and being wholly overcome with painful reflections, I returned to the coach, whither I was soon followed by my aunt, who waited only to give the old woman a present before she followed me. From that period I made it my business to seek out my school-fellows, but never could meet with any but Olivia, who has become a very amiable young woman, and was not sorry to improve her acquaintance with me, especially when she found the change, which, through the divine blessing, had taken place in my feelings. Olivia often visited me at Hartley Hall, and we often talked of the days which were past; but although we took the utmost pains to trace out Anna and little Minny, we never could discover what had become of them: it seems that they had left the country, immediately after the death of my governess, but whither they went, or what became of them, we never could make out. Thus with respect to these young people, we were left without other comfort than that which we were able to derive from Scripture, wherein, in many passages, the Almighty promises his protection to the orphans and fatherless, and especially to those who are of the seed of the righteous: "The poor committeth himself unto thee for thou art the helper of the fatherless" (Psalm x. 14.); "I have been young and now am old, yet have I not seen the righteous forsaken, nor his seed begging bread." Psalm xxxvii. 25.

Olivia was much with me during my youth; she often was our visiter for weeks at Hartley Hall, and I have, in return, spent many happy hours in the pea-green tea-room at her father's house. She was a particularly pleasant companion, both to me and to my aunt, because she possessed a larger share of Christian humility and simplicity than any young person I ever met with, always excepting the beloved Anna. These qualities I always attributed, under the divine blessing, to the instruction she had received at school, and to her early intercourse with Anna, the charming young creature above-mentioned. Olivia was accordingly my frequent companion in youth, and our friendship continued after we were both married, and became mothers: neither was there any interruption of our friendly intercourse till death deprived me of this my cherished friend.

It is some years since I lost my Olivia, but as I was her frequent companion during her gradual progress from youth to age, I have not that clear remembrance of her in her sweet girlish days, as I have of the lovely Anna, whose sweet figure and charming countenance is almost now present with me, as she stood under my window, blooming and sparkling with innocent delight, and crowned with her basket of roses. Nor can I, even to this moment, call this lovely creature to remembrance, without shedding tears of regret for the pain I gave her, and for my ingratitude to her beloved aunt.

And now, my gentle reader, having accomplished the task I proposed to myself, and set before you such passages of my life as were necessary to my purpose, I proceed to point out the end which I had in view in setting myself this task: namely, that I might afford a warning to young people:—that from the knowledge of what I have suffered at times through life, from the recollection of my proud and ungrateful conduct towards the friends of my youth, they may learn to avoid offences of the same nature towards their parents and instructers: for, let them be assured, that these faults, which now may appear so light to them, will, at some future time, arise like serpents, and sting them to the heart.

ERMINA;

OR, THE

SECOND PART

OF

JULIANA OAKLEY.

PREFACE.

If any of my present readers should happen to have read the history of Juliana Oakley, they will undoubtedly have some recollection of the lovely Anna and the little Minny; and though the younger was greatly inferior to the elder, yet I trust that what has lately come to my knowledge respecting these young persons may not be wholly without interest to those who are already in some degree acquainted with them. The sequel of their history was conveyed to me in a course of letters, written by Ermina herself, at that period of life in which she was enabled, through grace, to meditate with some advantage on her past experience; and as her account of herself contains some particulars and notices of a mode of life little understood in Europe, I no longer hesitate to give it to the little community of young readers who have hitherto accepted, with so much apparent satisfaction, many of my humble endeavours to amuse them.

ERMINA;

OR, THE

SECOND PART OF JULIANA OAKLEY.

CHAPTER I.

Ermina's account of herself.

THE history of my former companion, Miss Juliana Oakley, having been lately put into my hands, and there seeing my own name, and that of my lovely and beloved Anna, I have been induced to look back upon my own life, and have at length resolved to send you, my friends in England, some recollections of my former days, which I trust may not be wholly without interest.

I remember little of my life before I came to reside with my governess, or rather, I should say my second mother; she found me a little friendless orphan, and brought me to her own house, where I was never made to feel my orphan state. My parents had resided in Cornwall, where my governess had been paying a visit at the time of their deaths, and I never knew of any other relation than an uncle, who being a wild youth, ran from his father's house, went to sea, and was not heard of for many years; I shall say nothing of the happy days I spent with my governess, that period which was blessed to me through life, and will be so, through all eternity, for it was in that blessed abode of peace I acquired my first and most correct ideas of religion, and though the impressions seemed to wear away for a time, yet they were never entirely erased. After the death of my dear governess, I was left wholly destitute, and should have been without a home, had not an old aunt of my dear Anna's and a sister of my governess taken pity upon me; this good woman had come from Cornwall on hearing of her sister's illness, and had only arrived in time to close her eyes. Immediately after the funeral she returned with her niece Anna and myself to Falmouth, where she resided, and we made our journey in three days on the outside of a heavy coach.

I endured much fatigue on the road, and when we arrived at Falmouth, late one dark evening, at the end of autumn, young as I was, I felt myself shocked, not only by the dirtiness of the streets, but still more by the appearance of the house into which she conducted us. It was a kind of little low shop furnished in the roughest manner, and contained the wearing apparel of sailors, by making which Mrs. Finchley, for such was the name of my new protectress, obtained a scanty living; behind the shop was a small dark kitchen, and John Finchley, the master, was busy at his counter, serving two rough faced sailors, as we entered the door, carrying our own baggage.

I had been used to humble, but not to sordid life, and being wholly overcome with fatigue I burst into tears the moment I was set down in the kitchen.

Anna on this occasion looked sorrowfully at me, but she did not speak, and Mrs. Finchley's daughter, who was, as I afterward found, the wife of a sailor, then absent on a voyage, endeavoured to comfort me, saying, that I should soon be used to them all, and that then I should be as happy as I had been before the death of her aunt.

I thought that this was impossible, however I tried to hide my tears, and after having been refreshed with tea, I was shown to my bed-room, where I was rejoiced to find that Anna was to be my companion. Our chamber was up two pair of dark and narrow stairs; it was very small; the floor and ceiling were uneven; it contained only half of a window, the other half being cut off to give light to the next room; this window was a small sash, and as there was no curtain, admitted the light of a candle from an upper room in the opposite house; in one corner of the room stood the bed, the curtains of which being of tarnished green stuff, were nailed to a lath, fastened on the ceiling; a cracked looking glass, a chest of walnut drawers, a deal table, and two broken chairs completed the furniture of this wretched apartment: where, instead of being regaled with the taste of the fresh breezes among the trees, the song of the nightingale, the hoot of owls, or the murmur of waterfalls, together with the breath of many flowers, we were stunned with the oaths and songs of drunken sailors from the court below, where was a public house, and almost suffocated with the fumes of tobacco.

When Anna and I found ourselves shut up in this place, we looked at each other for a few minutes in silent despair: at length Anna began to shed tears, and I threw myself upon her bosom and wept with her till I could weep no longer, and being quite worn out and sick was compelled to undress and go to bed, where I presently found some relief in sleep.

The light of morning was so much obscured by the dinginess of the glass in the window, and the smoke and fog of the town, that we were not aware that the sun had risen till it was late; at length Mrs. Finchley entered our room and kindly assisted us to dress, then leading me by the hand down the stairs, she brought us into the kitchen, where our breakfast waited; there she sat down by us, and while she used her needle with much diligence, she thus addressed us. "My dear Anna and Minny, I am sorry I have no better home to offer you, I am sensible that this must appear a shocking place to you after your former delightful residence; but such as it is, I am thankful for it, many better persons than I am would be glad of such a resting-place as this; and thank God I live in hopes of a better home, even an eternal one.

"Finchley and I have gone through many sorrows, and endured many losses. It was thought when I was married, that my husband was a thriving man, and we possessed a hadsome shop and good business in an airy part of the town; we then looked forward to finishing our days in ease and affluence, but Providence ordained otherwise; we suffered many losses, and were at length reduced to live as we now do. Of six children who were born to us we have one only now living, four died in infancy and are now in glory, and our son, our hopeful and beloved, perished in the Eastern Seas as much as three years past; we were in the dark concerning his fate for many months, but at length were assured thereof by a comrade who saw him tumble overboard; it was a severe blow to lose our child in such a way, but it was a kind one," added the poor mother, "it has been blessed to us, it has driven us to seek comfort where we never sought it before, and we have been brought to say that which no man can say without divine help, *Thy will, O God, be done!*" In this part of her discourse Mrs. Finchley wiped her eyes, and then turning cheerfully to Anna, she added, "And now my dear niece, having told you my story, I must be plain with you on other matters: I shall never ask you, my child, to go into the shop, you are too young for such services in this place; but you will not refuse to help me with your needle, and in such household duties as can be performed in private, and I am sure this little miss will assist you, for the truth is," and she burst into tears. "I cannot, however willing, keep you my girls, unless you can help to keep yourselves."

I forget what answer we made, indeed I believe we made no answer whatever, but we both ran into her arms and all wept together, and from that moment we felt ashamed of ever expressing our uneasiness at our situation, even by a look; but what is more strange, after a time we became wonderfully reconciled to our situation, and though we remembered our happy home, from which we were now for ever parted, with a degree of sadness which we never overcame, yet we were blessed with a peace of mind while at Falmouth for which I could never acount; our feelings nevertheless partook of a degree of sadness at times, and our spirits were always in a state of something like depression; we enjoyed no pleasures, we were almost wholly confined in the dark kitchen above-mentioned, and we spent our time in making shirts for sale and committing hymns and portions of Scripture to memory; we seldom tasted the fresh air, and yet I have often looked back on that time as one of the most blessed of my life. I have often asked myself how I could possibly have been contented at that period, and have often inquired whence that peace proceeded which I then enjoyed. The answer which I have often given to this question was this, that at the period I speak of, I had in the first place been thoroughly humbled, for young as I was I had been made sensible of the desolate situation to which I must have been reduced had not Mrs. Finchley taken pity on me, and in the second place, my only companion, for I seldom met the rest of the family, excepting at meals, was my lovely Anna, whose sweet and pious discourse was ever tending to lift me above this world, and to give me interesting and glorious views of the next. Sometimes indeed we indulged ourselves in speaking of former days, in calling to mind our birth-day gambols, our garlands of roses, our violet-banks, and primrose-beds, the sweet stories our governess used to read to us in the long winter evenings, and the still more interesting tales which she was wont to recount when we gathered round her in the dusk, and I, as the youngest, was permitted to sit upon her knee; but we did not often permit this sort of discourse to ourselves, because these indulgences always ended in tears, and unfitted us for our duties; therefore Anna would not unseldom interrupt me when I desired to introduce these subjects, saying, "Let us look forward and not backward my dear Minny, being assured, as we are, that that which has gone before is not to be compared with those glories which are to come, when we may all hope to meet in the presence of our beloved Saviour, and when we may hope to be as He is, without sin and no longer subject to affliction."

CHAPTER II.

Character and conduct of Mrs. Finchley—Her delicacy and benevolence in the midst of poverty—Anna's distress during the walk on the sea-shore—Mr. and Mrs. Finchley discover the cause—Their generous resolution, followed by the arrival of two Strangers.

I SPENT nearly two years at Falmouth in the manner above described, during which time I rarely enjoyed the fresh air, excepting sometimes on a pleasant evening, when Mrs. Finchley used to take us to walk on the sands; for, with a delicacy rarely met with in persons of her station, she seldom permitted us to go out alone; it was certain that our health suffered from the close confinement, but our morals would probably have suffered more, had we been left at entire liberty, because in towns on the coast and where seafaring persons resort, there is often much to be seen greatly injurious to the minds of the unexperienced. Mrs. Finchley often lamented that she could not turn us out to play in the green fields, but, as she used to say, she had only a choice of evils for us, and she endeavoured to choose that which was the least.

I have often, on reflection, admired the character of this poor woman, though not a loud professor, or one who talked vainly of religion, yet I believe that her every action was influenced by religious principles, her whole life was one continued act of self-denial; she never seemed to think of herself, or provide for her own comforts; she had much to endure from a certain irritability in the temper of her husband, and much to suffer from real poverty, yet she was always calm and resigned, and when the subject of her afflictions was particularly pressed upon her, she invariably expressed herself as being thankful for the comforts she possessed, and as being happy in the prospect of a future intimate union with that dear Saviour whose presence she then felt, and whose secret consolations enabled her even then to go on rejoicing, under circumstances which most persons would havè thought truly miserable. I have little doubt that there are many characters which resemble that of Mrs. Finchley among the lower ranks of Christians in England, and yet these perhaps are not the persons most highly esteemed and best known in the professing world; but the Almighty knows his own, and the time will come when the secrets of all hearts will be made manifest. Oh may we all in that dread hour be found to have received renewed hearts, and to have been made one with Him, of whom it was justly said, He has done no violence, neither was deceit found in his mouth.

We remained nearly two years with Mrs. Finchley, and one circumstance which took place about that time I never can forget. I had grown rapidly during this period, and my little wardrobe was wholly exhausted; on this occasion poor Mrs. Finchley produced a gown of her own, and cut, and tucked, and new arranged it till she had fitted it for my wearing. She had but little stock no doubt, for she dressed very shabbily, but she could not bear to see the friendless orphan in a ragged state, and I can well recollect the pleasure with which she tied this frock upon me on a Sunday morning, and turned me round to see how well I looked.

Why should the recollection of this circumstance bring tears to my eyes even at this remote period? but there is something so inexpressibly affecting in works of real love and pure charity; something so divine in the nature of unostentatious benevolence, that that heart must be hard indeed which can contemplate it without some tender feelings.

At length the time of our residence at Falmouth was drawing to a close, though we were not aware of it. During the former part of our continuance there, Mrs. Wilmot, the daughter of Mrs. Finchley, had not heard of her husband, who had sailed a little before my dear governess's death, as a common sailor in an East-Indiaman, bound for the China Seas, and we could not have expected him back in less than two years.

From the circumstance, however, of his absence, and the increase of the family, owing to our having become inmates of it, there was evidently a considerable shortness of money, and though Mrs. Finchley, her husband, her daughter, and Anna, all worked hard, it was evident that it was often with difficulty that common necessaries were obtained; from Mrs. Finchley, however, I never heard a murmur, and though poor John sometimes looked blank when counting up his gains at the end of the week, he never seemed for a moment to grudge the food which fell to my share, and for which I could then make no remuneration.

Such was the state of things, when one fine evening in autumn, Mrs. Finchley proposed that we should walk out on the sands, before the night-service, for we often attended a church at six o'clock, which was situated very conveniently for our house.

It was a dry, fresh afternoon, and though the sun was low, yet it cast a fearful glow over the town, the bay, and the sands, which extended themselves before us. When clear of the suburbs, Mr. and Mrs. Finchley walked a little before us with their daughter, and I followed with Anna. We went on for some time without speaking, and as I rather wondered at Anna's silence, for she was generally cheerful on occasions of this kind, and looking up to her face, I saw that she was particularly pale, and had tears in her eyes.

"Dear Anna," I said, "what is the matter?"—"Oh Minny," she replied, "I am unhappy; look at my beloved aunt, see how shabby and patched her clothes are, and her bonnet, how brown it is, and her shawl, how old; and my uncle also, look at his clothes—his Sunday clothes too:—Oh Minny, dear Minny, I fear that they are very poor, and that we are a heavy burthen to them, and I cannot bear the thought," and her tears, which had at first only fallen drop by drop, now ran like torrents from her eyes.

I was quite old enough (for I was then near eleven) to sympathize in her feelings; we both wept bitterly, and I do not know that I ever felt more unhappy.

At length, however, we tried to compose ourselves, and I was much comforted by a quotation from Scripture, which my beloved Anna brought forward, viz. "Trust in the Lord and do good, so shalt thou dwell in the land, and verily thou shalt be fed." Psalm xxxvii. 3. While thus engaged with our own exchange of ideas, our elders, who were considerably before us, suddenly came to a stand; and Mr. Finchley, who had lived too long near the sea to be wholly unacquainted with maritime affairs, called to us to come up in haste, to see a large ship, which was sailing with a favourable gale up the channel. "Depend upon it, Martha," said he to his daughter, "that vessel is an East Indiaman," and he mentioned some indications by which he knew it; he also added, soon afterward, that he could plainly distinguish a boat coming from the vessel towards the bay.

This was an interesting sight to Mrs. Wilmot, and we stood and watched the boat till the sun was set, and we could distinguish it no longer; we then returned home, and sat down to tea, where I was no sooner in my usual place than Mrs. Finchley discovered the traces of tears on my cheeks, and the excellent woman asked me in sudden alarm, what could be the matter. I was then in a humble, and consequently a sweet state, and on her putting the question to me, I ran into her arms, and sobbed and wept upon her bosom.

She was alarmed, and begged me to explain the cause of my distress: I then told her all that had passed between me and Anna during our walk, on which Anna began to weep, and John Finchley, extending his big broad hand to Anna, at the same time drawing me to his heart, said, "Dear girls, dear children—wipe away your tears, fear not for yourselves, you shall never want a home, we will stand and fall, live and die together, so God have mercy upon us."

"Oh! we don't think of ourselves, indeed, indeed we don't," we both replied, "we think only of you, our dear father and mother, we are only sorry we can't help you."

I can hardly say what followed, but surely this exercise of tender feelings converted our dark and miserable kitchen into the gates of heaven. We had scarcely recovered any thing like composure before we heard a loud knocking, which was repeated again and again, till the whole house shook.

We looked one at another with amazement; Mrs. Wilmot turned pale, Mrs. Finchley set down the teapot, and Mr. Finchley stood up, and did not stir; the knocking continued, and then followed loud whoops and cries like that of a sailor calling to his companions.

"It's some wild chaps in a drunken frolic," said Mr. Finchley; "Is the door barred?" and he rushed out into the shop to ascertain the point, followed by us all.

"Are you all dead and buried," exclaimed a voice from without, "but I see the blink of a candle too."

"What voice is that," said John Finchley, "I don't know it."

Violent thunderings at the door again followed, after which came another cheer, and then these words, "Father — mother — Martha — are you all dead and buried?"—"What voice is that," said the mother, and looked the image of death.

Fresh thunderings at the door next followed, which, however, ceased the moment Mr. Finchley, with trembling hands, endeavoured to undo the fastenings, which he had hardly effected, when two young men, followed by an elder one, burst into the shop, and were saluted by a loud shriek on the part of the mother, who fell senseless the next moment in the arms of one of them.

CHAPTER III.

The Strangers' account of themselves, and the kind providence of their arrival to all the parties explained.

WHAT followed after this violent shriek I hardly know, for all seemed to be confusion to me—one and another were embracing each other, neither could I understand whether the tears which I saw were tokens of joy or sorrow, for I had never witnessed a scene like this;—the venerable father groaned—the daughter sobbed—and the mother remained long insensible, and at length when she opened her eyes, she shrieked again and sunk on the breast of the young man who had first flown to her. After a while, however, she spoke, and looking up in his face, "My William," she said, "can it be! Oh no, no; it cannot, my old eyes deceive me, and yet it is my William, my long lost William; my child whom I have mourned as dead so long; God be praised," she added, "but (clasping her hands and looking upwards), but he knows my gratitude; words cannot express it," and she became so agitated, so hysterical, that they were obliged to carry her into the inner room, where she was with difficulty kept from another fainting fit, by the application of water to her temples, and open windows, and every thing else which could be devised.

In the mean time the whole party were becoming more composed, and I was enabled to make out that the two young men whose arrival had so affected the family, were no other than William Finchley, whom we had all supposed to have perished some years since, and James Wilmot, the husband of Martha; but there was a third person, and this person was dressed as a gentleman, was a middle aged man, and looked as if he was no uninterested spectator of the present scene. He had taken Mr. Finchley's great chair in the kitchen, and there had sat taking now and then a pinch of snuff quite at his ease, till at length seeing Mrs. Wilmot so much recovered from her agitation as to be able to give some attention to ordinary things, he took two gold pieces from his pocket, and showing them to her, requested her to go to the next inn and order as good a supper for eight persons as that money would fetch; "and let it be brought here," he said, "for we will have one meal together, at least, before we part; and mind," he added, "that we have no salt meat, or ship provisions, but good Europe beef-steaks and fresh potatoes; let us have some porter too, and English cheese; none of your Dutch pine-apple, but good double Gloucester, if any is to be had."

I heard all this, and saw Mrs. Wilmot go out with her husband, and could not help wondering who this good gentleman might be, who called about him so decidedly and yet so good-humouredly; but I soon forgot him, for my attention was again drawn to William Finchley, who being seated by his mother, and holding her hand, was telling her how he had been saved from the waves after he had fallen from the ship's side, by a small country craft belonging to Madras, adding many other circumstances to his story, of great interest to his parents, and to all who heard it.

William's narrative was not, however, half finished, when it was interrupted by the reappearance of Wilmot and his wife, followed by two waiters, bearing trays, and then what a bustle were we all in, in removing the teacups, setting out a large table which had long stood disregarded under the kitchen shelves, and putting all things in order for the supper; while the old gentleman above-mentioned gave his directions and called about him in such a manner, that it was no longer even in Mrs. Finchley's power not to notice him.

"Sir," said she, "I beg your pardon, I hope, however, that you will excuse me, but I did not observe—"

"Ay, ay," said the gentleman, "I thought as much, you actually did not see me; I thought how it was, very well, very well; I am half-offended, however, and yet you ought to be very thankful to me, for had it not been for me you would not have seen your sons for some weeks to come, I can tell you that, and they must be off with me in a day or two for London, but they will not be long away."

"Bless you, sir," said Mrs. Finchley, "bless you, my dear good sir,—"

"Oh, I am a dear good sir, now," replied the old gentleman, smiling; "but mind this, my good woman, you never saw me till you began to smell the beef-steaks, and here they are smoking hot," and the old gentleman instantly set himself down to the table, and insisting that we should all place ourselves round him, begged that we would cut away and enjoy ourselves.

The gentleman had fallen on his hot steaks, without giving thanks, nevertheless, John Finchley would not be bribed, even by the smoking supper, to follow his example ; but rising up, and calling on his family so to do ; "My children," he said, "if we now fail to give thanks for this our happy and unhoped-for reunion around our table, we are undoubtedly without excuse, for never, Oh, my God, never I trust, may we cease to be grateful for the happiness of this blessed evening." Having thus spoken, we were all directed to sit down again, and notwithstanding our late violent agitation, we did credit to our repast, which was such a one indeed as few of us had tasted for some years.

The stranger, in the mean time, seemed to enjoy himself thoroughly, and when he had somewhat satisfied his appetite, "Mrs. Finchley," he said, "are not you anxious to know who I may be, who am dropped among you without invitation? for I am sure you never so much as once asked me to walk in, or even to stay when I was in ; well, but I won't be offended this time, though if you are not civiller the next time I come I shan't trouble you again."

"Sir, my good sir," said Mrs. Finchley, "I am sure I meant no manner of offence, but I was so overcome, and am so still, that I hardly now know what I am a-doing."

"Very excusable, very excusable," replied the gentleman, "such things as sons coming back after they have been dead three years, do not often happen, and so I believe I must pass over your want of politeness for this once, because I know you to be a good woman; but now for my name, if you won't ask it, to be sure I must tell you it, as well as my business, without being asked.

"My name, Mrs. Finchley, is Townley;" we all started, for that was my surname; "I had an only brother, and excellent parents," continued the old gentleman, "we lived near this place, and were a happy family, at least might have been so, but I was a rebellious son; I desired to go to sea, and my father did not wish it, in consequence I ran away, and got on shipboard: no matter what I suffered there, not half what I deserved; however, I went through many adventures, and was in the China Seas for several years; at length, however, I got a footing in Bengal, entered into some little mercantile concerns, married a woman who brought me some lacks, and am now as rich a merchant in my line as any one in India.

"For many years I heard nothing of my own family, though I was so happy as to have written and received a kind answer from my father, before his death, but I knew nothing of my brother's history till I met with your son, Mrs. Finchley, at Calcutta, and hearing that he was a native of Falmouth, I questioned him about my poor brother; heard he was dead, and had left a daughter, who was then actually under his aunt's care."

Mr. Townley had no reason to complain of want of attention to his story, as he proceeded, for we all looked eagerly at him, though no one spoke.

"As soon as I heard of my brother's child," continued he, "I resolved to come to England, and adopt her, if I could find her, for I have never had any child of my own; and accordingly I took my passage in the same ship with your son-in-law and son, and this evening, as you know, am arrived here, where, by-the-by, I can't boast much of my reception," added he, with a smile, "for there was not one among you who as much as said, Welcome to England, sir."

"Oh, sir," said Mrs. Finchley, "you must please to forget that; if you had intended for us to have made much of you, you should not have sent our dear William before you:" and the good woman in this part of her speech was unable to refrain herself from throwing her arms again around the sun-burnt, yet fine youth, who sat by her side.

"Come, come, Mrs. Finchley, do try to forget that wild boy, and pay some attention to your guest," said Mr. Townley; "and now, my good lady, can you tell me any thing of my niece? where is the little girl?" and he looked at Anna and me, and perhaps seeing something in our countenances which indicated more than he quite understood, "Surely," he said, "surely she is not present;" adding, as he looked at Anna, "my tender lily, surely you can't be my niece! No, I am mistaken, I see; then it must be the little dimpled one who clings so fast to Mrs. Finchley; tell me, my excellent woman, is this little girl my poor brother's daughter?"

"She is, sir, yes, she is," replied Mrs. Finchley, "this child is Ermina Townley, your own niece, if you are indeed the brother of Mr. James Townley; and you may guess how destitute the poor little thing must have been to have been reduced so such a home as this."

"A happy, happy home," I exclaimed, clinging to Mrs. Finchley; and I whispered, "don't let them take me away from you, my dear, dear mother."

My uncle seemed instantly to conceive what was the state of the case; for he immediately replied, "Dear child, don't make yourself uneasy, you and I shall be better acquainted by-and-by; but come to me, my little niece, and give me one kiss for your father's sake, and now back again to Mrs. Finchley's side." He then called for another draught of porter, laid down the money to pay for the supper, and promising to call the next morning, walked off to the nearest inn, leaving us behind to recover ourselves from the astonishment into which the various events of the evening had thrown us.

CHAPTER IV.

The proposed voyage to India—Mr. Townley's generosity to the Finchley Family—Ermina and Anna embark—Their feelings, and the subject of their conversation.

THE next morning my uncle came again to Mrs. Finchley, and had a long conversation with her, after which I was called, and asked if I should like to go with him to India. The idea of leaving all those I knew, and going with a total stranger, was dreadful to me, and I therefore answered that I would rather stay where I was.

I was then reasoned with, and my uncle promised me many fine things, among which I remember a coach and horses, if I would go with him; on which I replied, I would go if I might take Anna with me, but not without; "But perhaps," said my uncle, "your favourite Anna would not go with you."

"Then I will stay here," I replied, and at the same time made my escape out of the room.

In the evening I was called again to my uncle, and he then told me, that he had considered my proposal, and resolved to take Anna with me, adding, to Mrs. Finchley, that he considered this would be some kind of return to her excellent sister, for what she, during her life, had done for me; "and your niece," he added, "shall fare alike in all things with mine, on this condition only, that as she is much older than Ermina, that she take charge of her, and instruct her."

"She could do no less," said Mrs. Finchley, and the good woman expatiated largely in praise of my uncle's generosity.

"I see no generosity in the case," he replied, "I, who am rich, am doing no more than what your sister did in the utmost need."

"True," replied Mrs. Finchley, "and yet, sir, you must allow me to say that I feel your kindness deeply."

"And what for?" said my uncle, "I am doing nothing for you, and yet you have done as much for Minny as your sister has."

"Don't speak of it, sir," she answered, "I could not have found in my heart to let the poor thing want a home."

"Well," returned my uncle, "you shall be none the worse for what you have done; I am going to London, and your sons must go with me to meet the ship and receive their money, and after that I trust that we shall all meet again in this place, and then we will talk a little of your affairs; but in the mean time there are twenty guineas, Mrs. Finchley, rig yourselves a little better with them; and I shall be obliged to you if you will look out for a good day-school, and let Minny and her friend attend it, for I expect to be in England some eighteen months, or thereabouts, and should wish the girls to have every advantage of education."

The next morning my uncle set off to London in the inside of the heavy coach, while the two young sailors were on the outside; and Mrs. Finchley immediately set to work to fit us for our attendance on the only respectable school then in Falmouth; where we learned to read a little French, with the beginning of some other accomplishments which we never had time to bring to any kind of perfection.

My uncle was absent about six weeks, and when he returned, brought with him the two young sailors, who were both anxious to se tle at home; and then the kind gentleman, for he was indeed always kind and warm-hearted, made such arrangements for Mrs. Finchley's family as relieved them at once from all their embarrassments. He settled Wilmot and his wife in the old shop, and having got a situation in the dock-yard for William Finchley, he settled the old couple in a neat little cottage just out of the town, which he furnished for them, settling upon them twenty pounds a year for their lives, which, with the little Mrs. Finchley had received from her father, which might be about ten pounds more, and what she could earn with her needle, as she worked for her daughter's shop, with what her husband might obtain by any light labour he could perform, it was supposed they might live in comparative ease. In the mean time, while all these arrangements were going on, Anna and I were occupied continually with our school duties; and I do not recollect being affected, as I afterward was, by the prospect of the change of my situation; indeed, during the eighteen months of my uncle's residence in England, my heart clung so to Mrs. Finchley that I could hardly bear to hear of my voyage, and more than this, the truly discreet and pious manner in which this excellent woman always spoke of the various reverses of fortune, with the pomps and pleasures of this life, certainly was a powerful means of keeping my mind in a state of sobriety for it.

I have often thought that it is not so much the outward circumstances of pride and pomp which affect the mind of youth, so much as the comments made on these things by injudicious and worldly persons in their hearing; and hence the care which should be taken by all persons who wish to bring up their children in the ways of holiness, to avoid all worldly, ambitious, and covetous discourse in their presence.

As I have much to say respecting myself, after having left England, and as my adventures in a foreign country, though no way remarkable, may probably possess more interest for my young readers than any thing which I can tell them previous to my leaving Falmouth, I shall not say much of my separation from dear Mrs. Finchley and her daughter; of the tears of Anna in quitting her native shore; of the blessings poured upon us by the worthy old couple; or of the agitation of my young heart when I was lifted into the boat which was to convey me to the East-Indiaman; but will entreat my readers to endeavour, if they can, to conceive my astonishment when I found myself in one of the best cabins of the ship, surrounded with every possible comfort for a long voyage; with no other companions of my apartment but my dear Anna and a black woman, whom my uncle had provided as a servant.

At the back of our cabin was a window, in the quarter of the ship, and from thence I beheld the bay, the town, and the little boat which had brought us from thence, together with the figure of William Finchley, who had accompanied us. Anna stood with me at the window, contemplating this scene, but I should despair of giving any idea of our feelings: as the vessel was under-way, we were soon obliged to quit the window by a heavy sickness which came over us, and were forced to lay ourselves on the beds which had been provided for us on each side of the cabin. Being made thankful at the same time that we had one with us, viz. our black servant, who was too experienced a sailor to be affected by the motion of the vessel and swell of the sea. From that time we saw England no more; the wide waters had soon extended themselves between our vessel and the shore, and before I was able to leave my bed, we were past the latitude of the most southern point of Europe.

My uncle came into our cabin, soon after we were laid on our beds, and to my great surprise began to laugh heartily at our afflictions, at the same time saying, "Well, Minny, I think you have done well to bring a companion with you, for at any rate there is some comfort when in affliction, to have a friend who can sympathize with you."

Anna recovered from her sickness sooner than I did, for I remained a long time unable to rise from my bed, and during the whole of that time I felt particularly unhappy. I had a kind of feverishness hanging about me, which could not be overcome, and during that period I had such a longing for the green and fresh scenes where I had spent my early days, as I can in no way describe.

At this time the bleating of the sheep on the deck used particularly to affect me, as it reminded me of a breezy common near my dear governess's, where we used to walk and play on a summer's evening, drinking in the fresh air, and inhaling therewith all the fragrance of a thousand spicy herbs. Once in particular, these images of rural life had taken such possesion of my mind, that I started up in my sleep during the middle of the night, and calling on some of my old school-fellows, added, that I was ready to go out with them immediately, and then being half awakened, and hearing the rushing of the waters against the side of the ship, I began to sob violently, and could not be appeased till Anna came into my bed, took me in her arms, and promised to hold me during the rest of the night.

How sweetly, when I was come to my recollection, did she then discourse with me on the presiding care of Providence, and how beautifully did she enlarge on the mighty works of mercy and of love, as displayed in the salvation of man; and how tenderly did she sooth me to sleep on her blameless bosom. She was indeed a lovely example of all that is rare and excellent in youth; patient in adversity, moderate and humble in prosperity, ever devoted to the service of others, and never engrossed by self. But are not these the effects of grace? Man is naturally a selfish being, a stranger to that charity which seeketh not its own; and hence we may be assured that whenever the love of self is effectually subdued, the Holy Spirit has not only commenced His work but carried it on to a considerable extent.

CHAPTER V.

Ermina's recovery—Introduced to Mrs. Palmerston—Their profuse outfit—Observations respecting dress—Anna's gratitude—Mrs. Palmerston's affectation—Mistaken flattery—Her ideas of gentility and love of finery contrasted with Anna's agitated feelings and ingenuous sentiments.

When our vessel had passed the stormy neighbourhood of the Bay of Biscay and we were entered into calmer seas, I suddenly recovered—became eager for food—and found myself in a few hours as well as I had ever been in my life.

It was about noon on this day that my uncle came

into our cabin, bringing with him a Mrs. Palmerston, who occupied the cabin next to ours. This was the lady of a rich civilian in Bengal, who had been at home for her health, and was then returning to her husband with a large assortment of the latest Europe fashions, in which she no doubt expected to make a splendid figure among her old friends in Calcutta. "These, Mrs. Palmerston," said my uncle, "are my young ladies; I did not wish you to see them while they were unwell, for you would not have seen them to advantage, but now that they are fit to appear you will oblige me much if you will take them by the hand and introduce them to our friends on deck, and if you would add a few hints respecting their dress, you would greatly oblige me; they have hitherto, I believe, worn only their morning gowns, for I foresaw how it would be, and ordered the person in town who made their clothes to provide a box of these sort of things, but I will order up another box from the hold, and then if you will see that they are dressed properly—"

"Surely, Mr. Townley," replied Mrs. Palmerston, "I shall have the greatest pleasure in doing all you desire, only send up the box and I promise you that your young ladies shall have every assistance from me;" and she seated herself on my bed, which was converted into a sofa by day, with a sort of glee which people evince when they are about to have a great treat.

"Have we any more clothes, uncle?" I said, in a low voice. "More clothes than are there in that great box? What an immense quantity we must have!"

"What does she say?" asked Mrs. Palmerston.

"Nothing at all," replied my uncle, "nothing but nonsense;" and he gave me a look, by which I was made to understand that I must not say things of this kind again in the presence of Mrs. Palmerston, but why, or wherefore, I could not imagine.

We had been measured for our clothes at Falmouth, and our measures had been sent to London, and this is all we had known about our sea stock: accordingly when we saw one large box full of white linen wrappers, we had thought ourselves very rich indeed, and Anna having counted up the contents of this box had set herself in the most innocent manner to calculate how frequently we might put on clean things, in order to make our linen serve us for five months: neither she or

I had ever dreamed of other boxes containing dress suits of silk and muslin trimmed with lace, with sashes, veils, necklaces, and all those etceteras which after a while seem to become almost indispensable to the female sex. We had been early taught that our ornaments were not to be those of gold and pearls and costly array, but those of a meek and quiet spirit, which in the sight of God is of great price.

Oh happy simplicity :—how blessed was I while I retained that simplicity, and oh! how gladly would I often, in later periods of my life, have exchanged all the magnificent circumstances of oriental life, for the simple taste and innocent delights of my childhood, and the enjoyments of that simple period in which I had been accustomed to adorn my straw hat with a garland of roses, and to fancy myself splendidly decorated, and when a new penny book, with a gilt cover excited a degree of ecstasy which no acquirements however splendid could afterward inspire.

How particularly desirable is a humble spirit and moderate expectations; how many delights are within the reach of those persons who possess a simple and pure taste, from which the worldly minded are entirely excluded! but although a simple state of mind may be preserved in some degree in childhood, by judicious management, how is it to be retained in after years, when a person is compelled to see and hear so much which tends to corruption?

By religion only, I reply; by a constant recourse to the consideration of those first pure principles which are laid down in Scripture for the benefit of man.

He that is impressed with a deep sense of his own depravity and helplessness, must at the same time be led to feel, that all he possesses of worldly goods is more than he deserves, and hence, as his expectations will be moderated, his desires will be fewer. He who knows that if he is to be saved it must be through the pure unmerited favour of God, and not through any efforts of his own, must necessarily feel a sense of obligation which must tend to the humbling of self in a very great degree. And he whose hopes of future happiness are built on the foundation of Christ himself, must undoubtedly sometimes enjoy such foretastes of future blessedness—must behold such glimpses of future glory, as must in the comparison, throw all temporal magnificence into deepest shade. But I must not forget, while indulging in these reflections, what my uncle, with the assistance of his man-servant, who was a native of India, together with two or three sailors were introducing into our cabin, namely, one chest, which he immediately caused to be cleated down to the floor, together with two smaller boxes, one of which he presented to me and the other to Anna, at the same time giving to each of us a key of these last, which he took from his own pocket.

I received my box with the glee usual to youth, for I was then not thirteen years, but the tears stood in Anna's eyes; and as she looked up to my uncle, "Oh, sir," she said, "how can I bear all your kindness? I have no right to expect that you should treat me in this manner."

"Peace, silly girl," said the fond gentleman, "will you be content if I tell you that it is a pleasure to me to do any thing for the niece of your two most excellent aunts; and if Minny ever forgets what she owes to them, and to you too, I have done with her, so no more of this."

All this passed somewhat aside, for Mrs. Palmerston and our Indian servant, whom my uncle had taught us to call Ayah, were busily engaged in opening the great chest.

"I believe, Mr. Townley," said Mrs. Palmerston, "that I must call upon you for assistance; for this lock is too hard for me," and she rubbed her hand as if it had been grievously sprained by the efforts she had made; on which my uncle condoled with her, and she assumed the patient sufferer in a manner which almost made me laugh, as I had never seen any thing of this kind of affectation in any person before; however a grave look from Anna checked me.

When the affair of the sprained hand was settled, and it had been found that the blacksmith must be called to open the box, Mrs. Palmerston again seated herself on the sofa, and began to talk to my uncle. "Mr. Townley," she said, "you must now tell me which of these sweet girls is your niece: yet I think I can guess," she added, looking at Anna, who was much prettier and more delicate in her appearance than myself; "I think I know; I am sure I am not mistaken."

Anna and I were both silent, and my uncle not seeing

the tendency of her eye, replied, "Don't you think her like me; particularly about the upper part of the face; making allowance for wrinkles and sun-drying?"

"Very like," replied Mrs. Palmerston, still looking at Anna.

My uncle was a dark man with black eyes, and Anna was particularly fair, having an uncommonly soft and modest expression. However it was no matter what Anna might be, Mrs. Palmerston affirmed that she was excessively like my uncle. But on his calling me to him, and raising my hair from my forehead to show her the Townley brow, she perceived her mistake, and recovered herself with great dexterity, replying that the likeness about the forehead and the shape of the head was very striking.

I remember that when a very little child, my governess had corrected me more than once, for a mocking spirit, and I had for some years felt no inclination to yield to this spirit; indeed I had been kept too lowly, too humbly, and too piously, to admit of any thing of the kind, but at this moment I felt the temptation recur, and if I did not speak I looked many saucy things.

"What do you call your sweet little niece, sir?" said Mrs. Palmerston.

"Ermina, madam, or Minny, if you like it better," replied my uncle.

"Ermina! what a sweet name," said Mrs. Palmerston, "and what a lovely little girl belongs to the name," she added, caressing me. "But Ayah, we must have this pretty hair all nicely curled and parted, in this way. I will show the ayah by-and-by, and you must hold up your head, my dear; you have a pair of fine falling shoulders, if you would make the best of them: and those sweet coral lips, how lovely they are, we never see such things in India, do we Mr. Townley?" Thus she went on till the lock was undone and a warmer interest excited her, for she was precisely the person who delights in the view of fine clothes, even when belonging to another.

My uncle, when he had ascertained that all was safe, and no damage done to the box, made his escape, and Anna and I remained perfectly still and stupified, while Mrs. Palmerston and the ayah sifted the chest to the bottom, and displayed to our view all sorts of gay and rich dresses, for which my uncle could not have paid less than some hundreds of pounds.

I should despair to give any idea of Mrs. Palmerston's exclamations at the sight of this fine thing and that fine thing; but she scattered the whole cabin, every chair, table, bed, and couch, with the various suits, and looked at us from time to time exclaiming, "Well indeed, Mr. Townley has provided you well; these things are beautiful, but we know him to be worth an immense sum of money, I know not how many lacks, and his house at Garden Reach is one of the prettiest things in India. Miss Townley, you will live like a princess; I know that Mrs. Townley has a coach of her own, and your uncle his chariot, and I have heard that no one gives such dinners. Mrs. Townley has the most superb set of diamonds of any lady in Calcutta; they were left her by her father; he was an Armenian, and richer than any Jew. She was one of the Aratoons and a widow; your uncle did a very good thing when he married her, it was the making of him."

To all this I made no answer. "Well, but Miss Townley," continued Mrs. Palmerston, looking at her watch, "we must settle what you are to wear to-day. You know that it is not genteel to be over dressed on board ship. Come, what shall we select?" and she looked at Anna.

"What you please, ma'am," replied Anna, and the tears stood in her eyes.

Mrs. Palmerston looked at her for an instant with amazement, and then said, "Why, my dear young lady, what has grieved you? if you are hurt at seeing so many fine clothes, you are the very first young lady I ever met with who was ever afflicted by a circumstance of this kind; but we shall be too late for dinner if we do not set about what we have to do. She then selected two dark lute-string slips from the mass of rich dresses, and directing the ayah to dress us in them and curl my hair, she promised to come again when she was herself dressed and bring us out on deck; so saying, she left the cabin.

As soon as Mrs. Palmerston was gone, I proposed to Anna that we should open our boxes, but she advised me to postpone it till night, and she immediately set to work to restore the scattered articles to the chest, while the ayah was curling my hair. I observed as she was thus employed, that the tears fell, drop by drop, from her eyes, though she endeavoured to conceal them. I asked her no questions till the ayah went out to borrow some curling-irons from Mrs. Palmerston, and I then said, "What can be the matter with you, Anna?"

"Indeed, Minny," she replied, "I don't know, but I feel myself quite overpowered with the sight of all this finery, and the great importance which is attached to these things. How happy and easy were we, my dear Minny, with our excellent governess, when we had only one plain white frock apiece, which was kept for Sundays and holydays, and how proud we were (that is how pleased and grateful) when our dear governess gave each of us a yard of grass-green riband to tie our bonnets; and do you remember when one of the children's parents presented my governess with a present of five guineas over and above what he owed her, how I persuaded her to buy a new silk gown, and how she resisted my entreaties, and spent half the money on us and sent the other half to Mrs. Finchley, then in her greatest distress; but if you have forgotten all this, Ermina, you cannot have forgotten how Mrs. Finchley cut up her best gown to make you a frock, and how pleased she was to see you in it."

"I remember all these things, Anna," I replied, "but I don't understand wherefore they should make you unhappy now."

"I hardly know myself," said Anna, "but the sight of all these things has made me strangely sad. I know, indeed, that it is necessary to dress according to the company we keep, and the fortunes we or our friends may possess, therefore it may perhaps be necessary that we should have all these fine things, Minny, for I am no judge of these things, having only seen very humble life till now; but I am sure it is not necessary to make such a talking and bustle about them, and to speak of the clothes we put upon our poor sinful bodies, as if our eternal happiness depended on the colour and fashion of them, must be wrong, I am sure; and this makes me unhappy, and I can't help it."

She then repeated a part of that beautiful hymn of Dr. Watts's, viz.

How proud we are, how fond to show
Our clothes, and call them rich and new, &c.

"Well," I said, with some tenderness, "there is one comfort, our dear, dear governess is now clad even in finer raiment than any which your hymn describes."

She looked at me as if desiring to ascertain if I thoroughly understood what I had asserted.

"Yes," I said, "she is; for is she not arrayed in the righteousness of our Saviour himself, which is brighter and more beautiful even than the knowledge, virtue, truth, and grace of the greatest saints now on earth?"

The reappearance of the ayah put an end to this discussion, and here I close my chapter.

CHAPTER VI.

Anna and Ermina dress to be introduced to the company on board the Indiaman—They differ respecting dancing—Mr. Townley commends Anna's prudence—They arrive at Calcutta—Land —Delighted with the country.

About a quarter before two, Mrs. Palmerston entered our cabin again, and finding us dressed to her satisfaction, she led us out through the cuddy, or dining-room, on deck, where she introduced us to our fellow-passengers, among whom we found several ladies, and numbers of gentlemen; chairs being brought us, we sat under an awning to amuse ourselves with the novelty of the scene. The deck was more than 150 feet long, computing it from the stern to the bowsprit. At our end were all the persons of our own rank, including those who dined at the captain's table; and at the other end sat all the passengers of lower rank, among which were some private soldiers and their wives, who in such situations are exposed to hardship such as no cottager in England ever knows.

Immediately on our appearing, my uncle took Anna under his arm, and walked up and down the deck with her, but I was left with Mrs. Palmerston; and as there was no other child on board, every one began to joke, laugh, and romp with me. One asked me where I had got my coral lips, and another where I had stolen my bright eyes; another remarked the pretty curls on my head, and a fourth asked me if I would be his partner in the next dance, for it had been proposed that they should dance every night on board, now that we had left the more stormy seas.

I was at first confounded with all this, but I presently began to feel myself more at ease, and then my natural character, which as I before hinted, was that of a little pert, mocking girl, presently began to appear, and we raised such an uproar among us, that my uncle was presently obliged to call me to order. At length a drum and fife called us to dinner, and as all the ladies were handed to table, as if they had suddenly lost the use of their limbs or senses, I must also be led into the dining-room in great state, and no doubt thinking myself as good as the very best of them.

My reader will perhaps say, can this be the little simple, humble Minny, who sat but a few years past on her governess's lap, to hear the story of the little chuckoor, and the same little modest girl who shortly since spent her whole time in hemming and stitching shirts for sale, and committing portions of Scripture to memory? Yes, it is the same; and if you, my young readers, have never known yourselves but under the tuition of careful parents, and in scenes of trial and adversity, learn, from my example, what high prosperity and flattery is most likely to make of you, and join with me in this prayer:—Oh! Lord, restrain me as with bit and bridle.

At dinner I found myself seated near Mrs. Palmerston, and at a considerable distance from my uncle, to whom my beloved Anna had attached herself.

I remember little of what passed at dinner, where I was all amazement at every thing I saw; but I know this, that Mrs. Palmerston suffered me to drink wine with one or two gentlemen, who asked me, and that before I rose from table I felt it in my head.

The same scene which had been acted upon deck in the morning was repeated after dinner, and when we had taken tea and coffee, as it was a remarkably fine night, we began to think of dancing, and Mrs. Palmerston insisted that I should dance, which I was very willing to do. While they were settling their partners, I ran into my cabin to get a pair of gloves, and there I found Anna seated at the table, reading by the light of a lamp which hung from the roof of the ship, while the ayah was placed on the floor at work by her side.

"Where are my gloves, Ayah?" I said, calling about me as if I had been born a princess. The ayah rose and handed them to me, and I was running out again, when Anna said, "Minny, what are you doing? I wish you would not think of dancing."—"And why?" I asked.

"Because, if my poor aunt were living, she would not have approved it."

"Why, what's the harm of dancing?" I asked, stopping short.

"There is no harm in dancing itself," she replied, "you may recollect that we used often to dance on the grass-plat to our dear governess's guitar, but then you know that she always explained to us that what might be very innocent among brothers and sisters and school-fellows, was not so among strangers. You know that there is no harm in puss-in-the-corner and blindman's-buff among little children, but such games would be very silly among grown people, and people who are strangers to each other; and dancing is like these plays, innocent in itself, but not proper at all times and in all companies; and I do wish, Minny, you would take my advice for once, and come to bed instead of dancing."

"I can't see the harm of dancing now," I replied pertly.

"Very well," she replied, "and it is possible you may not; but this you do understand, Minny, that it is always right to take the advice of your friends, particularly those who are older than yourself."

"Older!" I said, "dear me! you are suddenly grown very ancient indeed, Anna, and yet you are not four years older than I am."

"There is one thing to be considered, Minny," she replied, "and that is, that both you and I are suddenly deprived of all our former guides and counsellors, and therefore it behooves us to be directors to each other; and therefore, in want of a better, it becomes your duty to attend to me, and if I give you bad advice, I am answerable for it."

"Oh, as to that," I said, "I don't suppose you will give me any bad advice."

"Well, then," said she, "that settles the matter, and I will send the ayah for your uncle, and we will be guided by him."

Accordingly my uncle was sent for, and Anna having informed him that she thought we were both better in our rooms at this hour, he commended her prudence, said he entirely agreed with her, and promised her to make some excuse to Mrs. Palmerston for my absence, and from that time we were not asked again to dance, though, I confess that I was sometimes mortified when I heard the tabor and fife upon deck.

As soon as my uncle was gone, we opened our boxes, and found an immense assortment of all kinds of trinkets, with scissors, needles, pins, thimbles, knives, ribands, necklaces, &c. &c.; and in arranging and rearranging these, I presently forgot my disappointment.

The rest of our days at sea during the fine weather passed much as this which I have described, but in weathering the Cape we had some severe storms, which put all vanities out of my head, and that no doubt of many others in the ship; and in the Bay of Bengal we were also much tossed about, so that I became heartily tired of the ship, and saw, with no small pleasure, the Island of Sauger, after a six months' passage.

When the vessel came to anchor in Diamond Harbour, which is at the mouth of the Hoogley, my uncle immediately forwarded a messenger to Calcutta, and in as short a time as possible afterward, a pinnace arrived to convey us to Garden Reach, where Mrs. Townley then was.

Into this pinnace we were shortly afterward conveyed with our baggage, and proceeding with one tide, arrived at Fulta, where was an inn by the water-side. I have little recollection of this inn, though it was the first Indian dwelling I had ever visited: it stood, as well as I remember, in a dry sandy plain, though in its immediate vicinity was a garden, which being well watered, produced all the plants of the climate, though the heat was such, and the glare of the atmosphere so great, that we could hardly amuse ourselves even with looking from the doors. We had a handsome dinner at Fulta, served up in a great hall, where at least half a score of my uncle's servants attended us, affording me much amusement by their turbaned heads, thick mustachios, and muslin habits.

The tide did not serve us again till near midnight, at which time we re-embarked, and lying down on our couches, enjoyed repose till morning, when waking we found all still around us—the pinnace fastened to the shore, and our windows opening on a beautiful garden, the trees of which feathered down to the water's side, and filled our small apartment with a fragrance which equalled that of the most aromatic spice, at the same time the warblings of small birds, together with the distant note of the dove, met our ears—and oh! how delightful, how inexpressibly delightful, were these sounds and odours to us, who had been so long pent up in an East-Indiaman.

I started up immediately, and not having been undressed, put my head as far as I could out of the window ; there I beheld a variety of the most charming trees and flowers, growing in groups and singly, on a lawn of the richest verdure. I knew not the name of a single tree, for all were equally new and strange to me, some being laden with thick foliage of a dark and brilliant green, and embellished with large spikes of flowers whiter than snow—others having leaves so fine and delicate that they seemed as if they would almost shrink from the touch—some being decorated with golden balls—and some with crimson, and star-like bells—while others raised their verdant coronets high above all the rest, as if they would assert a regal dignity above all the forest.

"Oh! Anna, Anna," I exclaimed, "how beautiful, how very, very beautiful! and is this India? it is surely more like Paradise!" Anna was equally delighted with myself, and understanding that our long, long voyage was at an end, we hastened to change our dresses, in order that we might be ready to go on shore whenever we might be summoned.

We were no sooner ready than my uncle appeared on the bank with two servants, carrying immense umbrellas; for as it was not more than seven in the morning, and the garden considerably shaded by the trees, he wished us to walk up to the house, and we were perhaps more impatient to accompany him thither than he to conduct us, for, as I afterward found, he had more domestic difficulties than he wished to have supposed.

CHAPTER VII.

Garden Reach described—Anna and Ermina introduced to her Aunt and to company—Mrs. Townley makes them presents—They ride in the coach, where Anna contrasts their present and former situations.

We had passed for a short space under an embowered walk of fragrant shrubs before we came out upon the lawn, and saw my uncle's house directly before us; and to the right and left, though at some distance, other houses of the same description, all of which looked like palaces. My uncle's house was a stone building, or at least one that looked like stone, of two stories in height, being encircled by columns which supported the roof. The roof itself was flat, and was guarded by balustrades; within the pillars, on the ground-floor, was a verandah, and on the second floor a gallery, into which every chamber opened by two or more doors; these doors were all latticed with green, and from the centre of the house large wings extended on each side, having also their columns, with their verandahs and galleries. Had I been a heathen I should have been almost inclined to have said that fortune was amusing herself in playing me tricks, and making me giddy, by raising me at once from the bottom to the very top of her wheel, for certainly nothing could well be greater than the contrast between this splendid habitation and Mrs. Finchley's kitchen in Falmouth. I was, however, too young to meditate very deeply on this extraordinary change of fortune; otherwise I might, perhaps, have been led to apprehend that the new lot which I had drawn might not be so entirely divested of its attendant evils as at first appeared. But young persons at the age I then was, are not deep or curious reasoners. I felt but little admiration and delight at all I saw, and though my uncle walked quickly, I was, I believe, always a few steps before him.

At length we reached the house, and passing through the verandah, stepped into a magnificent hall, which extended the whole length of the building, having large folding-doors open at the other end, through which doors I saw many trees.

There were three rooms on each side of the hall, in one of which was a superb hanging staircase, by which we ascended into an elegant upper room of the same size as the hall. This room was covered with a fine matting, and hung with chandeliers of cut glass ; there, a table of great length was set out for breakfast in such a style as I had never before even conceived, for the glass, silver, and china seemed almost sufficient to furnish a shop, and at the upper end of the room sat a lady, whom I was made to understand was my aunt.

I certainly was somewhat startled when I first saw her, for I had expected the lady of such a fine house to be something superlatively elegant: I therefore rather hung back, and required a little encouragement from my uncle before I could be persuaded to advance.

My uncle had appeared to me to be about fifty years of age, but this lady was certainly sixty; she was extremely stout, as well as tall, was highly rouged, had very dark eyes, and particularly strongly marked dark arched eyebrows, which met over the bridge of her nose; her complexion was sallow as well as brown, for she was of Armenian extraction, and her father's family having been long in India, it is probable that she was not wholly unallied to the natives, though probably remotely. Her dress was as singular as her person—it was extremely rich with lace, her hair was elaborately dressed, early as it was in the day, her throat bare, with the exception of a narrow black velvet collar, and her hands were covered with jewels. She sat on a large chair, with her feet on a footstool, called in India a mora, and was engaged in giving some orders to a native servant, who was himself covered with silver ornaments, and stood bowing, or rather cringing before her, with his hands in the attitude used by little children when they say their prayers, at the moment we entered.

As we advanced up the room she put her glass to her eye to look at us, but did not move, and as my uncle presented me to her, not a single line of her face changed, but she said she was glad to see me, hoped I was well, and said I was welcome to India, all of which sentences she uttered in a kind of foreign accent, and in as harsh a voice as ever issued from a woman's lips.

My presentation being over, that of Anna's ensued, and I then perceived that my aunt had meant to be gracious when she had spoken to me, for she threw such excessive haughtiness into her manner when she spoke to Anna, that it was with much difficulty that my lovely young companion could refrain from tears; my uncle, however, seemed resolved that Anna should not be left to doubt that she was welcome, at least to him, for he presently called her to the other end of the room, to show her the view towards the river, and then I heard him say to her, "You must not trouble yourself about Mrs. Townly, she is a foreigner, and does not understand our manners; but you may depend upon my friendship."

"I know it, sir," replied Anna, modestly, "I know your generosity."

"And my gratitude," said my uncle; "you have a right to my gratitude."

While standing at the window we saw several wheel-carriages drive up to the house, besides two palanquins, and a moment afterward half a dozen or more gentlemen were ushered into the room to breakfast with my aunt, who talked and laughed with them with as much vivacity as a girl of sixteen.

The gentlemen were scarcely arrived, and the ceremonies of introduction between ourselves and them had hardly taken place, before about a dozen servants entered in a long procession, with materials for breakfast; a moment afterward the table was covered, and a servant or more ranged themselves behind each chair. I think I counted four behind that of my aunt, and three behind my uncle. My aunt, however, soon directed one of hers to attach himself to my service, on which my uncle sent one of his to Anna, telling him that he was henceforward to be considered as her attendant. I observed all this, but I suppose that it was not generally noticed. We sat a long time, for the gentlemen and my aunt had their hookas or pipes, and there was a great deal of conversation, very little of which I understood. After breakfast the gentlemen took their leave, and my uncle then showed us a long suite of rooms, including a sleeping-room, dressing-room, and bathing-room, which he said were to belong to us; this room opened into the large sitting-room above stairs. In the bed-rooms were no carpets or curtains, but the floor was covered with matting, and there were two beds hung with fine China gauze. The dressing-room was furnished with couches, tables, and almiras or cabinets, and commanded a fine view over the gardens towards Fort William. Here the kind old gentleman shook hands with Anna, and kissing me, said, " My children, I trust that you will be happy, you shall fare alike, and be subject to no one's caprices. And you, Minny, I charge to love and obey Anna, for I have had proof sufficient of her discretion." He then introduced two ayahs and an inferior female servant, who were to wait upon us; he also told us that there was a dirge or tailor to be devoted to us; and promised us that when he went to Calcutta he would buy us a little carriage and horses, in order that we might go out when we liked. He then left us, and we looked at one another with amazement, to find ourselves in possession of such indulgences.

Soon after we heard my uncle loud in talk with his wife in the next room, shortly after which he left the house to go to Calcutta, which was at a short distance.

My uncle had not long departed before we were called into the presence of my aunt, who was much more gracious to Anna than she had been at breakfast, by which I was led to conjecture that my uncle had laid his commands upon her to that effect.

When we appeared before her, she was very busy with a cloth merchant, who was spreading before her a great variety of the finest worked muslins. She immediately presented me with several pieces, and gave as many of the same to Anna, desiring that they might be immediately made up for us, and only laughing when we told her that we had already more clothes than we could count. She then dismissed the merchant, and retired to her own apartments in one of the wings of the house, where she spent most of her time with her female servants; but how that time was employed I never could devise, for she neither worked, read, nor wrote, and as to music and drawing she never thought of such things, but she had three tailors always sewing for her, and she was much occupied in directing their employments, and arranging her jewels, trinkets, laces, and ribands.

We met at two o'clock to a kind of dinner; my uncle was, however, absent, and we should have been dreadfully dull had not two gentlemen dropped in who were distant connexions of my aunt's.

After dinner all our baggage arrived, having passed the custom-house, and we busied ourselves in seeing our things unpacked, and sent to be washed, and arranged in our cabinets, and we were utterly amazed when we put all together, and found how we were supplied.

We however were delighted to find a box of books, which my uncle had provided for us, and though we did not open it, we acounted it a most valuable treasure.

About five o'clock we were made to understand that we were to dress as smart as we could, and we then sat down under the hands of our ayahs, who arranged our hair most skilfully for us, and dressed us from head to foot without the smallest exertion of our own. Being dressed, we walked down into the hall, and there saw several carriages drawn up before the door. One was a coach precisely the same as an English one; another was a kind of open chair, carried by bearers; and I know not what else. But all these several equipages belonged to my aunt, and while we were looking on them we received a message from her, stating that if we wished for an airing the coach was at our service, as she was not going out.

This was too tempting an offer to persons who, as it happened, had never been in a coach in their lives, and an airing in a new country is certainly a very interesting thing, whatever it may be in one well known; and accordingly Anna and I entered the carriage, and were driven away we knew not whither.

"Well," said Anna, smiling, as soon as we found ourselves shut up together, and out of everybody's hearing, "so we are riding in our coach, and have our waiting-maids, and our fine dresses, and our footmen. Oh! Minny, Minny, what is to come next? I only wish that my aunt could see us, it would amuse her above all things, but I should not be the least surprised if, this time twelvemonth, we were both to find ourselves ladies' maids, or perhaps something lower."

"Why, Anna," I replied, "what chance is there that we should ever be ladies' maids?"

"What chance, Minny," she replied, "there is no such thing as chance—every thing, you know, is ordered by Providence, and no man is so great, or so sure of greatness, but that he is liable to fall, and no one so low, but he may be raised; and this reflection ought always to make us humble in prosperity, and cheerful in adversity; now for instance, Minny," she added, "when you and I were making the check shirts in my dear aunt's little kitchen at Falmouth—"

"Oh! don't talk of that, Anna," I said; "pray don't, you know my uncle does not like it."

"But your uncle is not here," replied Anna, laughing, "and I like to remember these things—the recollection is now so amusing, particularly when compared with our present grandeur. The change at first overcame me, because I could not bear such a waste of good things being made upon me; but now I see things in a different light, and think it my duty to take things as they come, and try to bear all changes with an equal mind; and ever to recollect that there are valleys as well as hills in this world, and that we must pass through one as well as another in our way to the celestial city, and before we can arrive at that blessed state of things in which the valleys will be elevated, and the mountains laid low."

I did not at this time enjoy all these grave discussions. I had not the relish for them which I had had at Falmouth; I had lately been highly excited, and I was in a state which required more and still more excitement, and I did therefore what I could to divert Anna's attention, by calling it to the objects which presented themselves from without.

CHAPTER VIII.

The country near Garden Reach—Conversation at dinner, and between Ermina and Anna on retiring to rest.

The carriage had by this time passed the gates, and traversing a way towards the interior between two gardens, we presently arrived at a long shady road, where fresh and striking objects met our view every moment—the horses' heads were towards Calcutta, though still at a great distance. On our left were the gardens and houses of Garden Reach, and on our right many native huts and tanks—there also we saw many of the native women walking about without shoes on their feet, and wrapped in webs of cloth, of which they formed petticoats and veils, some of them bearing pitchers on their heads and shoulders, as we often see in old pictures, and others carrying their little black naked children on their hips. We also passed by the door of a great pagoda, wherein we saw a frightful image, somewhat like a monkey, with many arms and three faces; and whereas this pagoda was quite dark within, we could not have seen the image had it not been for two lamps which were burning before it. We were at first much amused by these new objects, but the more we looked upon them the more we were made aware of the deep gloom shed over these heathen regions, and these habitations of the poor natives, when compared with the dwellings of our cottagers in England; and indeed no one who has not visited a heathen country can conceive a just idea of the human countenance when wholly divested of all religious feelings. Our coachman turned his horses almost as soon as we had passed the pagoda; but long before we reached home we perceived a heavy fog, which arose from the swamps, and tanks, and marshes, and rested like clouds on the thick masses of foliage on each side of the road; at the same time we observed a rank smell, such as may be perceived in woods in Europe at the time of the fall of the leaf, when the air is particularly damp.

It was quite dark, for the sun in these latitudes sets at six o'clock for the greatest part of the year, and there is little or no twilight, because the sun drops directly down under the horizon.

When we arrived in my uncle's garden the house shone like an illumination, long streams of vivid light issuing from every door and window, for the lamps in every girandole and wall shade were already lighted. In passing through the hall we were astonished to see a long table set out in the most splendid manner, and glittering with cut glass and gold and silver plate in the greatest profusion. We hastened up to our rooms, and remained there till my uncle came to fetch us, and to introduce us to a very large party, which was already assembled in the upper room, but which, as it consisted chiefly of gentlemen, and few young people, did not seem to promise me much amusement. I accordingly sat down, supposing that no one would think of me, but I was mistaken; for no sooner was it understood that I was Mr. Townley's niece, than one and another began to address me. I was desired to come forward and pay my compliments, and in return I had a thousand pretty things said to me on my fine fresh colour, sweet complexion, &c. by which my little head, which was never one of the steadiest, became completely turned. I tripped with short steps through the centre of the circle, lisped my words in a very babyish manner, and I have no doubt, looked not a little like a simpleton.

We were all handed down to dinner in great state, and I found myself seated between two persons who talked to me as if I had been a little princess, and asked me many questions about England, which country they either had never seen, or quite forgotten. I was very careful not to say any thing which might lead them to think that I had not been quite as great a person at home as I was in India.

I have often since reflected how very easy it is to destroy that simplicity which is so sweet in childhood, and to make would-be fine ladies of the most ignorant and superficial young persons. We sat a long while at dinner, and notwithstanding the novelty of the scene, I was most heartily tired, and truly glad when the ladies got up to leave the room.

We sat with my aunt and the other ladies till after tea, which was brought up on silver salvers; after which Anna asked my aunt if we might retire; and having obtained permission, we withdrew to our beds.

When in our rooms, Anna proposed that we should read our Bibles and pray, and I was ashamed to say that I was not in a humour for these exercises; I, however, made no objection, after which we went to bed, each in a separate bed, but as they were light, we pushed them so near to each other that we could converse conveniently.

"My dear Minny," said Anna, "I am glad to find that we shall have a good deal of time to ourselves in this place; we have no young companions, which I am very glad of, as there is a chance that they might not have been such as we might have relished."

"But it makes it dull," I answered, "to see only old people."

"Dull!" replied Anna, "did we find it dull, Minny, when we sat working together in Mrs. Finchley's kitchen? Ah! Minny, it was not dull then, for God was with us, and we were all in all to each other, we took sweet counsel together, and walked together in the house of God."

"What makes you so grave, Anna?" I asked.

"I don't know," she replied, "but I am almost afraid that all these fine things may divert us from our duty; but I will tell you what we will do,—we will make ourselves some rules for spending our time, and pray that we may be enabled to keep to them."

"We can't have rules here, Anna," I replied.

"And why not?" she said.

"Oh, I don't know," I answered; "we shall be wanted to go out, and to see company, and those kind of things."

"We will see about that, Minny," said Anna; "if interruptions occur sometimes, we must submit to them, but we will have as few as we can. Your uncle told me to-day, at dinner, that we were to have the little carriage to-morrow. We will get up early and take a ride, and then we will come home and be dressed for breakfast, and we will read while they are dressing us; we will read the Bible at that time, in order that our ayahs may hear it, for they understand English very well, you find, though it is rather an odd sort of English. Then breakfast will be ready, and that will take us up till near nine; then we can come back into our rooms, and we will read, and write, and draw a little, till one, and at one we will walk in the verandah, or read some of our new books; then will come luncheon, or tiffin, as they call it, and after that, if we find the heat great, we may lie on our couches and read again, and then we must dress and go out, I suppose, and after that dinner and company, which is tiresome enough, certainly, for who wants two dinners in a day? and then a little time with your aunt, and the Bible aagin, and to bed. This is the way in which we may pass our time very comfortably, if you like it, Minny."

"I don't know," I replied, "I want to look about me, and to go about; I don't like all this confinement,—I want to see new things; I want to see Calcutta, I want—" and here I stopped, for I really did not know what I wanted."

"Well," said Anna, after having waited some time, "please to finish your sentence, Minny, or shall I finish it for you?"

"You may, if you please," I answered.

"Well then, I will," she said: "you want somewhat of that humble, moderate, and contented state of mind which you enjoyed at Falmouth, when we sat together working for our bread, and thankful for a few potatoes and a little morsel of cold meat for our dinners—when we should have thought one of our morning wrappers a superb garment, and our very nightcaps the most elegant headdresses that could be devised! Oh! my Minny, let us pray that we may be enabled to bear our prosperity with moderation; it is certain that of ourselves we have not strength so to do, but the Almighty is all-sufficient, and he can make perfect his strength in our weakness; let us pray that we may be kept in this hour of trial; that we may be upheld, that we may be enabled to retain our integrity, that the vanities of this world may not have power to seduce, but that we may keep a calm and even course, being always in a state of preparation for whatever afflictions it may please God to try us with. For this world, my Minny, is not our home; it cannot be a resting-place to any one, because it is a place of sin; and where sin is, there necessarily must be sorrow, in one form or another. The times of prosperity, and those of adversity," added this lovely young creature, "are brought by reflection much upon a par in the mind of a true Christian; for independent of those secret consolations which the child of God experiences oftentimes in the periods of sorrow, from the sensible presence of his Creator, his experience of the variableness of human events gives him hopes that some change may occur to bring him relief, whereas the same conviction of the uncertainty of human affairs makes him fearful and moderate in prosperity, and induces him to make such a use of his good fortune as shall enable him to look back on his times of elevation with comfort. Now, my Minny, is the time for your exercise of moderation; and now you ought to think, in your turn, of what you can do for the orphan and friendless, not to speak of those who were your friends when you had no one to look upon you; and now, feeling your own weakness, and liability to fall and be carried away by temptation, you should be more than ever earnest in seeking the divine help, and using your privileges (as a child of God, which I trust you are) to throw yourself on the divine mercy, and to implore the divine direction.

"Let us pray every day," added she, "let us even now pray that the Lord may be our guide—that we may be the objects of the love of the Father—that we may be of the number of those who have been justified by God the Son—and that we may be sanctified by God the Holy Spirit, and finally be received into glory.

"If no other consideration can touch us, Minny, let us recollect that we are now in a country and a climate which has been fatal to many English people—a country over which even now, in the finest season, hang many heavy fogs and damps; and where we must expect much severer heat than we now endure; and where, if affliction should come in no other form, it is not unlikely that it will come in that of disordered health.

"Oh! Minny, my dear Minny, even now there is much which ought to make us serious, at least which ought to keep us from giving way entirely to vanity and folly."

Anna was proceeding, when hearing me sob on my pillow, she begged me to pardon her for speaking thus seriously; and then assuring me that she only did so from motives of real affection, she wished me a good night, and I presently afterward perceived that she had fallen asleep.

CHAPTER IX.

Anna's affectionate policy—Mr. Townley's advice to Ermina—The box of books—Account of Garden Reach—Mr. Townley's Seat—The Aratoon Family—Anna's ideas of them—She reverts with concern to their happy days when with their dear Governess at School.

I HAVE some idea that Anna, though unnoticed by me, contrived to gain my uncle to her side, with respect to the plans she had formed for the management of me; for immediately after breakfast, the old gentleman whispered to me to withdraw, adding, "And now, Minny, as I hope you have recovered your fatigues, I advise that you should return to your books; you know that your education is by no means complete."

I coloured at this hint, and looked at Anna, but obeyed immediately, and made no resistance to perform the exercises Anna required of me. This lovely young creature was not herself accomplished, but she was anxious to improve, and did her best to improve me: and under these circumstances I might have improved, and become a very different person to what I am. And here I must indulge myself in some reflections on the nature of ignorance, which is personified in its proper colours only by one author whom I ever met with; this author is old John Bunyan, whose character of ignorance is, a happy compound of *darkness*, *obstinacy*, *indolence*, and *self-conceit*. On reading the Pilgrim's Progress some years since, I was deeply struck with the justness of this description, and comparing it with Scripture, fully convinced of its deep foundation in the nature of the human heart; for St. Paul, speaking of the heathen, says, "Who having the understanding darkened, being alienated from the love of God through the ignorance that is in them, because of the blindness of their heart." Ignorance, therefore, is generally the consequence of obstinacy, and a determination of rejecting the truth; and idleness is, no doubt, the fruit of such determination in most instances. Hence it will generally be found, I am persuaded, that an idle child is an obstinate one, however that obstinacy may be veiled by a pleasing exterior, a gracious manner, or a smiling countenance; and this is a hint which, I trust, some of my readers may be induced to improve. But to return to my own history.

I worked with Anna during the whole morning, and at one o'clock my uncle came into our room, and the box of books was opened, where, to our great delight, we found a large assortment of the best books of that day, for young people, with many voyages and travels, and histories. My uncle directed us to place these books in one of our cabinets, and then took us into the verandah below, to show us our carriage, which was at the door, and was a kind of little vis-a-vis, calculated to hold two persons sitting opposite to each other, and drawn by two small horses, telling us at the same time that we were to have the sole command of this carriage;

but that he wished we would not be out in it after seven in the morning, or before five in the evening, excepting on very particular occasions.

Thus passed the morning of the second day at Garden Reach. After tiffin we lay upon our sofas and read our new books, and at five we were to prepare to go with my aunt to Calcutta, where she was to meet a few friends at dinner in her town house. A little before six we were ready, and accompanied my aunt in her coach.

I have frequently spoken of Garden Reach in the course of my narrative. It is now a line of noble houses, standing in gardens along the left bank of the Hoogley, as you descend towards the sea; but when I first went to India there were only a few scattered country houses along this bank, but these perhaps looked the more beautiful for standing alone. Fort William, which is situated in a line with these houses, but nearer Calcutta, was then very incomplete, though I believe that its buildings were then commenced. The habitations of the Europeans in Calcutta were also comparatively few, and mostly built round the old fort, which is in the centre of the town, beyond the residence of the English; yet still along the banks of the river was the Black Town, where the natives chiefly resided, though among these were some scattered houses of Europeans, or half-Europeans, Armenians, and merchants from other countries, some of whom were immensely rich, though they associated little with the English. My uncle was not in the service of the East India Company, and was therefore accounted of no rank; but he was always highly respected, and his riches and liberality gave him great influence. It was not a very light evening, therefore I saw but little till we arrived in Calcutta, where our way was sufficiently illuminated by the lights which issued from the houses, which were all large, and built with open galleries and verandahs.

My uncle's house was very large; it was situated very near the old fort, and the whole of the ground-floor was occupied by offices and warehouses. We ascended to the second floor by a wide stone staircase, as dirty as the streets themselves, and entered an immense range of rooms, which, though handsomely furnished, had a particularly gloomy appearance; here we were almost devoured by mosquitoes.

On this occasion we met with a large family of the

name of Aratoon, including a father, a mother, several brothers, four daughters, one of whom was married, and another about my own age, and sundry cousins and connexions, who were all more or less nearly connected with my aunt.

These persons were all of Armenian extraction, yet had somewhat of the appearance of the natives, which led me to suppose that they were somehow connected with them. Their dresses were very peculiar and very gay, as to colours, but their countenances were heavy, and their features strongly marked. The mother and married daughter were especially laden with jewels.

We had a very grand dinner, but conversed little, and indeed it was impossible to talk much, because there was such a bubbling with the water in the hookahs, for almost every one smoked, excepting the very young girls.

After dinner the ladies did not withdraw, as is the usual custom, but the party being only a family one, they sat together with the gentlemen, but we, that is, the younger girls, were permitted to escape, and we hastened into another room, where Anna and I should have found quite sufficient amusement in looking out into the street, and gazing by star-light at the tower of the old fort, which rose directly behind the opposite house, and meditating upon the bloody and strange deeds which had so lately passed there, of which we had so often heard my uncle speak, when miss, or mademoiselle, or whatever other title you may please to give her, Almeria Meriam Olivia Sophronisba Aratoon,—for the Armenians are exceedingly fond of long and fine names,—came to join us in the window, and instantly began a conversation with me.

I should despair of giving you any idea of the figure of this girl, who might have been about two years older than myself. She was extremely stiffly and tightly laced, or appeared to be so ; had a very long waist, and a gown or frock of exceedingly rich flowered silk ; her hair, which was black as a raven, was tightly drawn up from her forehead, and she wore a round silk cap. Her neck was covered, as I then thought, with green beads, but I afterward understood that they were real emeralds, and she had large drops of the same in her ears. Her complexion was sallow, and her eyes large, black, and bright, but not agreeable in their expression.

At first I could not comprehend what she said, not so much from her strange accents as from the entire novelty of the ideas which she endeavoured to express, for she talked of things and people I had never heard of, and uttered all the sentiments of a worldly old woman, in the shrill accents of a girl.

She took little notice of Anna, but insisted upon it that I should come to see her, informing me that she lived at a very little distance from Calcutta, and that I should find much amusement in her father's house. I at first, as I said before, could not comprehend a word she said, but her elder sister having engaged Anna in conversation, she presently contrived to make me understand her better, and she contrived, even during this our first intercourse, to put some notions into my head which I could not easily get rid of, and which worked a more pernicious effect because I could not bring my mind to impart them to Anna; and this first want of confidence in my real friend was the beginning of an alienation from her, which had an effect very little foreseen by me at that time. We had been about two hours with these young people, when we were summoned to the coach, for although my aunt had her apartments and establishment at Calcutta, she fancied she could never sleep well in the town; we accordingly went back to Garden Reach, and soon found ourselves again in our own chamber.

When alone with Anna, she without hesitation told me that she did not like the young people whom we had met that evening, and added, that she should do all in her power to avoid an intimacy with them.

I asked her what reason she had for disliking them.

She replied, that she hoped she had no bad feelings towards them, but that she believed them to be far from pious or even correct young people, and that she felt assured that they would never profit either me or herself, "and therefore," said she, "I shall endeavour to avoid an intimacy; and I blame myself much, Minny," she said, "for leaving you this evening, but I was off my guard. You and I must keep together, and then we shall be a protection to each other."

From that period, for several months, things went on with little variety. I remember few events :—Mrs. Aratoon had been taken ill, and we saw no more of the family for some time. My uncle was at home at breakfast and dinner, and kept up the authority of Anna. My aunt took little notice of us, but we were both flattered by the visiters, Anna by one set and I by another. I did not observe that Anna was the least changed by these flatterers, but I certainly from day to day became more full of myself—less occupied by religious feeling, —more indolent, haughty, and conceited,—more dissatisfied under the gentle control of my lovely Anna,—more unwilling either to look back on my past life in England, or on those things which were to follow at the end of time, the serious impressions which I had formerly received being only strong enough to give me some pain. Pleasure I had none, in any subject connected with my God, and I was so entirely taken up with my fine possessions, fine acquaintance, and magnificent modes of life, that the times when things had been otherwise with me seemed but as a dream or vision of the night.

If ever I was at all softened, it was when Anna reverted to our days at school, which she did in so artless and tender a way, that I could scarcely, on some occasions, refrain from tears. Once in particular, in the month of February, she said to me, "I wonder, Ermina, whether our dear governess's mezereon tree is already in blossom!—Does it blossom yet, Minny," she added, "though the hand that used to take care of and shelter it is no more!—Ah! Minny, had we but still that fostering hand, we might hope to flourish: but, alas! alas!" and she sighed deeply, "we are indeed deprived of a mother's care; your uncle is truly kind, but he cannot protect us from the lesser dangers which attend us in this life. O Minny, I already fear for you, and the more so because you have no fear for yourself. You are no longer the same child you once were,—the same modest, reserved, and humble little girl,—the same gentle and affectionate Minny!" and so saying, she burst into tears, and rested her fair cheek against the side of the couch near which she sat, and though I could not weep, I felt a degree of anguish such as I had never before experienced, though my painful feeling passed away too soon to be truly beneficial to me.

CHAPTER X.

The indisposition of Anna—Ermina's visit to the Aratoon family—Their house and its neighbourhood—Her indifference to Mrs. Finchley, and Anna's gratitude—She remonstrates with Ermina on her intended visit.

The weather was now beginning to be excessively hot, at least it appeared so to us ; I, however, retained a good state of health and spirits, but Anna was much affected by the heat. Her constitution, it now appeared, had been considerably injured by close confinement at Falmouth, and, perhaps, by anxiety of mind ; but although I saw her becoming more pale and languid every day, I had no apprehensions for her, and attributed what I saw merely to the effect of change of climate ; and as everybody about me was pale also, I had no uneasiness on my friend's account: indeed, my affection for Anna had lost much of its freshness. She who had been my only consolation in adversity was a restraint upon me in prosperity, and her blameless conduct a perpetual reproach.

It was in the middle of the month of March, that my aunt one day proposed to us to accompany her to visit her Armenian friends ; but Anna was really too unwell to be able to join our party, and my aunt, I believe, was not sorry to admit her excuses. It was a burning day, and the glare of the sun so great that we were obliged to lower all the blinds of the coach.

We passed quite through that portion of Calcutta which was occupied by the English, and at length entered the native town, where pursuing our way through many narrow streets and clay huts, we at length arrived at a more open space, of an irregular figure, on one side of which was a pagoda of a large size, standing in a court, and having its walls painted with flaming figures of dancing demons. The house of the gentleman whom we were going to visit occupied another. This house was encircled on the three sides by a court enclosed with walls of great height, which wholly concealed the lower parts of the building. Over these walls appeared the long and lofty branches of the bamboo-tree, and under the wall was a black and fetid tank or puddle, which must have been a serious nuisance to every house in the neighbourhood.

One side of the house of Mr. Aratoon was open to a lane or little street, of which it formed part, and there I perceived several irregular windows and balconies, where a person might sit and amuse himself with the humours of those who were in the street below, and even hear all that passed; altogether, nothing can be conceived more melancholy than the whole appearance of this great mansion, for it was evidently a very large pile of building. We drove into the court, through a wide gate-way, and then the whole extent of the chief front of the house appeared to us. It was an irregular building, of different heights in various parts, jetting forward in some places, and retiring in others; having here a balcony, there a turret, and there a gallery, destroying every appearance of order or plan in the building, and forming, upon the whole, a figure not unlike that which we may sometimes see on the surface of a china dish, or the bottom of a saucer. When our carriage stopped at the door, as no one came out to salute us, my aunt alighted, and being followed by me, entered an immense hall, where a variety of strange figures met my eye. The hall itself was as irregular as every other visible part of the house: at one end was a kind of dais or throne, that is, one part of the flooring was considerably raised from the rest, being covered with striped cotton carpeting; and on this place of honour sat a circar or shroff, weighing money which lay in heaps before him. Two or three Chinese were jabbering and winking, with their small eyes, in another corner; two half-caste youths, most daintily accoutred in white nankeen, were writing at a table at another end; and native men of every description were busy, or pretending to be busy, on every other side, coming and passing away through various door-ways, and evidencing by their free and careless manners that they were not quite under the same awe as they appeared to be in the houses of the English, where I had, hitherto, only seen persons of this kind.

My aunt spoke to several persons before she could

learn whether her relation was at home: we were, however, at length conducted up a wide staircase into a room above, which was the very counterpart of the hall, with this difference, that the one was devoted to the master, and the other to the lady of the family; the one being scattered with money, desks, account-books, and papers; and the other with women's works and garnitures; the one being the resort of shroffs, clerks, and circars, and the other of tailors, dhayes, ayahs, and children; but the same apparent confusion prevailed in both apartments, and women of various descriptions, some in petticoats of silk, and others in pagammahs of the same, were seen passing and repassing to and fro, as below.

It happened that none of the family were at home but the old lady and some of the grandchildren, which last went in and out with their dhayes and ayahs, being dressed in thin muslin trousers and coats, without shoes or stockings, and having nothing whatever to recommend them but their eyes, which were fine; but their sickly complexions, and their total want of manners, destroyed every pretension to the charms of infancy.

The old lady looked ill, though she was become excessively corpulent. Hot as the day was, she was wrapped in shawls and silks. She sat on a low sofa, and had a hookah near it, but she did not appear to have any occupation. She immediately entered into conversation with my aunt, but I paid little attention to what passed, till I heard my own name mentioned, and an invitation given to me to come and spend some time with her daughters; to which invitation my aunt gave no decisive answer, saying that the application must be made to her husband, whose niece I was. Before we left the house we were served with chocolate and rich cake, on a massive golden waiter, after which we returned home.

After this adventure, I remained at home for some weeks, and things went on as usual, excepting that Anna became decidedly more weak, and my uncle procured medical advice for her.

I often recollect this time, when my sweet young friend lay like a broken lily, gradually losing her strength and freshness. I often recollect, with the deepest anguish, my careless conduct towards her at that time, and the efforts she made,—those efforts which were evidently beyond her strength,–to instruct, to guide, and to preserve me, the object of her tenderest affection. Gradually, however, as her strength became weaker, her attempts to teach me began to relax. We were accustomed to translate French together, and I have still her book in which she broke off in the midst of a dialogue in Madame Bonne; but when she could no longer sit at the table and write with me, she used to lie on the couch and make me read to her, sometimes the Bible and sometimes books of another kind. In my little volume of Mrs. Teach'em I can still trace the mark of her pencil where I left off last.

She had a sweet voice in singing hymns, and she had also taught me to sing them. I well remember the last time I sang to her; it was by her own express desire; and it was that sweet hymn of Addison's—

"O God, our help in ages past,
Our hope for years to come,
Our shelter from the stormy blast,
And our eternal home."

There was no need that all my occupations with my lovely Anna should have ceased when they did: I was not so soon to be parted from my lovely companion; a little time yet remained, a precious little interval, which, had I used it well, might have saved me many an after pang. But my aunt had invited Miss Almeria Aratoon to spend some days with us, and she arrived precisely at this time, on which occasion I devoted myself wholly to her, and struck up one of those violent intimacies of which young ladies in their teens are generally so fond.

As to make any comparisons between Almeria and Anna, the thing was out of the question; but Anna's blessed conduct was always a reproach to me and made me miserable, whereas in the example of Almeria I found a kind of foil which set off my own superior good behaviour in a very agreeable point of view, as I chose to think, not considering that what might be passed over in one so very ill educated as she, was wholly inexcusable in myself.

However, I made no such reflections, but assimilated myself to all I saw and heard in this young person, however degrading. It would be difficult, perhaps impossible, to describe this girl to any one who has never been out of Europe. A creature so artful, so corrupt, and so full of the lowest information can scarcely be conceived in a Christian country. Added to these defects, she was wasteful in the extreme: at once haughty and familiar with her inferiors, and full of high expectations respecting her future lot in life.

My aunt was pleased at observing my attachment to her relation, and encouraged it to the utmost of her power; and with this view she invited me and Almeria to her side of the house, showed us her stores of rich silks, muslin, shawls, and jewels, and made us both some very superb presents. When not with my aunt, we used to romp about the verandahs, gossip with the ayahs, and sometimes take a turn to Calcutta, to visit certain of Almeria's acquaintance, who were not much better than herself. In the mean time, I saw very little of Anna, and as she could neither follow me nor expostulate with me, my alienation from her became more and more marked.

While things were in this state, my uncle was suddenly called up the country on some particular business, and it was expected would be absent some time. He took a very affectionate leave of us; particularly so (I thought) of Anna, of whom he was very fond, informing us, as he was going out of our room, that we might make up a packet for Mrs. Finchley, having spoken to a friend who was going to England, to convey it for us.

Dear Anna, immediately on this permission, busied herself as well as she was able, in seeing such things prepared as she thought might be useful to her friends at Falmouth: but I am sorry to say that I interested myself very slightly in this work, and a very few days after my uncle was gone, left it all to her; for he was no sooner clear of Calcutta than my aunt gave me leave to visit Almeria. It was on occasion of this visit that my rebellious spirit broke out without restraint towards Anna, and it was then I showed how thoroughly I had been spoiled by prosperity.

As my aunt never came to her room, and as she was not able to leave it from excessive weakness, they never met: it was therefore from me that she learned of my intended visit, and it was not till the morning of the day appointed for my short journey that I opened the subject to her

"O, Minny! dear, dear Minny!" she exclaimed, raising herself from the sofa, "don't go—if you love me, don't go."

"O, but I must," I answered, "I have promised."

"As you value me," she said, "as you love me—as you value the memory of your governess, of your country—as you fear your God, don't go, my Minny. I entreat, I supplicate you—" and she burst into tears.

"But I must," I replied, "I have given my word."

"Never mind your promise," she answered. "Say you will wait till your uncle's return—say any thing—say I am ill—say you can't leave me. Oh! Minny, Minny, don't go."

"Pshaw!" I replied, "but I must" (for I had learned to use many contemptuous expressions).

"Once again let me entreat you," said my precious friend, taking my hand, "if you love the memory of your early days—of those who took care of you in babyhood—grant me but this one request—don't go, dear Minny, at least till your uncle returns." I heard Almeria call me, and broke from her without giving any answer; and in a short time afterward I was on my way to Mr. Aratoon's house.

CHAPTER XI.

Ermina persists in leaving Anna—Her visit to the Aratoons—The society, conversation, and amusements there—Mr. Townley's unexpected return—Ermina returns home—Her alarm and remorse on finding Anna so much worse.

I CAN hardly suppose but that my readers will have lost all regard for me, before they have arrived at this point of my history; and yet, perhaps, they may wish to know what more I have to relate, if not for my sake, for that of my lovely Anna. I must do myself the justice to say, that I was very unhappy when I got into my own little carriage to proceed to the house of my new friend; and even as we were going along, when I looked on her as she sat in the place of the carriage opposite to me—that place which had so often been occupied by the sweet companion of my childhood, I could not refrain from many comparisons by which Almeria was no gainer.

I forget what passed during our drive, for I was not myself: my heart was far away from where I really was, and a thousand scenes of infancy were continually presenting themselves to my mind, in all of which my Anna acted some conspicuous part. We arrived at Mr. Aratoon's just as the family were sitting down to dinner, for the old gentleman chose to dine at an early hour, and surely such a motley group as assembled round this dinner-table, in a large shadowy back-room behind the hall, I had never before witnessed. Here were riches without elegance, magnificence without taste, and profusion without order. Every dish was spiced, seasoned, perfumed, and compounded in so strange a way that I could relish nothing; and though there were so many of us, conversation flagged in a most extraordinary degree. After dinner all the family dispersed, and Almeria with the sister next in age to herself, whose name was Sacharissa, or something very like it, withdrew me to a suite of rooms up-stairs, which belonged to themselves, and which was terminated by a little closet, where was a balcony, which hung over the wall of the house into the bazar, or narrow street below. This balcony was generally screened by blinds or checks, which last are blinds curiously composed of painted grass. I presently found that this closet was the favourite apartment of these two sisters, and here we lay down on low sofas, the two sisters having summoned their women to fan them, drive away the flies, and perform other services of the same kind. Among these women was one of superior dignity, who came waddling into the closet, as she was exceedingly corpulent, and sitting herself down in the circle formed by our couches, began to chew trawn, and roll it about in her mouth like one perfectly at her ease. I was presently made to understand that this old lady was Almeria's nurse, and a very great favourite of the family: hence the state she took upon herself.

We, the younger individuals of the party, talked to each other for some time, but my reader must excuse my giving any sample of the conversation of my companions. At length Almeria, taking a punkah, or fan, from the hand of one of her ayahs, tapped her nurse on the back with it, saying, " Well, old woman, have you nothing to say? tell us one of your stories, for the amusement of the little lady." The old lady gave another roll to the beetle-nut that was in her mouth, and then ejecting some of the juice on the pavement, she began her history, and told us a long story, somewhat in the style, though far more gross than those Arabian tales so well known in Europe.

As I understood but one-half of what she said, she soon talked me to sleep, and when I awoke it was dusk, and Almeria was waiting to lead me to the room belonging to her mother, where all the family were assembled.

There we found several strangers, and after drinking coffee, the young people left the old ones to converse, while we, being a motley assemblage of brothers, sisters, and neighbours, withdrew to amuse ourselves in dancing, romping, and various sorts of frolics. The day was finished by a heartless form of prayer, by which I was led to discover that I was with a set of persons whose mode of faith differed very considerably from that in which I had been brought up. I slept with Almeria in her chamber, which was next the closet above spoken of, and was kept awake for some hours by the gossip which passed between her and the old woman.

Of all gossip none can be worse than low Hindostannee gossip; and it appears to me that no young person can be even comparatively free from corruption who is exposed to hear the tittle-tattle of heathen servants.

We did not rise till late, and we spent much of our morning in lounging and looking over the stores of pedlers who came with boxes to the house, and thus one day after another passed with no variation, excepting from an airing, till nearly a fortnight had expired, during which time I had received only one little note from Anna, written in such a manner as rather surprised me, for the hand seemed strangely changed, the lines crooked, and some words omitted; it however contained only a request that I would return soon—very, very soon.

One afternoon, when, as I before said, I had been about a fortnight with Almeria, the old nurse informed us that there was to be a putulli nantch, or puppet-show, at the opposite house, that very evening.

"Oh!" said Almeria, "then we will go: Ermina has never seen a putulli nantch, and go we will."

The nurse began to expostulate, but her hopeful child bade her hold her tongue; and the next minute the young lady ran out of the room, and did not return for some time.

I heard no more of the nantch till we were withdrawn to our bedroom, and then, having dismissed the ayahs, Almeria said to me, "Ermina, I have settled it all. When they are all quiet, my brother Caratoon will come and bring the steps, and we will get out by the balcony, and go and see the nantch. Look," said she, calling me to the window, "the house is lighted up already; and don't you hear the tum-tums, and the music?"

"Music!" I said, "do you call that music. It is the most horrid noise I ever heard."—"Well, but," said she, "you will go with me." I refused at first, but my refusal became weaker and weaker, and when Caratoon came with his steps, which were those used by the bearers to light and dress the lamps, I suffered myself to be lifted down into the street, for the balcony was low, or probably the ground had been raised on that side of the building by the rubbish constantly thrown out into the street. I was certainly frightened when I found myself in an open street at this time of night; however, Almeria was presently with me, and her brother leading the way, we were the next moment at the door of the native house where were the lights, the crowd, and the music.

We were received at the door by a man who seemed half a European and half a Hindoo, and taken into a hall of a most shabby appearance, where they were playing off some frightful little puppets, with heads as big as all the rest of their bodies, in a little stage which was placed in one corner of the room.

The intense heat of the apartment, the wild appearance of the spectators, the smell of cocoanut oil, garlic, and tobacco, together with the squeaking of the man who played off the puppets, formed such a complication of disagreeables, that had my conscience been very easy, I must have been excessively uncomfortable; but as it was I was truly wretched, and after half an hour, I begged, prayed, entreated, to be taken back, but all in vain; for Caratoon seemed to be delighted with my misery, and kept repeating in my ears—"Are you frightened, Miss Ermina? Do you think the puppets will run away with you?—No fear of that, I assure you."

Never did any thing appear so long, so dreadfully long, as that frightful puppet-show. I verily believe that I never knew what misery was till that night. It was never, I think, till then, in that apparently unpropitious scene, that all I had learned in my happy childhood seemed really to begin to work within me for my good. The show was at length concluded, it was past midnight; and Caratoon drove me almost to agony by pretending that he did not know where the steps were, although he had himself seen them stowed away very carefully.

It was nearly one o'clock when I got to our chamber again, and what with shame and terror, I could not sleep till dawn of day, and when I did sleep, my imagination was full of terrors, and I again beheld before me all the serpents and horrible forms which had been represented at the nantch.

I at length, however, fell into a heavy sleep, in which even these horrors had disappeared, when I was suddenly awakened by Almeria, who said, "Ermina, your uncle is below. Make haste, and get dressed."

"My uncle!" I exclaimed. "What, returned so soon?"

"Yes," she replied, "he was not obliged to go so far as he first proposed."

"Is he very angry?" I asked.

"Angry!" she repeated, "what for?"

"For what we did last night," I answered.

"Why, what does he know of that?" she answered—"For the world's sake don't speak of it to him, or to my father and mother, but get up and get dressed."

"Is any thing the matter," I asked, "that my uncle should come so early?"

"No, nothing, not much," she said, "only Anna is worse, and she wants to see you."

"Worse!" I said, "my Anna worse!" and I burst into an agony of grief. "Tell me, Almeria—tell me, is she dying?"

"Dying!" repeated Almeria, "no, I hope not: come, don't frighten yourself."

"Oh, my Anna! my sweet Anna! my own Anna!" I

exclaimed, and fell back on the bed, and for some moments lost my recollection.

They were obliged to call my uncle to me before I could be brought to myself; but when I recovered my recollection, and had had leisure to observe his countenance, I plainly saw that I had the worst to apprehend.

My clothes were, however, at length put on, and I was put into the coach with my uncle, who had not one word of comfort to give me; for indeed he seemed by no means pleased with me, and once, indeed, asked me, "How I could have thought of leaving my friend, when she required my most tender care."

I could make no reply—I was self-condemned and miserable. And I was then made to feel that penury, with all its attendant inconveniences, was by no means the greatest evil to which human nature is subject. But what sufferings are intolerable excepting those which are mingled with feelings of remorse?

CHAPTER XII.

Ermina terrified and distressed at the danger of her faithful Friend—Anna's delirium and death—Its effects on little Minny and those who witnessed it—Conclusion.

Oh! with what anguish and terror did I ascend the stairs, to go to my Anna's room, when I entered the house at Garden Reach. The first person I met in the saloon above-stairs was Mrs. Palmerston, who, being at that time in Calcutta, had, as I afterward found, been in the habit of constantly attending on Anna during my absence. I had been accustomed to consider Mrs. Palmerston as a frivolous character; but when I then saw her drowned in tears, how did I love and respect her. She took my hand when she met me, and then turned again with me to Anna's room; indeed, I then wanted some one to encourage me.

Anna was in the dressing-room, where we had so often sat together. They had brought the sofa on which she lay into the middle of the room, and the physician was sitting by it, holding his patient's hand: several female servants were in other parts of the room.

Mrs. Palmerston drew me gently forward, for I became more and more terrified as I looked on this solemn scene; yet, prepared as I was for the worst, when I beheld my Anna pale as death, and lying without motion on her back, I believed she was already dead.

"Oh, my Anna!" I cried, and was pressing forward to kiss her sweet pale face. "Oh, my Anna—will you never open your eyes again!—never speak to me more!" But Mrs. Palmerston held me back. "Don't disturb her," she said, "we think that she is asleep."

My uncle had entered the room, and stood by the physician. He looked sternly sorrowful, and seemed anxious not to display his feelings.

Thus a few minutes passed. At length my lovely Anna moved, and opening her eyes, said, "Minny,—is Minny come?" and she looked up at Mrs. Palmerston.

"Here I am, my Anna—my sweet lovely Anna—here I am," I said.

She took no notice of me, but said again, "Will not Minny come?"

"I am here, dear Anna," I said, pressing forward and sobbing.

She again repeated, "Little Minny—Ah, little Minny!—will she never, never come?"

I could not bear this. "I am here, Anna dear, I am here," I exclaimed in an agony. "Place yourself in a light where she can see you best," said my uncle.

"She has known no one for some hours," remarked the physician. "She is too far gone; don't attempt to rouse her."

"What!" I exclaimed, "will she never, never know me again! Oh, my Anna!"

"Yesterday," said the physician, "she knew us all."

"And last night, at twelve o'clock, she knew me," said one of the black women, "and asked for Miss Minny."

"At twelve o'clock last night!" I repeated; and my reader may guess my thoughts. Our attention was then suddenly called to the lovely creature herself, for she began to start, and slight convulsions to agitate her features. I had never before witnessed convulsions, and was inexpressibly terrified. For a few seconds, she seemed to be considerably agitated, and then again closed her eyes and seemed to be sleeping.

"Surely," said my uncle, drawing a little from the

couch, " it was very strange that they should have allowed this disorder to gain such ground, without sending for me, or at least for Minny."

" You know, sir," replied the physician, " how rapidly diseases advance in this country. I had little fear for her till yesterday morning."

We were at this instant again drawn to the couch, where my beloved Anna seemed to be in a dreadful agony, every limb being convulsed. These convulsions, however, soon ceased, and she seemed to wish to be raised, opened her eyes, and, I thought, looked very like her former self.

Mrs. Palmerston was supporting her. She looked up to her, and knew her. " You are very kind, ma'am," she said, " very, very kind, and my uncle too, thank him for all his kindness. When I am gone, you will be kind to poor Minny; and don't be uneasy about me—I am very happy. I am going to my Saviour. Yes, my Saviour:" and her countenance changed its expression. A kind of glory, as I fancied, was suddenly shed over it. She looked up, as it were, to the very ceiling, and, joining her hands, " I come, my Saviour, I come," she exclaimed; then sinking back on her pillow, her eyes closed, and in a few minutes she breathed her last, leaving me most completely miserable, and utterly incapable of receiving any thing like comfort.

Thus terminated the earthly career of this most lovely young person; and from that period I felt the sentence of death passed on all earthly possessions and honours: an impression which, by the divine grace, has never worn away, though at some periods I have felt myself less affected with a feeling of this kind than at others.

I have reason, indeed, to think that the death of my lovely Anna was not only blessed to me, but to my uncle and Mrs. Palmerston.

My aunt, who had fled to her house in Calcutta, the moment that she was apprized of her being seriously ill, did not return till after all was over, and never evidenced any sorrow: but my uncle was a sincere mourner, and has often since been heard to say, that his first serious impressions of religion were received by the pillow of my dying friend, and the sweet companion of my childhood.

My aunt did not survive the lovely Anna more than

two years; and after her death, I lived alone with my uncle, and found increasing pleasure and comfort in his society.

I was married early in life, but still lived with my dear uncle, and he seemed to take as much delight in my children as if they had been his own. His death did not take place till an advanced age, and it was then most blessed.

Neither my uncle nor I ever again visited our friends in England, but we frequently heard of and from them, and every year sent them of our abundance.

Many years are now past since my Anna was in glory; but the recollection of her is now as fresh in my mind as in that sad day when I was first parted from her; and to this moment I cannot recollect my conduct towards her without a degree of anguish which time can never soften.

From my example, my gentle reader, be persuaded not to desire unmixed prosperity, remembering this—that adversity is the shining time of the Christian, and the period most commonly chosen for the purposes of divine mercy.

> "Judge not the Lord by feeble sense,
> But trust him for his grace;
> Behind a frowning Providence,
> He hides a smiling face."

THE END OF ERMINA.

EMANCIPATION.

EMANCIPATION.

THE late events which have agitated the minds of all the inhabitants of this once happy island have led me to so accurate a retrospect of my life, as, I trust, has not only had a good effect on my own mind, but is of such a nature, that, if put into a legible form, it might, I think, be useful to others. With this view, I have suddenly become an author; having resolved to give a faithful account of the leading events of my family history; rather choosing to incur the risk of being recognised in my *own* little circle, than to deprive the world of what I consider to be a very valuable and important lesson.

It cannot, under these circumstances, be supposed that I should choose to give my real name: I will therefore call myself James Penson.

My father was the cultivator of a small farm; part of which he held under a nobleman who resided in the adjoining parish, the other part having long been in our family. The tenement which my father occupied was called The Woodhouse, from its situation within the precincts of a wood belonging to his noble landlord; and the gardens and fields behind the house had been redeemed from the forest within the memory of my grandfather. The approach to the front of the house was through an avenue in the woods; and, from the contiguity of this front to the trees, it seldom saw the sun, excepting on a fine day in winter, when the woods were leafless.

Mine were as worthy parents as ever children were blessed with. They were simple people, knew little of the ways of the world, and had no ambition; having scarcely any other object in life, I verily believe, but to live inoffensively in the present world, and to be with their Saviour in that which is to come. Their gains were little, but their wants were less: hence they were rich.—They lived in comfort and in plenty; and they made it a rule never to send a poor person empty from their door. Begging in those days (for I am speaking of fifty or sixty years ago) had not become the system which it now is; and there was not then the risk of actually injuring society, and encouraging vice, which there now would be, in harbouring and feeding every wanderer who chooses to solicit our hospitality.

My parents had only two children; viz. myself and my brother Robert. There is only one year's difference in our age, and I am the elder.

I lived at home till I was ten years of age; and those were happy years. O how have I, in after-life, looked back with anguish and regret on those pure and innocent days—comparatively pure and innocent—when we followed our father to the fields in the morning, and finished the evening in reading the Word of God, verse by verse, to our mother! How dear, then, was Robert to me! how precious was he in my sight! How did I love my parents! What a number of innocent pleasures we then enjoyed! Who was the first to tell our mother when the chickens were beginning to break the shell, or when another lamb had appeared in the field—who knew where the first violets bloomed, or the first roses unfolded themselves—but Robert and myself? But, when I was ten years of age, a sad change for me took place.

My father's elder brother, who was a surgeon and apothecary in a small town in Devonshire, came to see us; and, having been married many years without hope of children, he persuaded my parents to permit him to adopt me; the good people consented, not knowing the character of the man to whom they were intrusting me: and thus I bade adieu, at once, to my home, my brother, and my happiness.

I still fancy I can see my Robert, in his Sunday coat of russet gray, rubbing the tears from his eyes, as he stood in the street of our village; and still hear the solemnly-pronounced blessing of my father, when he lifted me to the top of the heavy coach, by the side of my uncle.

It had been promised that I should return to the

Woodhouse for a few weeks during the next summer. But that summer, and many other summers, winters, springs, and autumns, passed away, before I saw my native place again. Our village is at least two hundred miles from what was my uncle's residence, and it was no easy matter for a child to undertake such a journey; therefore, during the first few years of my residence in Devonshire, my visit to my home was put off from season to season; and, after a while, I became so useful to my uncle in his business that he could not part with me: and thus, from the age of ten to twenty-four, I never saw my parents.

In the mean time, I was advancing in the way that I suppose my uncle intended I should go: that is, if I may judge of the end desired by the means which were used to obtain it. My uncle lived in a small town, where he was the only surgeon; and being also an apothecary, he kept a shop; and while he was busy in his shop, or with his patients, his wife was continually engaged in keeping up his interest, as she would have it thought, by paying and receiving visits. As to religion, I do not suppose that my uncle and aunt ever troubled themselves about it; but a rule or motive of action was soon given to me, which was quite independent of all pious considerations.

I was soon given to understand, that if I did not please the relations with whom I resided, I should be the worse for it; and, accordingly, I soon learned to accommodate myself to their wishes, at least in their presence; and I managed matters so well that I always retained my uncle's favour.

I was kept in my uncle's shop till I was twenty-one; receiving, in the mean time, occasional lessons in Latin, and other branches of polite education, from a schoolmaster residing in the town.

I have said that my uncle never concerned himself about religion. But he was a fierce politician, and talked of the tyranny of our governors, of the rights of man, and the privileges of women; of the cruelty of parents, and the pride of the great. He used to speak of the Almighty as of a kind of abstract Being, who, having made a race of weak creatures, was inclined to wink at their errors, and was ever ready to pardon their offences. He always smiled, if any one spoke of the influences of the Spirit in his presence; and it was well if he did not add some profane remark to this exhibition of contempt. He spoke of our Lord Jesus Christ as a fine example of human excellence, a dignified lawgiver, and a wise man; not considering, that if Jesus Christ was not really what he professed to be, viz. a God incarnate, he must have exercised the most awful blasphemy of which mortal man was ever guilty. And, finally, he spoke of my father as being a good, honest, simple man, who understood nothing of life or of human nature; directing me, at the same time, not to alarm his prejudices by introducing my own or his opinions in any of my letters.

When I had entered my twenty-first year, I was sent to London to walk the hospitals, and remained there for two or three years; being received for a time as an apothecary in one of the public infirmaries.

I was confirmed in all the false principles with which my uncle had inspired me, by the society into which I fell in town: for I attended a tavern every evening, where a set of ignorant young men used to meet, to sup, and discuss, over a bowl of punch, the laws of our country, the conduct of our rulers, and the defects of our church establishment. I was a leading speaker in these parties; and it was my favourite maxim, that all compulsion was to be avoided, as far as possible, in our dealings with our fellow-creatures; that universal toleration ought to be allowed to every religion; and that every man's house was his castle, and no one had any right to interfere with him within its walls.

I am ashamed to think what blasphemous nonsense I used to spout on these subjects; as if any society could hold together without the links or bonds of union that a regular government affords. It might as well be supposed that a human being might walk about, and be a perfect man, and yet be destitute of the back-bone, as to imagine that society could exist without laws.—But to proceed with my narrative, and to let my principles speak for themselves.

I had scarcely finished my time in town when I was called back in haste into Devonshire, and found my uncle very ill, indeed, in a dying state. I also found that a revolution had taken place in the family during my absence, which did not please me by any means. My aunt had introduced a young man into the shop, who seemed to have already become my lord-paramount, and was strongly upheld by her interest. My poor uncle was so ill, when I arrived, that he did not know me; and he died within two days; so that I suffered not a little uneasiness through the fear that he might, perhaps, have died without a will: for I was no longer in doubt that I had a very powerful rival in my aunt's esteem.

Immediately after the funeral, a will was, however, produced; and I found, to my great joy, that my uncle had left me a thousand pounds, with all his books, clothes, and surgical instruments; and that he had bequeathed, also, two hundred pounds to my father; and as much to my brother. I staid with my aunt till I had packed up and sent off my possessions, and secured my inheritance. I then coldly wished her adieu, and turned my views towards my home.

I had written one letter to inform my father of my uncle's death, and had despatched a second, to give an account of our legacies; a third had followed, to inform the family of my speedy return; though I could not name the day.

Since I had left my home, my once beloved home, such a revolution had taken place in my feelings, that I entirely ceased to look forward with delight to a reunion with my family. I had been in London, at the theatre, at the opera, at clubs, and in the gallery of the House of Commons; I had heard parliamentary debates, and could reason and talk, and was exceedingly clever and genteel in my own opinion; and I really had contracted a contempt for my father, and mother, and Robert; for I thought their mode of living utterly barbarous, while they sat in a kitchen with casement windows, and my mother wore a plaited mob-cap and a square muslin handkerchief pinned over her neck. My father, too, wore his own hair combed over his forehead, and a gray suit, all of one colour, even on a Sunday. As to Robert, I could not conceive what he might be like by this time; I remembered that he had brown hair when a boy, and that his eyes appeared to speak very often when his better judgment admonished him that it was needful to keep his lips closed. But I made up my mind that I should be ashamed of him, and I resolved to make my visit as short as decency would permit; though whither next to bend my steps I had not decided.

It was late on a Sunday evening in autumn, being precisely three weeks after my uncle's death, when I arrived at our village; and having deposited my luggage in a safe place, I set out on foot for the Woodhouse, which is about a mile from the village.

A very strange sort of feeling took possession of me as I advanced, and saw by moonlight (for, like most heroes of romance, I was favoured on this occasion of my return to my father's house with the light of the full moon) the various objects imprinted on my memory from early childhood; many of which, together with the circumstances connected with them, had glided away from my mind many years before.

At length, a light from the kitchen of the Woodhouse began to shine upon my path, and presently I discerned the outline of the two gable-ends of the old-fashioned mansion marked against the pale cold light of the sky, together with the high, clustered chimneys.

I advanced with quicker steps: I hastened to the door, and knocked. I heard a voice within—"Surely it cannot be dear James!"—and in the next minute I found myself in the arms of my relations. It was not till after various salutations had taken place in the little vestibule, or entrance of the house, and I had been led into the large kitchen, that I had leisure to look about and see what sort of people I had for my relations. It was much to the advantage of their appearance that they were all dressed in new mourning; the decency and comeliness of which are generally allowed. Notwithstanding this propitious circumstance, I had not sat five minutes without setting my father down in my own mind as a good sort of harmless but ignorant old man; and my mother as a specimen of a comfortable old woman, such as one should like to have about one when on a sick bed.

As to Robert, I was rather more at a loss to decide respecting him. He was not, indeed, a fashionable blade, such as I then thought myself, but his countenance beamed with intelligence and benevolence. There was no rustic sheepishness in his manner towards his town-bred brother; and when he spoke it was with correctness, and with little, if any, of the accent of a clown. He did not affect to be any thing but what he was, namely, an agriculturist. Nevertheless, he seemed to have conceived a correct view of what is proper, and even graceful in that character; and I found it was impossible to withhold respect from a person of his attractions.

In addition to my own relations, there were three persons who had been evidently sitting with the family before I had entered. Two of these were servants, a man and a woman; but the third was as lovely a young woman, of about eighteen, as I had ever beheld. She was soon introduced to me as a distant relation, an orphan, living with my mother. They called her Ellen, and I really was so much pleased with her appearance, that when I discovered, which I soon did, that she was a favourite of my brother's, I was displeased, and actually indulged the intention of attempting to disturb the good understanding which I perceived to exist between the young people. My mother busied herself to spread a table for me without loss of time; and as I had travelled all the last night, I was not sorry to get a good supper and go to bed.

A good night's rest quite removed my fatigue. My portmanteau had been brought from the inn, and having rendered myself as much of a beau as clean linen, powder, and pomatum could make me, I descended the stairs, and the parlour-door being open, I found that a fire had been lighted in it out of compliment to me; while my breakfast was there arranged on a small round table, with all the delightful appendages of thick cream, fresh butter, and white bread. The kettle was hissing by the fire. My first motion was to look for the bell-rope, but seeing no such specimen of refinement, I applied myself to a hand-bell which lay on the table, and rang authoritatively. The bell was immediately answered by Ellen, who entered in a morning-dress, the very pattern of rural neatness, and, begging me to excuse my mother, who had a little job to finish in her dairy, she sat down to make my tea.

It occurred to me that this was a most propitious occasion for showing off my superior breeding; and I scarcely know on what impertinences I might have ventured, had not the determined gravity and distant politeness of my companion thrown me into such confusion, that I scalded my throat, and was very near cutting my hand in attempting to help myself to a slice from the white loaf. The arrival of my mother, in a coloured apron, relieved my embarrassment, and restored my self-confidence; and when Ellen left the room, which she soon did, we had a long conversation, during which she opened to me many of the family arrangements and plans.

She told me that my brother and Ellen were engaged to each other, and were to be married as soon as the deep mourning for my uncle was laid aside, and that they were to continue to live with them; and she seemed to have great delight in the anticipation of this arrangement. She also added, that my father had a plan for me, which she thought very good, namely, that I should, if it could be managed, enter into partnership with old Mr. Southcott, the surgeon of the village; and thus, when he dropped off, as he was getting very infirm, I might fall into his place.

"My father," I answered, "will, I suppose, give me leave to judge in these matters for myself. You know, mother, that you and my father have always lived in this wood, and you can know nothing of life; but, at any rate, there can be no doubt that, in matters relative to my own profession, I must know better than people of your description."

"True, James, true, my dear," said my mother, colouring, and looking alarmed at the great man her son: "but I only gave you a hint, my dear, I meant no offence. To be sure you must know best." And the poor woman looked this way and that way, as if she thought that she had taken a liberty by sitting down in my presence.

I threw one leg over the other, and, looking up to the chimney-piece, began to make comments on a piece of embroidery in worsted, which had hung there in a frame ever since I could remember. "Mother," I said, "what an abominable smoky thing that is over the fireplace: why don't you make a bonfire of it?"

She replied, meekly, "It was my mother's work, James."

"Upon my word, the old lady was a second Arachne," I replied.

"Arachne!" she repeated, looking bewildered, "who is that, James?"

"One who adorns many houses, mother," I replied, "with her fine handiworks."

"Some London lady, I suppose," she answered: "but when Robert is married we are to have the parlour painted, and new curtains, and then Ellen's map of the world is to be put up in the gold frame, instead of that piece."

"Indeed," I said, "you will be prodigiously fine;" and, hearing my brother's voice, I sauntered to the window, whistling an opera tune, and saw him and my father come up to the house in dresses suited to their occupations, though perfectly neat. I turned to look to the door as they entered; and presently they came forward and shook me heartily by the hand; after which Robert kissed our mother, and asked kindly after her health.

I might have taken a lesson from my brother respecting my conduct to our mother; but I chose to despise him, and we never learn from those we despise.

I had no conversation with my father respecting my arrangements, until the evening, when we were all met round the fire. The plan at which my mother had hinted was then proposed to me; namely, that I should endeavour to be admitted into partnership with old Mr. Southcott.

"What sort of a practitioner may this same Mr. Southcott be?" I asked: "one of the old school, I have no doubt—ignorant, probably very ignorant—a mere quack."

My mother replied, that Mr. Southcott gave general satisfaction in the country, and obtained a handsome maintenance.

"Well," I said, "all that may be; and I thank you for your hints," I added, looking at one and the other of my parents; "but you must allow me to judge for myself. I have seen a good deal of the world; and at my time of life—"

I was proceeding, when Robert took me up, saying, "At your time of life, and mine too, James, persons are very apt to think themselves wiser than their parents. We have not even had experience enough to know our own folly."

I was offended, and did not endeavour to hide my displeasure. I measured Robert with my eye; and looked him for a minute in the face with as much contempt as I could summon into my countenance.

Our mother noticed my manner, and said, "James, dear, don't be offended at Robert; when you know him better you will find that he is the kindest, best creature in the world; but you do not understand him yet. You have lived with a very different kind of people: you have had a superior education. Robert does not understand the world." And then turning to her younger son, "Don't smile, Robert," she added, "you vex James; and you know that he is a stranger, and we must make much of him."

"I beg your pardon, James, if I have offended you," said my brother, offering me his hand, which motion I, however, affected not to see; and thus the conversation respecting my plans dropped for that time, and the discourse was turned into another channel.

During that evening, my father, who was as simple and good a man as ever existed, continued to give me such advice as he thought for my good; it not having yet entered his head that he had a son who was determined to abide by his own opinions, and to act as he thought right in his own eyes, without any reference to divine or paternal authority. The subjects which he pressed upon me were chiefly religious and moral: I forget precisely what they were, as I paid little attention to them; but this I recollect, that I gave him maxim for maxim, and opinion for opinion, till I had fairly carried him into the land of confusion; for, without meaning to speak disrespectfully of my parents, which God forbid, the fact is that they were not persons of superior abilities, though possessing that sort of sense which, when united with amiable tempers and true piety, fits persons above all others to get on comfortably through life.

While these things were passing between my father and me, Robert sat looking on the pavement: and I saw his colour change several times; but he did not speak till I made some remark respecting religion which did not please him; on which, looking up, he said, "James, do you remember our infant days, when we used to climb up the old yew-tree on a Sunday evening, to read the Pilgrim's Progress? those were happy times, James. I was very solitary in the yew-tree when you were gone. Religion in those days was very sweet to us. I can remember that you were then my teacher, and—"

"And now, I suppose, you would wish to become my teacher?" I said, interrupting him. "But, understand me, Robert, I am now for liberty of conscience, and emancipation from spiritual authority. I have no idea of one man dictating to another in matters of this kind;

and therefore I trust that you will not think of interfering with me."

"Please to explain yourself," said Robert.

"I do not see what explanation is necessary," I replied; "what I have said is very simple: all I would desire is, that men should exercise the same liberality one with another that God exercises towards us all. He created us with various intellectual endowments, and reasoning faculties; and with different innocent and pleasurable feelings; and he has placed us in a world where we find a variety of circumstances to gratify those feelings, but he exercises no further influence over us; he leaves us to judge and act for ourselves; and to suffer or to be happy, in consequence of our own evil or good conduct."

"According to your plan, then," replied my brother, smiling, "he ought to have turned us out of his hands full-grown; and not to have placed us, during the first years of our lives, in such a situation of weakness as to make us dependent on the mercy of others; and hence to become, in the natural course of things, subservient and subjected to parents, who, after having had the trouble of rearing us, think they have a right to counsel and influence us through life? And, really," he added, smiling still more decidedly, "Providence has made a great mistake by compelling us, according to the laws of nature, to enter life in a state of such entire helplessness: for to this cause we may attribute all the tyranny which exists in the world; for we find, from the notes of our old Bible, that, from the patriarchal government, arose the monarchical first; and then from this all other regular governments had their origin; moreover, from the necessities of man in his infancy, also proceed the dependence of the wife upon her husband, and many other systems of tyranny of the same kind; with all the various ties and clogs of domestic life; from all of which we might have been exempted, had we been introduced into the world full-grown, and entirely independent of each other."

"Dear Robert," said my mother, "how you talk! Did ever any one hear of a person being full-grown when he was born? How can you go on so; and presume to find fault with Providence?"

"O! Mrs. Penson," said Ellen, "you do not understand Robert; he is only joking. I dare say Mr. James understands him." And she then addressed me for the first time since our meeting at breakfast, saying, "You must not suppose, Mr. James, that your brother is ignorant, though he has always lived in the country; there is often a great deal of time for people to read, and think too, when they live in the country."

I found that I was likely to have two, instead of one, against me, whenever I attacked Robert; and that my brother was not quite so weak an adversary as I expected: I therefore closed the argument, by saying, that I should depart from my own principles if I did not allow my brother to enjoy his opinions as freely as I did mine; adding, that I considered emancipation from all prejudices to be a state of things greatly to be wished: and, thus speaking, I took up my candle, and went to my bed-room; resolving to get out of the house, and into a settled situation, as soon as I could.

I have now said enough to show my reader what he may expect of me; and shall, accordingly, pass over the events of the three succeeding years as succinctly as possible.

Notwithstanding my father's advice, I did call upon Mr. Southcott; and actually did contrive, with the consideration of a few hundreds, to persuade him to take me as a partner; and, more than that, within two years I married his niece Eliza; and entered, by his death, into full possession of his business, his new brick house with two bow-windows, his garden, his fish-pond, his paddock, his old horse, and his cow; with a quantity of ready money, in which sum was contained the premium I had given for the partnership. But, before I had the honour of leading Miss Eliza to the altar, Ellen had become the wife of Robert, and the young pair had fixed their residence with their parents at the Woodhouse; a scheme which, in this particular, answered to the extent of their wishes.

And now my reader may picture me to himself, a smart young surgeon; not indeed, perhaps, of the first style, but quite sufficiently polished for my line of practice; extremely well pleased with myself; and, as times then were, by no means deficient in the knowledge of my profession; with my smart house; a wife who was far less disagreeable to me than might have been expected, when it is considered that I sought her only from interested motives; and a sufficient income to enable me to live with comfort, and lay a little by. What more did I want to render me a happy man, it may be asked; and it may also be answered, I wanted humility; and, in wanting that, I wanted every thing: because humility is the only substantial basis on which happiness can be reared; for in wanting humility, as it concerns our spiritual affairs, we must ever remain ignorant of our need of a Saviour; and in wanting it in our temporal affairs, we must be ever going wrong, and heaping up stores for the future of regret and sorrow.

I am about to speak of my wife as she was, and as she would now speak of her former self, without the fear of incurring the smallest displeasure; for I trust that she is now, and has been for some years, a totally changed character.

She was young when I married her; and, being an orphan, she had been brought up at an ordinary school. She was handsome, and had acquired a taste for company, but was not a bad housewife; and, as I was much from home, provided I found a good meal, and my house neat, on my return, and discovered that my bills at Christmas were not larger than I had expected, I was very well satisfied; though, even during the first year of my marriage, my father hinted to me that there were some things in my wife's conduct which it might be well to correct. "Your wife, my dear James," my father said to me, one day, "is young, and you are a great deal from home: her dress is remarked as being too much in the fashion—somewhat out of the common way; and, as your family are known to be plain sort of people, it is not thought consistent. Perhaps a kind word from you might set this matter right;" and he was adding more, when I interrupted him, by saying, "As long as my wife does not do any thing actually immoral, father, I shall not interfere with her. If every person, in unimportant matters, were to be subservient to the will of another, what a miserable condition on earth would ours be rendered! I am a respecter of the rights of women, as well as those of men. The husband and wife bind themselves together in society for mutual convenience. The man takes his part, the woman hers; the woman manages matters in her sphere, the man in his. There is no need of interference on either side, so long as they respect each other's privileges. The shape and form of my wife's bonnets do not affect my comfort; she may fashion them as she pleases. In these matters I am for liberty of conscience."

"Your comfort, James," replied my father, "is not what we are talking of, but your respectability. If your wife is not prudent in such matters, you will be blamed. A man either derives shame or honour from his wife's appearance. He therefore cannot be so independent of her as you pretend."

"Your ideas, let me tell you, sir," I replied, "are quite old-fashioned—obsolete—out of date. Permit me to explain to you the change of views which has taken place since your juvenile days. The march of intellect, during the last thirty years, has been more rapid than for hundreds of years before. The present generation, instead of blindly following the past, has been brought to perceive the fallacy of many opinions which were formerly held as infallible. For instance: that system of domestic tyranny which has pervaded all ranks and degrees of men until the present time, is now exploded, and a new code of morals is introduced—one more suited to the weakness of our nature, and to the laws of the Divine government—one, in fact, more rational, and better suited to the amiable nature of man."

My father looked perplexed as I proceeded, and I was wicked enough to be amused by his very apparent confusion of manner. I was enjoying my triumph, standing behind my counter, and seemingly more engaged with my phials and drugs than with the argument, when a champion, with whom I never could grapple so successfully as with my father, entered the shop. This was my brother; who had scarcely appeared, when my father appealed to him, asking him if he had not heard some very unpleasant remarks made on the dress of his sister-in-law on the Sunday before, as he was coming out of church. "And I was just saying to James, Robert," continued the good old gentleman, "that, as his wife is so young, a kind word from him might be advantageous: not that I would make mischief, for the world, between man and wife; but, as James is five or six years older than Eliza, he might, you know, just give a gentle hint, and set things all right at once; for, after all, there is no great sin in these fine fashions; only, you know, people will talk."

Robert smiled, and shrugged up his shoulders, hinting that it would never do for him to interfere between his brother and his wife; and was proceeding to other matters, when I insisted on his hearing what I had to say.

"Robert," I said; "it would save a vast many contentions, in future, if my father could be made to understand my way of thinking; and could learn not to bring my actions to the standard of his own opinions; which, as I just now said, are obsolete and out of date. The progress of intellect," I continued, with much pomposity, "has, it is very certain, proceeded with increased velocity from age to age, in proportion as the shadows of ignorance and darkness have withdrawn. This progress has, no doubt, been precipitated, to an almost incalculable degree, by the art of printing, and the consequent general diffusion of learning." Here I paused, to take breath, and, indeed, to consider what I was going to say, for I began to feel myself somewhat bewildered; and Robert was so provoking as not to attempt any sort of interruption, which, of whatever description, would probably have relieved me considerably, and set me off again with renewed velocity. But he was mischievously silent, and stood in an attitude of mute and respectful attention, as if bowing to my superior genius. I was therefore obliged to proceed; and added, "In short—in short, owing to this rapid march of intellect," and there I hesitated again, for I did not like the expressive smile which rested on Robert's countenance; "in short we consider that—that many things which were once thought right are now wrong, and *vice versâ.*"

"And what was once thought wrong is now right," added Robert: "is that what you mean by *vice versâ?*"

"Vice! vice!" said my father, getting quite warm: "you may well talk of vice and wickedness; too much learning, I am sure, has made you mad, James. I fear you don't deal in such a drug as common sense in your shop, boy, or I should turn doctor myself, and prescribe a few grains for your own use;" and, so saying, he walked out of the door, sighing heavily, as he stepped into the street.

"There now," said Robert, with displeasure, "you have made our father unhappy with your abominable nonsense. Pray, is it among your new discoveries that it is a good and right thing to make a gray-headed parent weep, for I saw the tears in his eyes? but you cannot have taken leave of your senses altogether,

James. What do you mean by all this nonsense? you have some meaning, I suppose?"

I became angry in my turn, and spoke roughly to my brother; but we were both more calm presently; and, as I was just stepping out to visit a patient who resided about half a mile in the country, we walked together, and I then tried to make him understand what I meant. I first began by asking him if he thought that a custom or principle must be good because it was ancient?

He replied, "Certainly not; otherwise the customs and habits instituted before the Flood must have been the best, because they were the first established on earth."

I must remark in this place, that almost all my brother's learning is derived from Scripture.

"You grant, then," I answered, "that old customs may be bad, and old received principles may be false?"

"Neither customs nor principles are necessarily good because they are old," replied Robert; "neither are they necessarily bad for that reason."

"True," I replied; "I am willing to argue fairly."

"But is it not probable," I continued, "that, as science and literature advance, many things may hereafter appear right to us which now seem wrong, and the contrary?"

"I allow that every thing is capable of improvement, in theory, and in practice too," replied Robert, "excepting religion and morality. These, indeed, may, and we trust will, be better attended to in practice as knowledge increases, but their theory cannot be amended. We can have no new lights on these subjects beyond what the Bible can supply; and our fathers had the Gospel; and the moral law was declared ages past, and will continue in its perfection for ever. Therefore, I deny what you assert, that the opinion of religious persons can ever change respecting right and wrong."

"Surely," I replied, "the same things may be seen in a different point of view, by an enlightened and an ignorant person."

"Not simple matters of morality, and right and wrong," replied my brother. "In these things the conscience is an unerring guide. Every man is more or less aware when he is doing wrong. Else why have even the smallest children recourse to concealment when they meditate an immoral act?"

"The fear of shame or punishment," I answered, "is what induces this deceit or concealment, which we see in all children, when they seek to do what they think will not please their parents. And now I am come to the point at which I was aiming. Those persons who have received the new and improved light of which I am speaking would wish to see a more easy and charitable discipline established in the place of those severe laws by which offences are multiplied, and occasions of guilt are created."

"Really, James," replied Robert, "you must explain yourself further before I can understand you."

"For instance: let us first speak of our religious establishment as it exists in this country," I answered. "Why should it be a sin to preach without a gown and cassock? or to pray extempore, instead of using a prescribed form?"

"I do not know that it is a sin," replied Robert.

"It is so far a sin that those persons who do not conform to these rules are excluded from many offices in church and state," I replied.

"For the same reason," replied Robert, "that you would refuse to take a partner or apprentice in your profession who disapproved of your mode of practice."

"I don't say that I should refuse any partner or apprentice on that account," I answered; for I was determined to uphold my sentiments through thick and thin.

Robert smiled.

Nothing used to provoke me, at that time, so much as the playful way of my brother, though there was not the least appearance of sarcasm in his manner, or, I verily believe, in his mind. And I asked him what amused him so much.

"I was thinking," he answered, "what a plight the poor patients would soon be reduced to, when the doctor and his apprentice chose to think and act upon different principles."

"Robert," I said, "surely you can never be serious?"

"Well, I will," he replied.—"And to return to our religious establishment. I think it is reasonable that persons whose opinions do not agree with those of the bulk of the nation in spiritual matters should be excluded from situations of authority in the country; though I think it would be very hard to deprive them of the free exercise of their religion."

"I cannot see what religion has to do with government," I replied.

"Every man's principles," returned Robert, "must have much to do with his actions: for instance, do not your principles and mine operate powerfully on us both, in the management of our respective wives? Were Ellen to wear a cap or bonnet I did not approve, I should tell her of it immediately, and should be displeased if she did not change the fashion."

"In that case," I replied, "you would convert the simple act of wearing a top-knot which did not suit your taste into a breach of morals; and here is precisely an exemplification of what I began my argument with, namely, that offences may be multiplied, and occasions of guilt created, by too severe a discipline. And hence, I approve of the wisdom, and I admire the policy, of that system which I hope to see established in our island before many years are past. I would have every situation of authority and honour under government laid open, without test or inquiry, to every respectable person, of whatever creed he might be. I would have every assistance and every encouragement given to immoral persons, by which they might be brought back into the bosom of their families. I would have the utmost tenderness shown even to the felon, whom we are obliged to exclude from society in self-defence. And I should be sorry ever to exercise any thing like discipline over a faithless wife, or an undutiful son or daughter, so long as any hopes remained of reclaiming such a one by tenderness or forbearance, or by any conceivable exercise of charity or love."

I then proceeded to spout certain absurdities which I thought very fine, respecting universal love and charity, philanthropy, and benevolence; denominating indiscriminate forgiveness a godlike attribute; when Robert interrupted me, by simply asking, to what God I attributed this quality. "Not, I trust," he added, "to the God of the Christians? for the very foundation and basis of true Christians is this, brother; that the Lord our God, being perfectly holy and just, could not forgive sin as an absolute God; or without a sacrificial atonement. And hence, to harmonize the attribute of mercy with that of justice, he ordained, before the foundation of the world, his own Son to be a propitiation for the sins of the whole world; thus exhibiting his incapacity of forgiving sins (to speak after the manner of men), by the very measure which he took, in his divine wisdom, to show his infinite love towards his fallen creatures. Do not, therefore, think, James," continued my brother, "that you are imitating the divine character by this blind and indiscriminate benevolence which you so much praise; which, in fact, is but a device of the Evil One infused into the minds of men, in order, no doubt, to confound all proper distinctions of right and wrong; and actually to make it men's interests to do ill that they may obtain favour."

I was by this time at the door of my patient's house, and not sorry to part from my brother, with whom I found it impossible to coincide in any one opinion.

From that time my brother and I had many discussions of the same nature, but neither of us was in the least disposed to give way, and therefore our arguments only tended to make us uneasy in each other's company, and to discomfort both our parents and Robert's wife; all of whom, as well they might, thought me decidedly wrong; that is, as far as they could understand me.

After this, years passed on without any great changes, excepting that both families were augmented by the birth, in one of two children, and in the other of three. My brother's son was the eldest of this generation, and was called George, after my father. My son was his junior only by a few months: we called him William, after my deceased uncle. In two years more a daughter was added to our family, and another son to my brother's; and, as much as eight years afterward, a second daughter was given to me, on which dear child we bestowed the name of Sarah.

It was when my son William and my daughter Bessy had attained the ages of five and three, that the baleful effects of my false principles began to display themselves more evidently. My wife, as I before said, was young and inexperienced when she married me; and my absurd notion of not interfering with her caprices had deprived her in many instances of the benefit of my advice. There is an old saying, that "two heads are better than one;" and even granting that a man may not always be wiser than his wife, yet it may be naturally supposed that, when two persons having the same interests, take counsel together, some good may sometimes accrue from the very pause and delay which these consultations must occasion. But the independent principles which I entertained, as I before stated, had prevented me from holding any of these consultations with my wife; indulging the idea that I had no right to interfere with any of her little whims or caprices, or even with her opinions, so long as she allowed me the same liberty. If, therefore, she did not improve under my management, no one can wonder; and if our children were not guided in the best manner possible, it will not, I suppose, be a matter of surprise to my reader.—But to return to what I was about to say.

My mother was always anxious that all her family should meet on Easter Sunday at the Woodhouse to dine, and accordingly on that Easter Sunday which happened soon after William had completed his fifth year we all met under the paternal roof, and had an excellent dinner; after which, my brother and myself took a walk with our little sons, and were returning, when the boys picked up a little puppy which belonged to a dog in the yard, and brought it into the kitchen. The puppy made a whining noise, which attracting my brother's attention, he bade his son carry the little animal back to its mother. We then proceeded to the parlour, which was always used on this annual festivity, but were presently called out again into the kitchen by the loud cries of the little dog, which George had placed upon the dresser, instead of carrying it back to its mother. The creature had fallen from the dresser, and was considerably hurt. My brother no sooner understood the state of the case, than he took a small horsewhip from a peg in the kitchen and gave his boy a slight stroke over the shoulders, which made him roar louder than the puppy had done.

"Be silent, sir," said his father. "If you give another roar, I shall give you another stroke. Go up to your room, pray to God to forgive you for your disobedience, and don't come down till you are humble."

The little fellow was silent in a moment, and went stumping up stairs, half-frightened and half-sullen. My brother then turned round to put up the whip in its place, and, in so doing, stepped near my boy, who, starting back, said, "Uncle, you are not going to beat me! Father never beats me!" and he looked boldly up to him as if he dared him to it.

"It is not my business to correct you, little master," replied Robert, "while you have a father to do you that good turn; you have nothing to fear from me;" and he replaced the whip, and accompanied me into the parlour. There we found the rest of the family seated round the tea-table; and we also sat down: but I observed that my brother was thoughtful; and, on Ellen asking where George was, he answered that he had corrected him for disobedience."

"Yes," I said, addressing my sister; "he laid his horsewhip over his shoulders, and then sent him to his room till he had done roaring."

"He did very right," replied Ellen, calmly, "if he was disobedient."

"And don't you ask what mighty offence a child of five years old could be guilty of, sister, to deserve such a punishment?"

"I understood that he was disobedient," she replied.

"Disobedient!" I repeated: "giddy, thoughtless, forgetful. He did not put the puppy down, when his father bade him."

"Well, what was that, brother James, but disobedience?" asked Ellen.

Robert reddened, while this was passing, and looked as if determined not to enter into an argument on the subject: but I was equally determined that he should; and challenged him to the contest, by saying, "Surely, Robert, it would be better to reason with a child at that age, when he does wrong, than to use such violent measures. I have never laid a hand on William."

"So he told me just now," replied my brother.

"And you see the consequence, Robert: his will is free, his spirit unbroken: and he will tell the truth in the face of the whole world, whether it makes against him or not. But once lay the horsewhip across his back, and he loses that noble confidence for ever."

"Noble confidence!" repeated Robert: "might not another name be used for this sort of behaviour? Truth I delight in, but not when it proceeds from want of shame. Children should be taught to be ashamed of what is wrong, and be made to know that chastisements will follow bad conduct; and they should not be accustomed to suppose that all is right, when they acknowledge their faults without shame or penitence."

"You will make a canting hypocrite of your boy,

Robert," I said; "that is, if he does not, by-and-by, break the yoke, and leave your house. This sort of treatment might have done years ago, when children, by comparing notes, could discover that the same process of tyranny was going on in every other family as well as their own. But in these enlightened days, when the march of intellect is making such rapid strides, another system must be adopted. Man must now be governed by reason, or not governed at all. Blind obedience can no longer be expected, either from wives, children, or servants. Man has discovered his rights, and will require to be treated with justice. Every man's conscience must now be a law to himself, and the regulator of his actions. I desire not the blind obedience of any person connected with me; nor can I understand why any individual should demand such submission from another. I abhor the system of controlling the actions or principles of any free agent—such is man—and I reprobate every measure of government by which the reasoning and thinking powers of the subject are to be brought under the trammels of custom."

I was proceeding to this or some such effect, when the door was burst open, and George entered, his eyes being swelled, and his little features all blubbered and shining with tears; while his sobs were so loud as to shake his whole little body. Straight he ran to his father, and was on his knees in a moment before him, begging pardon; then to his mother; then to his grandfather; then to his grandmother; as if he felt that he could not have offended one without offending all: imploring, entreating, with all the energy of infant eloquence; and not being satisfied till he had received the kiss of peace from each honoured individual, nor being perfectly happy again till lifted upon the knees of his father: where, as from a place of perfect security and happiness, he humbly waited until his portion was administered to him from the hands of his mother.

"What say you now, James?" said Robert, at the conclusion of this scene. "Who is so happy now as the contrite child, received again into his father's arms? Would all the reasonings of the wisest man that ever lived have had such speedy and salutary influence on this infant as the chastisement, given by the hand of affection, which has produced these feelings in this short time?"

Where persons are resolved not to be convinced, no arguments will prevail. I determined to retain my own opinion, and Robert held as fast to his: and from that time, as if by mutual consent, we saw less and less of each other for several years; and, in consequence, our children met much seldomer.

About two years after that, I began to look out for a school for William. I sent him to one in the village; but, as I stipulated with the master that he never should use corporal punishment, and as my son was aware of this stipulation, it is not to be supposed that I could keep him there long. I therefore soon removed him; and, happening to meet with a schoolmaster at some distance, to whom the forty or fifty pounds a year I paid for my son was an object of some consequence, I failed not to hear an excellent account of the youth's improvement from vacation to vacation: and as fathers are sometimes blind to the faults of their children, I was by no means the first to observe that the reports of the master did not exactly tally with the manners, and appearance, and general improvement of the boy. Something, indeed, might be pleaded for me, in consideration of my constant occupation abroad; nevertheless, I had sufficient opportunity to see the faults of my son, had I not been blinded by self-conceit.

Bessy was sent to school soon after her brother. Her mother had chosen the same seminary in which she had herself been educated; and as I left the management of my girl to her mother, I cannot be supposed to have understood more of my daughter's character than of her brother's. Bessy was as much as eight years old when Sarah was born.

My wife was very ill soon after the birth of this child; and not being able to nurse her herself, the infant was sent to a cottager, who lived very near the Woodhouse, that she might be under the eye of my mother, whose talents as a good nurse were never questioned by me. The cottager was engaged to give the infant milk, and the little creature throve so well in her country abode, that we left her for several years where she was; and it may be supposed that she spent many hours each day with her relations at the Woodhouse.

When William was thirteen, he was brought home,

and bound to me, to serve in my shop, and to gather what he could from me relative to my profession, to which I purposed to bring him up. Two years after this, Bessy left school; and thus we had both our children at home again. And now the independent principles in which I had brought up my children, and which I had encouraged in my wife, began to display their riper fruits.

During the first few months, or perhaps I might say the first two years, of my son's residence with me, I had little to complain of in him but a sort of insolence of manner, now and then displayed towards me and my wife, and universally evidenced towards his relations at the Woodhouse. I do not recollect whether the noun *quiz*, or the verb which answers to it, had been brought into use at that time; but this I remember, that my son was continually employed in using that figure of speech which in these days we should call *quizzing;* and that his elders and superiors were almost invariably the objects of his exploits of that kind: not that his cousins escaped; for he was particularly bitter upon George, who was by this time become a very fine youth in appearance, and was, also, very well spoken of in the neighbourhood. I remember well, that, being in the shop on one occasion with my son, I was struck with his independent manner to a customer; and I argued the point with him, and told him, that, as we lived by our patients, it was necessary for us to be polite to them.

"I wonder then," he replied, "that you can submit to this manner of life, father. To be obliged to weigh out a scruple of magnesia, or measure a drachm of castor oil, for every fool who chooses to ask for such things, is a sort of servitude which is hardly to be borne. And then to make a bow, and say, 'Much obliged, madam,' to every old woman who chooses to lay out sixpence with one, really, father, it is what I cannot do."

"And pray," I answered, "what can you do then? or what situation can you choose in life, in which you must not submit to some of the humours of your fellow-creatures?"

In reply to this, my son muttered something, of which I only heard so much:—"When I am out of my time—when I am my own master—" &c.

"When you are out of your time," I answered, taking up his words, "you will have more sense; and will find, that, if you are to get on in the world, you must submit to the customs of the world, and the laws of society."

"You have often said, father," he replied, "that those laws and customs of society which prevailed in your younger days, and in my grandfather's time, are all absurd and out of date; that people know better now; and that the tyranny which was formerly exercised by parents and masters cannot at present be tolerated. I am sure I have heard you say such things a thousand and a thousand times."

"You have mistaken me, William," I said, "quite mistaken me."

"I am sure I have not though," he replied; "I have heard you a thousand times laugh at the old sayings of my grandfather and grandmother, and speak of the march of intellect, and say how things would be changed by-and-by."

"Ay, by-and-by," I said, "mind that, William; things will be changed by-and-by, but they are not come to perfection yet: people are not yet so far enlightened as not to demand submission from those to whose well-being in society they contribute. I have no doubt that as the march of intellect advances, these exactions will be no longer made; but, at present, we must bend a little to prejudices; and you must not offend our customers upon any account. There is no druggist's shop within many miles of this; and I can assure you, that ever since I have been settled in this place, I have gained a very considerable emolument by the sale of drugs, and turned many hundred pounds in this way."

"More than I shall ever do," muttered my son.

I felt my fingers itch, to use a rustic phrase, to apply a horsewhip on this occasion to the shoulders of the youth; and late in the day as it was, it would have been well if I had not resisted this inclination; but I had spouted so many absurdities for years past, upon the new mode of managing young people without coercion, that I was ashamed of departing from my own principles, and very unwilling to confess myself in the wrong. I therefore resolved to get on as well as I could with my son, hoping that time would bring him to reason; for I was utterly ignorant of the depravity of man's nature, and still believed that all I saw amiss in my fellow-creatures proceeded from ignorance, bad government, prejudices, ill examples, and narrow-mindedness.

Soon after this conversation, Mrs. Penson began to make complaints of her daughter; alleging that she would not give her any assistance in her household; that she spent half her day in looking out of the window; was always teasing her for new dresses; and was actually very insolent to her whenever she admonished her of a fault. These complaints, which were often repeated, and which came upon me at the time when I saw more and more every day of what I did not like in my boy, had rather the effect of making me irritable than of producing proper conviction; and I interrupted my wife several times in the midst of her complaints, saying, "I wish you would exercise a little liberality towards your daughter: you cannot expect gray heads on young shoulders: she will be wiser by-and-by. When her face is less blooming, she will be less anxious to show it; and when her person is less youthful, she will not feel so much pleasure in adorning it." Experience might have taught me that vanity and levity are not overcome merely by the influence of age; otherwise, how could we account for the number of vain old women who infest our public places, bringing shame and contempt on wrinkles and hoary heads.

After the return of Bessy from school, our ill-arranged family went on together in an uncomfortable way for as much as two years, during which I became increasingly dissatisfied with my son; and so did Mrs. Penson with her daughter. In the mean time, little Sarah, who had been brought home, was taken ill, first with the measles, and then with the whooping-cough; after which, she fell into so delicate a state of health, that I and her mother were very glad to yield to the solicitations of our relations at the Woodhouse, who requested that she might return to them; and, indeed, I was not sorry that this my little darling (for my Sarah was a lovely child) should be removed from the influence of her brother and sister, who now began to give me more uneasiness than I liked to confess; but as I had about that period of my life as much as I could possibly do in my profession, I had less time to give way to reflections concerning the state of my family.

About the time when William was in his eighteenth year, there came to settle in one of the handsomest houses in our village a sprightly widow-lady of about forty years of age. My wife immediately called upon her; and she took the earliest opportunity of employing me in a professional way, by sending for me to her footman; a youth who had been reared in the family, and was, I found, a great favourite with his mistress. This young man had met with a slight accident, which I soon remedied.

This lady, whom I shall call Mrs. Seymour, at first appeared to me to be a sort of blue-stocking, or female pedant; and, being certainly a very weak woman, I found that it would be no difficult matter to get to her blind side and win her favour, by using some of those hard words and fine-turned periods which I had so often used in vain while opposing the plain good sense of my brother Robert, and the straight-forward simplicity of my father.

Accordingly, in a very short time, I was told that Mrs. Seymour had declared me the most agreeable man in the parish; and, out of regard for me, she patronised my wife and daughter; and even began to complain of a nervous disorder, which made it necessary for me to call very often to inquire after her health. Thus the intimacy between the two families augmented; and, in the same proportion, the distance increased between ourselves and the worthy people at the Woodhouse.

Things went on in this way for more than a year, and I still retained Mrs. Seymour's favour; but, about that time, a middle-aged man, who was a native of the village, suddenly returned with a little independent property; and having bought a small piece of ground, built and opened a meeting-house, which was immediately filled. Truth obliges me to say, that the parish was prepared for an invasion of this sort, by the neglect of our own minister; who, being a relation of the nobleman whose tenant my father was, had several other pieces of preferment, and, in consequence, had never resided among us, or even supplied us with a resident curate. Religion, therefore, had been for a long time little attended to in the parish in general; and the state of the greater part of the inhabitants was that of the most profound ignorance. By reason of which, had the establisher of this chapel been a man who could have taught us the true doctrines of our religion, he might have been a blessing to numbers in our parish. But, unfortunately, this was not the case. Mr. Everard Johnson (for such was his name) was, to the extent, as ignorant as any journeyman curate in the United Kingdom, and, perhaps, I might add, as immoral as the very worst sample of these ; though he had some qualities which blinded his people, and made them believe that he was a prodigiously fine preacher, and a perfect pattern of all that is excellent. His voice was loud and deep; and he was even a greater adept than myself in using hard words and fine-turned periods. His person, too, was attractive, and he had a peculiar art in interpreting Scripture so as to confirm his own opinions. What these opinions were I should not soon have known, had not my brother Robert informed me, on an occasion which I shall presently relate.

Mr. Johnson had scarcely opened his chapel before Mrs. Seymour made her appearance there—was all enraptured—and insisted on my wife and daughter accompanying her in her next visit. My wife yielded to her solicitations, and came home in raptures, saying, that she had resolved she would henceforth be a constant attendant on Mr. Johnson.

"Do as you please, my dear," I answered: "I shall not interfere with your wishes on this subject, so long as you do not desire me to accompany you. I was brought up in the Episcopal Church, and am, for my own part, very well contented with the establishment."

Mrs. Penson smiled, and said, "Then why do you not go to church now and then?"

"Because," I replied, "my profession does not leave me the opportunity."

From that period, my wife continued to attend Mr. Johnson's ministry both on Sundays and week-days (for the chapel was open one or more days in the week); and soon after she became a decided follower of Mr. Johnson our annual meeting for dinner took place at the Woodhouse.

After dinner on this occasion, while all the family were present, Mr. Johnson's name was mentioned; and my father and mother both expressed strong dislike to the circumstance of a chapel being erected in the village, appealing to me on the subject to uphold their opinions: for neither of my excellent parents even then understood me well enough to guess how I should be likely to decide on any given subject.

"And pray, father," I replied, "why should you object to the erection of any chapel in which the poor are instructed? and in which the long-neglected flock may have a chance at length of receiving some improvement?"

"A poor chance, I fear, James," remarked my brother. "Are you aware what doctrine is preached in the new chapel?"

"No," I replied, "I never inquired. But my wife can inform you."

Robert turned his eyes upon his sister-in-law; and she answered his inquiring looks by saying, "I am sure, brother, that we hear nothing but what is particularly good from Mr. Johnson. He says, that without religion and virtue, no person can expect to be happy in the next world; and he talks of our Saviour in the finest imaginable way. He says, that he is the first example of human excellence that ever appeared."

"And does he tell you, sister," asked Robert, "that this Saviour is one with God, and equal with God? that he became incarnate? and that it was necessary for him to live and die for our redemption? Does he tell you that divine justice could not be satisfied with any thing short of perfect obedience? and that salvation could not be effected by any thing less than the sufferings of God in the human nature?" Then turning to me, and addressing me in a solemn manner, "James," he said, "I do not object to this self-appointed teacher merely because he does not belong to our excellent establishment, but because he is a teacher of false doctrines.—This is a fact which I was led to ascertain by a request made to me, a few days since, by George, that I would allow him to attend for once on Mr. Johnson's ministry; and I do not hesitate to say that, from the result of my inquiries, I am convinced his preaching is not conformable to Scripture: in consequence of which I have forbidden my family to enter within the walls of his chapel."

"And you would advise me to do the same?" I replied.

"I have no right to dictate to you, James," he answered.

"Certainly not," I said; "certainly not."

"But perhaps I might venture to advise," added Robert.

Here my father took up the argument; and remarked, that it was always dangerous to follow teachers who had no fixed creed, no written articles—and who might change their doctrines and their forms of instruction at their own pleasure: and he added much more to the same purpose; concluding his discourse with a high encomium on our Liturgy and constitution; and speaking of a sister of his, who had died years ago, and had been led from error to error, till, at last, she had herself finished in being a public preacher—from having taken a prejudice against the preacher of her own church when yet in her early youth; "at which period of life," he added, "the judgment is commonly very weak."

The old gentleman brought both William and Bessy upon him for this last remark; and I hinted, that, if the judgment of young people was not always good, that of older persons, being liable to be warped by prejudice, was often no better.

This remark displeased my mother, who took up the contrary side very warmly; and the evening was terminated in so unpleasant a manner, that my wife and I resolved to make our visits at the Woodhouse less frequent than ever; while William and Bessy, during our walk home, spoke of the whole family at the farm with the utmost possible contempt.

From that period my wife became more and more under the influence of the new teacher; and Mrs. Seymour, who was a lover of novelties, having declared herself the patroness of Mr. Johnson, nothing was heard of among a certain party in the village, but parties to the chapel, meetings in private houses, with other matters of the same kind; which are all in themselves good under proper regulations, and must be approved by every well-meaning person, with proper restrictions, but which, without such restrictions, are to be feared. Yet, as it was my principle to allow toleration to every one to the utmost possible extent, consistent with certain indefinite notions I entertained of the rights of man, I never inquired into the mode in which these things were managed, or attempted to control my wife in any of her schemes. But this new fancy of Mrs. Penson's had one effect which I did not immediately apprehend; it withdrew her from home and from attention to her family; and many things were thereby neglected, to which Mrs. Penson had formerly attended, as a wife should do.

About this time, my father and mother hearing certain reports which did not please them, ventured several times to advise me to keep a more diligent watch over my family. I say ventured, for I was in the habit of receiving their advice with so much insolence, that it must have been extremely painful to them to enter into any argument with me: but I had then unfortunately so much of the spirit of contradiction about me, that expostulations of any kind tended rather to confirm me in my errors than to lead me to a wiser mode of conduct. It would serve no purpose to repeat all the arguments used by my parents to induce a wiser discipline with my children; or to lead me to exercise that influence which every man ought to have with his wife to persuade her to keep more at home, and to practise her religious duties more in retirement than she was inclined at that time to do. Suffice it to say, that our last conference on these subjects ended in an open rupture. I gave my parents to understand that I desired no further interference by them in my affairs. And my mother, as she went weeping out of the house, said, "Well, James, I now give up for ever, that wish which I have long foolishly indulged, namely, that George and Bessy should make a match, and that the two brothers should thus again be united: for I now see the folly of entertaining such wishes; and I will henceforth endeavour to leave all to One who is as much wiser than I am as the east is removed from the west."

It was not long after this conversation that Mrs. Penson had a party; to which she invited Mr. Johnson, Mrs. Seymour, and all those persons who favoured their notions; and there was a great deal of talking, and many whisperings; and Mr. Johnson offended me by making a direct attack upon me, because I did not attend his preaching; my wife, Mrs. Seymour, and Bessy, all upholding him in their different ways.

I was plain with him on the occasion, and explained my principles to him, in the same way as I had done on many former occasions to others; observing, that although I had no leisure for going to church, yet, that I belonged to the establishment; had been brought up in it; and had no mind to leave it; thinking it as good as any other; adding, at the same time, that I was nevertheless a person of the most liberal way of thinking, and would allow the utmost liberty to my family; and should never think of interfering with their sentiments and modes of worship. And, having thus declared myself, I left the room, in order to cut the argument short. But, as I afterward found, my son took it up where I had left it, and uttered many disagreeable truths, which drew upon him the displeasure of the whole company, and that to such a degree, that many persons then present declared they would rather go ten miles for a drug, from that day forward, than enter my shop when he was behind the counter.

This animosity among my neighbours presently appeared in its effects, and threatened such serious consequences, that I, understanding the cause, became excessively angry with my son, and insisted that he should beg pardon of those whom he had offended. But he was violent, and not only refused to obey me, but insulted his mother, and told her that all this mischief had proceeded from her folly. "Why did you form this improper intimacy with such canting fools, mother?" he said: "all this trouble proceeds from your nonsense."

I was enraged at this insolence, and reproved him very severely; on which he became sullen, and we were all in confusion, when Mr. Johnson, either by accident or design, came in; and, the case being opened to him, he took upon him to give his opinion. He told me at once that my son was very much disliked; and that I certainly should lose all the customers who esteemed him as their friend, if I persisted in keeping the youth in the shop: and he advised me to let my daughter wait upon those whom William had insulted.

Bessy in her turn was offended at this proposal, and I myself did not like it; but Mrs. Penson approved of it, and asserted it to be very proper and judicious; and, being thus upheld, Mr. Johnson insisted more urgently upon the expediency of his counsel. On which William suddenly veered round to his side, saying, that he did not see what Bessy was more fit for than to weigh drugs; adding, that he would be bound to teach her in a month all she need to know: the young man inwardly chuckling and triumphing at the mortification which his sister betrayed.

I could hardly restrain myself from pointing out the door to Mr. Johnson, and bidding him avail himself of it, to walk out of the house; but he had scarcely taken his leave, at his own pleasure, when I burst out upon my wife with the more fury, from the restraint I had put upon myself in his presence, and said, "What does this puppy come here for, to dictate to me in my own house? What has he to do with the management of my family?"

"What did you let mother go to his chapel for then, father?" said my son: "did not uncle Robert, months ago, advise you to keep her and Bessy more at home?"

"What has attending the man's preaching to do with his ruling my house?" I asked.

"Why a great deal," replied William. "What are people governed by, but their principles? as uncle Robert says. If Mr. Johnson has taught mother to think as he does, why, to be sure she will act as he wishes. What else could you expect, father?"

"Cannot you be silent, William?" said Mrs. Penson. "Did you not, just now, say you approved of what Mr. Johnson proposed regarding Bessy? and now you are turning against him, now that he is gone away."

"No," replied William, "I am not turning against what he proposed about Bessy" (and he nodded provokingly at his sister); "but I do think that the man steps out of his place when he comes here, and lays down his injunctions in the way he does. And I blame you, father, for letting him come at all; for anybody of common sense might have foreseen how it would end, when he was gaining such influence over mother, and when his sentiments are so opposite to yours. For, if a man has any spirit in him connected with those notions he thinks highly of, he will be for making others do as he thinks right; and, for that reason, father, when I have a house of my own, and a wife of my own, and children of my own, they shall do as I wish, or I will know the reason why."

"Well, young man," I said, prompted by an indignation which, had I given way to it, would have induced me to lay my horse-whip over the young man's shoulders, "in accordance with what you have just said, I shall take the liberty of bidding you to be silent; and of hinting to Mrs. Penson, that I should be obliged to her to keep her doors shut henceforward against that pragmatical fellow, Mr. Johnson. And as to you, Bessy, you will understand, that it is my wish, when you see any person in the shop to whom your brother is disagreeable, that you go to them, and show them as much civility as lies in your power."

A very urgent call, from a patient at some miles distance, forced me at that moment to break up this disagreeable intercourse; but it may well be believed that my reflections, as I rode to and from my patient's house, were not the most agreeable. I, however, then resolved, though too late, to be firm; and not only to forbid my wife's attendance on Mr. Johnson's ministry, but also to forbid him the house, and never to allow her to visit Mrs. Seymour but in my company.

The case of my patient had not detained me so long as I expected; I therefore returned before it was supposed I should; and it was about seven in the evening. I saw my son in the shop; and he told me that my wife and daughter were at Mrs. Seymour's. I hastened there after them; and found Mrs. Seymour, Mrs. Penson, and Mr. Johnson in the parlour; but Bessy was not with them. I was asked to sit down, and tea was handed to me; after which, Mrs. Seymour said, that she had heard I was offended with Mr. Johnson; and then she proceeded to apologize for him, though he was present, and to say that he was too frank, and could not help speaking his mind. "In that respect, dear Mr. Penson," she added, "he resembles you—all warmth of heart—and now and then, perhaps, a little warmth of temper too. But allow me, my dear friends, to bring you together. Let the religion of one of you, and the benevolence and candour of the other, produce the blessed and lovely fruits of charity. Let me see you give your hand to Mr. Johnson, my dear Mr. Penson. Let me witness this work of peace. And may the remembrance of the unpleasant circumstances of this day be blotted entirely from your memories!"

Being thus urged, I shook hands with Mr. Johnson; though I secretly determined that my wife should never go to his chapel again.

It was getting dark, although it was summer-time, when this reconciliation was effected; and I had just solicited my wife to prepare to accompany me home, when I thought of my daughter, and asked where she was.

"O, Bessy is gone into the pleasure-grounds," said Mrs. Seymour, "to see the improvements I have been making. We could not think of keeping her shut up here with us old people." Mrs. Seymour then rang, and sent a servant to call her; and she presently came in, appearing heated and agitated, which I did not fail to notice.

As we walked home, I told my wife that I would have her stay more at home, and keep her daughter more with her; and I also gave Bessy a lecture: in consequence of which, we all arrived at our house in very ill humour, and in that state went to bed.

Mrs. Penson wept the greater part of that night, and the next morning complained of a headache: and in a few hours was really so unwell, as to be obliged to go to bed. She kept her room some weeks with a rheumatic and feverish complaint; and I was a good deal disturbed for some days about her health. But my fears of this kind presently gave way to unpleasant feelings of another nature: for when a little better, nothing would satisfy her but she must send for Mrs. Seymour; and this lady, when admitted, insisted upon it that Mrs. Penson's mind was uneasy, and that she must be permitted to see Mr. Johnson.

I persisted, for some time, in saying that Mr. Johnson should never enter my house again; but Mrs. Seymour appealed to my own principles, and reminded me of my own words. "Have you not often said, my dear Mr. Penson," said she, "that the old system of things is now about to be exploded?—that the principles of domestic tyranny, so long held as sacred, are now, from the rapid march of intellect, considered entirely wrong?—that you have no idea of influencing the opinions of your wife?—and that you think every human being's conscience ought to be a law to himself? Have I not heard you say, if your wife were an Hindoo, you would not hinder her having her little idol in her own chamber or on your mantel-piece? and if she were a Mahometan, she should have her mosque and her minaret in the corner of your field, if it would give her any pleasure? Why then deprive her of a rational and improving teacher? why deprive her of that which is necessary to the peace of her mind? You say that you are content with your own religion and your own forms of worship. Well and good; be it so. We may and do think you mistaken; nevertheless we will let you alone: yet, at least we have a right to demand the same forbearance from you which we exercise towards you."

"The same," I said; "but not more."

"Not more! what do you mean," she answered,

"Why," I replied, "that you should let me and my family alone. I do not come into your house, and meddle with your family as you do with mine. I have never given my opinion about your proceedings; or wished to have any influence in your affairs."

"Neither does Mr. Johnson wish to interfere with you, Mr. Penson," she replied: "all I ask for him is, that he may be permitted to administer spiritual comfort to her who is in so much need of such consolation."

I might fill a quire of paper with a relation of the various arguments on this subject which took place between me and Mrs. Seymour. Suffice it to say, that by dint of perseverance, she at length prevailed; Mr. Johnson was permitted to visit the house again; and from that time I was sensible, from day to day, that I was less and less the master of my own family. Not that Mr. Johnson, at first, openly interfered in my concerns; this he avoided doing on many accounts; but he was a man of strong mind, and had an object in view of which he never lost sight. He had been educated by Socinians; and the advancement of his sect, with the establishment of a congregation in the place appointed him by his superiors, was that at which he aimed with undeviating steadiness.

It was by gaining influence over the females of such families as he could find admittance to, that he thought he should best obtain his end; and no doubt he had hit upon a method most likely to ensure success. He had won the confidence of Mrs. Seymour and Mrs. Penson, by pressing upon them the importance of religion in general; though he had kept them in entire ignorance respecting the real nature of the true faith; and he was always ready to excite their fears, whenever they attempted to throw off his yoke, by making it appear that his cause and that of God's were one and the same;—an artifice which he upheld by the most flowery and impressive disquisitions, respecting the power of God, the beauty of virtue, and the horrors of death.

How far this man was sincere in his views of religion, and how far he was not so, I cannot pretend to say. But on this I cannot be mistaken, namely, that he was very sincere in attachment to his party; and, in consequence, left no means untried to gain proselytes to his own ways of thinking.

The first strong symptom which appeared of his influence in my family, when readmitted, was a request, on the part of Mrs. Penson, that I should have Sarah at home. "Bessy is no comfort to me, but Sarah would be a very great one," she said; "she is a dear little girl; and when she comes home for a few days she is so neat, and so obliging, and so pleasant; and she is so excellent a needle-woman, and reads so correctly, and sings hymns so prettily, that it would be quite a pity she should be spoiled. And they say she will be ruined if she remains at the farm much longer, she will obtain such false notions of religion."

"They say!" I repeated: "who are they?"

"Mr. Johnson and Mrs. Seymour," replied Mrs. Penson.

"I wish Mr. Johnson and Mrs. Seymour would let me and my family alone," I answered. "If you would be governed by your own good sense, Mrs. Penson, and not by the absurd arguments of these people, you would perceive, that if Sarah is a better behaved girl than Bessy, it is probable that is because she is better managed; and you would not wish to take her from those who have made her the lovely child which she is, to make her like the girl you have spoiled."

My wife gave up the point at that time; but, being urged by Mr. Johnson, she returned to the charge again and again; and, no doubt, would have carried her point, had not other circumstances intervened to alter her purposes.

When Mr. Johnson was readmitted into our family, my son took the liberty of telling me that I should repent my weakness sooner or later; and showed such marked insolence towards him and to all his party, that my wife became exceedingly angry; and I thought it right to reprove the young man; on which he submitted. But Mr. Johnson took upon him, soon after this, to give him a private lecture on his behaviour to his mother; on which he broke out again, and we were all in such confusion that I became weary of my home, and began to frequent a club in an evening, where I met my neighbours and enjoyed some quiet. But the more frequently I absented myself from home, the more influence Mr. Johnson obtained there; and such, at length, was the disorder among us, that I became thoroughly irritated; and, no doubt, often acted the part which I most opposed in others, namely, that of the domestic tyrant.

While things were in this state, a proposal was made to me, by the father of a young farmer in the neighbourhood, for Bessy. I approved this proposal, and mentioned it to my family. But it seems that Mr. Johnson had a friend of his own whom he wished to recommend, and my wife was, of course, on his side. My son also had some dispute with the young man I wished for a son-in-law; and Bessy had also ideas of her own on the subject. My proposition, therefore, met with general opposition; and Bessy told me, with a great deal of pertness, that she thought it very hard I should attempt to bias her inclinations; that the time was past in which parents were permitted to regulate their children's opinions; and that I had never thought it necessary to attend to my father's injunctions, and she did not see why she was to attend to me.

My wife also attacked me, pleading that the son-in-law I proposed was not a religious man, and that, therefore, she could not consent to the marriage. And William told me plainly that he would have nothing to do with him, and would not own him as a brother.

I was almost driven out of my senses by these provocations, and, in my passion, I told Bessy that she should either marry the man I proposed, or go to service; telling my son at the same time, that if he did not choose to submit to me, he might find another home and another master; and so saying I hastened to my club, where, meeting some of my old companions, I opened my whole mind to them.

"It is entirely owing to your new fancies, Mr. Penson," answered a respectable mercer, who was sitting at the same table; "all owing to your march of intellect business, your toleration, and your contempt of old saws and the wise ways of our ancestors. I expected how things would end, when you told Mr. Bell there, our good schoolmaster, that you never would have a son of yours corrected, although Solomon advised it; who, being the wisest of men, and more than that, inspired of God himself, might be supposed to understand these matters as well as you or I, and surely a little better. But it is of no use talking now the affair is past. I see nothing left for you to do but to stand to what you have said: if Miss Bessy continues refractory, just hand her up to her own bedroom and turn the key upon her; and if Master William is insolent, take a cane and lay it over his back. As to your wife, I say nothing; he is a bold man, indeed who meddles between man and wife. Only this much I will venture to affirm, if my wife did not choose to do as I bid her, why I should be apt to make a division of the house between her and me; and I would be liberal with her, and give her the largest share; inasmuch as the outside of a box, or cask, or house, or whatever it may be, is larger than the inside by the width of the wall, or the wood-work, or whatever else it may happen to be made of;" and he nodded to the gauger across the table, and appealed to him for the truth of this assertion.

Mr. Bell here interrupted the mercer, by saying, "Let us forbear looking back, Mr. Rickets; you only make Mr. Penson more unhappy, and that there is no need of; we have all judged amiss in our time. No man is infallible; and hence the wisdom of following the old, tried, and beaten path—the path which is sanctified by its agreement with the way of holiness. It is now our business as friends, to give Mr. Penson our best advice; as we would do to you, Mr. Rickets, if you had made a bad speculation in your business, or committed any other error. My advice is, that, as Mr. Penson is blessed with one of the best of brothers, whose children do him all the credit a father could desire, he should walk over to the Woodhouse to-morrow, before he takes any rash steps, and hear what counsel Mr. Robert has to give."

It would have been well had I followed this temperate advice of Mr. Bell; but the schoolmaster, having thus uttered his sentiments, left us, as he always did, after he had taken one cup of ale. And then the subject being re-discussed, with the assistance of a bowl of punch, I became so inflamed and heated, that I returned to my house intent upon the strongest measures. And, being again provoked by the manner of my wife and children, when I entered the parlour, I locked Bessy in her room, laid my walking-stick over the shoulders of my son, and sent my wife crying to her chamber; having attributed faults to her of which she was not guilty.

There was a large sofa in the parlour, and there I lay, after I had cleared the parlour, till the night-bell informed me that I must be up and away, my assistance being required at six miles' distance.

Roger the boy, whose business it was, called me immediately when the bell rang, and hastened into the yard behind the house to saddle my horse. Being already dressed, and finding that the horse was not brought to the door, I went myself into the yard, and, in so doing passed under my daughter's window. There was a light in the room, and as I stepped quietly along, Bessy opened the window, and said, "Roger, is it you?"

I stood still, but did not answer at first.

"I say, Roger," she continued, "is father going out? I heard the night-bell."

"Yes!" I thundered out, "I am going out, miss; but I shall be back very soon—before you want me. What do you require of the boy?"

"Nothing, father, nothing," she answered; "but I feared something was the matter."

"What," I asked, "did you never hear the night-bell before, that you should be calling to the boy at this hour? Put out your light, and go to bed, or I will make you know what it is to have an angry father." The window was immediately shut, and the light put out; and I mounted immediately and rode out of the yard.

I was detained with my patient till towards the afternoon of the next day; and my reader may be well assured that during that detention my uneasiness was very great. I can hardly account for the apprehensions I endured at that time; they were such, however, that when I alighted at my own door, I hastened into the shop saying, "Where is Bessy? where is William?" And thus speaking, I proceeded through the shop into the parlour, and there found Mrs. Penson in tears, while Mr. Johnson on one side of her, and Mrs. Seymour on the other, were engaged in consoling her, while she seemed to be refusing all comfort.

Mr. Johnson stepped forward immediately to explain the mystery to me. He told me that William had been missing ever since I had quitted home, during the night; and that a letter he had left unsealed on his table addressed to me, had left no doubt that he had formed his plans deliberately; had set coolly to work to make good his escape from the parental roof; and that there was little hope of his being brought back.

Mr. Johnson handed the letter to me as he spoke, but I was unable to read it at that time: my feelings were too powerful at the moment for my reason: I was like one beside himself: I wished myself dead, or rather that I had never been born: I know not what extravagances I uttered. But at length gaining more self-command, I read the letter, and then solemnly renounced my son; saying to those present, that, as I could only blame myself for over-indulgence and too great kindness, I should ever henceforward consider that young man as a stranger who could thus coolly and deliberately cut the ties which bound him to his family, and requite affection by the most base and black ingratitude.

Mrs. Penson here warmly addressed me. "Nay, my dear," she said, "surely you would not renounce the poor boy! Will you not try to trace him out? Will you not endeavour to bring him back? Will you not forgive him?"

"No!" I replied, in the bitterness of my feelings, "let him go; let him taste the fruits of his own evil works; let him know what want and hardships are. May he come to beg a piece of bread! or to feed with the prodigal on the husks which are thrown to the swine!"

Mrs. Seymour retorted severely upon me for this. "Mr. Penson," she said, "is this you? Have you wholly forgotten your own principles? Are you entirely departed from them? Have I not often heard you say that mercy is a godlike attribute; and that the Creator, having endowed us with fine reasoning faculties, and various senses by which we may receive pleasure from outward things, has placed us in a world wherein we find a variety of objects to gratify those senses; but exercises no further influence over us: on the contrary, that he leaves us to act for ourselves, and to suffer or be miserable in consequence of our prudent or imprudent conduct? Are not these your own words, Mr. Penson? Are not these your own principles? Why then should you be angry, past forgiveness, with your son, because he takes his own way instead of yours to make himself happy? Has he not always evidenced an aversion for the pestle and mortar? Why should you force him back to it? Why should you renounce him because his taste is dissimilar to your own?"

I made Mrs. Seymour no answer; but, turning abruptly to Mrs. Penson, "Has any money," I asked, "been lately paid into yours or your son's hands?—any large sum, I mean, by any of my customers?"

Mrs. Penson had been in the habit of sometimes receiving money for me and giving receipts.

She replied, that thirty pounds had been paid the day before, for which she had given a receipt.

"And where is that money?" I asked.

"I left it with my son," she replied, tremblingly · "and I understood that he had given it to you. He has often been intrusted to give you money which has been received."

Mr. Johnson and Mrs. Seymour here interfered, and begged me to look no further into this part of the affair; stating that my son's character would be for ever gone, if this part of the business were known.

I could make no reply; I sunk upon a chair; and my groans were so loud that the servant-maids were alarmed, and put their heads in at the parlour-door to ascertain if some one was not very ill. Certain however it was that my unhappy son had robbed me, and was gone; and the reason he gave me for thus leaving me was, that I had struck him. Unhappy young man! had I corrected him sooner, had I made him feel that I would be master while he was yet in tender infancy, all this misery might have been spared him. But, alas! the evil which was done could not now be remedied. And such was my pride, that, after the first burst of agony was over, I made light of the matter; and even gave out that, as I did not find my son suited for my profession, I had provided a situation for him at a distance. And this story I told at the Woodhouse; and though I was not believed, yet, there, as well as in other places, it had the effect of preventing any expressions of pity or condolence, which I dreaded to hear from any one.

In the mean time I thought it best to permit Bessy to come out of her room; and I rather hesitated whether it would be prudent to urge her to extremes by pressing upon her the marriage she professed to dislike. At the same time, I was very much hurt by her behaviour when she joined us again; and once or twice, when I hinted my wish to her that she would stay more at home, she was very impertinent. This impertinence being once exhibited in the presence of Mr. Johnson, he advised me to forbid her going out, excepting in company of her mother or with Mrs. Seymour; informing me that he had observed she was very fond of going to Mr. Rickets's, who had an only son of nearly her own age, to whom he suspected she was attached.

I told Mr. Johnson, that, as Mr. Rickets was an honourable man, and in good circumstances, and as his son also bore a very good name, I thought Bessy might do worse, and I would not interfere in the affair. But Mr. Rickets was a declared opposer of Mr. Johnson's party; and therefore, though I could not be induced to take any steps which might preclude the meetings between these two young people, yet Mr. Johnson so worked on Mrs. Penson, that she took care to break off the acquaintance, and would never suffer her daughter to go anywhere without her, but to Mrs. Seymour's.

While things were in this state, it was brought to my knowledge that Roger, who was an apprentice, had assisted to get my son's clothes out of the house, and had committed one or two other offences against strict honesty, of such a nature as would have entitled him to a severe punishment, that is, if the law had had its course.

When I found these things out, I was exceedingly angry, and was determined to bring the boy to trial: not that I had any wish or expectation of seeing him hanged, but I really did hope that he would be made to feel; and was about to take measures to this effect, when Mr. Johnson and the ladies all attacked me, Mrs. Seymour making the first assault. She began by stating that the poor boy was an orphan, wholly dependent on me; that he had been four years in my family; that his prospects were ruined for ever if I made the affair public; that public punishments had lately been found to promote the increase of crime; that severity led to deceit; that man, in the present condition of society, could only be governed by reason; that the present state of the march of intellect would no longer admit of those arbitrary regulations by which kingdoms in a more savage state were kept in order; and that, if I not only would forgive the boy, but allow him a little pocket-money, and a few more indulgences, she would answer for his future good conduct, as she had much influence over him; he being the first cousin of her footman Samuel, the young man who had been my first patient in the family.

When Mrs. Seymour ceased to plead, Mr. Johnson, my wife, and daughter, were all ready to second her arguments: and the end of this was, that Roger was called in, told that he was to be forgiven, admonished to do better in future, and informed that he was to have sixpence a week for pocket-money, that he might not be driven to dishonesty for want of a penny. And this matter being settled agreeably, as Mrs. Seymour said, to my own liberal principles, Roger was dismissed to his own quarter of the house, to chuckle at the folly of his master, and to enjoy the contemplation of the agreeable reward he was to receive for his various delinquencies.

Thus I was persuaded to go on from one folly to another; though by this time I more than half suspected that the new lights of which I had so long boasted were little better than so many Will-o'-the-wisps, which would lead all who followed them into bogs and quagmires, from which they would never help any to extricate themselves.

But I have scarcely patience to proceed narrating the wretched and low-lived perplexities in which my weakness and folly involved my unhappy family. It was not three months after the restoration of Roger to favour, that Bessy became of age; and received into her possession a hundred pounds, which had been left her by a distant relation of her mother's. And what was the step she took on finding herself mistress of this hundred pounds I am ashamed to say; yet truth compels me to say.—On my giving her some slight offence, she took an opportunity to run away; and the person she chose for the companion of her flight was the smart footman of Mrs. Seymour—the cousin of Roger; and no doubt this affair had not been helped forward a little by the boy whom I had so weakly pardoned.

Here was an unlooked-for blow; yet, when the thing was past, my wife recollected a thousand little incidents, which, had not her mind been turned to other matters, might have awakened her suspicions, and perhaps prevented the evil.

The naughty girl had managed matters so artfully, that she could not be traced till after she had been married some weeks. She was then discovered in a mean lodging, in a large manufacturing town at some distance from our village. She had wounded my pride too deeply to allow me to forgive her. I refused to see her; and I did right: and she would have had nothing to complain of had I from the first acted consistently with her: but I had brought her up without respect either for God or man; I had filled her mind with false notions of the Deity, and of herself; I had accustomed her to suppose that the blind obedience which parents require from children, in infancy, was a thing at once absurd and out of date; that the Almighty was weakly merciful; that no one man had a right to control another in matters which did not immediately concern himself; and that it was a god-like attribute to forgive offences, and to heap kindness on the offender, without even exacting a change of feelings or of habits in that offender. I had also taught her that it was cruel to exercise any thing like discipline over a faithless wife, or an undutiful son or daughter, so long as any hopes remained of reclaiming such a one by tenderness; and although I had not forgiven my son, she had not entertained the least doubt that I should be ready to do so the moment he chose to claim my pardon. She was, therefore, quite astonished when I gave her notice that I would not see her if she offered to come to our village; and equally so when she was informed, through Mrs. Seymour, that I would allow her twenty pounds a year, but only on condition that neither she nor her husband ever appeared before me, or was seen in the parish.

My mind, which had been gradually opening to the errors—not to say the wickedness—of my past life, was at this time in a degree of trouble which I cannot describe. I was made to see my sins in an awful light by their consequences—the ruin of my children—my unhappy children. I saw, too, that the present misery of my wife was owing to my conceited folly. Had I admitted her to my friendship and confidence when we first married, from how many follies and mistakes might I have preserved her!

In all these sad reflections, but one consoling thought remained; and that was, my little Sarah, now thirteen years of age, was as yet uninjured—she had been brought up in innocence and simplicity—and she might yet be a comfort and honour to her unhappy parents.

Though I had not followed William when he ran away, I had used every means, and employed every friend I had, to trace the steps of Bessy; but, as I before said, did not find her till it was too late, and till she had been actually married several days. 'I did not then see her; but, having ascertained her situation, I came home immediately; and there, being seized with a violent fever, was confined by illness so long, and recovered so slowly, that I was compelled to take an assistant for a term of years.

Thus was a considerable part of my gains cut off; and I was ashamed to look my father and mother, or my brother, in the face; neither could I contemplate their two fine and hopeful sons without a degree of anguish which it is not in my power to depict: and at one time, my sufferings both of body and mind were so acute that I became delirious; and in my delirium called vehemently for my parents and my brother.

They were immediately sent for; and were in the more haste to come, as I had before refused to see them; under the idea that they would triumph over me in my misfortunes. I knew them immediately, and begged my parents' pardon for all my undutiful conduct; and, stretching out my arms to Robert, I said, "O that I had cultivated your friendship!—that I had not despised my brother!—that I had not counted myself among the wise ones of the earth!—that I had not believed the present generation to be wiser than all which had gone before!—that I had not vainly supposed that new light could be thrown on those eternal truths which were taught by inspiration, ere yet our fathers or our fathers' fathers had seen the light of day!" I then wandered from the subject; and raved about my children, and called them my lost and ruined ones; neither could I be persuaded, for a while, but that they were both dead.

In this wretched and bewildered state I remained till the fever left me; and, as soon as it was possible, I was removed to the Woodhouse; where the best chamber in the house was allotted for my use; and my little Sarah was appointed to be my nurse, under the direction of my mother and sister-in-law; my wife being obliged to remain at home, to direct, as well as lay in her power, the new assistant in the management of the business. Poor woman! what must have been her sufferings at that time! being parted from all her children, and groaning, as she did, under the same blows which had reduced me almost to the gates of death.

But, as I was saying, my little Sarah was my constant attendant at that time; and I very well remember a conversation which I had with this child, one Sunday evening, when most of the family were at church, which made a deep and lasting impression on my mind. She began by saying, "Father, shall I read to you? I have here the Bible, and the Pilgrim's Progress;" and she mentioned one or two more books

"Dear child," I answered, "I cannot attend to reading: I can think of nothing but of your miserable brother and sister."

The tears came into her eyes, and she answered, "Cannot any thing be done for them, father?"

"Nothing! nothing!" I answered: "they are both ruined, and ruined by me, because I did not restrain them when they were children."

"Something might yet be done for them, father," she answered: "we might pray for them; and if we pray in our Lord Jesus Christ's name, and for his sake, our heavenly Father will hear us."

"I am not fit to pray, Sarah," I said.

"Then, father, you might ask our Saviour to intercede for you," she replied.

This was a new idea to me; and I asked her what she meant.

"Our Saviour is man as well as God, you know, father," she answered; "and, as mediator, and our friend and brother, he has prayed the Father for us: and his continued intercessions will be heard."

"How do you know this, Sarah?" I asked.

She immediately showed me 1 Tim. ii. 5—"For there is one God, and one mediator between God and men, the man Christ Jesus;" and 1 John ii. 1—"We have an advocate with the Father, Jesus Christ the righteous."

I held the book in my hand, and was lost in meditation; while my little girl, looking upon me with innocent glee, said, "Is it not so, father? have not we got a Friend to pray for us who will do better than we can? My aunt often tells me, when I do not feel in a state of mind to pray, to go into my room, and ask my dear Saviour to pray for me; and it makes me very happy when I do so."

"Happy!" I repeated; "are you ever unhappy, Sarah?"

"Sometimes," she replied, "when I cannot do well—when I cannot love God; and that often happens. My heart is very wicked."

I asked her what she meant by her heart being wicked—a question which seemed to surprise her; and she replied, "All our hearts are wicked; are they not, father?"

I asked her how she knew that.

On which, she showed me Jer. xvii. 9—"The heart

is deceitful above all things, and desperately wicked: who can know it?"

"You seem," I said, "to turn to the Bible on every subject, Sarah."

She looked more surprised than ever, and said, "Does not every Christian do so, father? My aunt tells me that we may find rules for every thing in the Bible; and she also says, that when people desert the Bible, to make out rules for themselves, they become puzzled and confused, and sometimes quite mistake what is right and what is wrong, and often, the more clever they think themselves, the more foolish they become."

"Did she mention to you the name of any particular person who has done this, Sarah?" I inquired.

"No," she replied, "she mentioned no particular person; but only told me, that if I grew conceited, and thought that my own opinion was better than the law of God, I should soon prove myself to be a fool."

"True; very, very true, Sarah," I said; "and she might have told you that your father has been that fool to whom she alluded: for I have not only despised the Bible, but all those persons who drew their wisdom from the Bible, and their authority from God; and I have ruined your brother and sister." I could restrain myself no longer; I burst into tears as I spoke; for I was very weak; and poor little Sarah mingled her tears with mine.

From that day, it pleased God so to work upon my heart, that I began to look upon my former life, and all my former false, conceited, and absurd opinions, with the horror and contempt which they well deserved. I was made to see that all these false opinions had been built upon an erroneous view of the nature of man. The Bible tells us that "the heart is deceitful above all things, and desperately wicked;" but the promoters of the liberal system, and the proclaimers of the march of intellect, tell us that man is good by nature; and that it is to the unwise and tyrannical measures of government, and the want of education, that we must attribute all the miseries we see in the world: and in agreement with this idea I had acted. I had taken my views of God and his government from my own vain conceptions; I had despised all authorities, even that most sacred of all delegated authorities, namely, the parental one; and, in the disobedience to my own parents which I had displayed before the eyes of my children, I set them the example of rebellion to my authority: and I had done more; in the abundance of my folly, and in the spirit of my absurd liberality, I had not guarded my privileges as a husband, as a master of a family, and a member of the church as established by government; and had allowed persons of principles dissimilar to my own to obtain influence in my family, and even to have a voice in my private consultations and domestic arrangements. But I had been made to suffer; and my sufferings were prolonged, through the mercy of God, till I had renounced for ever, I trust, all my absurd and impious notions, and until my rebellious will had been brought entirely under the control of that of the Almighty.

In the mean time I recovered my health, and returned to my house, leaving my little Sarah in the happy home where she had ever been; and, from that time, I and my wife (though, alas! in some respects too late) did all that in us lay to comfort each other, and to consult each other's happiness. Mr. Johnson soon ceased to visit us, when he found that the church and the state were united again within our *domicile*—by which my reader must understand, that the man and his wife were again of one mind, and were resolved to uphold each other; for it can only be states and houses divided against themselves into which the enemy can ever hope to gain admittance. I also failed not (God being my helper) to seek, repeatedly, the pardon of my parents; and to make up to them, as much as in me lay, the loss they had sustained by my long course of rebellion and disobedience: and then, and not till then, did my wife and I begin to derive benefit from the friendship of my brother and his wife. I consulted Robert about my poor lost Bessy; telling him, that, for Sarah's sake, I thought it was still my duty to refuse to see her. He agreed with me in this; but, as I could well afford it, he engaged me to increase her allowance to thirty pounds a year; undertaking, most kindly, to look after her affairs, and to give her the best advice of which he was capable. From that time, he never mentioned her name to me; though, at the seasons when I paid the allowance, he generally gave me such hints as he thought would administer comfort to me; assuring me, that, should her health fail, or any other circumstance call for my personal interference, he would give me timely notice. But I never knew, during all that time, where my poor child resided; and this was also kept a secret, by my desire, from Mrs. Penson; for I felt, that while Sarah was unmarried, we could not show too decided a displeasure at the conduct of Bessy.

In the mean time, I knew that my unhappy daughter was in better hands than mine; and I endeavoured to be as easy about her as possible. But I had many sad hours, and many, many bitter feelings, respecting my elder children: for years passed away, and I heard nothing of my poor boy; but I forgot all his undutiful conduct, and thought of him only as he was in his infancy; distressing myself frequently with the reflection of what he might have been had I acted the part of a Christian father to him. Nor were these reflections the least of my miseries. O how often, during that time, did I utter the exclamation of David, crying, "Oh, Absalom! my son, my son!"

And who could deny that I deserved all this suffering, and more than this? I am well assured that I did not receive one chastisement too much; for all was necessary to bring me to a sense of my sin; neither would any of these troubles have availed in the least to my reformation, had not the divine blessing been shed upon these afflictive dispensations. I was, indeed, as grass shorn and cut down to a level with the dust; but I should also have withered, as grass cut down, had not the dew of heaven descended upon me, and occasioned the withered blade to spring again.

It was during this period that circumstances led me to a consideration of the nature of our Episcopal church, on which I had formerly looked with such infinite contempt; and then I perceived that, notwithstanding there might be some little things connected with it which we might reasonably wish otherwise, yet that, taken as a whole, in its Liturgy, its Articles, its various forms and ordinances, man had never been able to produce a system at once so noble, so simple, so useful, and so happily conformed to Scripture. "And this," I said, "is the nursing-mother whom I have despised, and taught my children to despise! this is the mother whom I have hated, neglected, and endeavoured to despoil!" And, on remembering these things I have often wept like an infant, crying, "My Father!" I was then brought to see the beauty and consistency of our holy religion; and to observe how my errors of faith had, in a considerable degree, arisen from a false view of the divine attributes.

In common with many other pragmatical persons, I had formed an ideal deity to myself, as totally different from the God of Scripture as Mahomet is unlike to Christ. The god of my folly was a supposed indulgent parent; paying little regard to the proceedings of his children, so long as they transgressed not certain bounds; which, by-the-by, were always regulated by my own pleasure: but, when I came to examine the character of the Deity by Scripture, I discovered at once, to my utter dismay, that he is a God of purer eyes than to behold iniquity; one, in fact, that cannot tolerate sin; and one who, from the perfection of his nature, cannot pass over the slightest transgression without regard to justice or atonement.

The incapacity of the Deity (to speak after the manner of men) to overlook sin without departing from the perfection of his nature, was, accordingly, the truth which, being strongly fixed upon my mind, by the divine blessing, conducted me to the knowledge of other doctrines of true religion; for how could I rest under the impression of being continually beneath the eye of a perfectly just God, unless I had some means of appeasing his justice? I was not so ignorant of myself as to think it possible I could, by any efforts of my own, render myself acceptable in the view of perfect holiness; nor was I so absurd as to expect that if I could not find help and comfort in Christ, there was any prospect of obtaining it through any other mediator proposed by man.

To Christ then I turned my attention; and by the divine blessing on the study of Scripture, and the Articles of our church, the truth of the Holy Trinity was unfolded to me in all its glory, and all became plain and satisfactory to my mind: while the whole system of revelation was developed to me with increased beauties and glory.

My creed was then fixed; which may thus be stated: There is one God, eternal, infinitely holy, just, and merciful, omnipotent, omniscient, and omnipresent. This God, even the Lord Jehovah, cannot change; nor can aught be added to or deducted from his infinite perfections. In this one glorious Essence there are three Persons, the Father, the Son, and the Holy Ghost. These three Persons are called first, second, and third, in reference to the parts they take in the work of man's salvation. Man, having been made in innocence, corrupted himself through the malice of Satan, and rendered himself the heir of everlasting damnation. But his Father and Creator, having foreseen his fall before the foundation of the world, planned, in his infinite wisdom, a means whereby he should not only be set at liberty from the bondage of Satan, but be infinitely elevated in the scale of beings; and rendered more gloriously happy and blessed, in proportion to the guilt and misery in which he had been sunk; for *where sin abounded, grace hath much more abounded.*

I was further taught, that, in accordance with this everlasting purpose, God the Father had chosen from the mass of mankind, multitudes past all calculation to be rescued from destruction, and made heirs of glory. But inasmuch as (from the necessity of the divine nature) this could not be done, and mercy flow to us, till divine justice should receive satisfaction, God the Son descended from heaven within the four thousandth year of the world; and, uniting the two natures of God and man, fulfilled the moral law, and bore its penalties; and not only obtained our justification by his obedience and death, but through his infinite merit entitled believers to the enjoyment of everlasting glory. Thus God incarnate not only obtained for all who believe in him, and all, in fact, who do not reject his offers of mercy, eternal happiness in the world to come, but also entitled them in this world to the precious benefits conferred by the teaching of the Holy Spirit—that sacred Person of the adorable Trinity who has, in his infinite mercy, taken upon himself to call, to regenerate, to sanctify, and finally to glorify, all such as have been predestinated to salvation by God the Father.

Such is the outline of the creed which, through the divine blessing on the study of the Word of God, and the conversation of my brother, I was led to adopt soon after my misfortunes and my illness; and I do thank God that my opinions from that period have never varied in any one essential point.—But to return to my narrative.

Sarah was thirteen at the time of the marriage of

poor Bessy; and the next eight years were to me a period of deep distress, though, no doubt, they were the most blessed years of my life. What a change passed on me during that time—a blessed change I trust! for I then was taught to hate and loathe myself more, if possible, than I had ever admired and loved myself. The character of my wife, too, seemed, through the power of religion, to be entirely changed; and I was led to wonder how I could have lived so long with her without having understood her better, or loved her more.

The assistant I had taken, when I was very ill, had remained with me four years; and afterward, having taken my brother's second son into the shop, he proved a real comfort to me after my assistant left me; and from that period indeed he never left me, excepting when he went to London to finish his studies.

Dear Sarah remained at the Woodhouse, for I never would hear of her being removed; and I was never more pleased than when my brother asked her of me for his eldest son. We had all seen that these young people were attached for some years to each other, and therefore were not surprised at the request. The marriage, however, was put off a year on account of the death of my poor father; and as my mother was almost childish, and excessively fond of Sarah, we thought it would be cruel to part them, and it was agreed that George and his wife should still live with their parents; a plan which has been found to answer in my brother's family, though not generally, I think, to be recommended.

Sarah was in her twenty-second year when the wedding-day was fixed. It was the sixteenth of May, and happened to be remarkably fine weather.

It was not a very busy time with me, and things so fell out that I could allow myself twenty-four hours or more of holyday on the occasion; my nephew having most dutifully insisted on returning to the shop immediately after the ceremony; which I esteemed as a great kindness, for I much desired to make one of the happy bridal party; who, after the wedding-breakfast, were to take a little excursion, and not to return till the noon of the next day.

The marriage took place at the parish church soon after eight in the morning; and the party consisted of my mother, my brother and sister, myself, and my wife the bride and bridegroom of course, and my younger nephew; not to omit a little fair girl named Lucy Howard, who was bridemaid, and who was all innocent delight on the occasion. This little girl is now my niece, being married to my second nephew.

From the church we came to my house, where we had breakfast; and then my mother went home, while we proceeded in a hired coach to the place where we were to spend the day.

There is in our neighbourhood a famous ruin, near to which is a good inn, which I thought would be a very proper place for us on this occasion; but Sarah insisted on spending the day at a rural inn on the borders of the same extent of woodlands in which the Woodhouse is built, and just on the verge of the park of the same nobleman whose tenant my brother is, as much as four or five miles from the Woodhouse. I had seen this inn several times: it is a large black timbered building, having the high road and the park in front of it; and behind it a dingle, and the woods; a very pretty place, assuredly, but very much out of the way, I thought, for a bridal party. But Sarah had set her mind upon this plan; and if ladies are ever to pursue their own plans, surely it ought to be on their wedding-day.

Well, into the coach we all got, to the number of six, and as merry a party we were as ever met; for I tried to conceal any painful reminiscences I might have on that happy day; my brother and sister were the gayest of the gay, and their son the most happy looking being I had ever beheld; and we laughed as we went along, and talked nonsense; yet, from time to time, some pious expression of gratitude to God would drop from the mouth of one present; and the tears would tremble in every eye, and these again were chased away by the smiles of innocent joy.

Most of our way lay through woods, and it was scarcely noon when we arrived at our inn. Dinner had been ordered for us; and I remember that roast lamb and green pease made part of our regalement; and while it was getting ready we rambled in what directions we chose, two or more together. At two we met, and dined in a large low parlour, with casement windows, and hung round with rudely coloured engravings of the Prodigal Son.

The story of the Prodigal Son was a very affecting

one to me at that time; but every one was careful not to make any remarks on these prints.

We did not sit long after dinner, my sister Ellen having proposed a walk to a lodge at a very small distance from the inn, which she said opened into the park, and was reported to be one of the most beautiful structures of the kind which had ever been seen in the country. Having desired that tea should be ready for us on our return, we all set out, taking our course under a sort of avenue, formed on one side by the trees of the park, and on the other by the skirts of the wood. We started together, but soon dropped off in pairs, my companion being my sister Ellen; the little bridemaid making excursions in several directions; pleading for her excuse that she had no companion but an old dog of mine which I had cherished till he had not a tooth in his head, because when very young he had belonged to poor William.

My sister Ellen was always a remarkably pleasant, lively companion, in an agreeable way: yet I could not help observing, as we walked along, that she became absent, and that more than once she scarcely heard me when I addressed her. "Well," I thought, "it is natural; joy absorbs the thoughts, no doubt, as powerfully as grief."

At length the gates of the park appeared, and close to them, within the park, the roof of the lodge. In truth, it was a very pretty construction; it looked like some of those toys which ingenious children form of moss and pasteboard. I shall describe it as it appeared to me when arrived in full view of it. It was a thatched cottage of one floor, having a centre apartment, with a rural porch in front, and on either side the porch a casement window, pointed, and having its upper compartments filled with stained glass; the roof over the porch was rounded, and thickly set with thatch. On each side the centre room were wings terminating with gable ends, and windows looking to the north towards the park, and to the south towards the road. These windows were also gothic, and each of these gable ends contained two rooms. Behind was a kitchen-garden and small court, and in front was a little portion of ground richly planted with roses, eglantines, jasmines, hyacinths, wall-flowers, polyanthuses, ranunculuses, and every species of fragrant herb. The wall of this edi-

S 2

fice was rough-cast, and coloured, to resemble stone, and the wood-work was painted green. Some of the windows were almost overgrown with the luxuriant branches of odoriferous creepers. The view commanded by some of the windows of this cottage must, no doubt, have been beautiful in the extreme; for the glimpses I had through the openings of the trees, even from the high road, of the various lovely natural objects were enchanting.

But my reader will ask, "What is all this to me? is the doctor becoming sentimental and poetical in his old age? What have we to do with the beauties of nature and ornamented cottages? Had he not better stay at home and mind his shop?"—Well, then, we will have no more descriptions, but proceed with our walk.

The bride and bridegroom, who had walked first, stopped for us when they had reached the gate of the park; and we came up just as they had made themselves heard by the persons within the lodge, for the next moment, the door was opened, and two little girls, apparently of the same age (being perhaps about six years old), came quickly forward; and passing through the green wicket of the garden, stood before us on the other side of the gate. One held a key, but made no attempt to apply it to the lock; on the contrary, they both stood courtesying, and blushing, and appearing evidently alarmed at the party without.

"What pretty creatures!" exclaimed our merry little bridemaid: on which she was gently reproved by my sister Ellen; who seldom lost sight of propriety and prudence. Yet I could not help saying to my sister, in a low voice, "Those children are as remarkable, of their kind, as their habitation is. What little delicate beings! and how nicely they are dressed, in their pink-striped frocks! how fair and lovely they are! and what brilliant eyes they have! But, my little maids," I said, addressing them, "are we to stand here all day, looking at your pretty faces through the bars of this gate? Will you not open to us?"

"Mary can't unlock the gate, sir," replied one of the little fair ones, with a low courtesy and a deep blush.

"Then let the other try," I replied.

"Ellen can't unlock the gate, sir," replied the other, courtesying and blushing in her turn.

"Come, come," said my brother, laughing: "we will

soon settle that: give us the key, and let us see what we can do."

The key was immediately handed through the bars, and we found ready admittance. "And now," said Robert, "show us the way to your house, little damsels: you must go first, lest we should lose ourselves."

The two little ones then, taking each other's hands, walked before us through the green wicket up to the porch, which, by-the-by, like that of a Mahometan temple, was nearly as large as all the rest of the house besides; and the door being already open, we were introduced into a roomy kitchen, paved with square flags, neatly whitewashed, and in every respect as nice as hands could make it. One of the casements was open, and an eglantine had made its way through it in a most fantastic style. A fire of wood was burning on the hearth, and a hissing kettle was hanging over the fire; but not a living creature was seen within the apartment but a cat, which, at the sight of my dog, raised her back, and placed herself in an attitude of self-defence.

"This is Fairy-land, I suppose," said Lucy Howard; "for I see no inhabitants in this house, but these two fairies and their cat."

"Our cat's name is Tippet, ma'am," said one of the little girls, courtesying very low.

"Is Tippet a fairy too?" asked Lucy.

"We have got the story of the white cat who was a fairy," said the other of the little beauties, courtesying in her turn; "but Tippet is not a fairy."

"Indeed," said Miss Lucy; "are you quite sure?"

"There are no fairies now, ma'am," answered the first little speaker, laying a very strong stress on the word ma'am, and courtesying every time she used it; her little dimpled hands being placed very formally before her.

"Upon my word," I said, "you are the two most delightful and amusing little personages I ever beheld;" and I made each of them a very low bow, which they returned in the gravest manner possible by two low courtesies, which set Lucy laughing again: but I was surprised at the same time to observe that tears were in the eyes of Ellen and my daughter. I however asked no questions; for my spirits that day were in such a state that I did not dare to meddle with any thing which might excite any pathetic or tender feelings.

"But have you not a parlour to show us, little dames?" said Lucy: "where is your parlour?"

The little girls immediately moved hand-in-hand to a door on the left side of the kitchen, and opening it, we walked into a considerably large sitting-room, on the northern side of the cottage, in which a window at one end commanded a view of the park, where the deer were feeding in various groups. This parlour was hung with a green paper representing a thick foliage, and set round with chairs so painted and constructed as to resemble roots of trees; in each corner was an old-fashioned cupboard, painted with some curiously whimsical devices; and in the centre of the room was a table covered with a green cloth, on which lay several books, a flute, and some needlework. There was one thing, however, which surprised us much—there was an inner door in this parlour, and the outer door was scarcely opened, before my dog rushed in, and flew to the inner door, whining, scratching, and seeming as if he would have torn up the very floor. The children were frightened at this, and I was surprised; but my nephew drove him out, and shut the door of the house against him.

When the dog was out we began talking again to the little girls. "I do like to hear these children talk," said Lucy, "and to set them a courtesying, and saying, 'ma'am;' I must set them going again." And she turned to them, and said, "Are these your chairs, my dears?"

"They are our chairs, ma'am," was the answer she received; the little speaker courtesying low at the same time.

"Ladies come here and drink tea, ma'am, sometimes," said the other little blushing one.

"And sit on these chairs, ma'am," said the first.

"Well then," said my brother, smiling, "I suppose we may do as the ladies do. Suppose we were to seat ourselves, and then we might talk more at our ease. Come, tell me," he added, drawing the little girls towards him, each by one hand; "what do the ladies do when they come?"

"They do drink tea, sir," said one.

"They do eat bread and butter, sir," said the other.

"And we have the best china, sir, when they come," added the first.

"The china with strawberries on it, sir," said the second.

"Do the ladies love you?" asked Miss Howard.

"When we are good they do love us," they both answered.

"But you are never naughty, are you?" asked Miss Howard.

They both blushed at this question, and one answered, "Nobody is quite good."

"Why, what do you do that is naughty?" asked Lucy.

"That is not a fair question," said my brother; "we have no right to bring them to confession. See how the little things blush: their very necks are red. This is not a polite return for their hospitality."

"But they are such delightful creatures," said Miss Howard: "I never saw any thing like them: do let me talk to them. Please to tell me," she then added, "which of you two is the better girl. I must know."

"Mary is the best," replied one of them.

"No, I am not, Ellen is the best," replied the other; "but the ladies say we are neither of us good; and they showed it us in the Bible, and they made us learn it."

"What did you learn?" asked Lucy; "please to repeat it."

They both answered together, "'Foolishness is bound in the heart of a child, but the rod of correction shall drive it far from him.'" Prov. xxii. 15.

"But nobody uses a rod to you, I am sure," said Lucy; "you never saw a rod, I am certain."

The two little creatures reddened violently on hearing this question, and tears came into their eyes; and we all felt that Lucy was making too free with them, and had hurt their feelings; and she felt it herself; for she got up and kissed them both, and said she would not talk of such things any more. "But," she added, "now tell me, do you live here by yourselves? Is there nobody here to take care of you?"

"We must not talk about that," they answered.

"About what?" she asked.

"About our mother," they replied.

"Not about your mother! how strange!" said Miss Howard. "Why must not you?"

"Because she told us we must not," they answered.

"When did she tell you that?" asked Lucy.

"When she sent us to open the gate."

"But you may tell now about your mother," said my sister-in-law. And, as quick as thought, she rose up, and, taking the little girls each by a hand, she led them to me, and, directing them to kneel down, she said, "Join your little hands, my darlings, and say, 'Please, grandpapa, see and forgive your penitent and humble daughter. Please, grandpapa, forgive your own poor child, our dear, dear mother!'"

O my reader! conceive, if you can, what I felt when I beheld these two lovely babes kneeling before me, in obedience to their aunt, and lifting up their little united hands, their baby hands, while terror was depicted on their infant features—for they could not, and did not understand the affair. Conceive, if you can, what the feelings of my wife were, whose surprise was equal to mine on the occasion, as she had not the least suspicion of what was to be the result of our meeting at this cottage. I fell back in my chair—I groaned, I was unable to decide. I looked at the babes, my feelings were strongly drawn towards them, but I was motionless.

"They have only one parent," said my sister, "their father has long, long forsaken them; nay, he left your daughter before these babes saw the light. He can have no part either in your anger or your forgiveness; neither do we ask you to restore your daughter to the place from which she has thrown herself. We only ask you to pronounce your forgiveness; to give her your blessing; and to tell her that you look forward with hope to a happy reunion with her in that blessed place where all tears shall be wiped from every eye."

As my sister proceeded, I burst into tears; and, bending forwards, drew up the two little innocent ones into my arms. This action was interpreted in favour of the petition; and when I lifted up my eyes again all surcharged with tears, I saw the inner door of the parlour standing open, and in the doorway two figures, the one of a female and the other of a middle-aged man, a little retired in the background.

In the foremost of these I recognised my poor Bessy at once; but, probably, more because I was prepared to see her than from any other circumstance: but I had not the least recollection of the person who stood near to her, and should, no doubt, have supposed him to be her husband, had I not been just informed that he had long left her. I however did not bestow more than a single glance upon this second person, for my eyes were riveted on my daughter. But O, how entirely changed, how altered was my child! how suddenly passed away, as I looked upon her, the hope I had before entertained, in spite, as it were, of my reason, of seeing her blooming and lovely in person as I remembered her to be formerly! for Bessy once was a very pretty girl. But she who now appeared to me was sallow and broken down; and dressed, though neatly indeed, in a very humble style, with no pretensions to any thing of the lady in her manners; her person, too, was much sunk; and she looked some years older than she ought to have done. She stood trembling with her eyes fixed upon me, with that sort of imploring look which a criminal uses towards a severe judge; while all the rest of the party had gathered behind me, leaving the space clear between me and the offender, with the exception only of my wife, who had sunk upon a chair by my side, and was weeping audibly.

A minute or perhaps more elapsed before I could speak. At length I pronounced the name of Bessy; and at the same instant being admonished by a sign from my brother (as I afterward learned), she came trembling forwards, and with her the man before mentioned. And then, agitated as I was, I first discovered that this poor man had lost a limb, and was halting on a stump affixed to the knee. But they both advanced and knelt at some short distance from me, as if they dared not come nearer; and I heard some broken words, amid which I distinguished, "Father—father—pardon—pity —forgiveness—we have offended." I arose, and in rising pushed away the little twins, but stood fixed to the spot; my eyes being riveted on the man who knelt by my daughter. A poor, low person, I thought him. He was clad in very coarse garments, though he was perfectly clean. He had a sort of shabby military air, and wore a stiff black stock upon his neck; his features elongated and emaciated; his mouth was disfigured by a broad gash, which had probably been made by a sabre; while his complexion was sunburnt and weather-beaten, like one who had been long exposed to every variety of intemperate climate.

Such was the person who knelt by Bessy, and he seemed as deeply concerned as she could be in the result of the next word which I should utter; for his eyes were brim-full of tears, and some drops had already strayed down his rough cheek. Yet, intently as I looked upon him, I had not the smallest recognition of his person, and was ready to ask, "Who are you, who thus dare to intrude upon our retirement?" when my brother whispered the name of William; and the next moment I had fallen forward into the arms of my two children, weeping on their bosoms more like an infant than a man who had weathered so many storms of life.

I can recollect nothing from the time when, stooping to embrace my children, I had fallen forward into their arms; neither could I define my feelings, or say what they were, when, recovering my recollection and composure, I was enabled to look again upon my altered Bessy, and still more altered William. O what a conflict then took place within my breast, of tenderness, remorse, pity, and shame! Where was the once self-sufficient, handsome youth, who used to grace my shop? where was my once blooming, sparkling, gay, and saucy Bessy? Till that very day, nay, till that very hour, I had always thought of them as they were when I last saw them. O what a revulsion; what a violent and sudden change, was there now in my ideas and views respecting them! There was a degree of humility, contriteness, and tenderness in their aspects which was touching in the extreme. Bessy was no longer in appearance more than a sort of decent cottager; and poor William was completely fallen, in manners and deportment, into the rank of those with whom he had associated for the last eight or nine years; namely, the private soldiers, or, at best, the sergeants, of a marching regiment. For, as I was afterward informed, when he left me, he had hastened to the nearest seaport town, where, having soon spent all his money in riot and dissipation, he had enlisted into a regiment just embarking for foreign service, and had endured inconceivable hardships, until he lost a leg in the field of battle, and also received a severe wound upon the lip.

In looking upon my son especially, I felt that, much as I loved him, it would be totally impossible for me to restore him to the rank from which he had fallen; and, no doubt, the perplexed state of my feelings was observed by my brother, who, in his usually kind and cheerful way, said, "Come, my friends, I think it is time to put an end to this scene. I hope, niece, that you are provided with some person to whom you can trust the keys of your house and your gate for a few hours: you must get yourself ready forthwith, and follow us, with your brother and the two little fairies, to the inn; and we will have one happy evening together." And, so saying, he took my arm, and adding that he wished to speak alone with me, he led me out of the house into the park; and there we had a long conversation.

He informed me, that Lady —— (that is, the mother of his landlord, the nobleman in whose park we then were) had assisted him, from the very first, in his management of poor Bessy's affairs; that, after my daughter's husband had forsaken her, this excellent lady had placed her in some situation on her jointure land, which is in Yorkshire; and that, within a few weeks, she had brought her to the beautiful lodge where she then resided; "where," added Robert, "she lives rent free; and the pious old lady and her daughter-in-law often call upon her, lending her books, and directing her in the management of her lovely little girls. And the blessing of God, my dear brother," continued he, "has been shed upon the various endeavours of these noble ladies with your poor daughter: for Bessy is now as humble a Christian character as I ever knew; and she will be perfectly content, now that she has received her parents' forgiveness. But we have all agreed, and the ladies at the Hall are of the same opinion, that she should be left where she is, and not be again introduced into the society from which she is fallen, and for which she has rendered herself unfit. She will be very happy in her cottage, where her duties lie; and if once or twice a year we have a family-meeting in this place, our natural affection will be kept up, without doing any violence to the established customs and opinions of society. Neither," he added, "do we wish that poor William should be brought back to your house. He has wholly lost the habits which would fit him for it, and he does not desire it; on the contrary, he shrinks from the idea. But he wishes to live here with his sister; and he will find much pleasant employment in the large garden which is behind the house, and in instructing his little nieces; for he writes a good hand, and knows a good deal of some other things: and what (though I mention it last) is better than all, I verily believe that he is a true penitent, and, in one word, a converted character; for, when he came back to us, he had in his knapsack a well-worn Bible, which his sister tells me has been his constant companion ever since. He has a small pension," continued Robert; "and, with what you allow his sister, they will do very well."

"And they shall do better still," I added; "I will certainly make poor William's income equal to his sister's, as long as he behaves well. And may God bless my children, and give us many a happy meeting with them in this place! for I admire their delicacy in not wishing to be set on a footing with their unoffending sister; and I thank them for it, and shall take account of it. And now tell me whose scheme was it to bring us all together this day?"

"My wife's and your daughter's," replied Robert, smiling. "They would have it so: it has been long planned—ever since Bessy came into the country; and my little twin nieces were kept out of the way whenever we visited poor Bessy, that they might act their parts in perfect simplicity. But we little thought, when we formed our plan, that poor William would have his place in our drama. He came, poor fellow, to the Woodhouse three weeks since; but none of the servants knew him; and we got him away unsuspected."

I could not help smiling at this innocent contrivance of our fair relations, and said, "I shall remember them for this trick." But what man can anticipate the devices of the fair sex?

Was it any lingering remnant of natural pride which made me feel relieved when I found it was not expected of me to introduce my poor children again to my neighbours, or was it merely a sense of propriety? Certainly I was relieved when this dread was removed; and my brother and I were just turning about to leave the park, and to follow the rest of our party, who had already set out for the inn, when a little pony-carriage, containing two ladies, came out from beneath a grove, and approached us. "There are poor Bessy's best friends," said my brother, "the excellent Ladies ——"

The carriage drew near, and was stopped, while the elder of the two ladies addressed my brother. "We are glad to see you here, Mr. Penson," she said: "I trust that all has succeeded to your wishes. May we congratulate you on your son's happiness, and in the completion of the blessed work of reconciliation which was to crown this day?"

"Your ladyship may rejoice with us on both accounts," replied my brother.

"God be praised!" returned the pious lady: then looking at me, "I suppose," she added, "that I now see the elder Mr. Penson?" and she paid me a compliment on the act of forgiveness which I had just performed; and assured me that she and her daughter would have a watchful eye upon my children, and would do all in their power to serve them.

The carriage passed on before I could express my feelings in any other way than by the most profound reverence.

When my brother and I came opposite the lodge, we found that our friends had already set out; an old woman being stationed at the gate to lock it after us. When we entered on the road we saw the whole party before us; and the appearances of my newly-found children struck me again in a manner which I cannot describe. Bessy looked not a bit better than a decent cottager in her Sunday-dress; and poor William's figure, as he limped along with his wooden leg, his shapeless hat, and his sort of homespun coat, was even more strikingly pitiable. The dog was following his steps. The contrast of these figures with the gay bridal-party was at the same time so singular, that I no sooner observed it than I laughed aloud in a way most painful to me. I immediately checked myself, and then felt almost disposed to burst into tears. I could not conceal my agitation from my brother, but said, "Oh, Robert, Robert! look at that poor fellow there, and see the punishment of my pragmatical self-conceit. I was wiser, forsooth, than all who had ever gone before me. I must be for striking out new ways, and enacting new laws, and out-arguing Solomon himself; and see what I have made of it. Look at my son, and look at yours. See how blessed, how happy your George is, with his lovely young bride; while all the prospects of earthly prosperity are passed away already from before my poor, poor William. Lord, have mercy on all those who, forsaking the fountain of living waters, have hewed out to themselves cisterns, broken cisterns, that can hold no water."

My brother endeavoured to comfort me, and to show me that all was for the best; and that all which had happened had been wonderfully overruled for the good of my children. And so well did he argue, that before we arrived at the inn I was composed, and able to sit down with a smiling countenance to the refreshments which were prepared.

And now my wife and I had full leisure to examine and caress our charming little grandchildren; and it was with the greatest pleasure that I found they were entirely submissive to the will of their mother. As to my wife, I verily thought she would have turned childish, such was her delight in these little lovely creatures.

After our repast, my brother asked the company if they had any objections to reading and prayer.

"None in the world," I replied, speaking for the rest; "and permit me, dear brother, to choose our subject, viz. the first seven verses of the third chapter of the Second Epistle to Timothy:—"

"This know also, that in the last days perilous times shall come. For men shall be lovers of their own selves, covetous, boasters, proud, blasphemers, disobedient to parents, unthankful, unholy, without natural affection, truce-breakers, false accusers, incontinent, fierce, despisers of those that are good, traitors, heady, high-minded, lovers of pleasure more than lovers of God; having a form of godliness, but denying the power thereof: from such turn away. For of this sort are they which creep into houses, and lead captive silly women laden with sins, led away with divers lusts, ever learning, and never able to come to the knowledge of the truth."

My brother, having read these few verses, closed the book and turned to me, supposing that I had some remarks to make. Neither was he mistaken; for I took the occasion, first, to observe, that, by the latter times, in all probability, was meant the present period, as every thing tended to show that things were pressing towards their end; and I then pointed out how the verses my brother had read were applicable to the present day; in which men, despising all those who had gone before them, and all the wholesome rules and customs of their forefathers, are for establishing a new order of things,

www.ingramcontent.com/pod-product-compliance
Lightning Source LLC
LaVergne TN
LVHW011155110826
845150LV00006B/1230

* 9 7 8 1 4 2 5 5 4 6 2 3 6 *